Jack Bowman is a writer and a gambler. He does not blog; he does not tweet; he does not answer the phone or the door to unsolicited callers.

He is thirty-eight. Or was. Or will be soon.

He lives alone.

WITHDRAWN

www.transworldbooks.co.uk

HIGH ROLLERS

Jack Bowman

CORGI BOOKS

TRANSWORLD PUBLISHERS
61–63 Uxbridge Road, London W5 5SA
A Random House Group Company
www.transworldbooks.co.uk

HIGH ROLLERS
A CORGI BOOK: 9780552168458

First published in Great Britain
in 2013 by Bantam Press
an imprint of Transworld Publishers
Corgi edition published 2014

A CIP catalogue record for this book
is available from the British Library.

Addresses for Random House Group Ltd companies outside the UK
can be found at: www.randomhouse.co.uk
The Random House Group Ltd Reg. No. 954009

The Random House Group Limited supports the Forest Stewardship Council®
(FSC®), the leading international forest-certification organisation. Our books
carrying the FSC label are printed on FSC®-certified paper. FSC is the only
forest-certification scheme supported by the leading environmental
organisations, including Greenpeace. Our paper procurement
policy can be found at www.randomhouse.co.uk/environment

Typeset in 11/14pt Minion by Falcon Oast Graphic Art Ltd.
Printed and bound by CPI Group (UK) Ltd, Croydon, CR0 4YY.

2 4 6 8 10 9 7 5 3 1

To John Chandler – whether you like it or not

1

HALO JACKSON GRINNED at Chris Stern as the blades started to turn lazily in the fan casing of the CalSuperior Cargo 737.

He walked back into Hangar Six, put the snap-on wrench carefully back in its place in his roll cabinet, fastened the door firmly, then joined his friend squatting beside it. In the time it took him to perform those few simple actions, the sound of the jet had risen to alarming proportions. Half a dozen techs, who had been scurrying around the gleaming blue-and-silver giant, now dropped away from the unglamorous 737, grandly named *Pride of Maine*, pulled their Predator protectors from around their necks and dropped them securely over their ears. The triple layer of dense foam insulation with rubber seal deadened the rising howl to a stomach-wrenching roar but, still, an instinct for self-preservation made them back away, as though the few extra feet would protect them from the sound.

Under a large No Smoking sign, Chris pulled a Camel from his top pocket and put it between his lips without lighting it.

Cal Lemanski frowned at Halo and Chris and flapped his hands at his own ear protectors. Chris gave him the thumbs-up, and he turned away.

Kids. Cal was a bear of a man – big, bearded, barrel-chested. He was fifty-four and called anyone under forty 'kid'.

Halo and Chris grinned at each other – an unlikely-looking pair of friends. Halo was black, skinny, toothy, and with a non-haircut that verged on an Afro; Chris was as broad, blond and pink-cheeked as a drunken Minnesota hunter.

The roar gripped them like something physical. Halo cracked first – he usually did. He grabbed his Predators and clamped them on. Chris held on for another split second, to make a point, his eyes screwed up, his cigarette flattened between his gritted teeth. Then he pulled on his ear protectors, holding them firmly, like Munch's *The Scream*, crowing silently at Halo. He took a long fake drag on his cigarette – eyes narrowed, cheeks hollow – and breathed out luxuriously, as if he could still see the smoke leaving his nostrils in decadent trails.

Inside the huge engine the titanium-alloy fan blades – machined to a thousandth of an inch, in a feat as near perfect as makes no difference – sliced through the air at 5,500 revolutions per minute, a mere eighth of an inch from the lining of the engine casing, creating a diverse world of vacuum and violent turbulence.

Now, forty feet from Halo's head – but far below the nearly unbearable roar of power – there came another sound. Light and delicate. A sound like a gentleman toast-master calling for silence, with the silver tines of the best fork against the finest crystal. A single tone: so small that it was immediately sucked into the stomach of the engine, so genteel that it might have passed for imagination in a library.

And another revolution of the blades began.

Slowed a half-million times, a single blade swept past the tiny sound in a headlong suck of air and, safely cocooned by its neighbours' shrouds, spun laconically around to meet that crucial point once more. The point where the rubberized lining of the fan casing was abraded above and beyond the call of duty. Like old friends, another tink of greeting. Was it louder this time?

Halo and Chris were engaged in a silent game of Rock, Paper, Scissors when the number-two engine of the *Pride of Maine* tore itself apart.

Thirty-eight titanium-alloy blades, each shaved to a cutting edge and exerting an escape force equivalent to the weight of a Mack truck, shattered from the fan casing and ripped free in a catherine-wheel formation at a speed approaching 700 m.p.h. Some gouged troughs in the reinforced-concrete apron; others ricocheted backwards, kicking off the ground and slicing through the hangar. Some found even softer targets, then continued their escape stained red.

It was as if the devil himself had reached up from Hell to spray Number Six Service Hangar at Los Angeles International Airport with a short burst from an apocalyptic Uzi.

It was over so fast that when Halo got shakily to his feet he still had his 'paper' hand ready to go. He looked around him, at first unable to comprehend what he was seeing.

In an instant, the jet's fuselage had been all but severed fore of the starboard wing. Twisted metal, heavy drapes of colour-coded wiring and dark blue patterned carpet were exposed, festooned with fluffy white insulation. The wing itself had collapsed on to the ground, buckled and broken. Over Halo's head the hangar was split open in a rough line of gashes, each spikily framing twenty-foot blue swathes of the cloudless LA sky.

The number-one engine whined down slowly to a point at which a human voice could be heard. But there were no voices – not then, nor in the eerie silence that followed its complete cessation. Men in blue coveralls started to move, picking themselves off the floor, peering in disbelief from behind gleaming testing gear at the plane silhouetted in the giant doorway of the hangar.

Halo turned to share his amazement with Chris. But Chris wasn't there. In his place was a shapeless red-and-blue lump. Halo frowned down at it until his brain finally registered that the red-stained chunk of blue cloth was wearing Chris Stern's Nikes.

Then he fainted.

*

Tom Patrick felt his stomach lurch as the river card appeared on the scuffed green baize. Jack of diamonds – turning the pocket jacks he'd been nursing into something even more valuable.

If his gut rolled over, his expression was unchanged. The other players searching his face for clues saw only what they'd been seeing for the thirteen hours since the start of the tournament – weary, red-rimmed green eyes set deep in a pale face, darkened by the shadow that told of more than one day away from a razor.

Tom regarded the five cards on the baize carefully. Nothing else on. No straights, no flushes, no pairs showing. The only thing that could beat him: someone holding pocket kings to match the one on the table.

He glanced briefly at the other players.

After years of playing, he had this knack. He needed only a glance, almost over their heads – as if he was about to call for chips or food – to take in the faces of his remaining opponents. Other players would stare at a challenger, seeking the clues that might give them an edge. It wasn't necessary – not in Tom's book. This quick glance, perfected over years, was all he needed to size up the opposition left at this final table.

To his left was Corey Clump, big and bluff and easy, with his fat ass hanging off his seat and his dopey smile fooling everyone; but Tom had been watching Corey at the river, and he'd seen that little slump of disappointment. Corey would fold his hand.

Next to Corey was a player he'd seen around but whose name he didn't know. Same age as Tom – maybe thirty-six – clean-cut, wearing sunglasses day and night and with white iPod cables running from his ears. In his head, Tom called him the Pinball Kid, kinda like that deaf, dumb and blind guy in the movie. Except this Pinball Kid wasn't dumb. Not in the head and not in the mouth. This Pinball Kid was one of those players who couldn't shut the fuck up. It was like a tic.

Now he was grinning at Tom.

'Pocket jacks? I got the kings, man. Better fold, man, cos I got you beat . . .'

Tom let the guy drone on, filling the air. He knew it meant

11

nothing. The Pinball Kid might have the kings, he might not.

Behind the Pinball Kid stood a sexy dark blonde, with smoky eyes and a tight dress showing off spectacular curves. She'd been there most of the day, sometimes with a hand on the guy's shoulder, loose but proprietorial, a stand-out in a casino filled with a thousand men and maybe twenty women – and those generally over fifty and crammed into velour sweatpants. She met Tom's eyes briefly but neutrally. She must know what the Pinball Kid had, but her face gave nothing away.

Next to the Pinball Kid was Mr Ling, his face a cliché of inscrutability, but he had a big fat tell, and right now Tom could see Mr Ling's fingers sizing up his dwindling chips, estimating how many hands he could still play after losing this one. Tom was amazed Mr Ling had got this far in the tournament with such an obvious weakness.

He had his own weakness, of course . . .

A few years earlier, in a tournament right here at the Bicycle Club off the 710 freeway, Tom had bluffed everyone out of a monster pot. He'd held a pathetic seven and a two – the worst hand in poker – but he'd decided to make a stand anyway. As the last man shook his head and threw away his cards, they'd hit the dealer's over-eager hand and flipped over: pocket tens! The pair would have stomped all over his lousy hand if the other player had only had the guts to call his bluff. Just the memory sent a thrill up Tom's back as he debated his next move. So far, it was the pinnacle of his poker career – a moment to be taken out every now and then, pored over and savoured, then wound carefully in the soft cloth of memory and tucked safely away once more.

Four hands later, his own over-confidence had hustled him out of the game in a humiliating collapse.

It had been an invaluable lesson for Tom. His game could survive almost anything but his own ego.

But here and now sound judgement told him the Pinball Kid was his only danger. If he had pocket kings, Tom was finished. And, annoyingly, the sunglasses kept Tom from looking into the Pinball Kid's Hold 'Em soul and finding out.

All these thoughts flared in Tom's neurons in bare seconds, and he hardly paused before going all in, pushing what was left of his chips across to join the pot. He knew it would see off anything but pocket kings.

The Pinball Kid hesitated. Then laughed.

Then called his bet.

*

Tom was annihilating his sorrows when the smoky-eyed blonde was suddenly beside him. 'Bad luck,' she said, her voice turning it into a teasing question as she gestured to the barman.

He looked over her head to where the Pinball Kid, Mr Ling and Corey Clump were the only three left at the table, almost hidden by the throng of players and watchers looking for vicarious thrills.

Pocket fucking kings.

He shrugged. 'They say you've got to get lucky six times to win a tournament. I was up to four.'

'You ever been all the way?' she said, with a curious little smile.

He looked at her sharply. Was she coming on to him? Tom

was tall, dark, but only borderline handsome, so he decided to err on the side of caution. 'Cashed a few times.'

She nodded approvingly and looked towards the table. He took the opportunity to glance down at the back of her neck, where a small, curved wisp of hair had escaped her chignon, and now waved gently over her flawless skin in the oxygen-rich breeze being pumped through the club. Something about it thrilled him: he wanted to curl it around his finger and feel the silken softness run across his skin.

He blinked the idea away, and ran his hand up the back of his own neck, feeling the stubble there against his palm. A nervous tic – a tell all of his own – but one he made a monster effort to keep at bay at the poker table. The blonde was sexy as hell but she was with someone else. Poker was fraught enough without banging another player's girl between hands.

His phone rang. 'Shit.' He fumbled it out of his pocket and looked at the number. 'Excuse me.'

She raised a surprised eyebrow: most people who played cards devoutly had nothing better to do on a Sunday or, if they did, they were there to avoid doing it.

They both turned at the shout that greeted the demise of another player. The Pinball Kid stood up from the table and looked around for his girl.

She walked away from Tom without another glance.

*

Tom strode into the bright sunshine, the California heat a shock to his air-conditioned skin. 'Yeah, Pete, what do you want?'

'Hey! How'd you know it was me?'

Tom sighed. Unless it was about planes, Pete LaBello was a Luddite. He'd only just mastered faxes; cell phones were all *Star Trek* to him. 'Your name comes up on the thing. What's up?'

'You at the Bicycle Club?'

Tom deferred answering his boss for the five seconds it took him to make it out of the parking lot and into the honesty zone.

'No.'

'Good. Go Team's about to leave for LAX – got a 737 blade off on the ground. Thought you might like to be first on the scene as you're right there.'

'I'm not on the Go Team.'

Hesitation.

Embarrassment for sure.

Pity, maybe?

'No. Munro's leading.'

Tom let it go. He was still out in the cold, but this was a small indication that a thaw might be on its way. He'd have to swallow his pride and start from the ass-end up if he wanted to stay in his job. And – despite everything – Tom did want to stay in his job. It was the only damned thing he'd ever been any good at. Not just good. Damn good. A helluva lot better than Lenny Munro could ever dream of being.

'Tom?'

'I'm here.'

'You got your flyaway with you, right?'

'Always.'

'Well, if you don't mind doing the donkey work for Lenny . . .'

Pete tried to make it a joke but Tom couldn't humour him

– it was still too raw. Pete must've heard that in his silence because he went on, 'Three dead. They're engineers. I thought it'd suit you.'

Tom felt the unintentional sting of the words before he answered, 'I owe you one.'

'Nah!'

He could almost hear Pete wave away the debt with his generous Italian hands.

He hung up and stood in the unrelenting LA sun, frowning. Pete was kind but transparent.

They're engineers.

Tom knew what his boss had been saying. That he wasn't good with civilians.

*

Tom Patrick wasn't good with civilians. That was why Pete LaBello hadn't called him last night when a Jetstream 31 had gone down in Nevada with seven passengers on board – including a woman flying to see her oilman boyfriend with their six-year-old daughter along for the ride.

But engineers weren't civilians, they were industry, so Tom's investigative powers – which were held in some esteem throughout the National Transportation Safety Board, despite his recent history – would be invaluable. And unsullied by his second and more infamous characteristic: his monumental lack of tact.

Six months ago, Tom Patrick had been lead on a Learjet emergency landing during which a New York stockbroker got his neck snapped. At a press conference, in the full glare of the publicity that only the death of rich people brings, he

16

had bluntly told the hysterical widow – who was demanding the pilot's head – to 'Hold your horses, ma'am.' He'd already established, unofficially, that her husband had not been wearing a seatbelt on touchdown due to a combination of bravado, belligerence and Bell's whisky. And – breaking all NTSB protocols – he'd told her that right there and then. Live. On air.

He had been immediately suspended – and his replacement had taken another two months to make the same version of events a matter of official record. The hysterical widow – still stinging from her halogen humiliation – had tried her best to sue the department for a hundred million dollars. She'd lost, of course, but a rich and humiliated woman's best is usually pretty damn good, and can take a lot of money to beat off. After three months, Tom was quietly reinstated by the back door – on probation and half-pay.

In NTSB terms, the back door was – fittingly – pipelines. For three months and fourteen days, he had been investigating pipeline leaks and fires across the continental United States. Pete hated like hell to lose him from planes, but jumping the gun on probable cause was a cardinal sin at the NTSB – and jumping it on live TV while bad-mouthing a dead millionaire to his grieving widow was always going to mean more than a slap on the wrist for Tom Patrick.

The Learjet was only his most high-profile foot-in-mouth incident. Just from Pete's personal memory – and at fifty-nine his memory was not even that great – he could recall Tom being quoted variously saying that passengers in a stricken 727 were now 'in little tiny chunks all over the Gulf of Mexico'; that the pilot of a wounded DC10 had saved the lives of all those on board through 'brute force and ignorance'; and that a frozen-solid teenaged stowaway who'd dropped out with the landing gear over Casper, Wyoming, had killed a couple in their Ford Taurus 'like a big meat popsicle'.

Pete LaBello was ten months from his gold watch. He and Ann were going to spend their declining years in Vermont and fully expected to live out their retirement in the same unspectacular way they had hitherto achieved in their respective careers. His time at the NTSB and hers teaching high-school physics were unspoiled by drama or particular distinction, and that was the way they liked it.

Pete liked Tom Patrick – he really did. But Tom didn't make even that easy, and the closer to the watch he got, the more wary he was about putting Tom back on planes. At the same time, he knew he couldn't continue indefinitely to waste him on pipelines when they so badly needed his expertise elsewhere. Which was why, when the report came in from LAX shortly after the Jetstream went down, Pete figured sending Tom Patrick north across LA instead of east to Nevada would make the fewest possible waves.

Pete LaBello was wrong.

*

Tom stood on the apron outside Hangar Six and looked around in awe. He'd been with the NTSB for eleven years, but the scale of plane accidents still left him humbled. And this one hadn't even fallen out of the sky or ploughed through a city. This was minor. And yet there was barely a piece of flesh or metal left in the wake of the number-two engine that hadn't been wrecked, ruined or wrapped around another piece of flesh or metal somewhere else.

The plane had been wheeled out of the hangar for an engine run, and had been turned at forty-five degrees to it so the turbulence wouldn't blast the hangar clear into the Pacific Ocean.

He became aware of the huddle of men behind him, waiting for him to say or do something. The airport manager, Duncan Hancock, cleared his throat very slightly. Off to his left, the paramedics who hadn't taken the injured to hospital were waiting to take the dead to the morgue. He recognized the looks on their faces: even though he'd shown his ID and it had been checked with DC by a doubtful assistant, they still thought it unlikely that someone who looked the way he did was about to undertake an official investigation into a vending-machine malfunction, let alone this.

He knew he should have gone home first and got what the manual called 'appropriate clothing' – but what the hell? Lenny Munro and the rest of the team would be here in an hour or two and things would be taken away from him again. Every minute was precious to him, so he was wearing the same tattered jeans and Hollywood Park Casino T-shirt he'd played poker in for the past thirteen hours. He had his 'appropriate' NTSB cap, and that would have to satisfy their sartorial suspicions.

Tom bent down and unzipped the flyaway bag that investigators were required to keep with them at all times. It was packed with everything from paperwork, through a department-issue laptop, to his gym kit. Not that he went to the gym – or had ever been to the gym – but the track pants and T-shirt were good for watching TV in any motel in the south-western United States.

He took the digital video camera from its hard case and began to record the scene.

As always, once he'd started, the rest of the world melted away around him, and he felt the low-level adrenalin drip that made this job not unlike an afternoon at the Bicycle Club.

Tom panned across the scene once, then panned back with the camera pointed up at the destroyed hangar. Then he turned a slow circle, taking in the entire scope of the scene. Glancing at the LCD screen to ensure he was getting everything, he started to move and talk, giving time, date, location and brief circumstances of the incident so far.

'Six injured men have been removed from the scene to LA County Hospital. Two critical with amputations, two stable with open fractures, two with minor wounds and shock.'

He walked past the nose of the plane and into the hangar. The automatic aperture took a second to adjust to the gloomier interior.

'This is body number one – estimated to be twenty yards off the starboard side approximately in line with the . . .' he looked up '. . . main accessory hatch aft of the nose-gear.'

Still shooting, Tom placed a bright orange flag on a small weight beside the body. It was face-down on the cement. He zoomed in. 'Few visible injuries. Minimal blood from the nose and minor cuts.'

He stepped over the man's body, glanced up briefly to see where he was heading next, and stepped into the cool darkness of Hangar Six.

'Body number two.'

Tom raised the camera to show the tattered remains

hanging six feet up the wall on a hook made of twisted corrugated-iron sheeting.

When Tom was a kid the garbage men in his neighbourhood used to tie dolls and teddy bears they found in the trash to the front of their truck. Now he had to force that image out of his mind.

'Body is caught up on metal sheeting presumably torn loose by the incident. It is approximately eight yards from the tip of the starboard wing and approximately six feet from the floor.'

He placed a second flag in the puddle of blood under the dangling black work boots and stared up at the body.

'Cursory inspection shows multiple open wounds and massive loss of blood. Also . . .' He stopped and squinted into the evening sunlight that streamed through the torn metal, then used the camera zoom to help him out. 'Also a substantial piece of metal embedded in the lower abdomen, possibly a fan blade.'

He turned away and looked for body three. As he crossed the floor, he bent down and looked at something small and white. The stub of a cigarette. He marked it and moved on.

Nearby, the lower half of what used to be a man was sprawled on the floor beside a large metal tool cabinet.

'Body three.' Tom placed a flag beside a blue-coveralled knee. 'Part one.' He looked around him and found part two – the upper half of a man, his left arm severed mid-forearm, the right crooked across his chest, his eyes half closed and a spray of his own blood under his chin. Tom frowned as he noticed the man's right hand – frozen with its two forefingers extended like a V for Victory.

He became aware of someone standing beside him, and

turned to see a wiry black man in blood-spattered coveralls and a blanket. He was also looking down at the dead man's hand.

'Sir, you need to get back behind the tape.'

But the man seemed not to have heard him.

'Scissors,' he murmured. Then – never taking his eyes from the body – he held up his own flattened 'paper' hand to explain to Tom. 'He woulda won.'

2

IT WAS DARK by the time Lenny Munro led the Go Team through the small throng of reporters and out to Hangar Six.

Tom had already arranged eternal daylight, courtesy of high-beam magnesium arc-lights. That was the thing about working in LA – the town was never short of lighting equipment. One team of paramedics had departed with bodies one and two, and the pair who'd lost the toss were now picking up the disparate pieces of body three and placing them gingerly in the black bags.

'Tom?'

Tom looked up from his notebook.

Lenny Munro was a heavy-set man of forty-nine, with a ridiculous buzz-cut that he fondly imagined made him look like a retired astronaut, but actually made him look like the hopeless dad in a 1950s sitcom.

'Pete told me he'd sent you.' It was a statement of fact, but Tom could tell Lenny was pissed. What the hell? Let him be pissed. Tom wanted back in on planes, and if he was prepared to swallow his pride and be first-on-scene for a dick like Lenny Munro, then that was Lenny's good fortune.

Tom rose off his haunches and shook his hand briefly.

Lenny was flanked by two investigators in appropriate clothing – Jan Ryland, a slim, bookish woman in her early thirties, and Jim Crane, a tall, greying man with a salt-and-pepper beard.

'Hey, Jan, Jim.'

They nodded – embarrassed to see him. Lenny Munro got down to business.

'What are we looking at?'

'Secured area. Most of the injured were removed before-hand. Maintenance crew was ten-strong. Three dead inside, six in hospital, all hanging on.'

'What about the tenth man?'

'He's over there.' Tom pointed to Halo, who was now behind the tape.

'What's he doing here?'

'The paramedics have checked him out but he refused to go to hospital until his friend was accounted for.'

'Where's his friend?'

'Right there.' Tom pointed to the shapeless black body-bag being rolled into the nearest ambulance. 'And there.' Two paramedics carried a second bag between them.

'Talk to him yet?'

Tom looked at him soberly. 'Lenny, he's in two pieces.'

'You know who I mean.'

Tom shrugged. 'Hey, I'm just first-on-scene. You know I can't start an investigation without you.'

'Just asking. I'm not saying you'd do anything you shouldn't, Tom, you know that.'

'I know that, Lenny.'

They both knew they were being lied to.

*

Twenty-seven minutes before Lenny Munro made it to Hangar Six, Tom had finally finished initial documenting of the scene. He hadn't skimped and he hadn't hurried; he'd made sure that everything he did was done with the utmost efficiency. He'd asked the manager to inform him when the Go Team's scheduled Delta flight touched down from DC. Every time one of Hancock's staff came close to him he held his breath, but he managed to finish before word of the arrival. He'd done his job.

Everything he could glean now was a personal bonus.

Tom packed his flyaway bag, then ducked under the yellow tape to where Halo Jackson stood, holding his blanket tight around his throat. 'How you doing, Mr Jackson?'

'Fine.'

'You been to the hospital?'

'I'm fine.'

Tom glanced at the young woman paramedic who hovered near by. She rolled her eyes, and her silence said, 'Can't force him to go.'

Tom shrugged. If Halo Jackson wanted to live in denial, that was up to him. All it did was save Tom a drive to LA County and that sick, miserable feeling he always got in hospitals. A doctor taking his blood pressure once told him he suffered from 'white-coat hypertension'. Tom had been offended at the time, but once his ego had settled down he'd known the guy was right. Just being around doctors made him clammy.

'Mr Jackson, the—'

'Halo.'

Tom hesitated. 'The investigators will be here soon—'

'You're not the investigator?'

Tom handed him his card: 'I'm just first-on-scene – faster somebody gets here the better – while the Go Team gets together. They'll run the whole thing.'

Halo nodded.

'So,' said Tom, 'what can you tell me?'

Halo didn't say anything at first, and that alone endeared him to Tom. Everyone had an opinion and most people couldn't wait to share; he liked a man who thought about what he was going to say.

Then Halo Jackson shook his head slowly and looked straight into Tom's eyes. 'I have no idea.'

Some fucking bonus.

*

Munro and his team worked through the night, treading carefully around the worst of the drying blood as they started to number a thousand pieces of scattered metal. In the sunshine of the next morning they would go outside and log more. They would find a six-foot peel of engine casing creating havoc with commuter traffic on Sepulveda Boulevard, and a fan blade through the cab of an airport baggage-handling cart. The handler, Carson Holt, had been spared skewering by taking an illicit cigarette break. Later he would lose a day's pay because of it, and wouldn't even go to his union rep. Carson figured a hundred and twelve dollars was a small price to pay for escaping being pinned to his seat by flying debris, and lived his life better for a short time after that.

But for now the Go Team was there under the fake Hollywood daylight, starting the process of reassembling the plane so they could see what had gone wrong and where. It was a two-million-dollar jigsaw, with the pieces scattered in a half-mile radius.

But one piece interested Lenny Munro from the start: the quarter-inch piece of cigarette Tom Patrick had marked. Smoking was not banned in the airport for health reasons alone. More important – way more important to anyone who knew anything about flying – was FOD. Foreign Object Damage. It was a fancy term for litter. In most places litter was an eyesore; in airports it could be death. A knotted condom, a workman's dropped glove, a McFlurry cup: any of these could get sucked into an engine and bring down a plane, and airports around the world employed teams of cleaners – preferably with OCD – to avoid just such an outcome from a bout of minor litter-bugging.

So, Tom Patrick finding a cigarette in the hangar behind the *Pride of Maine* was a big deal to Lenny Munro. A very big deal. A cigarette alone was not enough. But cigarettes came in packs.

And when he presented his Air Accident Report four weeks later, Lenny Munro – quite understandably – placed the blame for the loss of the *Pride of Maine*, the deaths of three engineers and the injuries to six more squarely on the shoulders of maintenance engineer Christopher Stern.

Husband of Vee, father of Katy.

And best friend of Halo Jackson.

3

Tom could feel the heat still rising from the floor of Storage Tank Nine, Amoco farm, Santa Ana. All around him, charred and twisted metal smoked like a dung heap. Although pipelines were not his thing, he knew instinctively what had happened.

Storage Tank Nine had been emptied of gasoline at 06:30 hours. At 15:45 hours, some careless asshole had pumped diesel into it. At 15:59 a stray spark – probably caused by poor electrical bonding during the doomed transfer – had set the latent gas fumes off like a little bomb, and the brand-new diesel had fuelled the resulting conflagration.

Simple.

And yet it would take him a week of collating forensic details and interviews before he could present evidence of what was already as plain as the nose on his face. Tom sighed. There was no fun in pipelines, only grunt work. Now, take that storage tank, fill it with fuel, electrical circuitry, four thousand moving parts and three hundred passengers, then set it on fire as it hurtled across the sky at 500 m.p.h., and he'd be in business . . .

He squinted at the sun, thought of the casino he'd seen on the way into Santa Ana, and wished he were flicking up the corners of his cards to check his hand. A tiny shiver of excitement ran through him – the same way just thinking of pickles made his mouth tingle.

He heard a clanging near the top of the storage tank and looked up. A hard-hatted man was waving at him. 'Your phone's ringing!'

'Well, how 'bout you answer it and set off what's left of the gas fumes in here?'

The man almost did just that, before he realized Tom was being sarcastic. Then he looked sheepish and disappeared, clattering down the iron ladder in what Tom could tell were *not* rubber-soled safety shoes.

The phone was still ringing fifteen minutes later when Tom clambered out of Storage Tank Nine. He could hear it all the way across the site. Tom never set his cell phone to voicemail – he hated returning calls and figured if people really wanted to speak to him they'd call back – but whoever this was had just hung on, listening to the phone ring.

'Patrick.'

'Hey, Mr Patrick. It's Halo Jackson.'

'Who?'

'Halo Jackson. From LAX?'

Tom's mind clicked back to a skinny black man in a blue blanket and was immediately wary. That job was done. The findings had been made public. Blame had been assigned. Why was Halo Jackson calling him now? 'I remember.'

Now that Halo had eventually got him on the line, he was apparently at a loss for what to say. Tom resisted the temptation to say, 'What can I do for you?' It implied that he might be prepared to do something for somebody, and he hated that kind of commitment. The silence stretched between them so long and tight that it became uncomfortable.

'What can I do for you?'

Dammit!

'I called you for a second opinion.'

'On what?'

'On what caused that 737 blade off.'

Tom hesitated. 'Mr Jackson, I don't even have a first opinion. I was just first-on-scene there. That really doesn't involve any investigation. It just means preserving the evidence as early as possible for the Go Team. You'd need to speak to the lead investigator.'

'I already did. That Munro guy? No offence, but he seems kinda like an idiot to me.'

Tom tried not to laugh, and warmed to Halo Jackson for the second time. He wasn't about to volunteer to help him, but he certainly welcomed any anecdotal evidence against Lenny Munro. 'In what way?'

'In the way that means he's wrong. His report was all wrong. He said a cigarette pack got caught in the engine but that's bullshit.'

'How do you know?'

'I know cos Chris Stern din't smoke. He just kept one cigarette – not a pack – in his top pocket. He'd take it out now and then and have, like, a fake drag, then put it away and button his pocket down again. I saw him do it a million times.'

'Isn't it possible—'

'No. It ain't possible.'

Mentally, Tom rolled his eyes. He wasn't getting into this.

'You know, Mr Jackson, if you have any complaints you really need to be talking to the people in DC.'

'I already did. And the other team members.'

This surprised Tom. Jackson was a pretty persistent guy. 'So Munro didn't listen and DC didn't listen?'

'That's right.'

'And I'm your last port of call.'

'That's right.'

Tom was stung. He didn't want this man bothering him but, hell, if he was going to be bothered, he wanted it to be as a priority, not a last resort. The last vestige of his professional persona blew away like mist. 'Why do you give a shit?'

'He was my friend.'

'So? Being your friend doesn't mean he can't be careless. He shouldn't have been smoking.'

'He wasn't. He was giving up,' Halo countered, with spirit.

'Listen, I saw a cigarette myself – on the floor right next to his body.'

'You see a pack?'

'Could have disintegrated in the turbine,' said Tom.

'Not if it was in his pocket.'

'Listen,' Tom said impatiently. 'The guy was smoking. It's highly likely the cigarette was in a pack and just as likely the pack could have been sucked in. It wasn't found on his body.'

'You saw his body, Mr Patrick.'

Tom hesitated. He knew what Halo Jackson meant – Chris Stern's body had been severed mid-torso. The pocket of his coveralls was sliced in two. Who knew whether the cigarette and/or pack had spilled from it before or after the *Pride of Maine* had become a spectacular death machine? Lenny

31

Munro's probable cause relied on circumstantial evidence, but then, this wasn't an exact science.

Halo continued doggedly: 'They've taken his death benefits. And his pension. His wife and kid can't have them. They've lost Chris and they're losing everything else too. Now Air Maintenance say they might sue his estate to recover the compensation they have to pay out. They could lose their home.'

'That's not my problem.'

Halo was silent for a long moment. 'I saw you on the TV a while back. You were on the news. Telling some New York witch to get off some pilot's back.'

'So?'

'You get into trouble for that?'

Tom paused, glancing out at the godforsaken fuel tanks. 'Some.'

'Yeah, I thought you would. Soon as I saw it.'

'What's your point, Mr Jackson?'

'Well, my point is, I need someone who's not afraid of trouble.'

'Good luck finding him,' said Tom, and hung up.

*

The Rubstick was smaller and shabbier than the LA clubs, but once Tom sat down, everything was the same. Same game, same green tables, same people – men in net truckers' caps or comped casino jackets, a few women, all too fat or painfully thin.

He bought in for two hundred dollars on a no-limit Hold 'Em table. First hand, he was dealt pocket sevens. Another came up on the flop and Tom was off. He walked out at ten thirty p.m. a thousand dollars richer than he'd been at eight o'clock.

Tom wouldn't have left if he hadn't got to be at the Amoco farm tomorrow at eight and he was still buzzing from the high of winning. Half a mile from the Motel 6, he spotted the Sawmill, with its flickering pink neon sign and, underneath that, 'Gentlemen's Club'.

Tom didn't want to sleep. He felt better than he had in a long time. Since his rapid demotion to pipelines. Since he'd come home to find Ella sitting on the couch with her bags packed around her, and a cab running its meter outside.

'Hi,' he'd said.

'I'm going,' she'd said.

'Where?'

'Somewhere else.'

Shit, why'd he have to think about that just when he was feeling so good?

He swung into the Sawmill's parking lot.

Inside, it was cramped and foggy and cold from the dry ice wafting lazily across the stages. Two Vietnamese girls were dancing, their eyes half closed with concentration, their hard, lithe bodies turning like snakes around the poles. They wore only G-strings, and their fake breasts looked hard and awkward, like they might come off in your hand.

Tom sat down and ordered a beer from an angular red-head in a sequined bikini. The music ended and one of the Vietnamese girls gyrated over the customers, opening her legs. The silver-haired man sitting closest to Tom stuffed a twenty up under the G-string, and squeezed her inner thigh at the same time. Tom saw the girl hide a wince and smile a reptilian smile at the man. She drew away from him, and displayed herself to Tom.

'I only just got here.' What the hell. He wasn't paying for something he hadn't seen.

The girl only shrugged and smiled. 'Next time you pay me good.'

'Yeah, next time.'

A new song played through inadequate speakers that couldn't quite handle the bass, and two new girls came out. One was a pneumatic blonde with breasts the size of footballs. The other was a black girl with soft features, small breasts, a tiny waist and a big ass. The blonde started to work herself into a frenzy on the pole and several men got up and took seats closer to her. Tom stayed where he was. The black girl didn't seem to notice that she'd been deserted. She continued her sinuous dance with her brass lover, seeming to enjoy the reactions of her own body, lost in a world of her own, and not making eye-contact with her bread-and-butter customers.

Tom felt like a voyeur.

When the music stopped, the blonde's G-string was not enough to hold the tens and twenties she was getting. Tom and two drunken college kids were the only customers who'd stayed where they were. The college kids stuffed five each into the black girl's G-string. Tom handed her a fifty.

She smiled and said, 'Thank you,' in a soft Southern voice.

Her name was Lucia and, for three more fifties, she came back to the Motel 6 and he held her all night long. At dawn he awoke, hardening in her mouth, and she earned her money then.

He took her to breakfast at a diner on the strip, watched

her fill up on banana pancakes and insisted on paying for a cab to take her home.

When he got back to the room, she'd left the three fifties on the pillow.

Fuck, thought Tom, it comes to something when it takes a whore to make you feel all warm and fuzzy.

4

Frik Venter was stuck in traffic. The fact that he was stuck in traffic in one of the most beautiful places on the planet completely passed him by. He was too used to seeing Table Mountain with its cloth of cloud looming over Cape Town on his right, and the broad blue sweep of Table Bay on his left, for it to make a dent in his consciousness. All Frik Venter saw now was the back of the pick-up truck in front of him, which was packed with a dozen brown-skinned men in dirty work clothes, who apparently found him an object of some amusement. They stared at him boldly, then one would say something and the others would laugh so loudly he could hear them over his thrumming air-conditioning and Fleetwood Mac's *Rumours*.

Frik tried to ignore them, even though they were only ten feet away and entirely filling his line of vision. After about fifteen minutes of humiliation, he saw his chance and changed lanes. A woman in a Toyota Yaris sideswiped his Merc and – in the silence after the bang – he could hear the workmen almost hysterical with laughter. To add insult to injury, the line of traffic he'd just crashed to leave, started to move.

Frik Venter ignored the accusing glances of the first-class passengers and closed the cockpit door behind him. 'Sorry, Vernon.'

'You okay? Heard you had a bump.'

'Women drivers.'

'Tell me about it.'

Frik hung his jacket on the peg and strapped himself in. 'We all ready?'

Vernon nodded. 'I did the walk-around and went through work-ups with Toby.'

Vernon Langeholm and Toby Marais were both experienced pilots and Frik trusted they'd done the pre-flight work-up and done it well.

'Souls on board?'

'Hundred and twenty-four – now you're here.'

Frik told Air Traffic Control they were clear for pushback.

Flight SA77 to Johannesburg lifted off safely, then banked away from the city and the sea, made a lazy hairpin and climbed north-east towards the Karoo desert.

*

Harold Robbins Mhleli had been named for an author whose books he'd never be able to read. He had managed pretty well up to Grade Three, enjoying comics like *Mutant Ninja Turtles* and *Richie Rich*, then things had got away from him and suddenly the four-mile walk to school without shoes had seemed a high price to pay when his days were increasingly spent standing outside the hot, fly-blown classroom with palms stinging from the strap. Not that Harold really minded standing outside. He had a well-developed imagination, and spent hours being a soccer star or a cattle rancher while his more industrious friends were just children labouring over nouns and verbs and the value of x.

After the third bad report in a row, his father announced that Harold needed to leave school and get a job. His mother, who'd named him more in hope than expectation, sadly had to agree, and instead they put all their hopes for a child/pension-plan into Harold's younger brother, Sofiso.

Harold was twelve and had been working on the ostrich farm for two years. He liked it. After his first week – when he'd been kicked so hard he couldn't breathe for what seemed like ever – he'd learned to respect the big, fluffy-looking birds, and he got along fine with the half-dozen other boys who worked on the farm, turning eggs, feeding and cleaning out.

But his favourite thing was to ride the birds. Tourists came three times a week to see the ostrich races and, more often than not, stick-thin Harold was one of the jockeys. He loved walking out into the makeshift paddock in a brightly coloured nylon blouse, the way the tourists clapped and laughed, and the rich white children watched him, wide-eyed, wishing they could be like him – a jockey on an ostrich about to pound across the Karoo. For Harold, this part was almost better than winning the race, because if he won he was too excited to care and to see what anyone else was thinking or doing. No, he liked this as much – this complete awareness of himself and his brief appearance in the spotlight, looking grown-up and professional and courageous.

Today he was on Lemon, the ostrich that had kicked him that first week. Harold didn't hold it against Lemon. After all, the bird was named because he was so sour, so he should have seen it coming. But Lemon was also fast so Harold would have forgiven him almost anything.

Harold and five other boys got changed in the baking, buzzing air behind the thatched toilets, where black-widow spiders hung shinily under the eaves, protecting the unhatched offspring of murdered fathers. Harold's shirt today was sunshine yellow, which made his dark skin look exotic. The boys all wore proper riding helmets, and Harold adjusted the straps because Jonty had worn it yesterday and Jonty had the biggest head of any boy his age Harold had ever seen. The boys were always laughing at Jonty's head.

Harold loved the helmets almost as much as he loved the dazzling blouses. One day he imagined he would be walking out into a grass paddock, and getting on a horse instead of a bird, and thousands of people would watch him win races. Or maybe he'd just take Lemon up to Durban and enter him in the July Handicap and see how those thoroughbreds liked taking on the fastest ostrich in the Karoo.

The boys walked out into the desert sunshine and the thirty or forty tourists who'd braved the hot, dusty coach ride from Oudtshoorn broke into applause. Harold tried not to grin. He didn't want to look as if this was special to him. He wanted to look like an old hand.

Lemon's head twisted and darted under the canvas bag as Limping Andy jacked Harold on to the ostrich's back. With his knees, Harold clamped the bird's wings where they met the body, and took hold of the single rein, which led to Lemon's beak and enabled Harold to steer a vaguely circular path. At the familiar jerking, rolling movement of the big bird under him, Harold let his body go loose and roll with it, while his knees gripped like iron. He looked down at the tourist children gazing up at him and felt such pride that he thought his chest would burst with it. He scowled to show this was all in a day's work to him.

'OH!'

It wasn't the 'Oh' of a father whose child has just dropped ice cream down his pants; it wasn't the 'Oh' of a woman whose heel has broken.

It was an 'Oh!' so forceful and loud and startled that people turned away from the ostriches to look. What they saw was a young man squinting up into the sky, with a look of not-understanding on his face.

Everybody looked up. Even Harold.

A plane was falling out of the sky over their heads.

That was Harold's first thought, quickly followed by one that insisted such a thing was impossible.

'Shit!'

Harold glanced down as Limping Andy left his side – yanking the canvas bag from Lemon's head – and ran.

And suddenly that was what everybody was doing. Running and screaming. Harold looked back up – and the plane that had been picture-book bits of glittering silver was huge now and filled the air above him and he screamed at Lemon and kicked him so hard that he almost fell off, but the bird took off fast, faster than he'd ever run before.

Harold just clung on – he had no idea of steering Lemon: he just wanted to stay on and get away from where he'd been when the plane was right over his head. Lemon's mighty feet hit the ground concussively, shooting pulses up Harold's spine. There was a noise in his head like a bomb and the heat from the sun on his back seemed to increase impossibly as a wave of pressure propelled Lemon forward at an even greater pace. Harold buried his face in the black feathers and screamed and kicked and screamed and kicked until it slowly dawned on him that if he wasn't safe by now it would have been too late.

Almost a mile from the farm, Harold put his head up and started to turn Lemon in a wide circle to slow him down.

Something the size of a motorcycle hit the ground so hard in front of them that it bounced several feet into the air. Lemon skittered sideways and Harold fell off. The bird hammered away across the scrubby desert, leaving a comical trail of Roadrunner dust behind it.

'Lemon!'

He knew it was pointless. They never came back when they were called, and Lemon had the look of a bird that wasn't coming back, period.

Harold got up slowly and turned to find what he first took to be some kind of Ninja Turtle with a hi-tech shell. But as he walked round it he could see that it was actually Captain Frik Venter, still strapped into his seat, his staring eye-whites pricked with blood, his shirt ripped from his body, leaving only a Yogi-bear collar and tie, and with one arm cut off above the elbow as cleanly as if Harold's mother had been preparing him for dinner.

Harold got sick, but was careful to bend well forward so he wouldn't ruin his sunshine-yellow shirt.

*

South African jet crash kills 138

AP – A passenger jet crashed in South Africa yesterday, killing all 124 passengers and crew on board and 14 people on the ground.

Although the Boeing 737 came down in the remote Karoo desert, debris fell on a farm where tourists had gathered to watch the popular ostrich races.

None of the dead are believed to be US Citizens.

Well, that's okay, then, thought Tom, wryly.

Then, almost immediately: What the hell is an ostrich race?

He fired up his computer and checked out the crash online. It was a knee-jerk thing with him. He had to see it. Had to look for clues; had to imagine what the cause might have been, even if he had no connection with the investigation. Like an angler buying a magazine to see how his own catch matches up to carp caught a thousand miles away. Ella had called it obsession; he called it professional curiosity.

The South African *Weekly Mail and Guardian* had the best coverage. Pictures of the wreckage still smouldering. At least, one part of the wreckage. The plane had broken in two, with the greater part of the fuselage and wings landing on the farm in a blazing fireball. It had been only twenty minutes out of Cape Town, its fuel tanks still well over half full.

The cockpit and fuselage forward of the wings had come down about a mile away.

Tom scrolled down through the pictures of scorched

earth, black debris scattered in a wide radius. One picture was of Terrence Terblanche, forty-six, who owned the farm, crying over the body of an ostrich that looked like the crispy remains of a giant Thanksgiving turkey gone wrong. Tom snorted in amusement.

He looked again at the picture of the fuselage. Something about it bugged him but he couldn't quite get it.

The next picture was of a small African boy, whose wide, shocked eyes were focused on something behind the photographer's shoulder, as if the horrors around him were too distracting to allow him to look straight into the lens. He wore a bright yellow shirt in a silky material. The caption read: 'Harold Robbins, aged 12, who escaped on an ostrich'.

Struck by the left-field strangeness of the caption, Tom Googled, found a video link, and watched in wonder as brightly dressed boys raced seven-foot birds across a distant desert.

You learn something new every day, he thought.

5

Halo Jackson hadn't learned anything new for weeks, not since Tom Patrick's address, which appeared to have done his cause no good at all.

He hadn't seen the report of the crash of SA77 because it didn't make Fox News and the only newspaper he bought with any regularity was *Daily Racing Form*.

Halo had been granted three weeks off after what he now thought of as 'the Hangar Six incident'. Three weeks was apparently the time it took to get over seeing your best bud cut in half. His union rep moaned and bitched and told Halo he would be well within his moral rights to fake post-traumatic stress and bump it up to a few months on full pay.

Halo knew he'd never get over it. He didn't need to fake PTS: he had the uncomfortable feeling that he'd never get over that either. Just, different people handled it in different ways.

Cal Lemanski had gone right off the rails – had gone what Halo's grandmother used to call 'doo-lally' – and was looking at an early pension.

Some of the guys were envious of Cal and his imminent life of leisure, but Halo had gone to see him in the Packer Institute – what his grandmother used to call 'the nuthouse'

– and it had made him shiver. Chris Stern had been cut in half by the *Pride of Maine,* but Cal Lemanski had been scooped out like a tub of Ben & Jerry's at a kids' birthday party. The big Pole, with his thick black beard and booming laugh, looked like a half-deflated sex doll, sagging at the joints and barely able to hold the weight of his own head. He'd recognized Halo and thanked him for the *Juggernaut* without smiling; just left it on his lap, shiny and unthumbed. Then Cal's wife, Paula, had come in, so Halo had patted Cal's back and said goodbye. When he left, Cal's wife was sitting holding her husband's gnarled hand on top of a glossy blonde licking her own left nipple; Paula stared at Cal and Cal stared at the wall.

No. Halo reckoned going back to work ten minutes after the Hangar Six incident would have been better than what Cal Lemanski was facing.

Halo's three weeks off had been wasted anyway. He'd get up early because that was his routine, and watch *Judge Judy* re-runs until he was hungry enough for breakfast. Then he'd go to the park or the movies. Three times he'd gone to see Vee and Katy. Vee seemed constantly dazed, and Katy was by turn naughty and quietly tearful for Daddy, her little world rocked by something she didn't understand.

After the third time, he'd realized he was being no help and stopped going. Vee had her mother to lean on.

Halo had his own demons to face. He had to make a conscious effort to stand his ground the first time an engine was run in testing. He put his protectors on the instant it started, and felt it buzzing in his chest. Bile rose in his throat and he swallowed hard. None of the men on this shift had been in Hangar Six. All his crew were still in hospital or recovering slowly at home. No one would really understand if he spewed all over his shoes.

Then, a couple of months after he got back – just when he'd thought he was doing okay – he finished his shift and found another man using Chris's locker.

'What the hell are you doing?'

Everyone looked round at Halo. The fair-haired youngster at the locker stared in surprise. 'Uh, excuse me?'

'Who said you could use that locker?'

The kid blushed maroon. 'Um, Mr, um, Mr . . . the supervisor guy.' He was in his undershorts and a T-shirt, holding his spanking new coveralls defensively in front of him. 'I'm new. Aaron Perry.'

He held out his hand but Halo ignored it. Chris's possessions had been tossed into a file box. He stared around the locker room with tight lips. 'Who did that?'

Gully Johnson buttoned up his coveralls and nodded at the blushing Aaron, who said, 'The guy told me to put this stuff in a box and use the locker.'

'You just throw it in like that?'

Perry glanced around the room for support, but no one was taking his side. 'Sorry. I thought it was stuff nobody wanted.'

In another mood at another time, Halo would have agreed with him. Apart from a couple of plaid shirts and a pair of worn Reeboks, the box held a bottle of aftershave, another of L'Oréal shampoo ('Because I'm worth it,' Chris used to say), a few coins, a photo of Chris with Vee and Katy, a cross-head screwdriver and a creased poster of Scarlett Johansson with oily gum marks in each corner.

Perry moved aside warily as Halo came forward and

picked up the box. In his arms, he could smell the aftershave and he bit his lip as he shoved the box into the bottom of his own locker, on top of his training shoes. He slammed the door and clicked the padlock on it, then grabbed his jacket and left.

'Sorry, man,' he heard Perry say behind him.

The next time he went in to work his locker smelt like cat's piss. He threw away Chris's Reeboks and sprinkled Chris's aftershave around to try to chase out the reek. He took the file box and loaded it into his car.

On his way home that night, he put it in a dumpster behind a Taco Bell, then cried all the way through the drive-thru.

*

Four days afterwards, when Tom Patrick got back to the rented Long Beach condo he bitterly called home, there was a stack of bills on the mat and one white hand-addressed envelope. Inside it was a picture of Chris Stern before a 737 fan blade had sliced him in two like a slab of blue steak. Next to him was a pretty young woman with shining hair and big green eyes, and between them a girl of about five, with her mother's eyes and her father's wide smile.

There was an LA phone number scribbled on the back of the photo, which Tom didn't call.

6

THE PINBALL KID SAT DOWN beside Tom and they exchanged the briefest of eyebrow-raises as they bought their tournament chips. Tom waited at least half a minute before glancing up to his right. The Pinball Kid's girl was nowhere to be seen.

Tom's personal disappointment was tempered immediately by his rapid evaluation of how this desertion would affect the Pinball Kid's play. His ego might have taken a battering, therefore he might be more cautious at the table. On the other hand, playing with the hand of a beautiful woman on your shoulder might be a distraction. Although it hadn't proved much of a distraction last time they'd met, thought Tom, with a sour pang.

He didn't know any of the other players taking their seats at the table. He glanced at them, sizing them up with a single flicker. A Chinese woman, two Latinos in their forties. A girl in her twenties looked up for approval from her boyfriend, who stood behind her, just as excited. Amateurs.

A tall, reed-thin old man, who looked like he'd just walked from Nebraska, slid into his seat and gazed morosely at his two hundred dollars until it disappeared and was replaced with ten stacks of red chips. Then he stared at them as if he couldn't believe his hard luck already. Tom was wary of him.

The last person to take his seat was Halo Jackson.

*

'You owe me two hundred dollars.' Tom walked angrily to his car with Halo a few paces behind him.

'How come?'

'My buy-in.'

'I didn't ask you to stand up.'

'I should call the cops.'

'Why?'

'You're stalking me.'

'I was playing cards in a public place. It's a free country. How's that stalking?'

'What about the phone call? And the photo?'

Halo said nothing. Tom reached his car and opened the door. He turned to Halo.

'Look, I can't help you – I really can't. I wasn't part of the investigating team, and the report has already been published. To be honest, I'm not part of any investigating team right now. I'm on the outside trying to get back in. Helping you wouldn't help me to do that, even if I thought I could help you, which I can't.'

Halo stood resignedly in the humid LA smog. 'Cos of your trouble?'

'That's right.'

Halo gazed off towards where the mountains would be if only the smog would clear. 'I'm sorry.'

'Me too.'

Tom got into his car. Halo stepped aside so he could pull

out of his parking space, but the Buick coughed, caught and then died. He twisted the key again. Same thing. 'Fuck!'

Halo was hovering, which only made it worse. Tom tried again, feeling the heat rise in his face.

'Won't start?'

Tom wanted to punch Halo. Instead, exerting enormous self-control, he got out and flipped up the hood.

'This is a nice car,' said Halo, conversationally. He glanced down the battered driver's side. 'You should take more care of it.'

Tom ignored him. He knew the Buick was a piece of shit; his father had hated it before him. He slammed the hood down angrily, having barely glanced at the engine, and got out his phone.

'What you doing?'

'Calling a cab.'

It was busy. Tom gritted his teeth and hit redial.

'For a ride?'

'No. I want it to run me down and put me out of my misery. Or, even better, run *you* down and put me out of my misery.'

Halo apparently decided to ignore the sarcasm. 'My car's right here. I'll give you a ride. Least I can do.'

The cab number was still busy. Tom snapped his phone shut and glared at Halo. 'You're right,' he said. 'It is.'

*

Halo's car was an immaculate pale blue 1977 Mustang. Tom got into the passenger seat, then crossed his arms to show he was in no mood to be grateful.

Halo made a couple of attempts at conversation, which were met with angry silence. They drove to the 710 and headed for Long Beach. Halo sang along to Buddy Holly on the radio, playing with the hiccups and grinning when he got them right. Tom glared at him but without conviction. He couldn't quite work Halo out and suddenly wondered what kind of poker player he'd have been if they'd stayed. Halo gave the impression of being a flake. His wide, buck-toothed grin and his lazy, hooded eyes made him look like he'd just got high, but Tom knew there must be more to him. Hell, just to qualify for his job he'd have to be a pretty smart guy. Meticulous, organized – and his attention to detail also made him dogged. He'd already shown that in his pursuit of Tom and the rest of the DC Go Team. Right or wrong, Tom admired doggedness like a mall chick admires Miu Miu.

He realized he was veering dangerously close to the rocks of giving Halo an inch, and made up for it by scowling so hard at Halo's sing-along to 'Oh Boy' that Halo gave up and switched to KFI 690. The call-in was 'My Mother Rules My Life' and finally Halo and Tom both snorted at the same thing at the same time, and the atmosphere in the car cleared along with the smog, as the Long Beach breeze started to kick in.

'You mind if I make a call on the way? Something I gotta do.'

Tom shrugged. 'It's your car.'

Halo came off the freeway and took a left on to Bellflower. Then he swung a right off the strip on to an immediately residential street, with small but neatly tended front yards behind low chain-links. He pulled half on to the kerb outside one that had blazing flowerbeds but a shaggy lawn. 'Come in.'

Tom sighed, but Halo had already walked up the path, leaving him no one to protest to. He sprang his seatbelt.

As he came up the steps, someone opened the door to Halo – a small girl who flung her arms around his legs. A small girl Tom recognized. He stopped dead and Halo met his eyes guiltily.

Tom would have walked straight off the porch and tried again for a cab but, before he could, the girl's mother was at the screen door.

'Hi, Halo.' Tom couldn't see her yet, but she sounded genuinely pleased to see him. 'Long time no see! Come in.' The kid took Halo's hand and tugged him towards the door.

Halo looked round at Tom. 'Uh, Vee, this is a friend of mine, Tom Patrick.'

She stuck her head round the door and smiled at him. Green eyes, glossy brown hair pulled back off her face. The woman in the photo with Chris Stern. Except now she looked five years older, although Tom knew she wasn't.

'Hi, Tom, come inside.'

Out of the fierce sunshine, the interior of the house was dark and cool and uncluttered but for a dolls' tea party going on in the living room.

'Do you want some tea?' The child looked up at Tom earnestly and he felt himself redden. He had no idea about children or what to say to them.

'Okay.'

The child took his hand and led him to the couch. 'You sit here.'

Vee winked at him. 'Don't let her bully you now, Tom.'

Halo followed Vee into the kitchen and Tom sat where he

was told. He tried to hear what Halo was saying, but the child held out a tiny cup and saucer to him. 'Do you want sugar?'

Tom looked into the empty cup and wondered why he was even considering his options. 'Yeah. Okay.'

She picked up a little china bowl and a mustard spoon and spooned air into his cup. Then she fetched a little jug from the coffee-table. 'Do you want cream?'

'No, thanks.'

She frowned. 'But I have a cream jug.'

'I don't take cream.'

To his confusion the kid's sunny demeanour clouded. She looked forlorn. He felt guilty and irritated at the same time. Ella used to get that look when he'd come in from a long day at work and told her he only had time for a quick bite before going to the Bicycle Club. He'd asked her a million times to come with him but she wouldn't. Wasn't interested. Never would be. Not his fault.

'But the cream's the best bit!' Halo came back into the room and put two mugs of coffee down on the table. 'Can I have some tea, please, Katy? With cream and sugar?' Katy's face cleared and she fussed over Halo, carefully handing him a little teacup. Tom sipped his coffee from the mug, but Halo dipped his tiny teacup into his coffee and drank it from there. Katy giggled. 'Best tea in the world, Katy.' She snuggled on to the couch between them, totally happy. Tom felt stupid: that was all it took.

Vee came in with a cup of coffee and sat in the La-Z-Boy. A man's chair. Black leather, remote-control holsters, leg-rest levers. She was lost in it, curling her legs under her like a girl, and resting her coffee on the arm.

There was an uncomfortable silence. Tom wasn't used to making conversation for the sake of it.

Vee leaned her cheek on her palm and looked at him frankly. 'Halo tells me you might be able to help us, Tom.'

*

Tom slammed the door of the Mustang, hoping it would somehow break, but it was made of sterner stuff. Halo ignored him and waved at Vee and Katy on the porch as he pulled back round towards Bellflower.

'You mad at me?'

Tom's jaw worked but he didn't trust himself to speak yet.

Halo pulled out into traffic – he was a careful driver. 'Great girl, ain't she? We went to Vegas for the weekend and there she was, waiting tables. She and Chris did a bit of flirting and he gave her a twenty-dollar tip. Then we went to the Luxor to lose some money. Halfway through the night he disappears. I soldier on alone, determined to lose my quota, y'know? Finally get to bed around midnight – no Chris. Next morning he comes in to breakfast with her – married! Man! I pulled him aside and says, "Are you goddamned crazy?" I'm, like, "Get it cancelled, man! You don't even know this girl." But he wouldn't. I mean, it was nuts, right?' Halo glanced at Tom for confirmation that it was nuts, but got nothing. 'That was a pretty uncomfortable ride home, I can tell you. Kinda like this.'

Tom refused to play.

Halo sighed. 'I was so down on that girl. We come back to LA, they move in together, and bit by bit I realize she ain't here to break his heart or his bank. It's the real thing, you know? Love at first sight. You know?' Again he glanced at Tom.

A long silence, then Tom frowned, suddenly focusing on the road. 'Why are we going back this way?'

*

Halo pulled into the Bicycle Club lot, stopped the Mustang in front of Tom's Buick and waited.

Finally Tom sighed. 'You see the crash in South Africa?'

Halo looked surprised and shook his head.

'737. Like yours. But this one came apart in mid-air and fell on an ostrich farm.'

Halo seemed suitably bemused.

'Did you know they race ostriches out there?' Halo shook his head again.

'Yeah. They got little kids as jockeys and everything.' Halo looked dubious, so he added: 'Seriously.'

Halo obviously felt he should say something, so he said, 'Gee.'

'Looks like maybe it was a blade off.'

That changed the expression on Halo's face.

'Are you involved in the investigation?'

'Hell, no. Just looked at the pictures online. Seems to me like the fuselage split just fore of the wing.'

'Like the *Pride of Maine*.'

'Like the *Pride of Maine*,' agreed Tom. 'It might be nothing.'

Halo nodded slowly. 'But it's something.'

Tom shrugged. He wasn't making any promises – not based on viewing a couple of crash-scene pix on the god-damned Internet. But something in his gut had stirred and bothered him enough that, after he'd got over the ostrich

55

races, he'd continued thinking about what it might be. Like many of his best moments, it had come while he was asleep, nudging him awake at 3.02 a.m. so he could suffer in its grip until dawn. It was a tenuous link. Same kind of plane; the fuselage parting in the same kind of place. But Tom knew that instinct played a bigger part in investigations than anybody ever cared to admit. Sure, it always had to be supported by the evidence, but it was instinct that told him where to look for that evidence; what that evidence might mean when he found it.

If he didn't trust his instinct, he'd never have mentioned the South African plane.

'So you'll help.'

'Shit.' Tom was irritated with Halo for trying to make him commit right out in the open like that.

'You will, right? You said to Vee—'

'Christ, leave me alone, will you?' Tom shoved open the door and slammed it behind him. It still didn't break.

Tom ignored Halo and pulled out his phone, coming round the Mustang to stand by the hood of his own car.

Halo sighed and reached into the glove box; he held up a hose clip. 'Man, I'm not sure you'd even *be* any help. You know what brings down a 737 but you can't fix your own car?'

Tom recognized the clip that had previously held the fuel line to the Buick's carburettor. 'Sonofabitch.' He flipped his phone shut and snatched the clip from Halo.

'You have my number.' Halo waved and drove carefully away.

7

TOM FELT THE TIME had come to talk to Pete LaBello but he didn't know what to say to him on the phone, so – in a rare piece of forward-thinking – he caught the earliest flight he could to DC.

He hated to fly. Unlike most professionals in the field, familiarity had bred in him not contempt for the mundanity of air travel but a doom-laden feeling that every flight he took shortened the odds of his plane going down.

Tom asked for a seat fewer than seven rows from the wing exit. The Southwest Airlines attendant – whose badge read 'Gary Holstein' – raised a plucked eyebrow and looked into Tom's face with a suggestive smile. 'You a safety-first kinda guy?'

Tom nodded briefly, but the attendant appraised him over the counter and obviously thought he was worth a follow-up. He leaned forward conspiratorially as he held out Tom's boarding pass. 'Not as much fun that way.'

Tom glanced behind him to make sure they couldn't be overheard. He put his elbows on the counter, casually getting closer to the man, who gazed into Tom's green eyes with an expression that said he couldn't believe his luck at this turn for the intimate.

Tom's voice was soft, almost tender: 'Well, call me picky, but I think having a seventy-five per cent chance of getting out of a downed plane seems like a lot more fun than being trampled unconscious, then flash-fried to a carbon shell.'

It took a moment for Gary Holstein to register that what Tom was saying was not about sex. When it did, his face drained of a little colour and all its cockiness. Tom took the ticket from his slack hand. 'Thanks, Gary.'

On the plane, Tom counted the seats to the exit. He was four rows back. He closed his eyes and visualized getting out in the dark. Then he visualized getting out in the dark while crawling on the floor and holding his breath.

'You okay?'

He opened his eyes and turned to the woman beside him. A nice-looking woman in her forties, with short brown hair and hoop earrings. 'I'm fine.'

The woman patted his hand reassuringly. 'Fear of flying?'

It was the oldest cliché in the book, but Tom said it anyway: 'No, of crashing.'

She smiled as if he'd said he was scared of the Loch Ness Monster.

He took the safety card from the seat pocket in front of him and checked the brace position for his seat. Most people didn't even know there were different brace positions for different seats.

'Oh, I never read those dumb things,' said the woman. 'I mean, if the plane goes down, what good's that going to do you?'

Tom could have told her that it might make the difference between life and death; that 95 per cent of plane crashes were potentially survivable; and that, if you remained conscious and mobile when one of those planes hit land or water, it was these small things – these *dumb* things – that improved your chances of getting out. And getting out was what it was all about. He'd put flags beside enough bodies in the past eleven years to know that getting out meant everything to survival. He'd put flags next to bodies burned up in their seats because they'd forgotten the lap-belt was not a car seatbelt and, in their panic, had clawed frantically at their hips for the release; bodies that had collapsed in the doorway, choked by the toxic fumes just inches from fresh air, because they were eight rows away from the exit, not seven; drowned, bloated bodies in inflated life preservers – passengers who'd panicked and pulled the string before getting out of the jet, and who'd been pinned to the ceiling like bugs as the cabin filled with water.

He could have told her. There had been a time when he *would* have told her. When he'd started the job he used to tell people, hoping to help. But he'd soon realized they didn't want to hear the horror stories. They wanted to eat their peanuts and believe it would never happen to them.

So he just smiled at the woman in the hoop earrings and watched the safety demonstration intently while everyone around him read their newspapers.

*

The United States passed beneath Tom in a vast brown and green patchwork quilt until Kentucky popped into view, all dark woods and brilliant grass, like an emerald in dirt. Thirty-five thousand feet up was as close as he'd ever been to Kentucky, but he could never fly over it without thinking of

Fort Knox – and then of the billions of dollars' worth of horseflesh standing in the bluegrass paddocks below him, with only a bit of creosoted post-and-rail between them and any man with a rope halter who cared to take his chances.

Gold was cold and garish. But Galileo, Tapit, Frankel? Living, breathing poker chips in a high-stakes game played across the world by men and women with nerves of whip-steel.

Tom never bet on the horses, but he was in awe of the stud industry. Poker was a game of odds, but breeding was a seemingly impossible shot in the dark. A heady voodoo of parenting and progeny, genetics and eugenics, nature and nurture to produce the *über*-horse, whose heart and mind and legs and lungs made it a winning machine and – even more lucratively – a template from which more winning machines might be reliably churned out. The odds made him dizzy. Even when the breeder's work had been done to perfection, the rare talent might be sent to a trainer who didn't understand that the horse needed bar shoes behind, or a sheep for company, or to be stabled next to this filly or that colt to give of his best. And even if he did, then this precious gem, having been cut to a pinpoint of brilliance, could be ridden by the world's greatest jockey and not care for the smell of his aftershave, or the way he fiddled with the reins, or how the grandstand at Keeneland looked in the afternoon sun, or the feel of grass instead of dirt, or the shadow of the winning post as he came up the stretch.

A million and one things had to go right – and each at the right time. Miracle odds. It made getting lucky six times to win a poker tournament seem a ridiculously simple task, and – as always – by the time they were over Lexington and the truly great farms, Tom felt both poverty-stricken and inadequate.

Thank God, Kentucky passed quickly and he could rebuild his self-esteem over West Virginia, as the dirt-poor coal-mining towns passed miserably below.

*

'Tom!' Pete's PA, Kitty Rees, was obviously surprised to see him – and not in a good way, Tom thought, when he saw her face.

He liked Kitty. She'd been with Pete since joining at the age of twenty-two, ten years before, and she and Tom had sort of grown into their jobs together. They'd even fooled around once after getting drunk at the only office Christmas party he'd ever attended. It hadn't been much – her hand up his shirt, his hand high on her thigh, and an exchange of alcohol-flavoured saliva, Rolling Rock and white rum. He always thought of Kitty when he tasted rum, but that was the only legacy of a long-gone incident. For a while they'd been sheepish around each other, then Tom had snapped out of it and helped her do the same. 'What the hell, Kitty?' he'd told her. 'No one's going to blame you for being unable to resist me.' They'd both laughed and gone back to being friends.

But now she didn't seem happy to see him.

'Don't worry, Kitty, I'm not here to make a scene.'

'I didn't think you—'

'Yeah, you did.'

She hesitated, then admitted, 'Yeah, I did.'

They smiled.

'Pete in?'

61

By way of an answer, Kitty got up and tapped lightly on his door before opening it and speaking quietly. Tom noticed she'd put on a little weight, but it suited her. She turned round and caught him looking. 'What?'

'Nothing.'

'You think I look fat?'

'I think you look sexy as hell.'

She gave a mock-frown. 'You're so going to get sued one of these days.'

'Or laid, I'm hoping.'

Kitty smiled. She didn't look like she was about to call any lawyers. 'Go on in.' As he passed her she looked at him properly for the first time and said accusingly, 'You lost weight?'

'God's a man, Kitty. Suck it up.'

She punched his arm.

Pete got up as Tom came in, and shook his hand.

'Hi, Pete.'

'Good to see you, Tom.'

Silence.

It had been months since they'd seen each other. Anyone else, and Pete would have expected some mild chit-chat – 'How are you, Pete?'; 'How's Ann?'; 'How long to retirement now, Pete?' He sighed and knew that Tom Patrick was not the man to make those enquiries.

He indicated a chair and Tom threw himself into it. The silence stretched between them. Pete felt irritation rising. He knew he'd have to kick things off, even if it was Tom who'd flown all the way across the country to see him. The guy didn't have a socially adept bone in his lanky body.

'What's up, Tom?'

Tom ran his hand nervously up the back of his neck and Pete knew it was coming – whatever Tom Patrick couldn't say on the phone. As usual, once he decided to get in the pool, Tom went straight off the high board . . .

'That LAX cargo plane. You happy with Munro's findings?'

Pete frowned. He'd expected a back-and-forth about the state of Tom Patrick's non-career, an attempt to barter his way back in – even a resignation speech – but this was out of left field.

'Camel pack pulled into the engine? Yeah, sure.'

'C'mon, Pete! They fire frozen turkeys at these fuckers in type approval and they don't come apart like that. Munro didn't find any evidence of the pack in the compressor or turbine.'

'I don't know. Maybe the guy kept his Zippo in the pack. That'd make a dent. But based on surrounding evidence, the disturbance causing the disintegration of the compressor, it's a sound conclusion.'

'It's circumstantial at best,' said Tom.

Pete leaned back in his chair. 'That's why they call it *probable* cause.' When Tom didn't smile at his NTSB humour, he asked, 'Why?'

Tom paused. 'I don't know. Just a hunch.'

'Care to share?'

Tom looked as embarrassed as he ever did. 'It's very . . . hunchy.'

Pete prepared himself. 'Hunch away.'

'The jet that went down in South Africa. The 737?'

'I saw that.'

'You see how the fuselage was sliced apart just fore of the port wing?'

'Yeah.'

'Like the LAX 737.'

'What's the connection?'

'Like I said, it's just a hunch. This Chris Stern . . .'

'The smoker?'

'The quitter. Apparently he'd take a smoke from the pack, have a drag, then button it back into his coverall pocket. Never carried the pack. His buddy told me Stern was real careful about it.'

'His buddy would.'

Tom nodded in tacit agreement, but raised his eyebrows at the same time to show a question still lingered.

'There was a cigarette on the cement, Tom. Not in Stern's pocket.'

'I know. But Stern was cut in half right under the chest. His pocket too. That could be how the cigarette ended up on the floor.'

'But you don't know.'

Tom came back with an edge. 'Maybe if I was lead on the case instead of Lenny Munro, we'd *all* know.'

'Maybe. And maybe we'd all be up to our asses in lawyers.'

Tom shrugged.

Pete let it go. 'Then what do you think caused the engine to tear apart like that?'

'I don't know, but one thing's for sure. The South African jet wasn't brought down by a Zippo at twenty-five thousand feet.'

Pete sighed. 'Munro's investigation was by the book—'

Tom gave a disparaging snort and Pete frowned. 'Don't snort at the book, Tom. The book is good. The book is what we do around here. The book is why you're on the outside looking in right now and why I have to watch my best investigator crawling around in sludge-pits in Buttkiss, Arkansas!' He calmed down and spread his palms. 'Munro's report adds up. There's no reason for me to question his work here, Tom. And sure as hell no reason for you to question it.'

Tom nodded slowly. He knew Pete was right. He'd known it before he got to LAX this morning. He'd just hoped that coming all the way to DC – looking his boss in the eye – would make him seem more convincing. But now he realized that if he'd had a convincing argument he wouldn't have needed to come to DC: Pete would have believed him over the phone.

He looked at him apprehensively. Pete felt warily that he was about to be put on the spot.

'So you won't sanction a second investigation?'

'Are you fucking joking?'

Tom got to his feet, unwilling to leave and let it go, even though Pete's chin was set stonily. 'How about on my own time?'

Pete was surprised. 'What's the deal, Tom? What's making it personal?'

Tom flushed. 'Nothing. It's just bugging me. That's all.' He tugged the door open.

Pete sighed. 'Tom. Don't do this. You're on your way back in. If you get sidetracked now you may never make it. Let it go.'

'I can't.'

Tom strode past Kitty. He ignored her smile, as he ignored the sound of his boss yelling at him to come right back here.

8

TOM SPENT THREE HOURS on the phone to the South African Civil Aviation Authority before being put through to an investigating officer on the 737 crash. During that time he'd been cut off three times, listened to around an hour's worth of hits from the 1970s played on what sounded like a glockenspiel, and introduced himself twice to the same person – who'd turned out to work in the staff canteen.

The line was variable, and punctuated by clicks and weird whirring noises. All Tom could do was sit and suffer, and try to tune out the vagaries of a phone system ten thousand miles away.

So he was sprawled on his bed, watching *The Hunt for Red October* with the sound down, eating a cheese and bacon sub, and tapping his fingers idly against his chest to the infuriating rhythm of 'Me And You And A Dog Named Boo', when a woman's voice said, 'Pamela Mashamaete.'

Tom swallowed his mouthful fast and almost choked as he introduced himself.

With only the evidence of their switchboard operator to go on, Tom was wary of the level of efficiency he'd find at the SACAA, but Pamela Mashamaete quickly allayed his fears. She was the lead investigator and sounded young but smart and – more importantly – she had no qualms about sharing information with him once he'd explained the purpose of his call. There was no hesitation, no need to refer to a higher authority for clearance, no reluctance to speculate on initial findings. It was refreshingly, if haphazardly, useful and they were quickly on first-name terms. At least, they were after Tom's initial manful attempts to call her Miss Mashamaete.

'I think you'd better call me Pam.'

'Thank God for that. I'm Tom.'

'Well, thank God for *that!*'

Pam couldn't tell him much at this stage. The wreckage had been laid out at a site near somewhere called Oudtshoorn. They had recovered virtually all of it, as the desert scrub was easy to search.

'Is that where you are now?'

'Yes.'

Apparently he'd got through to Pam on her cell phone. He grimaced at the thought of the non-claimable bill. 'So, what's your initial feeling about the cause?'

'Oh, we don't have *feelings*,' she laughed, 'we're only allowed to have *theories*.'

Tom smiled to himself. Pam understood. 'So what's your gut *theory?*'

There was a good pause and he imagined her standing somewhere hot and dusty, surrounded by scrub and ostriches and little-boy jockeys. As the silence stretched out, he liked Pam more and more for the weight she was obviously giving his question and her answer.

'The fuselage came down in two pieces – the break occurring just forward of the wings. Initial inspection shows no evidence of metal fatigue around the break.'

'So what caused it?' He tried to keep the impatience out of his voice.

'At first we thought maybe a bomb, but once we'd assembled the aircraft we could see something had hit it from the outside on the port side. The majority of the damage was caused right there, but there's also evidence of at least two major breaches elsewhere on the passenger cabin. They weren't serious enough to cause further complete breaks, but passenger injuries support that scenario.'

'Yes?' He was sitting straight up on the bed now, stiff with anticipation.

'The *theory* we're working on is that the number-two fan let go and the blades tore through the fuselage.'

There it was. Tom nodded dumbly, heady with the possibilities raised by a connection between the two incidents.

'Tom?'

'I'm here.'

'Does that help?'

'You betcha ass it does.'

'Oh, I would never place a bet that big!'

Tom grinned as she laughed at her own joke. 'Any idea why it may have come apart?'

'Not yet.'

'Birdstrike?'

'No evidence of it yet.'

'Hey, Pam, thanks. Anything I get now I'll share with you.'

'That would be great.'

'You want to give me your cell number? Cos I'm sorry, but if saving lives means sitting through "Jive Talking" on the xylophone one more time . . .'

They exchanged numbers and Tom bounced off the bed,

tightly coiled with excitement for which he had no outlet. He wanted someone to share with, someone to throw their arms around him and tell him he'd done good.

But there was no one.

He took a slip of paper off the floor next to the bed. Halo Jackson's number. He crumpled it and dropped it. What was he thinking?

Then he picked it up, raised the phone and dialled the number, but didn't hit the call key. After a moment he dropped the slip back on to the carpet, grabbed his jacket and car keys, and left.

*

It took him an hour to drive to Santa Ana only to find that the girl called Lucia wasn't at the Sawmill. The manager wouldn't give him her number either, even when he flashed his badge at him and told him it was for official business. The man – tubby, middle-aged, with dyed black hair – chuckled. 'So that's what they call it these days, huh?'

Tom sat in the Buick for twenty minutes before he'd swallowed enough of his pride to go back in and ask the manager to give Lucia his cell number. Then he drove half a block to a KFC and got a bargain bucket.

Some celebration.

His phone rang and he fumbled it hurriedly out of his pocket with greasy fingers. 'Lucia?'

'It's Halo.'

'Shit.'

'Thanks.'

'What do you want?'

'Who's Lucia?'

'What do you want?'

'You hear about John Wayne?'

'Still dead?'

'Saab 340 crashed on take-off.'

John Wayne Airport.

Tom felt a knife twist in his heart as he realized he was now hearing about crashes on his doorstep from virtual strangers before getting calls from Pete. He felt his grip on his job loosen a little bit more, as his chicken-greasy fingers scrabbled for purchase.

'Tom?'

He hung up on Halo without answering, and called Pete at home. He knew he shouldn't – it was two a.m. in DC – but he couldn't help himself.

Pete answered groggily.

'Pete? It's Tom.'

Pete grunted.

'I just heard about the Saab at John Wayne.'

'Yeah?'

This had been a stupid thing to do, Tom knew, but he couldn't back down now. He had to bulldoze his way through. 'Can I get in on it?'

'Jan's there.'

'Jan! Christ, she's only been on the job two years!'

'Seems the pilot ran out of runway. Human error. Couple of minor injuries, no deaths. I thought it would be good for her to cut her teeth on it.'

Tom heard Ann mumble, beside Pete, 'What time is it?'

The sound of Pete clicking on a lamp. 'Shit, Tom, it's two in the goddamned morning!'

'I know. I'm sorry.'

'If you were, it'd be a first.'

'Seriously, Pete. I know I shouldn't have called. It's just . . . It's driving me nuts, seeing other people picking up the slack, working jobs that should've been mine.'

'And you figure waking me up at two a.m. to whine about it is going to get you back in my good books?' Pete banged the phone down.

It felt shitty to be hung up on and Tom kind of wished now that he hadn't done it to Halo. The night that had started so well had ended with a sour feeling in the pit of his stomach.

He shoved aside his bargain bucket. A ragged man who was gnawing on a wing at the next table looked at it, and Tom pushed it towards him.

'Thanks.'

Tom nodded at him and got up, feeling empty.

He couldn't face the drive back to Long Beach, so checked into the Motel 6 he'd stayed at before. On a whim he asked the clerk for the same room, and used the memory of him and Lucia in that very bed to make himself come, so that he could finally drift off into a fitful sleep.

At five a.m., Pete called and sent him to Boise, Idaho, where an oil pipe was leaking into a stream.

Tom didn't actually apologize, but he didn't bitch either, and did his penance like a man.

9

THE HONOLULU COULD NOT have been less aptly named. The club north of Long Beach was little more than a vast marquee in the middle of an even vaster parking lot, cleared between strip malls and ugly prefabricated buildings housing hardware stores and plumbing-supply merchants.

Tom didn't like the Honolulu. He preferred the Bicycle Club or the Normandie, which both possessed an olde-worlde charm of LA sorts – made of bricks and mortar and the baize had had time to get scuffed. But the Honolulu was his closest casino and Sunday was jackpot day at the church of the damned.

Two giant plastic palm trees made a feeble nod at a theme. Poker players didn't need themes, though: all they needed was cards, a dealer and someone to lose to. They wouldn't have cared if two giant plastic turds had been displayed either side of the entrance, thought Tom.

Inside the marquee, thick, garish carpet was laid on the asphalt, and cool oxygen pumped gently through the air.

He couldn't see anyone he recognized, which was unusual. He'd seen the Pinball Kid here plenty on a Sunday, and occasionally Corey Clump. Sometimes he and Corey would even grab a bite after they were knocked out. They didn't know each other – all they ever talked was poker: pots they'd won; pots they'd lost; pots they'd seen others win or lose. Never tactics: that was way too revealing. That was the difference between nodding politely at the guy you were pissing next to, and comparing dick sizes.

Tom dropped a hundred dollars on a cash table, and was dealt in. The first few hands were nondescript, but after that he started to get a good feeling about his game. He took a two-hundred-and-twenty-dollar pot with a five-high straight, beating out jacks and nines held by a wizened Latino man in a Raiders vest, who kept holding up play to fiddle with his food. Tom wondered whether it was a tactic, but once he'd beaten him, he didn't let it bother him.

Soon his hundred-dollar investment had grown to over a thousand. And this was real money, not tournament chips. He looked around for a chip jockey so he could change it up and avoid the temptation of blowing the lot. There was none near by and it was his turn to play. He glanced at the cards he'd just been dealt: nine of clubs, ten of clubs. Because he was on the dealer button, he played them.

The hand unfolded in an almost scripted manner. The flop showed the seven of clubs, the queen of hearts and the queen of spades, and a ripple ran round the table at the pair showing. Boosted by his winnings, Tom raised recklessly, then called the re-raise on the back of the seven, hoping for a straight or – even better – a back-door flush of five clubs.

The six of clubs came on the turn. Tom was outwardly relaxed but inside he felt the familiar build of tension and excitement that started just above his balls and spread into his belly. Six, seven, nine, ten of clubs were his. The only thing missing was the eight. The straight flush was on but was disguised by the pair of queens. The queens were the obvious threat to all at the table, and it was easy to overlook the seven and six. Sure, they were both clubs, and possible straight-flush candidates too, but it was the queens that were the dazzlers, blinding the hasty or the unskilled to other options. And this was not a high-rollers game: it was a run-of-the-mill Sunday-afternoon cash table where some players were only a step up from buying a scratchcard to satisfy their need to lose money. There were two young friends in Long Beach State jackets who hadn't even had the sense to play at different tables so they weren't winning each other's cash; a crumpled brunette, who had earlier failed to raise when she'd held the nuts – which she'd then stupidly shown to everyone; a smooth-faced Asian boy, who'd thrown in virtually every hand he'd been dealt; then the Raiders fan. Next to him was an angry-looking, pockmarked man, whose compulsive leg-shaking made the whole table tremble. He'd won a couple of small pots – once on what Tom was sure had been a bluff. A very fat woman dressed in what appeared to be a counterpane made up the rest of the table. She was a tutter – someone who couldn't let any play or card go untutted. In Tom's experience, tutting was the most negative thing you could do at a poker table and he discounted her ever winning through anything other than dumb luck.

The Raiders fan, the college kids, the crumpled brunette and the Asian had all folded at the sight of the queens. Their pre-flop money had swelled the pot nicely, though.

The tutter tutted, then checked, but the leg-shaker threw in his bet, staring straight at Tom as he did so. Tom ignored him and raised. The tutter grumbled and matched Tom, and the leg-shaker glared angrily at Tom before re-raising. Tom grinned inside at the man's pointless anger and raised again.

The tutter tutted loudly. Then get the hell out, thought Tom, and after a few moments of lip-biting and chip-counting, she spun her cards back to the dealer.

Tom could feel the animosity of the leg-shaker coming at him in waves as he called Tom's bet.

It was all on this last card. If it was the eight or any club, Tom was probably home free. Anything else was a disaster.

The painfully thin Chinese girl dealer with translucent skin flipped over the five of diamonds. Tom didn't have the straight or the flush or anything else. His heart banged in his chest. The dealer directed a tiny finger at the leg-shaker, indicating it was his bet.

Tom's forearms had rested on the fake-leather padding around the edge of the table throughout. It was through this that he'd felt the small vibrations of the leg-shaker ever since he'd sat down two hours before. Now his forearms told him that – just for a second – the man had stopped shaking his leg. He started again almost instantly, but it was a clue that Tom seized on. Something had made him stop. The cessation of leg-shaking indicated that he'd had to think for a moment, and thinking was all about reassessment. And reassessment meant compromises and a lowering of expectations.

It was a small chink of hope but Tom went with it and decided to go with the bluff: make the guy think he had a pocket pair that matched one of the lower cards on the table, and was therefore sure to beat trip queens with a full house. When the leg-shaker pushed his bet into the centre of the table, Tom shoved in the rest of his chips. The man looked uncertainly at his cards again and Tom knew he had him.

With the pot at more than fourteen hundred dollars, and a small knot of people forming to watch the action, the leg-shaker lost confidence, stood up and folded, angrily flicking his cards at the dealer. As the last man folded, he turned his cards face up. Pocket tens!

Tom met the man's eyes and grinned. He couldn't help it. He knew he'd bluffed well, but bluffing three-of-a-kind clear out of the game was an almost sexual thrill.

'Get your fucking hands out the way!'

The dealer ignored the pockmarked man – used to the abuse of losers.

'Waving your hands about, you fucking amateur.'

'It's over. Leave her alone,' said Tom, casually, without looking at him.

'Fuck you. Let's see what you got.' The leg-shaker stared at him with angry eyes.

Tom never showed his cards unless someone paid to see them. He peered at the pot innocently. 'I got about fourteen hundred dollars.'

People round the table chuckled.

'You gonna show me, dick?'

Tom shrugged. 'Yeah, I'll show you dick.' He pushed his cards carefully back at the dealer. She quickly absorbed them into the pack, hoping to dissipate any trouble once the evidence was gone for ever.

'Fuck!'

Tom said nothing, just started stacking the chips into neat piles in the little plastic trays the club provided. A thousand dollars per tray for the ten-dollar chips. He needed more trays and looked around for a chip jockey.

From the corner of his eye he saw the leg-shaker coming at him and managed to get an arm part-way up in front of his face. The deflected blow still spun his head round and knocked him off the chair. The man was on him in an instant, almost under the neighbouring table, dropping his knee into Tom's groin as he pounded his fists on to his face.

It was over quickly, but not quickly enough. Security guards pulled the man off him and Tom curled up tight on his side, not even feeling his face as the pain in his balls swept over him and he threw up on to the garish carpet beside his head.

He felt a hand on his shoulder, but resisted the attempt to roll him on to his back. He needed to be in this position for a while yet. Maybe for ever.

He was dimly aware of people's feet moving around him as he breathed hard into the carpet, which smelt of vomit over shoe-dirt. Two pairs of shiny black military-style boots were scuffing and bracing either side of an incongruous pair of red cowboy boots, which Tom registered must belong to the leg-shaker.

Stupid red boots.

Another wave of nausea hit him and he spewed again. This time the hands didn't try to turn him over, just pulled him a little away from the puddles of vomit. Tom was pathetically grateful that he wasn't lying in his own puke.

Slowly, slowly, the agony between his legs subsided and he started to breathe again. At the same time his face and head started vying for attention from his central nervous system. His face pulsed with pain, and he tasted blood in his mouth.

This time when the hands touched his shoulder, he allowed them to help him to sit up. Someone handed him a bar towel with Bud Lite on it, and he spat blood and flecks of vomit into it, then wiped his mouth. He winced as he scraped across his torn lip. Blood dripped into his eyes and nose and trickled down his throat. Fuck – what a mess.

He remembered his chips and looked up to see the dealer holding his trays for him. She met his eyes reassuringly.

Then he looked round to see who'd given him the towel and met the dark grey eyes of the Pinball Kid's erstwhile blonde.

'Okay?' she said.

Before he could answer, a boy of about twelve dressed as a medic hunkered down in front of him and shone a torch into his eyes, making Tom feel old as well as beat-up.

'How many fingers?'

'Three.'

'Good. You think you can stand up?'

'Not straight.'

The kid grinned at him. 'Take one in the nuts?'

Tom nodded weakly and the medic stood up. 'Get the ice bag, Lis!'

By the time Lis appeared with the ice bag, Tom was resting his forehead on the table where he'd been playing, although the Honolulu staff were hovering nervously with towels in case he threw up on the baize and put the table out of action all night.

The medic put butterfly plasters on the cut over his eye and dabbed stinging disinfectant into his other cuts and scrapes. Tom felt like a five-year-old who'd come off his bike. He sure smelt like one.

The blonde was still near by, he was embarrassed to note.

A narrow, weather-beaten man in a tuxedo, with a tag reading 'Manager', appeared at his elbow and spoke to the medic. 'He okay?'

'He will be. The cut above his eye needs stitching.'

'Okay. I'll take it from here.'

The medic hesitated. 'You'll have to sign off on that, sir.' The manager said okay, and Lis fetched a clipboard. Tom watched dully as the guy signed for him like a pound puppy, then asked Tom to follow him. Tom straightened with difficulty, clamped the ice to his groin and managed to walk after him with only a hint of a limp and a pained expression. The blonde caught his arm. 'I'll wait here for you.' He nodded, wondering why.

The manager walked slowly so Tom could keep up. The dealer walked behind him with his winnings.

'Would you like us to cash that up for you, sir?'

'Please.' The dealer peeled off.

By the time they reached the door marked 'Manager', Tom's head was clearing and the ache in his balls was bearable.

Inside, two burly security guards with buzz-cuts stood at either side of the leg-shaker, who glared at him, chin and crotch thrust forward belligerently. The manager sat behind his desk and motioned to a chair. 'Sit, please.'

Tom adjusted the ice bag he held over his balls. 'I think I'll stand, thanks.' The manager nodded his understanding.

Tom noticed a CCTV camera in the corner above the desk. Behind him the dealer came in and handed him his money in a thick roll.

'Thanks.'

'You're welcome,' she said nervously.

The manager asked her what had happened and the dealer gave a brief and accurate account of what had taken place. The only defence the leg-shaker could muster was that Tom was 'a fucking wise-ass'. He didn't even look as though he'd convinced himself.

The manager sighed and addressed Tom. 'Mr . . . ?'

'Patrick.'

'Mr Patrick, I am Robert Tarryk, the manager. I can only apologize for the assault you have suffered at the hands of another player. My security staff stepped in quickly but I'm afraid when these things happen they happen very fast, as you'll appreciate. I do hope it has not put you off returning to the Honolulu.'

Tom shrugged noncommittally. 'Have you called the cops?'

He saw the look Tarryk gave the leg-shaker. 'Not yet. I thought I would let you decide how to deal with this.'

Tom was caught off-guard for the second time in five minutes. He gave Tarryk a questioning look.

'Obviously we like to maintain our image as a desirable addition to the neighbourhood, Mr Patrick, and for that reason we prefer to handle things without recourse to the law whenever possible.'

Tom's interest was sparked now. He dabbed at his eyebrow with the towel and waited Tarryk out.

'If, for example, Mr Stanley here . . .' Tom glanced at the leg-shaker '. . . was prepared to make some kind of reparation?'

Stanley didn't react. Tom didn't react. Tarryk tried again. 'For instance, how does two thousand dollars sound?'

This time Tom couldn't hide his surprise. Tarryk was offering to pay him off.

'I don't want *your* money. He's the one who stomped on my balls.'

'And I'm sure Mr Stanley sincerely regrets it.'

Tom glanced at Stanley: he didn't look sincere or regretful as he shot a glance of suppressed fury at Tarryk. But it dawned on Tom that *that* was what would make him feel better: an expression of sincere regret on Stanley's face.

'We're all reasonable people. I'm sure we can work this out, Mr Patrick.'

Tom hesitated, then said slowly, 'I'm sure we can.'

'Good. So, two thousand, then?' He opened a cheque book.

Without warning, Tom turned and kicked Stanley straight in the balls. As with the perfect golf swing, everything fluked into place, and when he connected, he felt the power of the strike right up to his teeth. He thought Stanley actually left the ground, but he couldn't be sure.

'Yo!' one of the security guards shouted in surprise and, behind Tom, the dealer squeaked.

Stanley dropped as if his legs had been cut off. Tom watched him try to breathe, making a painful, high-pitched sound as he rolled gently back and forth on the carpet, clutching himself. Tears squeezed out of his tightly shut eyes and his gritted teeth were stained with blood from his bitten tongue. Tom figured that was as close to a look of sincere regret as Stanley was ever going to get.

Tom turned to Tarryk. 'You're right,' he said. 'These things do happen fast.'

Tarryk merely closed the cheque book and sighed.

Tom tossed his ice bag at Stanley, and walked out with the giggling dealer behind him. A few paces outside the manager's door, Tom turned and peeled a fifty off the roll and handed it to her. She grinned broadly and bobbed her head in thanks, then hurried away, still laughing.

For some unfathomable reason, the blonde was waiting right where she'd said she'd be.

10

HER NAME WAS NESS FRANKLIN, and by the time the waiter brought their second bottle of Pinot Noir, Tom was in lust.

Every damn thing she did was sexy. The way she murmured, 'Thank you,' and looked at him from under her dark lashes when he opened the door for her into the Honolulu parking lot; the way her midnight-blue dress split open to reveal a long, pale thigh as she slid gracefully into the Buick; the smooth feel of the small of her back under his palm as he ushered her gently to their table at Divo's; even the fact that she ignored the salad and ordered lobster in butter sauce, which proceeded to glisten on her full red lips as they ate and talked.

She did most of the talking and most of the eating while he sat and watched, listened and wondered how long it would be before his battered groin could muster an erection. It would be just his luck if Stanley's knee-drop had done irreparable damage just when he'd met the sexiest woman in the world, he thought wryly, as Ness dipped her red-tipped fingers into the lemon-scented finger bowl. If that proved to be the case, the kick in the groin was not going to be payback enough: Tom would have to hunt Stanley down and kill him. Slowly.

Ness sucked each of her fingers clean – not as a turn-on, but slightly absent-mindedly – while trying to catch the waiter's eye for more butter. Tom's stomach rolled slowly with desire, which only translated into a sharp pain in his balls that made him wince.

'You okay?'

'Yes, fine.'

She gave him a wry smile. 'You sure?'

'Well, as fine as a man can be after having some Neanderthal squish his balls and pummel his face to a pulp. That kind of fine, y'know?'

She laughed and ran her eyes over his face. 'I know that guy. He's an asshole.'

Tom raised a glass to that and she clinked hers against it.

Before they'd left the Honolulu, Ness had led him into the ladies' room and tried to clean him up, but he knew he still looked like a crash-test dummy. The cut over his eye did need stitching, but the butterfly plasters would keep it together until tomorrow, he reckoned. He wasn't going to spend his first evening with this woman in the emergency room with a bunch of drunks.

His nose hurt a lot. 'You think it's broken?' he'd asked.

She'd touched the bridge gently. 'No. Just cut and bruised.'

'Shame.'

She'd looked at him quizzically.

'I always kind of wanted a broken nose. Don't you think it's manly?'

She'd screwed up her face, making herself even more desirable in his eyes. Up close, he noticed a small white scar striped across her chin like a shooting star.

'Manly is as manly does,' she'd said at last.

When they'd first walked into Divo's, he'd felt every eye in the place turn towards him and it took him a moment to realize that they weren't admiring his taste in women. Whatever. Let them stare at his face – he was just grateful he had something prettier to look at across the table.

The waiter had brought the butter, and now Ness dipped a piece of lobster into it. When she put it between her lips, a trickle ran down her chin. She touched it casually with a napkin, as if she didn't really care whether it carried on down her neck or not. Tom winced again.

'So, Ness . . .' he searched his brain for the right words so his question would not seem presumptuous or downright dumb '. . . to what do I owe this pleasure?'

She shrugged, her pale skin hollowing deliciously around her collar bones. 'You impressed me tonight.'

'Yeah, I'm pretty impressive when I'm getting beat up.'

She smiled. 'You remembered your chips.'

The statement surprised him.

'You'd hardly stopped throwing up before you remembered your chips and wanted to check on them.'

'It was a big pot.'

'Hard won.' She toyed with a claw but didn't crack it.

'You were watching?'

She nodded and picked the meat out with her elegant fingers. 'Was it a bluff?'

Tom felt himself close off to her as surely as if an iron door had slammed into place. It was the one question serious players never asked and never, ever answered. He tried to hide his knee-jerk defence with a smile and took a sip of wine even though it hurt his lip. Her eyes held his, so he said, 'Winners don't tell.'

'Not even me?' She almost pouted and looked so erotic that he had to swallow to clear his airway. This was crazy. Why not tell her? All she was doing was flirting with him. Why not play the game?

But something in his gut kept him silent, although he raised his eyebrows to show he wasn't angry. 'Not even you.'

He thought she might be offended but, after a momentary hesitation, she smiled and cracked the claw. 'You're right. Winners don't tell.'

'Did the Pinball Kid tell?'

She looked at him, confused.

'The kid with the shades and iPod.'

'Oh, Garvey.' She nodded slyly. 'Yes, he told.'

'Is that why you dumped him?' He held his breath – it was pretty much a make-or-break question.

Her eyes slid slowly up from her plate and gazed into his with an expression that made him shiver, although he didn't know whether it was lust or something far more strange.

'That's why.'

She sipped her wine, then folded her hands demurely on the table. 'I have a proposition for you,' she said.

'And I've got one for you. You think they're the same?' He grinned and she smiled but shook her head.

'I'd lay odds against it.'

They weren't the words he'd wanted to hear.

Her eyes still danced at him, but there was a subtle change in her voice that had taken the playful banter out of the air. He took another mouthful of wine, then decided to behave like a grown-up. 'I'm all ears.'

'I work for a consortium. When they – when *I* – see a card player I think they should . . . invest in, I tell them.'

Tom tried not to let the disappointment show on his face. This was a business meeting, nothing more. He nodded so he wouldn't have to say anything that might betray him.

'I've been watching you for a while.'

He flushed. 'Not last week when I went all-in on queen high, I hope?'

She raised one perfect eyebrow drolly. 'That was ... surprising.'

They smiled, which broke the tension a little. Her shoulders relaxed and she leaned slightly towards him; he caught a whiff of scent – something spicy – which sent a small thrill through him.

'It's more than just the cards, Tom. You know how to hold your nerve. The money my clients invest, sometimes the amounts are large. And nerve-holding is ... an admirable quality.'

His eyes fell on her scar again. The idea of touching it with his fingers – maybe even his tongue – suddenly seemed very important to him. 'How large is large?'

The corner of her mouth flickered. 'Very large.'

Tom knew that his next logical question should be: Who are these clients? But he didn't ask because he already knew she wouldn't tell him the truth. And instinctively he knew, too, that in this context curiosity would not be seen as quite the admirable quality that nerve-holding obviously was.

What she was asking him to do was illegal. It was money-laundering, pure and simple. Dirty money converted into small round ceramic chips and gambled on the tables of Atlantic City, Nevada and LA. If losses could be minimized or – even better – turned into wins, the money that would be counted out from behind the casino cash windows was clean. Maybe even tax-free, if the casino was in on it.

He recognized the swell of his own ego that came with the offer, and immediately attempted to correct it. He'd been working on his ego ever since the Pinball Kid – Garvey – had beaten his pocket jacks. Bastard. 'Why me?' he asked. 'I'm not that good.'

She gazed at him coolly, not attempting to dissuade him from the truth, which he appreciated on some level. Like all gamblers, he didn't like to dwell on his losses, but it didn't mean they weren't there. Sometimes they were all he had.

'You're good enough,' she said quietly.

He understood. The last thing her 'consortium' needed was some Stu Ungar whizz-kid making a celebrity of himself – and his crooked money.

Tom's synapses were firing fast now – faster even than when he made his customary sizing-up glances around the poker tables. His job was in the toilet – nearing the U-bend, if it was to be judged by his latest trip to Boise to watch a small oil slick meander through an already polluted and litter-strewn stream. He was still on half-pay – an option he'd chosen in preference to outright suspension on full-pay. He could do with the money. And the tug of his ego was still there. Still needed work.

'What's in it for me?' God, he sounded like a criminal already.

'Ten per cent of winnings. No charge for losing – although, of course, we'd rather you won. If we ask you to play out of town, all exes paid. Motels, food, drinks . . . company . . .'

For the first time he saw her straightforward confidence waver, but almost immediately she was back on track, looking into his eyes with not a little humour as she added, '. . . within reason.'

He couldn't help smiling. 'Who decides what's reasonable?'

'I would be your liaison. So I guess that would be me.'

'Do you work on some kind of formula?' he teased.

'Sure. Twice a month is enough for any decent person.'

His eyebrows shot up. 'Can we haggle?'

'About frequency? Or decency?'

Her smile made up his mind – or what passed for it at that moment.

The smile faded. 'One thing, though, Tom.'

'What's that?'

'Your mouth,' she said seriously. 'It draws attention and gets you into trouble.'

He said nothing. What could he possibly say in his own defence that would be anything but a lie?

'Attention and trouble are two things we really don't need.'

The waiter brought coffee and Ness folded her fingers together in a businesslike manner. 'Would you like time to think about it?'

'No,' said Tom. 'I think thinking would be bad.'

*

Tom got home at ten p.m. The condo sprinklers had been on and there was the faint reek of the sewer from the reclaimed water that made the grass grow so goddamn green in this desert state. Kentucky-by-the-sea.

He stopped dead halfway up the path.

Halo Jackson was sitting on his doorstep, bleeding into a Taco Bell box.

'Jesus!'

Halo pointed at Tom's face half-heartedly. 'Back at ya.'

Tom let him in, but made him stand in the tiled hallway until he had fetched a pan he could bleed into.

'It's stopping now.'

'It can stop in the pan. My security deposit's already teetering on the brink. What happened?'

'I was getting food. For Vee and Katy, y'know? Just tacos 'n' stuff. Got back to the house and I was getting out of the car and this guy slams me up against it and, like, twists my arm up my back. I thought it was going to break.' Halo rubbed his shoulder and grimaced at the pain that lingered there.

'Then what?' Tom poured a couple of fingers of bourbon into a tumbler and put it down next to Halo.

'Thanks,' said Halo, but ignored it. 'Then he goes, "Stay out of other people's business" – and then the sonofabitch pulls all the tacos out of the bags and, like, stomps them into the ground!'

Tom couldn't help grinning. Halo seemed more upset about the food than his bloodied nose.

'Was there just one?'

'One was enough.'

'Then he hit you?'

Halo's eyes flickered sideways. 'Good as!'

Tom raised an eyebrow, and if Halo could have blushed, he would have.

'He drove off. I slipped on a burrito and cracked my nose on the side-view mirror as I went down.'

Tom grinned – although he stopped fast and sucked in air when he found he'd almost split his lip again.

'Not fucking funny. I cracked the mirror. That's seventy bucks they'll rip me off for that! Just cos you got a classic car, folks think you're made of money. Nearly ripped my goddamn nose off too!'

'So what the hell d'you come and see me for? I thought some guy had beaten the crap out of you!'

Halo looked defensive. 'He almost did! And what he said, "other people's business" – he must've meant the *Pride of Maine*.'

Tom grunted disparagingly. 'Get real. He's probably some guy who's got his eye on Vee now that your smoking buddy's gone. What did he look like?

'Big. White. Bald. Nice eyes.'

'Good sense of humour?'

'What?'

'Nothing. Anyway – who'd be interested in the plane?'

'Maybe someone trying to keep from paying up on Chris's insurance or something.'

'You been talking about it to people?' asked Tom.

'Only to you and Vee.'

'What did she say?'

'I didn't ask her. I didn't go back in. I just came straight here.'

'Nice job. Lead the bad guys right to me.'

Halo looked alarmed and apologetic but Tom gave a little shake of his head to show he was kidding.

'You mean Vee and her kid are still at home waiting on their tacos?'

Halo shrugged, embarrassed. Tom sighed. 'You want to call her?'

Halo hesitated. 'Can I?'

Tom handed him the phone. He watched while Halo dialled the number.

'You want to eat?

'Eat what?'

'Pasta.'

'What kind of pasta?'

'The kind I'm making.'

'Yeah, okay.'

Halo talked quietly on the phone to Vee while Tom made pasta. It was all he was really good at. Well, adequate. It was hard to go wrong with pasta – although not impossible, in his experience.

Halo got off the phone and came to lean against the kitchen door. 'Told her I got in an accident. A small one. Thought it'd cover the nose and the mirror.'

Tom handed him a bowl of pasta and a fork, then stretched out on the couch with his bowl on his chest.

Halo took the easy chair next to the TV and looked around at the sparsely furnished condo. One couch, one chair, a TV on a crate, a stereo with cables trailing across the floor. Not even a coffee-table or rug. 'You get robbed?'

Tom gave him a puzzled look and Halo waved his pasta-filled fork briefly at the furnishings. 'Empty.'

It was empty. Ella had sent for her stuff and Tom had been surprised to find that he was left with pretty much just what he'd moved in with two years before. He'd thought he'd been making progress but it had turned out that Ella had been progressing just fine without any help from him. 'I like it like this,' he said. 'Don't bleed on my chair.'

Halo touched his nose but the bleeding had stopped. 'So what happened to you?'

'Some angry loser at the Honolulu.'

'Just random?'

Tom sucked spaghetti into his mouth and shot Halo an impatient glance. 'Nah. All the time he was hitting me he kept yelling, "*Pride of Maine! Pride of Maine!*"'

Halo eyed his food for a moment. 'You think I'm paranoid.'

Tom's silence spoke louder than words.

Halo sighed, and gestured at Tom's face. 'How does the other guy look?'

Tom prodded his pasta and gave a mean little smile. 'Sincerely regretful.'

11

P̲ᴀᴍ Mᴀsʜᴀᴍᴀᴇᴛᴇ ᴄᴀʟʟᴇᴅ two days later. Just hearing her voice put Tom in that hot, dusty place with ostriches flapping, or whatever ostriches did. He didn't want to ask Pam what her surroundings were really like: he enjoyed the image in his head too much.

'I've emailed you some pictures.'

God, he loved the way other countries dealt with confidentiality issues.

Twenty minutes later Tom called her back. 'You got scoring on the disc flange!'

Pam laughed, a rich, joyous sound as if she really was enjoying her joke. 'I know!'

Tom's mind ticked like a Geiger counter on Bikini Atoll. The fan blades were attached to the fan disc, a ring of intricately tooled titanium alloy, which in turn was bolted to the flat face of the drive shaft via perfectly matched flanges. The integrity of the bond between the two flanges was crucial. There was no margin for error when two surfaces were required to maintain synchronicity at 5,500 r.p.m. 'How the hell did that happen?'

Pam made a long musical hum of 'Who knows?' 'We're thinking it may be nothing to do with the crash at all. That maybe it was scratched during maintenance or something.'

Tom heard the subtle inflection in her voice. '*We*'re thinking?'

'The team.'

'But not you?'

A long pause from Ostrich World. 'We-ell . . . the *team* thinks it can't be relevant, that if the scoring was caused during operation, it would have been picked up before . . . this.'

Tom nodded. Movement between the fan disc and the shaft would certainly have been picked up by the airborne-vibration monitoring system and gauged on a small black-faced dial on the cockpit's central pedestal. The dial was calibrated up to five units. Any vibration over two was reportable by the crew on landing, although it wasn't a fail-safe system. *Change the crew, change the defect* – the long-suffering engineers' mantra was cynical but true: what one crew refused to fly with, another cheerfully ignored. And even if a 1.9 reading had been noted and reported, small random vibrations were notoriously difficult to replicate in tests. 'Transient', they were called. Sometimes they were there; sometimes they just went away.

And sometimes they came back.

'You got the shaft?' Matching score marks on it would indicate the damage had been caused during operation.

'No,' she said, 'not yet.'

'You find the black box?'

She must have known he was going to ask about vibration readings. 'The VDM showed a vibration of just under two units.'

'But then it stopped working.'

'That's when everything stopped working.'

They paused for a moment, respecting the euphemism.

Two units of vibration weren't enough to make the scoring the cause of the crash. But something about it had obviously kept niggling away at Pam, and now it was bothering Tom, too. He itched to see the fan disc; burned to run his fingers over the faces of the two connecting flanges.

A jet engine was so precisely machined – and operated at such enormous speeds – that the tiniest problems could become fatal flaws in the blink of an eye. The fan blade-tip speed could approach Mach 1 a mere one-eighth of an inch from the fan casing. The slightest imbalance . . .

The long silence across the miles was filled with their minds addressing a previously unconsidered problem, mentally dissecting the engine of a 737, stripping it down to its heart, then poring over every part of the assembly, probing for chinks in its armour.

'Maybe the scoring's a symptom, not a cause,' he said. It was possible that something had gone wrong somewhere else and that the disc and the shaft had parted company as a result. In that case, scoring – and even deeper gouging – could easily have been caused as the two metal faces ripped apart.

'Hmm,' said Pam, sounding unconvinced. 'Or maybe there was something wrong with the manufacture.'

That possibility was so frightening that Tom actually shivered. If there was a fault in the manufacturing process, then who knew how many planes might be in the skies right now with the same fault lying dormant in their engines, waiting to manifest itself in wholesale carnage? 'Have you checked the trail?'

'Yes. Everything's properly papered.'

He sighed with relief. Every airline part imported into or made in the US was numbered, logged and had a paper trail stretching back to the manufacturer. That paperwork outlived the part it documented. Years after a part was destroyed, its paperwork still languished in old files. For some years the paper trail had been converted to computer records that could be printed off as required. But in many countries, when a plane was sold, the paperwork transferred with it was taller than a Harlem Globetrotter.

'Where did the plane come from?'

'Hold on.' He could hear her shuffling papers. 'It was a twelve-year-old jet bought by SAA six years ago from Avia Freight.'

'Converted?'

Silence again while she checked. 'QC.'

QC was Quick Change. The 737-400 QC could be quickly refitted for passengers or for cargo.

'How about yours?'

'I don't know. I'll check. I'll get back to you.'

'Okay.'

'Hey, Pam, thanks.'

She laughed again, as if she had nothing better to do with her time than discuss downed planes with him half a world away.

Tom looked up Munro's report online. It told him only that the *Pride of Maine* had been manufactured thirteen years before its untimely death. He called CalSuperior and asked for their operations department. When he identified himself to a chirpy-sounding man, all the chirp went out of his voice and he became sullen, as if the investigation into the demise of the *Pride of Maine* was a personal insult.

'I thought this investigation was over.'

'You thought wrong.' Tom waited irritably while the guy got the information he needed. The *Pride of Maine* was a second-hand purchase – as so many cargo planes were. This particular 737 had been bought a mere three years before.

'Where was it purchased?'

'Purchased from . . .' Again, the formerly chirpy man took a good long time to find the information for him, then told him so grudgingly that Tom wanted to reach down the phone line and throttle him.

'. . . Avia Freight.'

Tom felt a little thrill up the back of his neck.

*

The Avia Freight offices in LA were on Sepulveda Boulevard, sandwiched between a Denny's parking lot and the Sunny View Motel. The Sunny View, in turn, was permanently in the shadow of the neighbouring office block, making it quite possibly the only motel in LA without a sunny view – or a view at all, thought Tom, as he looked round at the eight lanes of traffic pumping smog just inches from the car-sized motel pool, which oozed under an opalescent slick.

The interior of Avia Freight had a clean, corporate look that made Tom feel immediately like a bum. He'd put on his badge and his NTSB jacket, but the pretty young clerk (actress-slash-clerk, no doubt) glanced at his sneakers and dismissed him out of hand. She asked him if she could get him anything – coffee, water, juice? – without smiling. Tom shook his head and picked up the first magazine on the table beside the leather couch. Embarrassingly, it turned out to be *Hustler* and, although he could feel his ears burning, he felt obliged to flick defiantly through it under the gaze of the girl, who had no doubt placed it there for her own amusement.

'There's a great *article* in there about paragliding,' she said, barely able to keep a straight face.

'That's okay,' he said. 'I'm only looking at the pictures.'

The surprise in the actress-slash-clerk's eyes was worth it. To hammer home his admittedly small advantage, he let the magazine drop open and carefully tugged the centrefold clear of the staples. He raised his eyebrows at her. 'You don't mind, do you?' She shook her head, clearly dumbfounded, as he folded it neatly into his back pocket.

A tall, bulky man with a Saddam moustache emerged from an inner office and walked over with his hand stuck out for Tom to shake.

'Bruce Allway? Tom Patrick, NTSB. We spoke?'

Allway's office smelt newly carpeted, although Tom noticed that the carpet was old and unravelling a little round the edges. Maybe it was a spray – like that new-car smell. Tom toyed for a moment with the concept of a world where nothing was ever renewed or replaced, just sprayed to make it smell as if it had been.

Allway could have done with a spray to clear his desk. Papers and folders spilled across it in thick, uneven piles; Day-Glo notes stuck seemingly randomly to things; an ironic desk-tidy overflowing with pens festooned with rubber bands.

''Scuse the mess,' said Allway, with a hopeless shrug that seemed to indicate that if Tom had come on any other day things would have been pretty much the same. He held up a grey folder. 'Found what you're looking for.'

'Really?' said Tom, in genuine amazement.

*

Tom read the file in the debris of his Denny's lunch. The *Pride of Maine* had gone into service with Avia Freight from new. Avia was a major cargo player, and the maintenance records were what he'd expected – regular and comprehensive. Every nut and bolt that had been checked or replaced on the 737 had been logged. Tom ran his poker glance down the pages, looking for information about the number-two engine. Nothing. According to the records, the compressor fan disc was the one the *Pride of Maine* had been born with, and the engine had been properly maintained up to the point of sale. No connection with the South African jet. If something had gone wrong with the fan disc, it was nothing to do with Avia.

Back to square one. Now he'd have to go back to the chirpy sonofabitch at CalSuperior and go through their maintenance records with a fine-tooth comb as well.

He sighed. He ran his hand across the stubble on his chin and felt a rare pang of embarrassment that he'd forgotten to shave. It was quickly subsumed by the more familiar burn of frustration at the way his career was trickling away, like sand in an hourglass.

He'd accepted Boise without a murmur. He knew Pete was pissed at him for the early-hours call, so he'd gone to Idaho

100

and done the job with his usual thoroughness. But he'd also known he couldn't go on like that indefinitely, poking around oil waste pipes and mucky fuel tanks looking for clues while his heart was in the sky and his head was up his ass. Sooner or later it would break him, and right now he figured on sooner.

How long would it be before Pete let him back in?

Tom knew he'd fucked up. His brain was a scientific wonder but his mouth belonged to a knee-jerk teenager who'd been left alone in his parents' house for the weekend with only sex, drugs and rock 'n' roll for company. Not for the first time, Tom wondered when – if – his big mouth would ever be wholly under his control. He wasn't about to hold his breath.

And, if that were the case, shouldn't he just get out now? Why hang around up to his armpits in toxic sludge, waiting for each humiliation to be over just so the next one could begin?

He looked down at the file that the by-then-slightly-less-hostile actress-slash-clerk had copied for him.

A wave of self-loathing swept him up. He knew why he was helping Halo Jackson. He might have been kick-started by Chris Stern's young widow and her daughter, but he *needed* to find out what had happened to the *Pride of Maine* because he *needed* to show that he could still do the job he loved – even if it was after the event and unofficial and made no goddamn difference. He realized he was holding on to his old life by this one slender thread, and if it snapped, he was lost, cast adrift on a sea of failure and leaking pipes, dead fish and pollution.

And so the waves of self-loathing deposit me on the shores

of self-pity, he thought wryly, and grinned at himself. What a fucking loser. No wonder Ella'd run a mile.

'More coffee, sweetheart?' The waitress, a harassed woman in her forties, saw his grin and took time out from her shitty job to smile back at him before passing on to the next booth. Tom gathered his papers, got up and dropped a good tip on the table.

His phone rang and Ness's name came up on the display. 'Hello?'

'Hi, Tom.'

Her voice alone made his heart bump.

'Want to play some cards?'

*

She met him at the Bicycle Club, looking spectacular in a clingy green dress. But he figured she'd look that way in pretty much anything. Her glossy hair was tamed into a small clip at the nape of her neck, leaving delicious tendrils to escape across her milky skin.

She handed him two rolls of cash. 'Change them up one at a time. They draw less attention that way.' She reached up and he thought for one dizzying second that she was going to stroke his cheek, but her hand moved round to the back of his head and then he felt her fingers press gently into the hollow at the nape of his neck. 'When I touch your neck like so, it's over, okay?' He nodded silently, not trusting his voice. 'There's a doughnut shop down the strip. I'll meet you there.'

They went to the floor man's pulpit-like plinth and he asked for a fifteen-thirty table.

'Number thirty-two.' The man indicated it with a jerk of his head.

Tom started towards it, but Ness put a hand on his arm and shook her head at the floor man. 'What else have you got?'

He stood and craned so he could check out the tables. 'Forty-one?'

This time Tom stood and waited while Ness scanned it. 'Know anyone?' she asked.

'No.'

She nodded briefly and they walked through the room. 'What was wrong with thirty-two?' he asked.

'Two to the dealer's left is a Chinese man in a red shirt. He plays for the Triads. We try not to step on each other's toes.'

The phrase 'honour among thieves' sprang to Tom's mind, and he pushed it away, suddenly feeling awkwardly like a thief himself. The enormity of what he was about to do made him falter. A beautiful woman had appealed to his ego and he was about to make the leap from law-abiding citizen to money-launderer.

He hadn't thought about it in such bald terms before. It had all happened so fast. He'd been dazzled by Ness, and by the idea of playing with big money – a real high roller. But now he was about to become a very small cog in a piece of illegal machinery.

He stopped – uncertain.

Ness reached table forty-one and turned to him, raising her eyebrows questioningly. When he didn't move, she came back over. 'First-night nerves, Tom?'

'Yeah. I guess.'

'Only the good guys get them.' She smiled.

'I'm not the first?'

'Nope, but you're one of the few. I like a man who takes things seriously.'

He nodded and she waited, but he still didn't move. The dealer at forty-one glanced up to see where his ninth man was and Ness gave him a holding wave.

She gave Tom another moment, then leaned in close, so that he could smell her skin. 'All you're doing is playing cards, Tom. Nothing more. Using your talent to make a living.'

She made it sound like the American dream. And who knew? If his career didn't get back on track soon, he would need *something* just to pay his rent. Poker and planes were all he had.

He followed her to table forty-one.

It was close to the centre of the room. As they approached, Tom was already sizing up the opposition. He had never sat at a big-stakes table – all his big stakes had been with cheaply bought tournament chips – but table forty-one summed up one of the things Tom loved about card clubs. Any one of these players could have taken their place at a lowly one-two table without a second glance from their opponents. Even though they were playing a high-stakes game, they looked no different from any other player in the place.

Tom took a seat opposite the dealer. To his left were a slender Latino in a loose-fitting suit, then a bottle-blonde fifty-year-old, with gold on each finger and dripping from her ears, an emaciated black man with grizzled hair and beard, two middle-aged men with bulging waistlines – one in a sports coat and the other in a club jacket that read 'Normandie – Five Card Stud'. On his right were a slim, unshaven white man in a net cap and with dirt under his long fingernails, a good-looking dark-haired woman in her thirties, and a skinny Chinese man who could have been thirty or fifty.

The dealer was a portly Latino with a Zapata moustache and a bored expression in his small dark eyes.

It was only when Tom changed one of the rolls of money for chips that he knew it contained ten thousand dollars. He felt suddenly ill. Intellectually, he'd known that he wouldn't be playing for peanuts, but the thought of losing ten thousand dollars of someone else's money – especially when that someone else might not be firmly bound by the law of the land – made his guts clench. If the other roll contained what this one had, then they – whoever 'they' were – must be prepared to lose twenty thousand in the experiment to see whether he was worth 'employing'. He hoped that people who could throw that kind of money away on an experiment wouldn't bother killing him for losing it. But he could only hope that. He couldn't know it unless – until – that happened.

The chip jockey handed him two trays filled with chips.

As Tom placed them on the table in front of him, he flicked a glance at Ness, knowing it was the last honest one he'd be able to give anyone for the duration of this game. He didn't care. Like a novice high-board diver seeking a nod from his coach far below, he needed to know he was going to be okay.

Ness read his face and cocked an amused eyebrow. She leaned against him and he felt her soft skin brush against him as she breathed into his ear, 'It's only money, Tom.'

*

It was only money. But it was a lot of 'only money'. And, thank God, by the time Ness touched his neck with those warm, soft fingers five hours later, a good sum of it had accumulated in a navy-and-white cityscape in front of Tom.

The relief that washed over him was almost palpable. He'd played out the hand because he'd been dealt a pair of eights, but he was almost relieved to see the old black guy turn over a straight. Tom didn't even want to delay long enough to count another pile of chips into another plastic tray.

As the other players put out their blinds, Tom slid a fifty-dollar chip to the dealer and stood up.

'You leaving with our money?' The bottle-blonde looked at him through lizard eyes.

Tom swallowed his knee-jerk response and bobbed his head to her. 'Ma'am.'

'Don't you "ma'am" me, you chickenshit homo.'

Tom piled his racks on top of each other, while the eyes of every other player at the table bored into him. After what seemed like for ever, he turned away from the table. Ness was nowhere to be seen.

'That's right,' the bottle-blonde said loudly. 'Go home and jerk off your boyfriend.'

'Yes, ma'am.'

He didn't wait to watch the woman's reaction, although he wanted to quite badly.

He went to the cash window where a wrinkled Filipina gave him a brief smile. 'Congratulations, sir. Would you like a cheque?'

'Uh, no. Cash will be fine, thank you.'

'Yes, sir.' She leaned slightly away from the window

and called down the row. 'Mr Collins! Cash going out!'

Collins, a muscular, shaven-headed man in a tuxedo, stood and watched with gimlet eyes as the cashier counted out $37,700, encased it neatly in elastic bands in three ten-thousand-dollar piles and one $7,700 pile, and slid it under the window to him. 'Thank you for playing, sir.'

He waited for her to ask for his ID, but she said nothing.

'Would you like an escort to your car, sir?' Collins asked.

'Er . . .' Tom glanced around as if a mugger might be waiting patiently behind him right now. 'No, thanks.'

Collins nodded. As long as he'd asked, and someone had heard him ask, he'd done his job. This guy was on his own.

Tom pushed the thick wads of money deep into his jeans pockets. They bulged like football pads on his thighs. He felt self-conscious walking out, but nobody looked at him. He glanced back at table forty-one, but even the bottle-blonde's back was turned.

He drove a quarter-mile down the strip, buzzing with the joy of winning – almost hard with it. Every time he looked into his rear-view mirror he realized he was grinning like a kid. He hadn't felt this goofily good since he was nine and his dad had bought him his first real bike. An ice-blue-metallic Peugeot racer with ten gears. It was a bittersweet memory: eighteen months later he'd left it unlocked outside Target's, and come out to find it gone. The two memories – joy and loss – were locked together inside him for ever. Now he brushed the loss aside: *getting* the bike had felt like this.

Ness was already picking at a bear-claw in the doughnut shop. She looked up as the bell announced him, and gave the half-smile that made her look so desirable he could hardly believe it was for him. He realized she must be amused by his beaming good mood. Her eyes flicked down to his jeans. 'Is that thirty-seven thousand dollars in your pocket, or are you just pleased to see me?'

They grinned and he slid into the plastic chair opposite hers. He jammed his hand into his pants to retrieve the money but she gazed out through the window and said, 'Not here, Tom.'

He was surprised, and she explained, 'I only came in for the doughnut.'

In her car – a small black Lotus – she allowed him to hand her the winnings, along with the untouched ten-thousand-dollar stake money. She peeled off $2,700 and handed it back to him. 'Nice job.'

He smiled, still buoyant, the way he always was after a win.

She dropped the rest of the money into a cloth bag and pushed it under her seat. Then she put the key into the ignition and looked at him expectantly.

He wondered what happened now. Decided to find out. 'Buy you a coffee?'

'Sorry, I have to get going.'

She smiled to soften the blow but Tom felt suddenly abandoned. 'Sure.'

'Tom,' she said, a little awkwardly, 'I have a boyfriend.'

He shrugged. 'Is he bigger than me?'

She laughed.

He sighed and got out of her car, then watched, like a dog tied to a gate, as she drove away.

For the second time in a month Tom was deprived of someone to celebrate with.

12

IRVING, TEXAS, WAS no place for a Chinaman. This thought passed with ever-increasing bitterness through the mind of Chuck Zhong about fifty times a night as he made the rounds of the WAE plant.

Two years ago he'd thought this was a vacation job, something to keep him out of the hellhole of a summer kitchen at the Lucky Eight restaurant in downtown Irving. Two years ago he'd enjoyed the irony of the fact (or what he'd believed then would be the fact) that he was working security at the plant where soon he hoped to be making a living as an aeronautical engineer.

That first summer he'd made his beat a constant one. While Jeff and Lyle huddled together and played gin rummy with their backs to the security screens, Chuck had walked every inch of the place, soaking up every aspect of the first aircraft-engineering plant he'd ever be a part of – even if he was just security for now. Soon he'd be part of it for real, testing, improving, hypothesizing, showing them all how good he could be.

He wanted so badly to show everyone how good he was, and graduating top of his class in aeronautical engineering at the age of twenty-three was no bad way to start. Chuck was the first person in his family to go to university, and he was already the biggest success in his particular branch of Zhong family history. That was what his parents always said anyway, not wanting to disrespect their ancestors by setting Chuck up as the evolutionary pinnacle of the entire Zhong dynasty.

But, hell, thought Chuck, to find someone who'd done better you'd have to go back to goddamn Genghis Khan or some such shit. If he discovered that a Zhong had built the Great Wall single-handed, then maybe – just maybe – he'd concede defeat.

But that success was two years ago.

For the thousandth time since he'd got the job, Chuck ran his flashlight across the rows of parts waiting to be packed and shipped, each with an FAA Form 8130-3 attached – its own birth certificate, a white docket of authentication that allowed airlines to trust a million lives to each tiny part.

That was the pinnacle, as far as he was concerned. These gleaming, virgin pieces of metal, tooled and machined and filed and polished until their surfaces were jewels, precious gems in reverse, which had begun pristine and priceless and would be buried in the innards of an engine for the rest of their lives, fated for their beauty to be hidden from all eyes but those of common grease-monkeys. Their appreciation could never match his, of course, but they would at least treat those metal jewels with respect every time they were exposed to the light of maintenance.

Chuck Zhong sighed heavily. The production line was starting to turn from a thrill to a taunt and – not for the first time – he laid the blame for everything that had gone wrong in his life at the door of his parents.

They had been in Texas for forty-seven years, transported as children to a new world from an ancient one in the wake of the war, with no expectations other than avoiding starvation. They had met in Irving, married in Irving and – apart from a single trip to China – Chuck couldn't remember the last time they'd been outside Irving. Maybe they never had. They hardly went outside the Lucky Eight.

Neither Ling nor Tong Zhong could speak English, and Chuck's Cantonese was so rusty that he barely spoke to his parents any more. He hardly saw them, now that he'd chosen not to sweat himself into a pork-scented grave in the restaurant kitchen. They had brought up three children and had named them Chuck, Billy and Mary-Lou, as if their names alone would earn them a welcome in a place where at best they would never feel accepted, and where at worst they'd suffer lifelong discrimination.

Chuck felt a familiar hot anger rise in him at his parents' ignorance. He always tried to suppress it but he never could. If they'd meant so well, why not move to a city that had a decent Chinese-American population, where they wouldn't stick out like sore thumbs? If they were so keen on integrating, why had they never bothered learning English? Then maybe Chuck wouldn't have had to spend his childhood interrupting his homework to translate from drunken Texan to Cantonese, and watching rednecks laugh at his father's mangled greeting at the door of the Lucky Eight, or see them pull their own eyes into slits and mimic his mother's smiles as she asked them to say the number of their orders off the arduous menu. Chuck's parents could count to 125 in English. He knew, because that was the greatest number of dishes the Lucky Eight menu had ever offered to the rude, loud populace of Irving, Texas.

111

He knew his parents had made every conceivable sacrifice to keep the three of them in school, let alone Chuck's four years at Texas State. But he still hated them, and it was a hate they, and he, could do nothing about, because he hated what they were and what they would always be.

Texas State had finally sprung him from the Lucky Eight, and from his own heritage. There were other Chinese kids there. Not many, but some, although Chuck steered clear of them. And Mexicans too – so many Mexican students that the white boys were less likely to be overtly racist, simply out of self-preservation. Chuck was pleased to discover that the white students hated the Mexicans so much that a Chinese classmate was almost a relief. For the first time in his life he didn't feel like the bottom rung of the ladder, and it was heady stuff.

He excelled at his studies and went out for the baseball team until his final year, when he did nothing but work.

He even got a white girlfriend, Verity, although he never told his parents about her. He knew they wanted him to marry someone from the old country – from the old village, preferably.

Chuck had been to the old village once on a trip it had taken his parents six years to save for. It had made him sick to his stomach. The mud was made of shit and the extended Zhong family had cut the throat of a small white dog for the homecoming feast. Chuck had cried and his father had slapped his face in embarrassment. Years later when Chuck had graduated, his father had wept loudly through the ceremony, drawing sniggers from the other students, and Chuck had wanted to slap him back.

When he'd made his application for one of three

entry-level WAE engineering vacancies, he'd pointed out with some pride that he'd taken this summer job in order to be close to the action. Or, at least, closer to the action than he'd have been at the Lucky Eight or at McDonald's. Chuck liked to think he had a sense of humour, and that other people appreciated it. And he liked to think that the humility he'd shown in pointing out his own humble beginnings at WAE would translate into the sort of paternal admiration that would lead to a job offer.

Chuck had been wrong.

He had waited three weeks for an invitation to an interview that never came. Then, on 13 September, alone in the human-resources department, he'd found a letter addressed to himself in the out-tray. Chuck thought he'd save them time and a stamp.

Inside were three impersonal lines saying his application had been unsuccessful.

Chuck had almost fainted. He actually felt the room swim around him, like something from a movie-of-the-week melodrama.

He didn't tell his parents. He didn't tell anybody; he could barely acknowledge the shame himself. He kept going to work, kept hoping that someone somewhere had made a terrible mistake, that it would all be okay in the end.

It wasn't.

Over the next month he noticed a change in three of the desks in Engineering. New people had taken up residence – three new engineers fresh out of college, who left little clues to who they might be. A photo of a WASPy girlfriend and a teddy-bear clutching a heart that read 'Congratulations' on one desk. On the second, a hefty gilt trophy declaring Neil

Abbotsham to be the 2007 Northwest Collegiate backstroke champion.

But it was the third newly occupied desk that cut Chuck to the quick. First he noticed there was a footstool in front of the chair. Then a few nights later he found a box of tampons in the not-yet-cluttered drawer.

A woman.

A woman had taken his job.

There had been two women on his aeronautical-engineering course. One had dropped out after getting pregnant in her sophomore year. The other was a willowy, spot-ridden girl called Fern Lipschitz. Fern wouldn't have needed a footstool: she was taller than Chuck.

He didn't know who this woman was, but he hated her anyway. In his mind, he knew he must have been bumped because of some ridiculous quota to be filled, whatever the quality of the applicant.

Chuck took the tampons with him, then tipped the whole box into the single, little-used ladies' toilet. They swelled in an instant and clogged the pan. When he flushed, only half of them disappeared. There was an ominous gurgling sound and the returning water crept high up the sides of the bowl. Maintenance would have to be alerted before the toilet could be used. He hoped it would cause the woman inconvenience and embarrassment. But, even if she got sacked for blocking the toilet, and bled to death on the way home for want of a tampon, she would not suffer one-tenth of what he was suffering right now.

He stayed in the security job out of a self-destructive need to show he could take the rejection. And from fear of being dragged back to the Lucky Eight if he was unemployed for more than about twenty-five minutes.

Once he saw the woman who had stolen his job working late. She was a girl, really, early twenties; small and pretty. Maybe Vietnamese. She'd looked up and said, 'Hi,' as he stuck his head round the office door. He didn't say anything, just started strolling round the small office as if it was part of his beat. He knew she was uncomfortable – a woman alone in a deserted building at night, with some creepy, silent security guard prowling around her – and it gave him a thrill. After that he always looked forward to checking her office, but she didn't work late again. Or she took her work home.

The work *he* should've been taking home with *him*.

*

Just as Chuck was coming to the slow conclusion that being a security guard for ever was possibly not the way to make the world pay for appointing the quota bitch in his place, Lyle got fired from the WAE plant for blowing Jeff in the engineers' office.

Chuck was surprised by every aspect of the sordid episode.

He was surprised that they swung that way; surprised they could be so stupid; surprised that the day staff had bothered reviewing the night tapes, which showed the deed in grainy black-and-white; surprised that Jeff somehow *didn't* get fired; surprised because he'd never seen Lyle or Jeff anywhere but the security office; and most surprised of all by how hard Lyle fought to keep his job. Chuck heard he'd actually cried when they'd told him he was canned. You'd have sworn the guy was pulling down a hundred grand per annum, instead of a lousy twenty-one and a half before taxes.

Come to think of it – and Chuck eventually did come to think of it – Chuck was also surprised by how Lyle managed to be driving a neat, two-year-old Suzuki 4×4 instead of the piles of rusted steel he and Jeff drove.

Now it was just him and Jeff, alone in the security office at night, until they could replace Lyle. Jeff was older than Chuck and a lot bigger; the two of them stepped warily around each other and Chuck made even more rounds than normal. They didn't speak about Lyle.

But somebody else did.

Spoke about him without ever mentioning his name.

Eight nights after Lyle had left, Chuck was off, and having a beer at a sports bar. The Cowboys were playing, so Chuck was rooting for the Jets, enjoying the rising wails of misery in the bar as Dallas got hammered.

Fuck Texas.

He stayed through the third quarter to make sure they were going to get their asses kicked, then left his money on the bar and got to his feet, swaying just a little. He went to the men's room and almost fell asleep as he fumbled with his zipper over the urinal. Shit. He was hammered and he'd only had five beers.

Someone entered behind him but he didn't turn round. If he had, he would've seen it coming . . .

Chuck came round face-down in the back seat of a car, tied, gagged and blindfolded. Someone was sitting on his legs and he grunted. Someone was heavy and fidgety against the tender backs of Chuck's thighs.

One of them was shaking; Chuck figured it was probably him.

'He's awake. Pull over.'

Chuck felt fear envelop him, making him panicky and breathless. He didn't want to pull over. Driving around for ever like this would do just fine. Pull over, and whatever was going to happen next would start to happen . . .

The car stopped and the door at his feet opened. The man on his legs got off and dragged him out on to the ground by his ankles. His face dug into a field that smelt fragrantly of grass and horse manure, and something hard and metallic poked at the back of his neck.

'Hey, Chinky.'

He'd always known Irving, Texas, was no place for a Chinaman.

Chuck squeezed his eyes closed behind the blindfold.

Now the blood of the first Zhong (in his branch of the family) to go to university was going to be a permanent part of this godforsaken piece-of-shit place. He felt his groin go hot as his bladder let go.

His *fucking* parents!

'We want to give you a lot of money.'

Chuck stopped breathing to hear better. The man couldn't have said what he just thought he did. Could he?

'You hear me, Hop Sing? We want to give you a lot of money.'

Chuck was so still he could hear his own heart thumping.

'Or we could just as easily kill you.'

The man laughed and was joined by another.

The man who was holding what Chuck had to assume to be a gun to his head pushed his face into the earth, and

Chuck felt grass and damp soil fill his mouth. 'You choose,' the man said.

So Chuck chose.

Two hours later he was back home. Shaking, piss-stained, with the real taste of Texas between his teeth – and with enough money in his pocket to put a down-payment on a neat little Toyota Rav 4.

13

'OFFICIAL BUSINESS AGAIN, PAL?'

Tom cursed his luck as he turned to see the manager of the Sawmill grinning. Tom ignored him.

'Lucia's in tonight, stud.' Tom ignored him some more but felt a warm glow at the information. He bought a six-dollar beer and found a table near the stage where two hard-bodied redheads were faking a lesbian thing.

They were followed by the same blonde he'd seen before, and a statuesque black girl, who was obviously a favourite with the crowds, judging by the amount of money she scooped up after her show.

Tom resolutely refused to tip any of them more than five bucks. He was keeping his powder dry.

Finally Lucia appeared and Tom felt the comforting glow of knowing he'd been right to make the drive to Santa Ana. She looked soft and pretty, especially alongside her dance partner, a painfully thin Korean, whose sinews ridged the skin of her pelvis.

Among the other customers there was a definite feeling of anti-climax after the tall black girl had gone, and many drifted to the bar as the two new girls started to dance.

The Korean gyrated hard and fast, her face a mask. Lucia

was again lost in herself as she performed, her eyes distant.

When the music stopped and she spotted Tom, she smiled and he unexpectedly felt himself blush.

She made the rounds, collecting fives and tens, then stopped in front of him.

'Hi,' she said.

'Hi.' He was stuck for what to say next. He had a fifty in his hand but he forgot he was supposed to give it to her. Suddenly it seemed like the whole room could overhear them. If he spoke, everyone would hear his voice. He couldn't do it.

Why was this so hard? Last time he'd just asked her to go for a drink with him and she'd said yes. Why was this different?

The Korean girl had collected her few tips and was walking offstage. Any moment now Lucia would follow her and his chance would be gone.

She saved him: 'You want to buy me a drink with that?'

This time he actually did buy her a drink. Not at the club, but in a small bar she knew down the strip. She ordered a Coke and he didn't press her to drink anything harder. He got a Jack Daniel's because he needed the courage. Fucking a girl like Lucia was one thing; talking to her was a whole 'nother ball game.

'It's good to see you again.'

Her words surprised him. Then he remembered how little she'd had to do to earn her money last time and figured, No wonder.

Once again the silence stretched between them and Tom downed the Jack in one in a bid for help.

This was a bad idea. They should've gone straight to the Motel 6 where he knew exactly what was required of him. He didn't find it this hard to talk to Ness. Maybe he should offer *her* fifty bucks for a blow-job . . .

The mental image of Ness on her knees in front of him forced words from his mouth to cover his sudden discomfort. 'How's work?'

'Late.' She smiled. 'I never get enough sleep.'

He made himself believe she meant the dancing. He didn't want to ask any more about her lifestyle, in case she told him.

'How about you? What do you do?'

'I'm an accountant.'

'Really?' She stared at him. 'You don't look like an accountant.'

'Oh, yeah? What does an accountant look like?'

She studied him, from his faded blue polo shirt to his scuffed jeans and his Converse sneakers, and gave him a lopsided grin. 'Like the anti-you!'

He laughed, then stopped short. It was so long since he'd heard that sound come from his own mouth that it had sounded strange to him.

'What's up?' Her eyes were actually concerned.

'Nothing. You're funny, that's all.'

She shrugged. 'So. Public or management?'

'Huh?'

Lucia half closed her eyes into a parody of suspicious slits. 'What kind of accountant? Public or management? Or auditing? Or panicky, now that you realize you should've chosen to lie about a profession you actually know something about?' Her tone was light and teasing and, instead of feeling

121

defensive, Tom put up his hands in surrender and grinned.

'Okay. I'm not an accountant.'

'Let me guess what you are.'

At least that would mean an exchange where she had to come up with all the questions, he thought, and where his answers had only to stretch to 'yes' or 'no'.

'You're like a cop but not a cop.'

Shit! This was going to be a short conversation! Was she psychic?

Lucia smiled at the surprise on his face. 'Close?'

'Maybe. How'd you figure that?'

She sipped her Coke, then picked a piece of ice out of the glass and played with it in her hands as she spoke. 'For a start, the accountant thing. I mean, who the hell pretends to be an accountant? So, I think you must have a job that's a lot more interesting than that.'

She stopped and looked to him for confirmation but he only shrugged. 'You don't say much. So unless your head is, like, totally empty, I guess that means you listen. That you've learned that listening gets you places that talking doesn't.'

He finished his Jack Daniel's and pointed the bartender to his glass for another.

'Which means that in your work, listening pays dividends.'

She looked at him expectantly, and he nodded. 'You're good.'

'Yeah?' Her face split into a grin of delight. 'I'm a psychology major! Final year. I love doing this stuff! Specially when I'm right.'

She'd surprised him. He'd thought the dancing and other . . . was what she did, what she *was* . . .

'Well, you're right so far. Want to see how close you can get?'

She nodded enthusiastically, and suddenly Tom didn't care if she nailed it. Keeping his occupation and identity from her didn't seem that important, compared to seeing the pride on her face.

Her brow furrowed and she studied him more closely this time, ending with a long stare into his eyes that made him uncomfortable. Hers were pale brown, and the black lashes around them were thick and spiked. The whites were very white and clear. He took a slow hit of Jack Daniel's so he could close his eyes and shut her out for a moment.

'Okay. You look tired.'

'Thanks.'

'Well, you do. That means you have a job where you're not being like a cop all the time. You couldn't be this tired all the time. Sometimes you have time to recover. Then you start again. So you have, sort of . . . cases. It's not a nine-to-five job. Am I right?'

'Right on all counts.' He hoped she'd smile again, but she was too engrossed to be deflected now by mere enjoyment.

'I bet you're good at your job, because of the listening thing.'

'Right again,' he said, with deliberate arrogance, making her laugh a little.

'But something's wrong. You seem . . . disappointed.'

Suddenly he didn't like this game so much any more. He looked for the bartender. 'You want another drink?'

'Coke, please.'

'You ever drink anything other than Coke?'

'Sometimes. With my friends.' She frowned, realizing what she'd said. 'Sorry. I just meant—'

'Forget it.'

'No. I didn't mean it like that. I just meant, it's bad to get drunk when you're working, so I only drink on my days off. That's all.'

He got them both a Coke. He was driving, after all, and the JD was still pumping through him nicely.

'So what is it? Tax fraud?'

He realized she was still trying to guess what he did. He shook his head.

'Security guard? Corrections officer? CIA?' This last thought made her eyes widen as if she feared being right.

She obviously wasn't going to give up so he told her. 'NTSB.'

'Plane crashes and stuff?'

He hadn't expected her to know it but she'd surprised him yet again. He nodded, not wanting to bother with the details of how plane crashes were no longer on his particular NTSB agenda. He hoped she wouldn't ask him about the bodies he'd seen. It was the reason he'd stopped telling people what he did for a living. He understood it – most people would never see a dead body, let alone one that had been torn apart mid-air and then driven two feet into the soil, or decapitated and impaled on a post-and-rail fence. People were curious. But he didn't like to think about the bodies, and those questions made him do that.

'I don't like to fly,' she said abruptly.

'Me neither.'

'Really? I'd have thought you guys were used to it. Like those people who go on and on about how you're more likely to die on the way to the airport than in an air crash. I wish they'd just shut up. I mean, you get car trouble on the 405, you just pull over, right? No off-ramps at thirty-five thousand feet.' A little shiver ran through her and she masked her discomfort by taking another cube of ice from her Coke and holding it in her fist while it melted on to the carpet. 'Sorry. I didn't mean to, like, diss your whole industry.'

'Hell, diss away. It's not my industry – I just pick up the pieces. Literally. If God had meant us to fly he'd have given us more leg-room.'

The tension that had built up through her little speech dissipated visibly and she dropped the ice, now half its original size, back into her Coke. 'Do you believe in God?' she asked.

'No.'

Her face betrayed no judgement on his answer. She swirled a finger in her Coke, clinking the ice. 'Can I kiss you?'

Tom wasn't sure he'd heard right, but she was looking at him in a way that made him think his ears hadn't played tricks on him – hopeful and shy, and sending fleeting glances towards his mouth.

Feeling like a teenager, he leaned towards her. She met him halfway and he felt her warm lips under his. The kiss was chaste and brief, but Tom realized he'd closed his eyes and held his breath through it. He felt a little dizzy and foolish as he straightened on the bar stool.

She gave him a dazzling smile and said shyly, 'Thanks.' She turned away from him to watch two truckers play pool. They had nearly finished.

Tom cleared his throat. 'You want a game?'

'Sure. Yeah. But we have to play for money,' she said. 'I always play for money.'

'How much?'

'Ten bucks a frame?'

'Make it five,' he said. Tom hadn't played for a few years but he'd always been a pretty decent bar-room player and didn't want to fleece her.

He needn't have worried.

She took him apart.

Lucia played like a man, getting down low, bridging strongly, stroking the cue smoothly and firmly, cutting back and fine, and spinning off balls and cushions to ensure a good position, seeing three or four shots ahead of her game, adapting to new lies quickly, never panicking.

Tom enjoyed watching her more than he'd enjoyed anything in a long time. Anything since they'd slept together, he realized.

When she'd fired the black into a middle pocket, she laid down her cue and gave him a wary look in case she'd overstepped the mark.

For only the second time in about a year – both in the past hour – he burst out laughing. 'Where'd you learn to play like that?'

She started to smile. 'College.'

'Well, forget that Freudian crap.' He grinned. 'You got a big future in pro pool, baby!'

'It was probably a fluke.'

'I'm hoping. Double or quits?'

She smiled teasingly. 'You're a sucker for punishment.'

This time he took it seriously, paying more attention to the table and a little less to her. He made a match of it but she still whipped his ass with two of his stripes left on the table. This time she allowed herself to crow a little, with a wide smirk. 'Again?'

'Hell, no! I won't have enough cash on me to—' He stopped himself, realizing what he'd been about to say and glanced round to make sure he hadn't given her away.

She got it too. She leaned into him. 'I don't want your money,' she said softly.

'Why not?'

'Because I like you.'

Tom finished his drink in a couple of slugs. 'I bet you say that to all the boys.'

He might as well have slapped her. She blinked, then looked away from him, her face losing its soft charm and becoming smooth and blank. 'Yeah. Whatever.'

'What?'

'Nothing.' She rolled her cue across the baize and picked up her purse, then turned back to Tom with a bright smile, but her eyes were focused away from his now, somewhere just to the right of his face. 'You want to go to the motel?'

Did he? All of a sudden he wasn't sure.

'Time is money, y'know?' Her voice had an edge to it now and made him feel bad.

Guilty.

Christ, thought Tom, if he'd wanted this kind of mind-fuck before sex he might as well be married! He'd be damned if he was paying to have her go down on him with that blank, accusing look, like he'd just cut her housekeeping.

He wondered briefly how he'd insulted her – how it had gone from so good to so bad so fast – but he stopped himself making the effort. She wasn't his girlfriend, for God's sake. He didn't owe her a dozen roses for being a dick. Being a dick was not only what he did best, but was his prerogative as a paying customer. It was his goddamned consumer *right* to be a dick!

Tom put down his cue and looked at her calmly. 'You have a lot to learn about being a whore.'

The hard look in her eyes cracked apart and her face twisted with the effort she made not to cry, but as she walked out of the bar, he saw the tears spill down her cheeks.

Tom stared into his empty glass until he was sure she was gone, his neck burning with what he assumed must be anger.

14

CALSUPERIOR CARGO'S maintenance records were a mess. A disgrace. Tom sat on the cold concrete floor of their storage facility, surrounded by a half-dozen boxes filled with the *Pride of Maine* paperwork that had been brought here after the plane was scrapped, as was usual after the publication of the NTSB report.

His ass ached. He'd been here since nine forty-five a.m. and it was now . . . He checked his watch. It was now three fifty-six p.m. Shit. He hadn't even found the FAA forms for the number-two engine yet. He'd found number one's in the first box he'd examined, but Murphy's Law decreed that that would be his only glimmer of hope the whole day long.

The thought of coming back tomorrow made him shudder. And the thought of not finding the paperwork at all made him feel sick. Not because missing paperwork was a bad thing. Missing paperwork could be a clue in itself. But if it wasn't in the final box, he'd have to check the whole lot again much more carefully to make sure it really wasn't there.

He unwound himself from the floor and groaned as his knees and back popped. He limped stiffly to the coffee machine and bought two cups of what was misleadingly described as espresso. He downed one instantly and took the other back to his temporary residence in the cardboard-and-paper city. He'd drunk twelve cups of this muck today and eaten nothing, and his stomach squealed in outrage to find itself awash with more bitter coffee-cum-sludge.

He sat down again and picked up another handful of random paperwork.

Tom had had some shitty days in the past year, but this was right up there. And, infuriatingly, he knew that it wasn't just because he couldn't find what he was seeking.

He'd woken up feeling miserable and empty. He'd made a stab at improving his mood by getting angry with Lucia. He'd tried his best to work himself into a bitter fury as he scraped dangerously at his stubble with a razor blade that needed replacing. But by the time he was showered, dressed and covered with bits of tissue paper, he felt even worse than he had before.

However hard he tried, the image that kept popping into his head was the hurt in her eyes – and the tears on her cheeks as she turned away.

It was too fucking bad! Why was he even thinking of her? He had a lot to worry about: the *Pride of Maine*; how he was going to worm his way back into air-crash investigations; his poker game; Ness.

He knew somewhere in the back of his mind that he was hoping the *Pride of Maine* would be his ticket back. There was something not right about it. The very fact that Lenny Munro was an asshole somehow lent credence to his gut feeling on that. And Pete LaBello couldn't keep him out in the cold for ever. He knew Pete must be missing his skills on planes, and he wasn't pulling his weight anywhere else right now. The pipelines and tankers of the western USA had been sound and non-flammable for a few days, for which Tom was grudgingly grateful. If he never saw another fifty-four-inch NS carbon-alloy pig receiver, it would be too soon.

He'd made a good start to his pro poker career. That was how he was trying to think of it, rather than as his slide towards the criminal underbelly. But he should take it more seriously. He should read some books, get some new angles, stay ahead of the game. That would impress Ness.

Ness.

He tingled at the thought of her. Impressing Ness would be a good thing in so many ways . . .

Anyway, it was challenging stuff and it was going to take all his concentration to keep those balls in the air. He had no time to waste on some weepy whore.

A bolt of guilt brought him full circle to Lucia.

Shit.

'How're you getting on, Mr Patrick?'

Tom looked up to see Mr Chirpy, who had turned out to be Lowell Dexter, a prissy-mouthed young man with foppish hair, trendy horn-rims and a suit so ugly and badly cut that Tom figured he must be heterosexual, despite compelling evidence to the contrary. 'Like shit. You call this a filing system?'

Dexter pouted and his small eyes flashed angrily. 'I called your office.'

Tom didn't answer.

'In DC?'

Tom pulled the last box towards him and opened the lid.

'They say you're not on an official investigation.' Dexter's tone was triumphant.

131

'Oh, yeah?'

'I spoke to a Mr Munro? He said you had no official sanction to do what you're doing.'

'Is that right?' Tom flipped through the box, his practised eye running desperately down random dockets, hoping against hope . . .

'Actually, what he said was, you're a fucking asshole who'll be working as a department-store Santa by Christmas.'

Tom snorted. He knew it was over – but he couldn't stop searching for what his brain had decided suddenly to narrow the search down to: the fan disc. Disc. Disc. Disc. His eyes were like heat-seeking missiles homing in on those four letters in the hundreds of thousands of combinations in front of him on the pink, yellow and white papers.

'So I'm gonna have to ask you to leave.'

'Oh, yeah?' Tom never even bothered looking at Dexter.

'Or I'm gonna call security.'

'Okay.' He didn't stand up. It had to be here somewhere. It *had* to be . . .

He'd hoped Dexter would have to go somewhere else to call security, but instead the man pulled out a phone and stood with one hand on his cocked hip while he asked them to come on down. No chance for Tom to stuff paperwork down the back of his pants.

A small, depressing part of Tom recognized how far he had fallen at this precise moment, but he forced it to the back of his mind as he scooped up handfuls of paper in his impossible quest.

Dexter snapped his phone shut and put his other hand on his other hip, looking like a puny, petulant Clark Kent. He was too nervous to come over and snatch the paperwork from Tom until reinforcements arrived.

Tom's eyes found disc. Disc. Fan disc. There it was!

He made himself riffle past it a few pages, all too aware of Dexter's burning gaze, but leaving the document protruding from the pile. From the corner of his eye he saw two uniformed men walk briskly into the room, both shorter than him, but a lot wider. He stood, holding the sheaf of papers.

'Okay, okay, I'm going.'

'Without the papers, please, Mr Patrick.' Dexter was enjoying his power-by-proxy to the full, now that someone had his back, front and both sides.

Tom dropped them back into the box. They hit his espresso on the way down and half a cup of black sludge poured into the box with them.

'Fuck!' yelled Dexter and hurried over, trying to shake coffee off the maintenance records.

'Shit. I'm sorry.' And Tom genuinely was sorry – sorry that he hadn't bought a *mucho grande* cappuccino from the crappy machine. Then Dexter could've made himself some nice *papier-mâché* hats from the wet pulp in the box. As it was, there was only enough spillage to create a distraction, but that was all Tom needed. As Dexter fussed over the boxes, Tom fed a single folded sheet of white paper up his sleeve with the skill of a grifter.

Then the security guards gripped him by the arms and showed him the door.

*

The white docket was the 'Serviceable' tag, and told Tom a story just as if it had been a novel.

His ability to picture a whole series of events suggested by the briefest of information had always been a joy to him. As a boy, an old English racing almanac he'd found in a thrift store had consumed him for the best part of a year as he deciphered its archaic shorthand: 'Ld 1 to 8; blndrd 9; went 2nd rdly run-in; just fld, shhd.' Eventually it revealed to him that a horse named Rum Shooter had led from the first fence to the eighth, blundered at the ninth, come back to take second place readily after the last fence and was gaining on the leader before being beaten by the then smallest of racing margins – a 'short head'. The book was his Rosetta Stone and fostered an addiction to gleaning the whole picture from the bare minimum of seemingly meaningless information. The fact that the race referred to was an amateur steeplechase that had taken place twenty years earlier some six thousand miles away in a muddy English field for a purse of twenty-five pounds and a pewter mug was immaterial: it ran fresh in his head every time he read the summary. Everything he needed to know was there in that old cold print. It was all about knowing how to read it, and imagination.

No wonder he missed air crashes, he thought, with a pang. His favourite part of the job was when every piece of wreckage that could be found was laid out on the floor of a hangar in an exploded view of the aircraft it had once been. Tom felt his stomach clench in excitement just at the thought of it. The knowledge that somewhere among the thousands of twisted, charred scraps of metal and foam, rubber and cabling lay the solution to a puzzle that seemed to have been devised and presented for his exclusive gratification.

Other investigators preferred the computer-aided reconstructions, the simulator rides, the eyewitness accounts, the cockpit voice-recorders of pilots reacting to the unexpected, spiralling from professionalism into panic as their planes shuddered and screamed towards the ground. Other investigators hated picking painstakingly through the wreckage looking for tiny, sometimes microscopic, clues, but Tom lived for it. Holes in oil pipes didn't compare – didn't even come close.

He sighed at the aching, plane-shaped space he realized it had left in him, and slid on to his back on the beat-up leather couch, careless of his sneakers scuffing the armrest. He twitched a lip in a self-mocking half-smile. He hadn't even felt this miserable when Ella left. What kind of man was he? Lying here alone, friendless, sexless, and mourning not his girlfriend but a hangar filled with scrap metal that held secrets in its very molecules.

Tom sighed and rubbed a hand over his face.

Loser.

He picked up a doughnut – the fastest coffee-sponge he'd been able to think of after his unceremonious exit from CalSuperior – and got back to the task at hand.

The scrappy white *Pride of Maine* print-off, annotated here and there with biro and oily mechanics' fingerprints, told him the story of the fan disc.

It was a short story.

Tom was surprised to see that this was a replacement fan disc, two years old. That worried him on two levels. Either it meant he was hopelessly wrong to suspect that the fan disc had had anything to do with the *Pride of Maine* or the South

135

African crash – or it meant the replacement fan disc had been badly flawed. The mechanic who'd installed the replacement disc had signed the job: N. Alvarez.

The phone rang and Tom looked at it suspiciously. The answering machine kicked in and he heard Lenny Munro's tight, angry voice.

'Patrick? What the fuck are you doing, you piece of shit? You fucking second-guess me to Pete, then go poking around my investigation like I don't know what the fuck I'm doing? You go anywhere near that investigation again and this time I'll see your ass kicked clean out of the board! Asshole!' And he slammed the phone down so hard that Tom winced a whole continent away.

His only emotion was relief that he hadn't picked up. He still felt queasy from the so-called espresso and had no stomach for trading insults.

He ran his eyes down the docket again.

The new fan disc had been supplied by Avia Freight and installed by CalSuperior. Nothing unusual about that. It was common for big companies like Avia to keep a stock of parts, and for smaller companies, like CalSuperior, to buy from them. CalSuperior had bought the plane itself from Avia: it was only logical they'd go back to them for parts.

The fan disc had spun through nearly five thousand cycles since then. Around seven start-ups a day for two years, with time off for maintenance. Not enough to fatigue, not enough to shift out of alignment, not enough to get scored in any way, shape or form. Not nearly enough.

Tom was frustrated by the paucity of information on the docket. If the fan disc had been the original, it would have run to six pages. As it was, all he had was the installation date, the disc serial number – B501-7776512 – the initials and signature of the mechanic who had performed the task, and three subsequent maintenance checks, each one unremarkable, adding more to his well of knowledge about dirty fingerprints than about the possible causes of the failure of the number-two engine.

The original manufacturers' paperwork wasn't even attached, although it might have been in the box he hadn't finished searching. At least he had the serial number. If Lowell Dexter hadn't been a prick, he could have checked that on their computer records.

It was frustrating to have to rely on ephemera like paper and digital records when what he really wanted was to hold the fan disc in his hands and run his thumbs and eyes over its surface, checking for imperfections.

He frowned. The *Pride of Maine* wreckage was long gone.

But there was still the South African jet.

The phone rang and he looked at the ceiling while he waited to hear if Lenny had anything else to say.

'Hi, Tom. Want to play some cards?'

*

Tom had lost sixteen thousand dollars when Ness put her hand on his neck. He felt himself flush with embarrassment. He was being pulled out of the game, stuck on the bench.

He'd played a stinker.

Outside she hitched one perfect shoulder and half smiled. 'That's just the way it goes sometimes.'

She was wrong and they both knew it. He'd been beaten by

his own arrogance. Any pocket pair in Hold 'Em was a big deal; kings were even better. But he'd hung in there too long with too much pouring into the pot, not wanting to believe the low straight that was unfolding on the table. His ego refused to let him throw in pocket kings: he wanted to beat someone with them, to be called and flip them over and see the looks on the faces of the other players.

Tom felt the sun warming his shoulders after the cool air of the club, and shivered.

'You want to get a drink or something?'

He grimaced. 'A pity drink? No, thanks.'

She smiled. 'You have your pride,' she teased, and the Lotus beeped and flashed as she unlocked it.

He held the door open and watched her slide in and drive away.

'Yeah,' he said, under his breath, 'for whatever that's worth.'

15

'YOU KNOW THIS GUY?'

Halo peered at the signature on the white tag Tom had stolen from CalSuperior, while Tom leaned against his Mustang in the LAX lot. He noticed the side-view mirror glass had been replaced.

'Sure. Niño Alvarez.'

'He here?'

'Nope. Three days off now. Back Friday. Why?'

'He replaced the fan disc on the *Pride of Maine*.'

'You think there was something wrong with the job?'

'Maybe. I don't know. The job or the part. Maybe. That's why I want to talk to him.'

Halo nodded but looked away. Tom could almost see the cogs whirring.

'You know where he lives?'

'You want me to show you?'

He had known Halo would offer.

Strangely for a Latino in LA, Niño Alvarez lived in Koreatown, with its ugly stone-coloured buildings covered with boxy, garish signs in a strange language. Tom realized why when the door of the apartment was opened by a

Korean woman looking harassed and hot, with her sleeves rolled up and a paste brush in her hand.

'Oh, hi, Halo.' She looked perplexed now as well as harassed, and shot a wary glance at Tom.

'Hi, Sylvia. Decorating?'

'Wallpapering.'

'Need a hand?'

Surprise pushed the other expressions off her face, then she smiled. 'You can paper?'

'I bet I could . . .'

She laughed then, and Tom was amazed to see her relax visibly as she pushed a strand of hair away from her eyes with a wrist. It was like magic. How the hell had Halo done that?

'You want Niño?'

'He in?'

'He'll be here in five minutes. He went to get batteries for the remote.' She rolled her eyes and this time Halo laughed. Tom felt like they were speaking a different language – one with which he had only a passing acquaintance.

'Coffee?' she offered, and they both nodded.

She went into the kitchen and Halo and Tom appraised the half-papered wall. Tom had rarely seen uglier wallpaper – big black chrysanthemums on a gold background. He was no real judge, but it made him flinch.

'You're doing a good job here,' Halo called.

'You like it?' she called back.

'Yeah. Goes with the couch.'

Tom glanced at the couch and found it did. Unfortunately.

'That's what I said! Niño's like, where? How? Why?' Again she laughed, then walked through with two coffees.

'Oh, Sylvia, I didn't introduce Tom. Sorry.'

She shook his hand and Tom could feel warm dampness where she'd washed it and hadn't dried it thoroughly.

'Tom's with the NTSB. He's been helping out with the *Pride of Maine* investigation.'

Halo had been a lot more subtle than Tom would have been: he'd have flashed his badge right at the door, before any of this. Even so, her face tightened. One day, he mused, he was going to introduce himself as a member of the International Paedophilia League and see if that look could get any colder.

'Nothing to worry about, Sylvia. Tom just thought Niño might be able to help too.'

'Oh.' She relaxed a little, even though Halo's words changed nothing.

Damn, he was good. Tom thought he should hire Halo to shove his hand up his ass and work him like a glove puppet every time he needed to interact with real people. The idea made him smile a little and Sylvia misinterpreted it as reassurance. She smiled back.

Behind them, the door opened and Niño Alvarez walked in. He stopped and raised his eyebrows briefly at Halo. 'Halo. Whassup?'

'Hey, Niño. Nothing. We—'

'He's with the NTSB.' Sylvia cut right to the chase, searching her husband's face for clues.

Niño shrugged, as if it made no difference to him, but he also immediately turned his back on them, dropping a pack of double-As and some change on the hall table.

Then he yanked open the door and ran.

'Shit!' Tom took off after him, vaguely hearing Sylvia shout behind him.

141

Niño was thick-set but fast, and knew where he was going. They both banged through the door to the stairwell and started down, their heavy, reckless footfalls echoing around them to join the sound of blood pumping in Tom's ears.

He heard the stairwell door bang again above him and hoped it was Halo.

He was gaining on Niño. He had a great rhythm going where he actually jumped down half of each flight, holding the rail for support, then slingshot round each corner to the next flight of concrete steps. He could hear that Niño was taking each step – albeit fast. He'd catch him before the first floor. He could do it. They were almost there.

Niño's fist connected with his cheek as he spun round the final corner. The blow itself wasn't much, but Tom's own speed upped the force of it considerably, making it enough to throw him off balance and send him crashing down the last flight, hitting the edge of every step on the way down. He smacked into the wall at the bottom and groaned loudly, dimly aware of Niño's feet in Timberland boots scraping past him and out of the door. He rolled and made a desperate grab for one of them but missed and Niño ran over his thumb for good measure.

'Jesus!' Halo hurried down the last flight and bent over Tom, touching his shoulder. 'What happened?'

'I fell down the stairs, you fucking idiot!'

'Well, excuse me for giving a shit.'

Tom rolled slowly to his knees and let out a sharp 'Ow!' as pain shot through his back and knees.

'Does it hurt?'

'No – I just thought I'd say, "Ow."'

'You're hard to help, you know that?'

'Shut up or fuck off.'

Halo shut up. But he didn't help Tom to his feet. That took Tom several wincing attempts to do all by himself.

*

'I guess we surprised him.' Halo stirred sugar into his coffee.

Tom pursed his lips irritably. 'You think?'

'You dropped your coffee on the couch. Sylvia's mad as hell.'

Tom shrugged.

'Niño's a good guy.'

'With a good left hook.'

Halo sighed and gave up.

There was no part of Tom's body that wasn't painful. He could feel welts striping his back from the stair edges, and wished they'd taken a booth where the seats were deeply padded, instead of these crappy metal chairs.

'I only wanted to know about the paperwork.'

'Maybe he thought it was about something else.'

'Like all the other bogus parts he may have installed, you mean? That's reassuring.'

'Should I tell Vee?'

'Tell her what?'

'How the investigation's going.'

'Shit, Halo!' Tom was angry with him on so many levels he could barely articulate. 'What the hell have you told her?'

'Just that you're trying to narrow down—'

'Well, don't! I don't want her thinking I'm gonna have answers for her soon – or ever! And don't call it an investigation!'

'But I—'

'It's not official. I don't have access. In fact, I probably have less access than you do, now that Lenny Munro knows I'm poking around. And that's what I'm doing – poking around with a stick in the dark. A small stick. A big dark. So don't fucking tell her anything! Don't even go round there!'

Halo stared into his coffee. Tom was no connoisseur of body language but the embarrassed cast to Halo's shoulders spoke loudly even to him.

'Oh, shit. You're fucking her, aren't you?'

Halo's eyes flicked up at him warningly. 'Not fucking.'

'Oh, I'm sorry! Making love! You're making love to her, aren't you?'

Halo shrugged. Tom pushed his chair back from the table and winced at the pain in his back. He got up and threw a couple of bills on the table. 'Great. Just great.'

'What is?'

'Every bastard's having sex but me.'

*

He waited for Pete to call him to chew him out for hassling Niño Alvarez or to send him on a pipeline job, but no call came. Tom figured it meant Alvarez had something to hide.

Ness didn't call either. Big surprise there.

A week ago he'd had two jobs. Two shit, half-hearted, not-what-he-really-wanted jobs, but two jobs nonetheless. Now it seemed he could be out of both of them.

Fuck it. He still had his unofficial probe into the *Pride of Maine*. And a week of vacation time to take. He called Kitty and took it.

The phone rang as he was stuffing his trusty sweatpants into his flyaway. Once he'd taken all the NTSB crap out of it, he was surprised to find how much it held.

'Hi, Tom.'

'Ness?'

Shit. Now she calls.

'Want to come play with me?'

Had she meant it to sound the way it did? Probably not: her voice could make the back of a cereal packet sound sensual. He bit back the suggestive comeback and went for the mundane truth. 'I can't. I'm going away for a week.'

'Oh.'

The silence was brief – more a hesitation, really.

'Somewhere nice?'

'South Africa.'

'South Africa!'

'Yeah.'

'That's sudden.'

'Yeah.'

'Business or pleasure?'

'Business,' he replied truthfully, even though he wished he could've said 'pleasure' and made her think he was the kind of guy who'd pop across the world for a week on a whim.

There was silence at her end, then a muffled voice. Tom wondered if it was her boyfriend. Wondered what it took to keep a woman like Ness Franklin by your side and in your bed.

Then she was back with him, saying words he'd never expected to hear. 'You want company?'

16

THE ROAD TO OUDTSHOORN through the Karoo desert possessed a brutal, stark beauty for the first twenty-five minutes of the drive. After that it was just tedious. Tedious and dusty.

Between hazy mountainous horizons, the flat plains of pale brown dust were spotted uniformly with tufts of coarse, reed-like grass, and dusty pale brown Merino sheep that did not look up as the rented Honda kicked up a trail that hung behind it for miles in the still, baked-dry air.

The only radio channel they could find and keep, played what he imagined was South African country dance music, all squeezeboxes, plucking and reedy old men – 'Duelling Banjos' meets German oompah – punctuated by bursts of guttural Afrikaans.

After a particularly ugly interlude between songs, Tom glanced at Ness. 'Hardly the language of love, is it?'

She raised a single amused eyebrow, then turned her gaze back to the interminable flat strip of dirt ahead of them.

For the hundredth time since they'd met at LAX, Tom wondered what the hell she was doing with him. It was an almost indignant feeling – like he was her father. 'What the hell are you doing with him, girl?' That was how he sounded in his own head. Was she crazy? Was her boyfriend crazy? Of course, he wasn't going to ask her any of those questions. He didn't want to give her a chance to tell him the truth.

She'd shown up looking a million dollars, with a set of matching Louis Vuitton luggage that looked real to his untrained eye. Beside her in the check-in line, with his fly-away slung over his shoulder, he felt like some kind of Skid Row junkie. As they approached the counter she'd taken his ticket and passport from him and had walked ahead. She took the lead in checking them in while he skulked behind her and – lo and behold – found himself upgraded to first class on her beautiful coattails.

'That's good,' was her matter-of-fact reaction. 'It's a long flight.'

Evidently Ness was so beautiful and elegant that she more than compensated for his tatty presence.

They'd spent the night in a hotel on the waterfront at Cape Town. She'd paid for another room, even though he'd offered to sleep on the couch in his. When they were told they could have one room with twin beds, she still went ahead and paid for the second.

He tried hard to take it as good practice for the subjugation of his ego.

*

They'd driven through the most beautiful countryside Tom had ever seen – or could ever imagine seeing. He wasn't one for noticing that kind of crap, but it was breathtaking. Once she'd asked him to stop so she could take a photo of purple mountains looming over striped vineyards under an azure sky. She snapped away, then put the camera on the roof of the car and insisted that he join her in a second picture. As he stood awkwardly on the dusty shoulder, she slipped a slender arm around him, resting her hand easily on his hipbone. He could feel the press of her fingers through his jeans and still couldn't speak when she showed him the picture. Just nodded.

They'd stopped for gas on the outskirts of Somerset West – a single-pump shed where an ancient, weathered attendant had spoken slowly so Tom could almost understand his strange English, with its clipped vowels and odd, choked *r*s, as he gave him directions. Thank God, those directions consisted of staying on this one road for the forty-mile journey.

As the Honda bottomed out in yet another pothole, Tom wondered idly how bad a back road to Oudtshoorn could be. He glanced at his watch and pushed the Honda up to 65 m.p.h. This wasn't his car, and if Avis were dumb enough to rent out in a country where this kind of infrastructure existed, then he would take full advantage of it.

'What's your boyfriend's name?' he asked, without knowing why – or how he should respond to the possible answer.

'Why do you want to know?' She was staring out of the window at the flat Karoo, her voice expressionless.

'Just making conversation.' If she said she didn't want to talk about her boyfriend, then she was thinking about sleeping with *him*, he thought. Make it so, he chanted in his head. Make it so make it so make it so . . .

'Richard.'

Whatever. Richard was ten thousand miles away and Richard's girlfriend was here with him. More fool Richard. He still had a chance.

Tom glanced to his right and hit the brakes hard.

The car slewed sideways before he caught it, corrected, and came to a tight halt in a cloud of dust. Ness looked round at him and he grinned. He hadn't needed to brake so hard, but it was fun to do it, out here in the *bundu*, with nothing more than knee-high tufts and the occasional sheep to hit.

'What was that about?'

He nodded into the desert. 'Look.'

The ostrich strutted fifty feet from the road. Tom could see its beady black eyes, and the sun glinting off its jet feathers. It picked up its dinosaur feet jerkily, as if pulling them out of mud each time. It was hard to tell, but the bird might have been limping.

He noticed something hanging from its head. A string, maybe. He opened the door and got out, shielding his eyes from the sun, and the bird immediately spooked and ran, its neck stretched upwards, its feathers a bustling pom-pom, its feet hitting the ground so hard that Tom could hear them from where he was standing. It scattered a half-dozen Merinos, which bolted all of ten yards, then went back to yanking at the grass while the ostrich kept going, leaving dust in its wake.

Tom grinned back into the car at Ness. 'Cool, huh?'

'Cool,' she agreed, but something in her tone made him feel stupid for stopping.

Within half an hour that feeling was compounded as they started to pass farms where ostriches were as numerous as cattle. Maybe she'd known.

'They race them, you know,' he said, trying to claw back an advantage.

'Race ostriches?'

'Sure. With kids as jockeys.'

'Are you teasing me?'

Tom looked at her and saw the smile hovering tentatively at the corners of her mouth. She was unbearably beautiful and, for the first time, he saw vulnerability in her uncertainty, and was surprised by a jolt of affection divorced from lust. He shook it off almost physically but it had knocked any kind of snappy answer clear out of him.

'No,' he said simply. 'I'm not teasing.'

*

Pam Mashamaete in the flesh was even better than she was on the phone.

The moment Tom shut the car door, a big woman in her thirties emerged from the shade of a ramshackle half-barn, let out a high cry of pleasure and broke into a grin he could've seen from space. She jogged to him like he was the Prodigal Son, testing her cream pantsuit to the outer limits, then ignored his outstretched hand and enveloped him in a bear-hug of epic proportions.

'Tom! You're here! I'm Pam!'

She released him so he could breathe again and he grinned, despite his embarrassment. 'Well, that's a relief.'

She shouted with laughter, her gleaming teeth framed by lips painted fire-engine red.

He turned to see Ness sporting a friendly smile. She gave him an expectant look and he realized she was waiting for him to introduce them. How did that go again? He jerked a thumb over his shoulder. 'This is Ness.'

Pam laughed another greeting and shook Ness's hand, then took his arm. 'Come meet the team.'

Tom was used to the three-ring circus that was 'the team' around any big air crash in the US. NTSB would have a team of fifteen to twenty investigators and support staff and then there were assorted airline officials, aircraft manufacturer's investigators keen to deflect blame from their plane, union representatives from ALPA keen to deflect blame from their pilots, media hounds keen to deflect blame somewhere new every day to make for fresh headlines, and grieving relatives, who didn't care who was to blame, but wanted them blamed fast.

Therefore Tom was astonished to see that Pam's team consisted of four youngish men dressed smart-casual in khakis and shirts, all wearing their badges – appropriately clothed, even all the way out here, Tom noted. Each of them also had a brightly coloured fly-swatter hooked into his belt, hanging down his thigh like a six-shooter.

Tom thought seriously about emigrating to join the SACAA. Being stuck with a skeleton crew and a wrecked 737 out in the middle of a desert was his idea of Paradise.

Paul Baputo, Clint Lenyani, September Sikeli and Rian Botha shook hands and smiled, and Rian handed them both ice-cold Cokes.

Tom had never felt so welcome anywhere. He hoped it wasn't because they were expecting him to be of any help whatsoever.

The hum of a generator was the only sound for miles, and he noted that its sole purpose seemed to be to keep a large ice-chest running for the sodas. He liked Pam more and more.

The seven of them walked to the barn, which was merely a vast roof on steel supports. No walls. So, as they approached, Tom could see the outline of the 737 emerging from the deep shade, the nose cone and tail fin pretty much intact, the rest just bumpy lumps of metal and grey-green upholstery, like the tufty Karoo between the mountains.

His throat actually tightened at the sight.

Ten thousand miles he'd travelled across the world to a foreign and exotic continent, yet this was a homecoming of sorts, and it felt like for ever since he'd been here.

*

Tom stood at what would have been the leading edge of the port wing of Flight SA77. Flies hummed somewhere, not near him, but in the desert stillness he could hear one twenty or thirty yards away. Still, he idly flicked the yellow plastic swatter in front of his face in a pre-emptive strike, and took another gulp of Coke.

A cold soda and a thirty-nine-cent fly-swatter. He knew his fly-swatter cost thirty-nine cents because the price tag was still on it. They'd bought it specially for him, and even put a little spring-loaded hook on the end so he could fix it to his belt loops. Paul had given his fly-swatter to Ness with an insistent smile.

Tom had spent two hours wandering about in the wreckage with Pam and the team. They had been thorough: pieces smaller than a quarter had been recovered and carefully positioned. The 737 and the fly-swatter smacked of the same attention to detail without pressure of time – an unusual situation for an air-crash investigator to be in.

'We don't get that many,' said Pam, when he mentioned it. 'We don't have the volume of traffic you do, and we have pretty stringent safety laws for our own jets and for those entering our airspace.'

'How many teams have you led?'

'This is my third.'

Tom's eyebrows shot up. Pam was obviously a natural. He didn't say so, but she smiled at his expression, confident enough in her own ability to know he wasn't being critical.

'You must be good.' They turned to look at Ness. She must've read his mind, thought Tom.

'Well, we try,' said Pam, modestly. She laughed generously and added, 'Hard!'

Tom was surprised that Ness had stuck with them this long. She hadn't said much, for which he was grateful. There was nothing worse than someone babbling on about something they knew nothing about. She'd stayed at the tail of the group, lazily flicking Paul's red fly-swatter around her, listening with apparent interest every time they stopped to discuss something. The only time she'd spoken before now was to offer to get fresh Cokes. She'd come back with a can for each of them, even remembering that September preferred a weird green cream soda, although he'd been too polite to ask for it specifically. It gave Tom a little twitch of proprietorial pride. He was glad he'd brought her along, even if she hadn't slept with him.

They passed a hand-painted sign in three languages. In English it read PLEASE DO NOT REMOVE ANY PARTS. Tom smiled, as did Ness. He caught Pam's eye. 'Isn't that like having an honesty box at Fort Knox?' he asked.

'It works,' she said. 'People understand what we're trying to do.'

As they walked, Tom said little. The few questions he had were brief, and were answered just as succinctly. If they didn't know something, Pam said so.

To Tom, the walk around the wreckage was two hours of foreplay. He knew where he wanted to end up, but he had to go through the motions to get there – had to make a show of objectivity, of open-mindedness. Investigators were trained to work crashes from the outside in, but all the time he stepped slowly and gently around the wreckage, he had only one destination in mind: one target that sucked at him like a black hole.

Finally they reached the number-two engine.

The number one was one of the more complete pieces of wreckage, stuck in the sand like a beached whale. But number two looked as if it had gone through a shredder. What was left of its smooth, round bulk was now splayed into a dozen jagged aluminium fingers.

The fan disc was laid out flat in the dust, like a giant's ring, twisted and broken open. A half-dozen fan blades were still whole and attached via their machined dovetails; others had snapped or torn free.

'Can we turn it over?'

September and Paul helped him, and Rian bent over it with a brush to clear the fine desert sand off the now-exposed face that had once bolted on to the matching flange on the shaft.

'See here?'

He walked round to see what Pam was pointing at with her swatter. He got down low, finally dropping on to his stomach to get the best angle. He patted his ass and slid a credit-card flashlight out of his pocket. In the shade afforded by the barn roof, it made a big difference.

The fan disc had been split open by the forces exerted by the blades tearing free, leaving the metal twisted and jagged.

The face of the flange was smooth almost all the way round. Then it wasn't. Here, in this one place, were the two shallow score marks, maybe half an inch long, that he'd seen in the emailed photos. They were almost parallel but connected at one point, running with the grain of the alloy. 'Witness marks', they called them. Imperfections that told a story. The story they told was still secret, and might never be known, but they teased him like a cinema preview of forthcoming attractions.

He shifted the flashlight and – just for an instant – saw something else. He played the sharp white beam over a shallow angle across the metal and saw it again. He got even closer and ran his thumb across the metal in case his eyes were playing tricks.

He frowned and Pam saw it.

'What?'

'Got a graze here too. Under the scores.'

Pam was flat on her belly in a second, her shoulder nudging his. He watched her manicured thumb run gently across the metal surface. She looked over her shoulder at the rest of the team, who leaned forward in anticipation. 'Grazing,' she said to Tom. 'What made that?'

'I don't know,' he said. She opened her mouth, then saw his closed look, and left it.

Tom noticed that the holes for the ring of bolts that had once held the disc to the shaft were all empty. 'Find any flange bolts?' He knew the answer would be no. If they'd found them, they'd be here.

'Not yet,' said Pam. 'Small things like that . . .' She trailed off.

Tom switched his attention to the curled and spiked surface of the once-perfect fan disc. Everywhere there was evidence of where the blades had torn free of the metal disc – jagged edges, virgin shards of metal exposed suddenly to the air for the first time since manufacture.

He examined what was left of the assembly, waiting for something to come to him.

The Karoo faded around him as he let his mind drift idly, like a child in a hayfield, wandering and meandering, brushing his hands through the high grass of information around him, plucking at seed-heads, then letting them fall and scatter.

He could feel himself coming close and let the idea take him there, following, not chasing.

The fan blades that were still attached to the disc were clustered together right over the place where the graze and the score marks were.

He rolled on to his side in the dust, away from the disc, and propped himself on his elbow. A fly buzzed close to his ear. Rian leaned down and casually flicked it away with a swatter.

Nobody spoke to him or asked him anything, and the silence of the Karoo fell softly over them all, like a shady veil.

Tom's mind raced in short, tight circles. Scoring and grazing; scoring and grazing. It meant something but he couldn't think what. He tried to let go and get back to the hayfield of discovery, but his mind felt more like a combine harvester, churning about noisily. There was too much to process right now: he couldn't do it. Scoring and grazing were important. He just didn't know why.

He looked up into five hopeful faces, got to his feet and

brushed the desert from his jeans. He should've worn shorts – or chinos at least: jeans were like Bacofoil in this heat.

He owed them something. He felt it even as his more-cynical self scoffed and laughed: *What? For a thirty-nine-cent fly-swatter and a can of Coke you owe them a probable cause?*

He didn't want to build it up – didn't want to let them see how his instinct was screaming at him that this was it, this was the key.

He tried to keep his voice neutral: 'This is important. I think. I don't know how yet but I think the fan disc is the thing.'

'The graze?' Pam watched his face closely, as if it would give her as much information as she'd hear from his mouth.

'I don't know. I don't want to jump to any conclusions. And I don't know what conclusions I'd be jumping to any-way.' He opened his palms in a vague gesture of ignorance. 'Maybe I should sleep on it.'

Pam nodded, but none of them pressed him further, for which he was grateful. He had no idea why the graze was more important than the scoring. But he had confidence that his brain would go on working on the problem without him, and inform him when it had come to a decision.

'Any more Coke?'

'I'll get it,' said Clint, but Tom was already halfway there. He grabbed six Cokes and a cream soda and lowered the lid, revealing a mirage-like figure floating towards the barn on watery legs across the mirrored sand.

Tom let the lid of the chest drop with a dull thud and, without taking his eyes off the figure, hissed open one of the Cokes and took a long swallow. He was aware of the others joining him and following his gaze.

'It's a boy,' said Ness, as if announcing a birth.

It was a boy. A small, skinny boy with knobbly knees below bone-thin thighs that disappeared into over-large red soccer shorts.

Tom frowned. 'Where the hell's he come from?' He felt Paul shrug beside him.

'Kids out here. They walk a long way to school.'

They stood in the shade and watched the boy approach with an easy, loose-limbed gait, his round head rolling slightly backwards with each stride, his chin bobbing into the air in modest pride.

Finally he got close enough to smile a greeting, but he didn't. He walked right up to them, and now Tom could see that, despite his lanky appearance, the boy was small, his extreme thinness making him appear much taller. His skin was dark and smooth and perfect, his ears tucked close and neat against the sides of his head, his hair shorn to mere circles on his skull. His eyes were everything in his face and, even though he hadn't said hello yet, Tom felt the sad anxiety coming off the child in waves.

He raised a hand in a tired greeting. '*Sanibonani.*'

They all murmured their own versions of 'hello' and Pam held out a Coke to him. He almost stepped forward to take it, then saw September's drink, and his eyes darted quickly between Tom and Rian – the two white males, Tom noted. 'Can I have a cream soda, please, *baas*?' he asked quietly.

They all took a step backwards so Tom could get another cream soda from the chest.

'Thank you, *baas.*'

The boy didn't open the can, just touched its iciness to his cheek and then his slender neck, which disappeared into a

158

baggy blue-and-yellow-striped T-shirt. 'Have you seen my ostrich?'

There was silence after his question, then Rian said: 'What does it look like?'

Tom snorted laughter at the absurdity of the question, but nobody else did.

The boy had perfected his description. 'He's a big male. He has a ring on his left leg, and there is a lead on his head. His name is Lemon.'

This time they all laughed a little, and even the boy grinned – just a brief flash of white.

Suddenly Tom realized that this was the boy in the picture – the boy whose face he'd last seen in the relative comfort of his living room: the ostrich jockey with the memorable name.

'Harold?' The boy turned surprised eyes to him. 'Harold Robbins, right?'

This time the grin broadened and Harold beamed at him. He ducked his head shyly. 'Yes, *baas.*'

'I saw you on the Internet after the crash.'

'Yes, *baas.* I was in the newspaper. And on the TV at DuPlessis's shop.'

None of them knew what this meant, and Harold tried to explain further by pointing back in the direction he'd come. 'In De Rust.'

They nodded, still not sure, and Harold Robbins Mhleli took the initiative once more. 'Lemon's very scared. He's lost and I want him to come home.'

'I thought the ostrich farm was destroyed,' said Tom.

'No, just . . .' He twitched a shoulder, not finding the right words, and settled for: 'Not all destroyed. But I lost my job.

Some ostriches were killed and Lemon ran away. So, too many boys and not enough tourists or ostriches. If Lemon comes home, maybe I can get my job back.'

They nodded silently at the simplicity of the equation: that meant a twelve-year-old boy's livelihood depended on a giant bird.

'You been looking for him ever since the plane crashed?' said Pam.

'Yes, madam,' said Harold, and – for the first time – his eyes flickered past them to the twisted wreckage he'd last seen smoking in the ruins of his dreams.

September waved an arm back towards the unseen town over the horizon. 'Can't you get work in De Rust?'

Harold faltered. Tom could see his brain working fast and, for a moment, thought he was going to lie to them. But then he dropped his eyes, as if ashamed, and mumbled, 'But I want to ride again.'

Tom understood. Harold might get work in De Rust, might pick up litter or run errands or dig ditches, but he was clinging to the fading dream that he would find Lemon and be allowed to go back to the job he loved. The parallel with his own situation made Tom's eyes burn. He turned away under the guise of finishing his Coke and tossing it into the bin.

'We saw an ostrich on the way here,' said Ness. 'Didn't we, Tom?'

He turned back and nodded.

'That was a big male,' she continued. 'Well, it was male anyway. I don't know how big they get.'

Harold's eyes were warily hopeful in a way that Tom recognized meant he'd been disappointed before. Carefully he added, 'He did have something hanging off his head. Like a bit of string . . .'

'Yes!'

'I couldn't see that well, but I noticed it as he turned. Very thin.'

'Yes!' said the boy again. He held out his left arm and quickly ran his right forefinger from his shoulder to his wrist. 'Two times this long?'

'About that. And he was limping, I think.'

'Limping?'

Clint demonstrated and Harold understood. 'Maybe he's hurt.' Then he looked at Tom again. 'Where is this?'

Tom pointed back towards Oudtshoorn. 'About ten miles that way.'

Harold followed his finger with his eyes and nodded determinedly. 'Thank you, *baas*.'

He immediately started walking away from them, as if Tom had pointed out a bus stop a hundred yards up the road.

'Hey!'

Harold glanced back, impatient.

Paul laughed. 'He could be anywhere by now!'

Harold shrugged and kept going, holding the cold cream soda against the back of his neck.

Ness shook her head. 'Unbelievable.'

They leaned against the ice chest and watched Harold Robbins Mhleli become a watery-legged mirage once more.

*

Pam had the paperwork for the fan disc to hand. Ever since

they'd found the scoring, she'd kept it in the nearest thing she had to a filing system: the glove box of her battered government-issue 4×4, along with 'Serviceable' tags on a missing rudder servo and on a flap track they'd found that looked as if it might have been hit by something. They were the Holy Trinity of her investigation: any one of them could be the probable cause of the downing of Flight SA77. Or none of them, of course – she was no fool.

But the fan-disc paperwork had just moved right to the top of her mental list of suspects . . .

She laid out the paperwork on top of the ice chest. Having obtained it by fair means, not foul, she had the full story of the SA77 fan disc at her fingertips, including the crucial FAA Form 8130-3, the 'birth certificate', which reassured them that it was an approved part manufactured to the highest standards and tested under the most stringent conditions at the WAE plant in Irving, Texas. Beside it, she smoothed out the CalSuperior 'Serviceable' tag for the *Pride of Maine*, and six heads bumped as Tom and the South Africans ran their eyes over them, searching for something that would connect the two parts.

'They're both replacement parts from WAE,' said Rian.

'So's every 737 fan disc replaced on the North American continent, and this jet was bought from there,' said Tom. Suddenly he put two dusty fingers on the two dockets. 'Same batch.'

'What's that mean?' asked Ness.

'See here? The SA77 fan disc has a batch number on the release certificate: WAE 8989-B501. And the serial number of the *Pride of Maine* fan disc is B501-7776512. The serial number starts with the batch number.'

'Is that good?'

He nodded slowly. 'It might be. It's something. I mean, it's a link at least. If we find something wrong with this fan-disc assembly, it's probably enough to justify getting WAE to check all the others from the same batch, but without the disc from the LA plane it's tenuous.' He sighed deeply, suddenly weary beyond belief. 'Goddamn Lenny Munro to hell! If we still had the other disc he could compare it to this one and be sure that the faults were the same.'

'Where is it?'

'Gone – recycled into dog-food cans. Fuck!'

He stepped away from the others and back to the fan disc, his mind overloaded with information and swirling anger.

He felt Ness come up behind him and touch his arm. He didn't turn, but she ran her hand soothingly across his shoulder-blades, where his shirt stuck to his back in a line of perspiration. She put her Coke can down beside the fan disc and took his hands in both of hers. 'Come on,' she said. 'You need to sleep.'

*

Pam and her team were booked into a rickety guesthouse half an hour away in De Rust and suggested Tom and Ness join them.

The dust kicked up by the 4×4 ahead of them made the ride unpleasant, even after Tom dropped a quarter of a mile behind. The particles hung seemingly for ever in the still evening air, and were efficiently scooped up by the Honda's vents to circulate up their noses.

De Rust was a one-horse town where the horse had died:

a single main street, with a hardware store, a liquor store and a scattering of tin-roofed houses with broken-down corrals between them. Desultory livestock – goats, sheep, donkeys – stood, heads drooping, in the dust, pelvic bones on sharp display.

The guesthouse didn't have a name, but it had a small, clumsily made Voortrekker wagon on a plinth beside the front door; Tom idly wondered how the apparently Afrikaner owners felt about having four black guests demanding breakfast and messing up their sheets less than a generation since their own separateness and superiority had seemed enshrined in law.

He quickly realized that the owner, Lettie Marais, didn't give a shit, as long as they kept her in cigarettes. Tiny, wiry, brown and terminally creased after seventy years without sunscreen – but with the constant companion of the cigarette smoke that curled around her head like a pale blue permanent wave – Lettie was an equal-opportunities scowler.

Between photos of white-haired grandchildren and whip-thin mongrels, the mantel in the breakfast room held a cigarette on a pair of chopstick holders. Lettie had written on it 'The One I Didn't Smoke' in a proud but empty boast. By the look and smell of her, Tom figured it was the *only* one she'd ever declined to light up.

Pam and her team said good night almost as soon as they got through the door, Pam giving Tom a quick hug at the foot of the stairs before she turned away. It was a confidence-giving hug. Even though Tom hadn't had one since his mother had died when he was fourteen, he recognized it immediately.

Lettie said, 'Good night,' to the team in a puff of smoke,

then squinted at Tom, picking stray flecks of tobacco off her tongue with yellow fingers. 'What kind of room? Single or double or twin?'

Tom suppressed his own desires and looked at Ness for guidance.

'Two singles?' she suggested.

Shit.

'Haven't got two singles.'

Tom warmed fractionally to Lettie.

Ness hesitated and Tom was gripped by the fear that she'd ask him to try another guesthouse. Then she said, 'Twin should be fine.'

'Haven't got a twin.'

This was getting better and better, thought Tom, his stony face hiding his growing enjoyment.

'What have you got?'

'One double.'

Ness shared with him a brief exasperated look that begged, 'Then why bother asking?'

Tom sighed. He hated to be a gentleman. 'You take it. I'll find somewhere else.'

Lettie snorted eloquently. 'There is nowhere else. This is it!' Then she eyed them both more carefully. 'You not having sex, then?'

Tom saw Ness blush.

Lettie lit a fresh cigarette from her old one. 'You should. Life is short. Wish I'd had more.'

Ness started to giggle, then sighed. 'Okay. Whatever.'

Hardly a landslide vote in favour, but it was better than nothing, thought Tom, as he picked up their luggage and followed Lettie's baggy butt up the stairs.

Just because they had to share a bed, he wasn't assuming anything. He showered standing in a rust-stained bath, then pulled on fresh boxers and a T-shirt. He took a towel with him, drying his hair as he entered the small, dingy bedroom with its dusty picture frames and the faded home-made quilt on the lumpy-looking bed.

Ness was already changed into plaid shorts and a white tank top. It was not a classically erotic combination, but somehow she looked just perfect.

Distracted by the way her nipples showed through the thin cotton top in the half-light of the bedside lamp, it took Tom a second to realize she was holding her phone.

'Calling Richard?'

She ignored the little edge to his question and smiled. 'No, I was just turning it off.' She put it on her woodworm-ridden nightstand, then gracefully threw herself across the bed on her back so she could reach his phone, which he'd left on the non-matching nightstand on his side. She turned that off too and he looked at her questioningly.

She shrugged almost shyly, and for a second time, Tom was moved to arousal by her sudden vulnerability. He turned to hide it from her and slid quickly into the bed, rolling on to his side to face away from her. He felt the mattress move as she slid beneath the covers beside him.

He felt her warmth seeping across the cool sheets towards him, and had to battle a compulsion to turn and take her there and then, rolling on to her, pressing her into the mattress, pushing her legs apart ... He squeezed his eyes shut and breathed. He thought about the plane. The wreckage. The fan disc. Think about the fan disc.

He focused and found it depressingly easy ...

Scoring *and* grazing.

Where each of the blades had ripped loose, the edge of the disc was torn and jagged – sudden failure written all over it. But there, over the site of the graze – in that one place alone – the disc must have shifted ever so slightly before it tore free. The fretting showed there had been movement between the flanges of the disc and the shaft. Small movement, but not sudden, one-time movement. Rather a sliding, rubbing motion.

Tom felt his body begin to relax as his mind picked up the slack. His breathing was easier now, the pressure in his groin lessening. Just as he had replayed that muddy English steeplechase in which Rum Shooter always just failed to catch the winner, a clear view of the spinning fan disc now filled his head. Somehow moving off-centre despite the ring of bolts gripping it to the shaft. Somehow shifting, taking the fan blades with it. And one of those fan blades digging into the abradable lining of the engine casing – digging in just enough to touch metal. A chaste metal kiss just a hair's breadth deep. And, a nanosecond later, another. Slightly deeper but still not enough to notice without mathematical instrumentation.

And what was causing this sudden imbalance? The integrity of the disc itself? Or something else, which had made the disc shift? Something like an insecure fan blade? A faulty flange bolt?

He needed to see the fan disc again, with this moving picture now playing in his mind. He needed to look more closely at the point of attachment. They didn't have the flange bolts, but there should be clues in the X-rayed metal of the disc as to whether it or the bolts were at fault. He had to see it. He had to go back there. He had to touch it, feel the movement. He—

Ness's fingers slotted gently between his ribs. Fire spread from them across his chest, down his belly, while his mind continued to feed him the wrong pictures – pictures he'd tried so hard to see that now he couldn't look away . . .

Tom mentally braced his hands on the fan disc and felt it move minutely against the face of the shaft – maybe a couple of thou of play . . .

She sighed against his hot skin.

Play.

Not sudden and catastrophic tearing of metal, but a slow, repeated movement where the imbalance increased exponentially and inevitably . . .

Play.

Just enough to throw the whole assembly out of alignment, for the blade to hit the casing, for the engine to rip apart . . .

Play.

A funny little word for what had caused 124 people to die screaming in the wreckage of a stricken Boeing 737.

He was out of bed before he could think, pulling on his jeans in a frenzy.

'Tom?' She sat up and he turned on the lamp to see her looking hurt and a little startled.

'I'm sorry,' he said. 'I have to go back there.'

'Now?' Her voice was tense with disbelief.

'I'm sorry,' he offered again, uselessly. His fingers were awkward and he flinched as he realized she was watching him trying to button his jeans over his erection. 'Shit.' He left it for a moment, pulling on his shirt and shoes instead. He knew he looked like an idiot. But he also knew that this thing would burn in his mind until he saw it. Saw the evidence he was certain was there. Felt the probable cause under his fingers.

He had to go.

'I'll come with you.' She flung back the sheets and swung her legs off the bed.

Tom hesitated. Was she nuts?

Then he picked up the car keys and managed – finally – to button his pants.

*

The flurry of the bedroom gave way to the far more difficult silence of the car as he swung away from De Rust.

Tom glanced at Ness in the pale green glow of the dials and couldn't read her expression as she stared at the tunnel of illuminated brown dust that raced towards them out of blackness, became darkroom red behind them under the tail-lights, then died away into blackness once more.

The further they got from De Rust, the more uncomfortable Tom felt.

His desperation to see the fan disc again was still there – the need to know whether the play had been caused by one bad bolt or a weakness in the integrity of the entire disc – but the thought of advancing a mere hunch as an excuse for choosing work over her was pathetic. He couldn't insult her by attempting to give it validation, so he said nothing, instead feeling the silence smoulder between them. He couldn't look at her face, but her hands were clenched on her thighs, and he wished he could reach out and take one – the way he would if this were a movie and he were a hero, instead of a fucking asshole.

Sudden headlights lit them up and lasered at him off the rear-view mirror.

'Tom!'

Her shout and the sudden blindness hit him together. A bang of metal on metal, and he wrenched the wheel violently to the left to avoid worse. He felt the Honda slide and grip and slide again, then came the spin and the thuds and bumps of hitting the surprisingly solid desert tufts, as sand spewed over the windshield like a dry brown wave.

They came to rest facing the direction in which they'd been travelling and, as the clearing dust brought the night back into focus, he could see the tail-lights of the other car speeding away.

'Jesus! Where the hell did he come from?' He looked at Ness, who was panting, her hands braced on the dash. 'You okay?'

She turned frightened eyes towards him, but nodded slowly.

The car had stalled. Tom turned the key but the engine choked apologetically. In the vast and sudden silence he could hear it ticking like a quiet little bomb.

He tried again. 'Shit. Come *on.*'

She touched his hand. 'Give it a minute.'

Tom sighed and turned off the headlights to conserve the battery, for what that was worth, and they were plunged into blackness.

He looked at his watch: twelve forty-three. Pam and the team wouldn't be out until six or seven at the earliest.

170

Tom checked his phone. Shaking it didn't help it find a signal. 'You got your phone?'

Ness gave a wry half-smile.

This was just great – worth halting sure-fire sex with the hottest woman he'd ever known. He wished feverishly that she'd stayed at the guesthouse and not been witness to this latest display of incompetence.

He got out and went round to the front of the car, shivering in the cold desert night.

The stars here were extraordinary; they seemed so close and bright, and were thickly spread in places as if someone had spilled a packet of star seeds and they'd grown haphazardly where they fell. Clustered in places and bare in others. A patch immediately overhead was naked indigo with only a single lonely point in the middle of it, light years away. Tom wished he were there.

Ness was beside him, following his gaze to the same star. He could feel her shoulder nudge his companionably as she leaned against the car. Her throat was slender, white and vulnerable where it stretched upwards under the starlight.

'The carburettor's probably just flooded,' she said softly.

Her voice made even such mundanity sound sexy. He gave her a cheeky grin. 'Are you coming on to me?'

There was a moment of silence and then she started to laugh.

He turned, trapping her body between his and the car.

He could see her teeth as she giggled, and was aware of her warmth heating his chest, hips and thighs. He felt himself grow hard against her and suddenly her teeth were hidden from him, and he could feel her ragged breath on his throat.

'Yes,' she said, pressing her hips into his, 'I'm coming on to you.'

Ancient stars bore witness as they explored hungrily, using hands and lips as substitutes for eyes and words in the darkness. He felt Ness moan low into his mouth, and pressed her down to the still-ticking heart of the Honda. For the second time in thirty minutes his out-of-practice hands fumbled with his button-fly – and suddenly they were illuminated in the lights of an oncoming car heading towards De Rust.

Tom straightened and Ness propped herself on her elbows and quickly pulled her dress down over her thighs.

The car passed them, leaving them in the blackness again, breathing in its dust.

The moment was gone.

In the ensuing silence, Ness levered herself off the hood and smoothed her clothes. She didn't look at him as she slid back into the passenger seat.

With a groan he couldn't suppress, he realized he'd never even got his jeans undone.

*

This time when Tom turned the key, the car coughed into a semblance of life and – after a brief, heart-sinking wheel spin – he swung it back on to the road towards the wreckage.

They didn't speak. Tom didn't know what to say and her face gave nothing away – she was as calm and unruffled now as she had been when they were standing at check-in at LAX.

He'd like to track down the inventor of the button-fly and make him suffer . . .

The barn's skeletal silhouette loomed out of the darkness

unexpectedly soon. Tom parked the Honda so it lit their way to the barn and he and Ness walked the short distance in silence. His flashlight was still in his pocket, he was relieved to find, as they reached the remains of the engine housing on the port wing.

But the fan disc was no longer on the ground.

Tom frowned and swept the dust with the thin beam.

'Where is it?' said Ness.

'We left it here, right?'

She nodded, confused. 'Sure. You and Paul turned it over and laid it flat right here, see?' With her toe she pointed at the faint, broken ring the fan disc had pressed into the dust.

Tom illuminated the mark. A footprint bisected it. He checked his own, and then Ness's. Neither was a match. 'Someone's taken it.'

'Taken it?'

Tom squatted to touch the footprint. 'This print was made after the fan disc was lifted up.' He was aware that his voice was calm, and realized it was because he was numb with disappointment. He stood up and waved the flashlight beam pointlessly at the road. 'The other car. They must've been on their way here. No wonder the bastards didn't stop to help.'

'But why would anyone take it?'

'It was the only evidence that there might be something wrong with the disc. The only proof. I should never have left it out here. Fuck!' He kicked impotently at the dirt.

'It's not your investigation, Tom. It wasn't your call.'

He waved her logic aside. He was a jerk. Possibly the only material evidence to two fatal crashes, and he had left it out here in the middle of a desert without security. Without even a door. With a polite little sign asking passers-by

173

not to steal souvenirs. He needed his ass kicked, and hard.

Like missing paperwork, stolen wreckage told its own story, and the only pinprick of light in the tunnel of his stupidity was that the theft of the fan disc proved he was on the right track.

It was a small and feeble pinprick.

Tom stared sightlessly into the dust between his feet, the tiny grains thrown into relief by the narrow beam of his torch, which moved gently with his breathing.

He felt Ness's hand on the back of his neck and almost laughed at the bitter irony. Out of the game and back on the bench for you, Patrick.

'Maybe we can catch them.' The thought jumped into his head, and before the words were out of his mouth he was running back to the car, heedless of leaving Ness in the dark.

'Tom! Don't!'

He jumped in and started the engine, threw the car into gear and gunned it forward, sliding to a stop beside her. 'Get in.'

'But, Tom—'

'Get in or stay here!'

He saw the flash of anger in her eyes. He wondered if he'd meant it but, before he could decide, the door opened, then slammed and he hit the gas with a vengeance. 'They won't be expecting us to follow. They won't be going as fast.'

She was fiddling with the heater.

'Cold?' he asked, trying for reconciliation.

'No,' she said. 'I'm fine.' But she continued to adjust dials and buttons and slides, and he knew it was so that she wouldn't have to look at or talk to him.

Fuck it.

The Honda had recovered from its bronchial moment and was roaring along. Tom started enjoying the chase, even though the quarry was not in sight. Adrenalin surged through him. He glanced at Ness's fingers exploring the air-con. Those fingers had touched him, held him, pulled him urgently towards her. Whether or not they caught the other car, he wanted to get back to De Rust as quickly as possible. They were both strapped in, and it was just as well. He threw the car around like a toy, careless of consequences. They'd had their crash of the night, he figured, so now they were protected by the god of lightning, who wouldn't strike twice in the same place.

Once, a Merino loomed in the headlights and Tom detoured crazily across fifty yards of stone, sand and tufts at sixty m.p.h. It made him want to whoop, but he kept his mouth shut and his hands on the wheel.

'Lights,' Ness said, without inflection.

There was a faint red glow up ahead. In this black wilderness, they would be able to see even the tail-lights of a car from a long way off. They were gaining quickly.

They went into a shallow dip and lost the lights, but as the road rose on the other side, the glow was much bigger, and Tom realized it didn't come from car lights – it came from a fire.

There was a short drop into De Rust and they could see a building ablaze. Before his mind had even worked out the geography, Tom's gut told him it was the guesthouse.

17

IT SEEMED DE RUST had no fire department. But it had plenty of people who were apparently well qualified to stand on the wide sidewalk in their PJs and gape at a house burning down.

'Water!' Tom yelled, as he scrambled out of the car. 'Water!' His original intention – to rush into the blaze – was snuffed out instantly: the heat was a physical wall that bounced him back and kept him at bay with the rubber-neckers. The fire was a raging, living thing that roared and screamed and cracked wooden fire-knuckles in its blazing fury as it consumed the clapboard house. Tom could feel the air around him bulge and sway as the flames sucked greedily at the oxygen-rich sky; it was as if they might decide at any moment to escape the confines of the guesthouse and tear hungrily up the main street, leaving blackened homes and residents in their hungry wake. The little wooden wagon on the front porch was blazing like a prop in a John Wayne film.

'There are people in there!' he yelled. 'Where's the fire crew?'

An elderly man in a T-shirt and baggy Y-fronts held up his palms expressively. 'No firemen here, *baas*.'

'What about water?'

'No water here,' he replied sadly.

'Did anyone get out?'

The old man shrugged. 'No one, *baas*.'

'Fuck!'

Tom was vaguely aware of heads turning towards him disapprovingly. His language had offended, while the fire that was incinerating six people provoked only interest. 'Fuck you all!' He shouldered his way past them and ran round to the back of the house. 'Pam! Paul!' The names of the other members of the team died on his lips. He'd hoped to see a way in to them, or a way out for them, but the fire at the back burned even more fiercely. If they weren't out already, they weren't getting out now.

In the backyard a large brown dog barked hysterically as sparks floated down around it. It was straining at the end of a chain attached to a stake driven into the ground not twenty feet from the back porch, crazy with terror and pain as bits of debris caught and smoked in its shaggy coat.

Tom ran to the dog, intending to release the chain from its collar but it went for him, and he felt sharp teeth sink into his left hand. He yanked himself free and scooted away from the animal, which came after him in a frenzy of flashing teeth and self-defence, yelping in surprise as its tether yanked it backwards off its feet and it landed on its side, scrabbling for purchase.

Tom stood out of range, nursing his bloody hand, already thinking of the rabies shots he'd need, and wishing the dog dead, while knowing he'd have to try again.

A tall, skinny boy with a pudding-bowl haircut was suddenly beside him. The kid was maybe seventeen, with a prominent Adam's apple, flaming acne and a bicycle. He spoke quickly in Afrikaans, then read on Tom's confused face that English was called for. 'We'll go to the stake, *ja*? Behind this, *ja*?' He tapped the bicycle.

Without thinking it through, Tom followed the boy back towards the flames.

The dog came at them with renewed vigour, but every time it launched itself at them, the boy parried with the bicycle, knocking it back, sometimes clear off its feet. Tom thought, This is nuts. Why are we trying to release a fucking mad dog? But the plan was in action now – a plan that meant he could save *something*, even if it was only a dog – so he ducked his head away from the heat and kept close behind the boy as the dog hurled, snarled and yelped.

They reached the iron stake and Tom grabbed it. It was hot enough to make him howl and leave a layer of skin behind. In a fury of anger, pain and helplessness, he kicked at the stake with his heel while all the time he could hear the boy covering his back with the bicycle. The stake finally popped free of the sun-baked earth. The dog was skulking warily now, having taken a few good blows from the bike. It wasn't crazy then, thought Tom. It had the sense to back off when it was beaten.

Tom and the boy retreated slowly. A chunk of burning wood popped off the house and fell in a shower of sparks near to the dog, and it turned tail and ran, the chain and stake clanking along the asphalt behind it.

'Jesus.' Tom sank to the high kerb and the boy sat beside him, staring at his bicycle and coughing into his fist.

'Broke the . . . things,' he said mournfully.

Tom looked. 'The spokes,' he offered.

'*Ja*. Spokes.' He coughed again. 'Broke them.'

Tom felt the heat of the burning house on his back. It was making his hands swell. His lungs were stifled with heat and smoke. A disjointed air of unreality settled drunkenly upon him. Pam and Paul, September, Rian, Clint and Lettie Marais were all dead. And he and Ness would be dead too, if they hadn't driven back to the wreckage.

What would it be like to die in a fire like that? To feel the pain he felt now in his hands but a dozen times worse, all over his body, searing his throat . . . His elbows on his knees, his hands splayed in the cool night air, Tom hung his head between his legs and stared at the little bits of desert grit between the flat gravel of the blacktop as he coughed up what felt like a lung.

Suddenly he was on his feet, pushing through the little circle of onlookers who had gathered to stare at a real-life victim, however low on the scale.

Pam's truck was parked across the street. Tom's hands flared with pain as he opened the door. Surprise registered, and somewhere in his mind was the mental image of Pam locking the car after they'd parked. He couldn't be sure, but—

'Tom, what are you doing? Your hands . . .' Ness hovered beside him.

Tom waved her away, coughing, then gritted his teeth and pulled open the glove box. Inside was the paperwork on the suspect parts. Tom pulled the forms out carefully, every finger protesting now, and looked at them.

There were only two dockets: one for a rudder servo and the other for a flap track.

'Tom, what is it?'

'They've taken the paperwork on the fan disc.'

*

The boy with the bicycle was called Johannes Jonker, and his mother ran Tom's hands under the cold faucet and a guttural barrage of what sounded like severe chastisement for not getting there sooner. They were ballooning and blistered, and felt like he'd plunged them into the heart of the fire and not yet taken them out.

Ness sat quietly at the opposite side of the old oak kitchen table.

Mrs Jonker emptied the freezer of surprisingly heart-shaped ice cubes and made Tom dig his hands into a bowl of them. The relief was fleeting but welcome. The boy sneaked an ice cube and sucked it, his face red from proximity to the fire.

'I always said she'd die in a fire,' Mrs Jonker pronounced smugly. 'All that smoking. All that wood. It was bound to happen.'

'But it happened tonight.' Tom's voice was dull, and husky from the smoke.

'And that's a new bike too, *domkop*! *Nou is it verklapte!*'

The boy nodded morosely in acknowledgement of his own stupidity at braving a fire and a mad dog with only a bicycle for protection.

Mrs Jonker sighed at him and turned to Tom. 'Better?'

'Yes. Thanks.' His hands were no better, but Tom wanted the woman to stop fussing and talking. He wanted to think.

Ness was quiet. He liked that. Her face was streaked with smoke-black, and her hands and arms were dirty from where she'd helped the boy to get him here.

The boy seemed to understand. He took another ice

heart and ran it carefully over his own face, his eyes distant.

'Look at you in a *dwaal*!' his mother chided him, as though he'd done something to be ashamed of. 'I'll go get Dr Viljoen.' She bustled out noisily.

Quiet descended on the little kitchen with its wooden drainer and its 1960s lino, worn and torn in a half-dozen places.

A small black dog had fallen asleep on Tom's foot. Now its hind leg twitched and half scratched at its belly as it dreamed of fleas.

The window was open, but no air stirred through it. Instead, insects whirred out of the blackness and into the light, like homing spacecraft. Moths clattered against the bulb and hard, shiny brown beetles hummed and dropped on to the table on their backs, their barbed black legs waggling robotically. A long green mantis sat on the dirty shade and cocked its alien eyes at the free meals orbiting its head.

'You think it was deliberate?'

The boy – Johannes – didn't look up at Ness's question, but continued to run ice around his raw face. Tom figured he was in low-grade shock, so he discounted his presence. He nodded slowly at Ness. 'Yes. Maybe.' He winced. 'I don't know.' The ice was melting fast around his flaming hands. 'If not, it's a major coincidence.'

She nodded.

'And I don't believe in coincidences.'

She nodded again, but Tom couldn't tell whether it meant she didn't believe in them either or whether she was just humouring him.

'Someone runs us off the road. The fan disc's stolen. The fire. All in the space of a few hours.'

'If we hadn't . . .' She tailed off and her eyes overflowed with tears that left silver rivers down her cheeks under the harsh white light.

Tom reached for her unthinkingly, then hissed in pain when he touched her, and snatched his hand back. 'Ness . . .' He stopped. There was nothing he could say to make it better because it wasn't getting any better. Anything he said would be meaningless noise.

To his surprise, the boy got up and sat on the oak bench beside Ness, awkwardly putting a consoling arm about her shoulders, even as he slid ice across his brow and lips.

Tom nodded his thanks at him, then carefully put his hands back into the ice and sighed in relief.

Ness snuffled quietly into the boy's shoulder, then palmed her eyes hard and sat up straight again. The boy got up and left the room. The dog sensed him go, woke up and tottered after him.

'This ice is melted.'

'You should go to a hospital.'

'I just need some aspirin.'

'Please, Tom . . .'

He sighed and took his hands out of the bowl. Iced water dripped across the stripped oak table, making big ugly marks, then on to the cracked lino as Tom walked to the back door.

When he got there he had to look pleadingly at Ness. Slowly she stood and opened it for him, then followed him out into the night, which was lit up with orange on two fronts – one of the dying flames, the other the rising sun.

18

THE NEXT TWENTY-FOUR hours passed in a haze for Tom. Ness drove him to the tiny cottage hospital where he drifted in and out of a drug-induced sleep and where, every time he woke, the long white voile curtains seemed to be blowing softly in the breeze, even though the air never reached his heated skin.

His hands burned, and when doctors and nurses touched them, he swore at them, which shocked them into silence and left them thin-lipped with disgust. Even through the haze, Tom was beginning to realize that when it came to profanity rural South Africa did not have the same experience or tolerance of it as urban LA.

Sometimes Ness was there, sometimes she wasn't. Sometimes she read to him from the local paper: Sakkie Mulder's prize-winning bull, Justus, had written off a motorcycle and injured its rider on the road to Oudtshoorn; baboons had stolen new science equipment from De Aar primary school; a truck had overturned on the N1, killing three giraffes it had been transporting to a private reserve near Stellenbosch.

She read all the stories in a monotone, giving each one equal weight; only the lowering or arching of an eyebrow gave him any clue as to her opinion of each tale of woe. The nature of the news added to his feeling of unreality.

She held his phone to his ear while he told Pete LaBello that he'd been in a car crash while on holiday. He'd be late back. Pete didn't sound like he was missing him, had been missing him, or ever would miss him. He said something about Lenny Munro but Tom was too tired to take it in.

Then Pete added grimly, 'When you get back, come to DC. We need to talk.'

Tom agreed because it was the easiest thing to do. He had a rough idea of what Pete needed to talk about and he couldn't imagine it was going to work out well for him, so he shoved it to the back of his mind. He was good at denial. Air-crash investigation, being a dick, and denial. Those were his things.

And listening. Who'd told him that? He was good at listening too, apparently. Tom couldn't remember any supporting evidence for that one, but he was prepared to annex any possible good qualities anyone had ever attributed to him and add them to what was an admittedly paltry store.

He drifted in and out of drug-induced sleep but whenever he was conscious the twin subjects of the fan disc and Ness made him equally crazy with frustration – one mental, the other physical.

With his hands useless bandaged blobs, he figured he had more chance of resolving the mental itch, so tried hard to think more often of the fan disc: who had known about it? Where had they taken it? Had they identified its importance already or had they waited for him to do it for them? If he'd stayed in LA, would Pam, her team and blunt old Lettie Marais still be alive?

More often than not, though – especially when Ness

thought he was asleep and closed her eyes in the chair beside his bed – the fan disc receded and the thought of her drove him quietly insane.

They still hadn't spoken about the almost-sex, but she touched him sometimes and made longer eye-contact, often breaking it with a secret smile, so he guessed they were okay. He sure as hell wasn't going to ask and give her the opportunity to evaluate just what she might be getting herself into, just what he had to offer. What he was prepared to offer.

He looked at her now. It was around ten p.m. and the only ward in the little hospital was almost silent. In this strange place in this strange, dry, harsh land, she was an oasis of cool and beauty. She sat in a sagging armchair she'd had to man-handle through from another room, her knees drawn up and swung to one side, her bare feet tucked under her; one arm was propped against the chair back, cradling her head, the other lay, palm up, in her lap, silently begging.

Tom shifted his head a little so he could more easily follow the lines of her calf to where her slim legs disappeared under the cream linen of the simple shift dress that made her look like a waif in a perfume ad. His eyes lingered on the shape of her thigh through the dress and a jolt of electricity ran through him. He let out an involuntary groan at the sudden memory of her strong legs wrapped around his waist, the skin of her inner thighs like silk under his fingers.

He squeezed his eyes shut but it didn't help. When he opened them again, Ness was staring at him, although she hadn't moved. 'Okay?' she whispered.

He nodded. If you could call having a persistent hard-on with no means to relieve it okay, then he grudgingly guessed he was.

She uncurled and stretched like a cat and he ached as he watched her breasts rise against the linen, then disappear again. She leaned forward and he looked at her cleavage, seeing the pale breasts dissolve softly into darkness. She became still and finally he realized she was watching him watch her.

Busted.

He swallowed.

Shit. He was behaving like a teenager. She was leaning forward now, probably to slap him.

Instead Ness put the flat of her hand on his bare chest. He felt his breathing become laboured and shallow, like he'd forgotten quite how. She didn't move her hand, but gently extended her thumb and ran the nail across his right nipple.

Tom bit back a moan and shifted. He flushed when the movement made Ness glance down at him. The thin sheet did nothing to hide his feelings.

She trailed her fingers down his ribs carefully, as if counting each one on the way to his hip; she circled his hip bone once and then Tom watched in tight agony as her hand swept downwards, pushing the sheet away. She touched him tentatively and he whimpered as his injured hands tried reflexively to ball into fists of control.

But fists and control were beyond him.

He lifted his head to see himself, dark and hard in her pale hand.

If ever he was going to tell a woman he loved her, this was the moment, he thought dizzily.

So he bit his lip hard, threw his head back and let Ness do whatever she wanted with him.

And she wanted to do plenty.

*

The next day – just as the doctors were reducing his pain meds, out of what Tom could only imagine was spite – a cadaverous man, in an ill-fitting dirt-blue uniform, came into the room. He ignored Ness and came round the bed to stare down at Tom. 'I'm Sergeant Konrad, Mr Patrick.' He was five ten but looked six two, due to his extreme thinness. It seemed the Karoo undernourished its residents with a dry glee.

Konrad's greying hair was slicked across his pate with something that made it flat and shiny, and he had small, pale eyes and wet lips under a scrappy moustache. His uniform consisted of a short-sleeved shirt and matching shorts, into which his knobble-kneed hairy brown legs disappeared in strict parallel, as if they would never come together in the perspective of his pelvis. He wore long blue socks, dusty black shoes and a black leather Sam Browne belt, with a small revolver tucked into a hip holster.

Tom thought he looked like a poorly armed Malaysian postman.

Konrad pulled up a chair and sat down. He took a battered little notebook from his breast pocket, but never bothered opening it, or even getting a pen out. 'The fire,' he said. 'What can you tell me?'

Tom glanced fleetingly into the beady blue eyes and failed to detect any spark of real intelligence. 'Not much. We weren't there at the time.'

'Why not?'

Tom told him briefly. 'When we got back, we saw the fire. Looked to me like it had started downstairs, probably in two sites, maybe more.'

Konrad stared at his book as if he'd made copious notes.

Tom got impatient. 'What did Forensics find?'

'It was a fire. Everything was burned up. People. Clues. Everything.'

Tom felt dawning suspicion. 'Was there a forensic investigation?'

'You let the dog go?'

Tom was confused enough, by this sudden change in tack, to answer, 'Yes.'

'The dog was chained up for a reason. It's a vicious dog.'

Tom mentally shook his head in surprise. 'So what? It would have died if we'd left it there.'

'We?' Konrad looked at him sharply.

Something told Tom that being involved in the dog's release was a bad thing. 'Me. It would've died if I'd left it there.'

'After you let it go, it bit someone.'

'Yeah, well, it bit *me* but I was too busy worrying about six people burning to give a shit.'

Konrad shook his head disapprovingly. 'I've been told about your language, Mr Patrick. Here in South Africa we don't think it's clever or funny.'

'Fuck off.'

Konrad glared at him. 'You let the dog go. It bit someone. You're responsible.'

'Okay, fine. I'm responsible. Sorry. What about the six dead people? Who's responsible for that?'

Konrad shrugged. 'Mrs Marais. She smoked a lot. People said it was only a matter of time.'

'So that's it? She smoked a lot. Case closed? What about

the car that drove us off the road? What about the stolen wreckage?'

'There's no point spending taxpayers' money if you know what happened.'

'Six people died in that fire, asshole! Five of them were government employees! Two of them were even white!'

Konrad stood up abruptly and, for a moment, Tom thought he was going to hit him where he lay. Ness obviously thought the same thing because she rose and took a protective step forward.

Instead the policeman dug out a creased bit of paper from his pocket and dropped it on the bed. 'Here's the fine. You can pay it at any police station.'

He pushed past Ness and left.

*

Tom left the little hospital with a bottle of painkillers rattling in his hip pocket and the hostile stares of the staff burning a hole between his shoulder-blades.

Ness went to open the car door for him but he beat her to it. 'I'm fine,' he insisted.

She rolled her eyes, then waved cheerfully at someone back at the hospital.

'What makes you so popular?' he asked, as he dropped heavily into the passenger seat.

'I think they feel sorry for me,' she answered, with a little smile, and got behind the wheel.

For the first time in a long time, he couldn't think of anything clever to say.

*

Ness drove away from De Rust. Tom didn't like being a passenger but Ness was a fast and good driver, shifting and cornering smoothly, even on the challenging dirt road. After she'd caught her first slide and locked swiftly to get them back on track, he relaxed and stopped worrying.

There were other things he didn't have to worry about. Ness had arranged for new passports to be picked up in Cape Town and had bought them both clothes from the only store De Rust had to offer, leaving Tom looking like an extra from *The Dukes of Hazzard*. Of course, Ness still looked incredible – even wearing something that looked like it might once have contained flour.

They passed the unmarked turn that would have taken them to the barn.

'You want to go to the plane?'

He shook his head. There was no point. He wondered idly if the Cokes were still cold, then realized he'd left his thirty-nine-cent fly-swatter there. If he'd been alone he'd have turned round and driven to fetch it, even though he knew he could pick one up in any convenience store in South Africa.

She seemed to realize where his thoughts were and took her hand off the wheel momentarily to graze his cheek with her knuckles.

His hands were still relatively painful, but the miles of crêpe bandage had now been replaced by a minimal covering, and he could use them almost normally if he was careful.

'Have you taken your pills?'

'They make me sleepy.'

'So? Sleep.'

He dry-swallowed two painkillers. Within fifteen minutes he was unconscious.

*

Tom slowly became aware that the car had stopped. First he felt the complete calm that follows the engine switch-off. The quiet was so all-encompassing that it actually started to push him back into sleep.

He heard distant voices and wondered why Ness was so far away when she should have been in the driver's seat.

Then he heard another voice, high, sing-song, luring.

It was this that finally forced him to open his eyes groggily and look around.

The car was stopped on a nondescript stretch of straight Karoo dust road. As he looked to his left he could see only sheep and shimmer. He shifted his gaze to the right, where the driver's door was open. It afforded him a good view of Ness standing about fifty yards away, one hand on her hip, the other shielding her eyes from the fierce sun.

That soothing sing-song voice rose again, but this time ended in a sharp, frustrated cry, and Ness bounded into action as an ostrich hammered past, not ten feet from her. With a start, Tom realized she wasn't trying to avoid the bird, but was making a grab for it.

The last of his drug-induced cobwebs were brushed aside as he hauled himself out of the car. The ostrich had dodged Ness, but had stopped only a few yards past her, its head poking this way and that as if it were weighing up its options.

A hundred yards away, off the Honda's left flank, was

Harold Robbins. The boy was jogging towards Ness now, and Tom could see he was in the same clothes he'd worn when he came to the barn, and held a square plastic storage container in one hand. As he approached Ness, he dipped his hand into the container and held out something to the bird, his sing-song appeal coming again.

'*Leee*mon! *Heeeeeere, Leeeeeeee*mon!'

Lemon scooted away a few paces and now Tom could see that the bird was definitely limping – much worse than before. No wonder it had let them get so close.

Harold reached forward but Lemon stalked off slowly, staying just out of reach. Tom noticed the boy didn't try to make a hopeless grab at the narrow leash dangling from the bird's head. That would surely have spooked Lemon into flight. Instead the child – with the apparent patience of a saint – merely sauntered over again, while Ness circled widely behind Lemon, like a sheepdog cutting off an escape route.

Tom didn't know whether to help or just enjoy the odd spectacle of the skinny child and the woman trying to capture a racing ostrich in the middle of the desert. Then Lemon skittered sideways again and Tom trudged towards the action. Lemon had the look of a bird that was sick of running and was only protesting now for show.

Ness and Harold glanced at him as he made the third point of a rough triangle around Lemon.

'Hello, *baas*,' said Harold, conversationally.

'Hi, Harold.'

'We're trying to catch Lemon,' the boy added, somewhat redundantly, and once more pressed on towards the ostrich. The bird now realized that Ness and Tom were closing in behind it and did a confused, lopsided little dance on the spot. Tom wondered fleetingly whether it might bury its head in the sand, even though he'd heard that was a myth. Still, it would be cool to see.

But Lemon didn't bury his head. Tom and Ness stood still about ten yards either side of his flanks, and Harold licked his lips and moved in. Lemon let him get just a single step too close this time: when he made a break for it, Harold grabbed the leash and shook the container at him. Lemon resisted for one last moment, then dug his beak hard into the grain.

Ness broke into spontaneous applause and Harold's beam split his face with delight.

Ness and Tom approached, although Harold deflected them quietly. 'He will kick you, madam!'

Now they were closer, Tom could see dried blood on the big bird's left leg. The wound was up under the feathers and out of sight, but it must be large to have caused the amount of blood it obviously had.

Harold saw Tom staring and his smooth forehead creased in concern. 'He is hurt, *baas*?'

'Looks like it.'

Harold turned to Ness. 'Will you hold Lemon, madam? I will catch his leg.'

Ness took the leash warily and, without a moment's hesitation, Harold ducked under the bird's chest and grabbed its scaly left foot with the giant dinosaur claws and pulled it up. Incapacitated, Lemon stood stock-still as Tom carefully moved in and parted the jet-black feathers.

There it was. The almost vertical gash was about four inches long, open and festering. At the bottom of the wound and between the rough quills, Tom could feel something hard under the skin.

Lemon hopped and staggered sideways and Harold cooed reassuringly to him as if the huge bird was a kitten. Tom found the place again. 'There's something stuck under the skin,' he said, with disgust. 'The whole thing's infected.'

'Can you take it out?' Ness was looking at him with hope and expectation, and he realized, with a sinking feeling, that now he'd *have* to take the damn thing out. Now he'd *have* to perform makeshift surgery on a leftover dinosaur in the middle of a fucking desert, all because Ness had given him the best blow-job of his entire life.

That was what it came down to.

Tom shook his head in amazement. Sometimes life was so bizarre that it didn't bear close examination for fear of insanity ensuing. 'Sure,' he said, sounding a lot more confident than he felt.

He pulled his Swiss Army knife from his pocket. It was nothing fancy and he couldn't remember ever having unsheathed the blade, although the bottle-opener was a godsend.

Parting the feathers once again, Tom licked his lips and wondered about the best way to do this. He was uncomfortably aware that both Ness and Harold were gazing at him with identical expressions of confidence, and that the longer he delayed, the less confident they'd all become.

Fuck it.

'Hold on tight!'

Feeling slightly sick, Tom dug the knife into the bird's flesh, quickly continuing the existing gash to expose a lump of something, before a fresh supply of blood welled up and hid it from view. But Tom grabbed it quickly, wincing at the sudden pain in his hand, and took it out of the bird with a single movement. 'Got it!'

Lemon – contrary to all logic – merely twitched and quivered, then dug his beak back into the grain that Ness was now holding.

Harold dropped Lemon's leg, and he and Tom stepped rapidly away from the bird.

'What is it?' said Ness, as she handed the leash back to Harold and came over to peer at the bloody lump in Tom's hand.

He picked at it, turning it over, suddenly surprised to see a glint of metal through the blood.

Ness saw it too. 'Is it a bullet?'

At that, Harold craned to see, pulling a reasonably compliant Lemon with him.

Tom saw that his plaid shirt was already bloody from the impromptu surgery, so he wiped the lump on the tail of it.

The air left his lungs in a single harsh whoosh. His practised eye told him instantly that what he'd dug out of an ostrich called Lemon was a flange bolt from the CFM56 engine of a Boeing 737.

*

They had left Harold walking Lemon happily to God knew where. He had thanked them effusively, waved goodbye and set off purposefully as if he knew exactly where he was going. Tom assumed he must, however unlikely it seemed.

Ness had tipped most of a bottle of Scotch over the wound. She'd bought it at LAX and left it in the car. They'd had just a couple of nips each, Tom thought mournfully. He tried reminding her it was a single malt, but she shook the rest over the ostrich for good luck.

Tom sighed. It seemed Ness had a stubborn streak.

For comfort he turned his mind, and his fingers, back to the bolt in his jeans pocket. He couldn't leave it alone – had to keep touching it. He drew it out for the tenth time since they'd set off again, looking at the three bright gouges in the shank, and the way it was cranked – just a little kink in the smooth line under the head. The grazes on the flange faces had told a story. That story had been stolen. But the same story was retold here on the bolt: the story of the disc ring shifting back and forth at least three times, each movement leaving those fresh-metal witness marks on the shaft of this bolt.

If Tom had found a diamond in Lemon he couldn't have been happier.

They barely spoke on the drive back to Cape Town. Tom's mind was whirring as he turned the bolt over and over like worry beads. Ness seemed preoccupied too, which suited him fine.

It was dark by the time they got to the city and booked into a hotel. This time Tom requested a double and Ness smiled. Despite her ministrations at the hospital, he was still relieved and a little disbelieving that this was happening. Some small – okay, not so small – cynical part of him had been wondering if, back at the hospital, she'd simply seen he had a problem and done him a favour. Strictly medicinal. Like he'd pick up her groceries if she were ill – that kind of thing.

Once he put it in that context, he realized how stupid it sounded. No woman went down on a guy as a favour between friends. Not unless Ness were some new and exotic kind of woman brewed up in a fantasy lab run by unattractive, halitosis-plagued virgin geeks.

Still, it had been a relief when she'd smiled.

Ness showered and Tom was just debating whether she was the kind of woman who'd welcome company – or kick his soapy ass out of there – when his phone rang. The thought that it might be Pete with a job made him scramble about looking for his cell and he banged his hand on the table as he answered.

'Mother*fucker.*'

'Tom?'

'What?' Tom snapped and dug his hand under his armpit – like that would help.

'Halo.'

'What do you want?'

'Er . . . Niño Alvarez is missing.'

'Good. I hope the bastard's dead. He stood on my thumb.'

There was a confused silence in which Tom started to feel just a little childish. He suppressed it by snapping at Halo again: 'Anything else?'

'No. Just that.'

This time Halo's silence was hostile, and Tom remembered that Alvarez was a friend and colleague of his. Shit. 'What's his wife doing?' He couldn't remember the woman's name but he hoped his slightly less aggressive tone would be enough to placate Halo.

'Sylvia,' Halo provided, as Tom had known he would – cos that's the kinda guy Halo is, he thought, a little bitterly. The pain in his hand was subsiding now and he was definitely feeling guilty.

'She's called the police but they don't give a damn. I mean, he's a man, not a little kid or some such. I guess they figure he's in Tijuana tying one on, or with a girlfriend.'

'You don't think so?'

'I wouldn't be calling you if I did. He hasn't been back to work since that day.'

'Well, what can I do about it from here?'

'Why? Where are you?'

'Cape Town.'

There was a surprised pause, then Halo wondered, 'Does that mean this call is costing me a fortune?'

'Yep.'

'Shit. I gotta go.'

'Suck it up, Halo. I found some stuff out.'

'*Pride of Maine* stuff?'

'Possibly. The 737 out here – it looked like the fan disc or the flange bolts failed. I have one of the bolts, which might help.'

'What about the fan disc?'

'It got stolen. And the investigation team were all killed in a fire the same night.'

'Sheee-it.'

'Sheee-it is right. I'd be dead too if I hadn't got up to go back to the wreckage on a hunch. Even then they drove us off the road.'

'Us?'

Tom kicked himself. He didn't want Halo knowing his personal life. 'I'm with a friend.'

'You getting laid?'

Tom's hackles rose at the surprise in Halo's voice. 'So? What's the big shock?'

'I'm not shocked.'

'You *sound* shocked.'

'Well,' Halo started haltingly, 'congratulations. Who is she?'

'None of your business.'

Tom heard the smile in Halo's voice as he said, 'My friends get laid, that's my business.'

'I'm not your friend, Halo. You're just some guy who calls me up and hassles me to do work he doesn't pay for. And gets my thumb squashed.'

Once again, the hurt silence. What *is* this? Tom thought irritably. Everyone's a goddamn *wife*.

Except Ness. So far Ness had played things very, very cool, and he liked that about her – liked that she hadn't tried to make them something before they were ready to be that. Of course, Richard probably had something to do with it, but Tom pushed the thought to the back of his mind.

'When will you be home?' said Halo, and Tom snorted. Halo had completed the wife analogy.

'Couple of days.'

'Can you call me?'

'Yeah. Okay.'

'Okay, then.' Halo sounded subdued. Tom tried to ignore it and hung up. He wondered if he should have asked after Vee. Too late now.

Ness emerged, managing to look better in a hotel towel than most movie stars did on the red carpet, and all thoughts of Halo, Vee, Niño Alvarez – in fact, all thoughts bar one – drained from Tom's brain as if they'd never been there.

Halo stared at the phone and thought about Niño Alvarez. They weren't good friends but they were colleagues and that made them friends of sorts, didn't it?

Two months before, some of the guys had asked him to make up the numbers in a Friday-night softball game they had running. Halo had struck out three times and Niño was the one who'd made him feel better about it. Playing catcher, it was Niño who'd yelled, 'Strike three!' then jabbed a finger towards an imaginary dugout and laughed. 'You're gonna fit right in here, man!'

That meant he owed Niño some loyalty, didn't it?

Tom Patrick, on the other hand, was a bit of an asshole, even by Halo's charitable standards. The NTSB man was an arrogant, tactless prick, with the sensitivity of a very large bull in a very small china shop. But if he had to pick sides, Halo realized, he would have a hard time deciding which way to go. He didn't think it was only his need for Tom's help that motivated him. There was something about the man – something deep under that thick skin – that Halo believed was worthy. Logically, he knew this theory lacked the tiny sticking point of hard evidence. Tom had never been anything but rude, offhand and dismissive around him.

Apart from that one time, Halo realized. The time he'd made him pasta.

Halo almost laughed at the thought. He was not some lonely sonofabitch who could mistake a bowl of spaghetti for friendship. He had pals, he had colleagues – hell, nowadays he even had Vee and Katy, and they would be enough for any man, all by themselves.

But something in the gruff, grudging gesture of offering food spoke to Halo of something else going on in Tom Patrick that was masked by his cynicism and prickly shell. *Well* masked, thought Halo, with a smile.

He sighed and wondered whether a choice was actually necessary. Finding Niño and working with Tom were not mutually exclusive activities. In fact, they were part of the same thing. This *Pride of Maine* thing.

Halo felt a nudge of guilt at Tom's bitter words about the *Pride of Maine*, then almost immediately suppressed it. He owed it to a much older friend to clear his name, and if he had to bully Tom Patrick into helping him do that, then that was what he would do.

*

Tom woke to find Ness standing over him, naked, with the bolt in her hand. She flinched when he opened his eyes, then smiled quietly. 'Sorry.'

''S okay.'

'I couldn't sleep. I was thinking. About this.' She shrugged, dismissing her own interest, and placed the bolt back on the table.

'Couldn't sleep, huh?' He reached out to pull her down to him. The smell of him was still on her; he'd marked her as his territory, and the thought made him hard again. She felt it and closed her hand around him.

'Don't want to waste that,' he mumbled, into her throat.

19

LYLE'S REPLACEMENT WAS a bald man almost as wide as he was tall, which was not very. His name was Nicholas H. Nicholas, and he wouldn't tell them what the H stood for. Jeff ragged him for a while about it. 'Humphrey. Harold. Harmony Hairspray.'

Nicholas said nothing and watched the screens.

Jeff rocked back creakily on his swivel chair and pursed his lips. 'Horatio. Henry. Herbert. It's Henry, right?'

'What does this do?' said Nicholas Nicholas, and Chuck leaned forward.

'You can toggle between screens, see? Here you got your assembly line, your meeting room, your cafeteria, your engineering section—'

'Cafeteria open?'

'Closes at six.'

'I didn't bring anything.'

There was a pregnant silence. Chuck had cold pork and peanut dumplings. They sat clammily in an old scratched plastic container in his backpack, waxy and flat, with pinched, corrugated edges, like a box of ears. He knew Jeff brought sandwiches – corned beef usually – with the crusts cut off. They never exchanged food.

But Nicholas didn't seem to be angling for charity. He sighed.

'Hobie. Harlan. Harlan Globetrotter.' Jeff laughed at his own wit, stretching the laugh in the hope someone would join him.

'There's a vending machine. Full of shit.'

Nicholas looked perkier at that. 'So do we get a break?'

'Jeff has twelve till twelve thirty. I take twelve thirty to one. You have one to one thirty.' Chuck got up and picked up his flashlight.

'Where you going?'

'The rounds.'

'Chuck likes to make the rounds, right, Chuck?'

Chuck shrugged. Jeff grabbed his own flashlight. 'I'll come with you. The new guy's pissing me off.'

Chuck was surprised. Jeff had never joined him on his rounds before. As far as he knew, Jeff never made rounds.

He glanced at Nicholas but the man simply turned his back on them and toggled between the screens the way Chuck had shown him.

'It's okay. I don't mind doing them. You grab some coffee – and make me some for when I get back.' He hoped his tone was light and bored but couldn't tell.

Jeff glanced at him and, for a split second, Chuck thought he saw knowledge in the bigger man's eyes. Then Jeff stretched, yawned – and flicked on his flashlight. 'Let's go.'

Chuck's palms were clammy and he fought illogical panic. So what? he told himself. So Jeff was making his rounds with him. He could make them again at four a.m. and do what he needed to then. It made no difference. All he had to do was act casual with Jeff. Everything would be okay.

Slowly Chuck's breathing came back to him and he started to relax.

Jeff shuffled along beside him, his height and slight stoop making him look like a man who was trying to go unnoticed. 'See the Cowboys lose again?'

'Yeah. Fuck.' Chuck hadn't seen the Cowboys lose, although he was pleased to hear they had. Every redneck in the state seemed to mourn every beating those bozos took. Lumping Jeff with them made it easier for him to handle the man being with him now.

'Yeah,' said Jeff. 'Fucking play-offs.'

Whatever that meant, thought Chuck.

The plant was dark and secretive, and the beams of their flashlights darted about, making barely any impression on the blackness. Chuck never turned on the lights any more when he made his rounds. He preferred to imagine he was a spy, a James Bond hunting down a secret formula, and would be tortured and killed – slowly – if he was discovered. It gave every work night a certain frisson. But he didn't need that fantasy tonight. Tonight he had all the frisson he needed.

Jeff didn't seem to mind the dark. Maybe he thought that was the way rounds were made, thought Chuck. The lazy bastard probably hadn't made rounds since the invention of the electric light-bulb. They walked in silence. Chuck opened the door to Engineering. He knew she wasn't there – the light was off – but he always hoped. Although he would have been disappointed to find her while he had Jeff in tow. He'd have had to be professional.

'You see the chick that works here?' Jeff waved at the girl's desk.

Chuck nodded briefly.

'Fucking hot little bitch, in't she?'

Chuck was surprised and stood still in the doorway while Jeff shouldered past him. 'You seen this?' Jeff opened her desk drawer and found a box of tampons. He grinned at Chuck. 'Whore,' he said, as though the tampons proved that.

He peeled a bright yellow Post-it note off a pad on her desk and reached up to cover the lens of the CCTV camera with it. Chuck felt disquiet blossom in his belly, like a rain-cloud gathering on the horizon.

'Why you standing over there, man? Come on in. Take a load off.' Jeff sank into the girl's chair and put his work boots on her neat desk. He pulled open another drawer and extracted a pad of white Authorized Release Certificates and dropped it on the desk beside him. Chuck's heart lurched into his mouth and Jeff grinned at him, his eyes glittering.

'This is what you came for, right?' The thick fingers of his big hand played a little drum-roll on the pad. 'It's what Lyle used to come for. We used to have another guy before you. Steven. Or Stevie. Whatever. He used to be you, y'know? A fucking suck-ass, making his rounds like a good little security guard. Before that we had Douglas. Ellery J. Douglas. Guy had the biggest biceps I ever seen. And he made the rounds too. Like the skinny little farmer before him. Me and Lyle, well, we used to just laugh it up when those assholes would sigh and pick up their flashlights. Just like you.'

Chuck said nothing. His mind was too numb to formulate any thought other than that Jeff knew. Had always known.

He felt sick.

'So, anyway, one night before you come Lyle suddenly gets

up and picks up his flashlight and announces he's making the fucking rounds! I mean! Goddamn!' Jeff showed his teeth at the memory, but Chuck wouldn't have called it a smile – or anything close.

'So he keeps doing it and I keep ragging him, but all the time I'm thinking, What the fuck – y'know?'

Chuck blinked. He knew.

'Then, out of the blue, he gets that little Suzuki Jeep. I mean, this is a guy who borrowed money off me for pizza! The fucking mooch!' Jeff's outraged indignation was almost funny. He was quiet for a moment, his jaw working in annoyance, his eyes narrowed under sandy brows, his fingers toying with a short stack of Post-it notes.

'So I followed him. Followed him in here. Into Engineering. Saw him steal these. Just a couple at a time. One from this pad, one from another. They're supposed to be logged an' all but, fuck, these people are slack. Every fucker's slack, y'know? Don't matter if they're pulling down a hundred grand or working for food. Every fucker's slack.'

Chuck nodded. Every fucker *was* slack. Even him, eventually, he realized with a pang.

Jeff got up, tiring of his own tirade. 'So, anyway, I figured, if he's getting something out of it, I'd better get something out of it too.' His eyes met Chuck's and he grinned broadly. 'You understand?'

Chuck saw his lips moving but the roaring of blood in his ears was such that he could barely hear the words.

'So when Lyle left, I figured you'd be stepping into his shoes. Young. Stupid. Greedy.'

The words stung Chuck. He was better than Lyle! Better

than all of them! Yet young, stupid and greedy seemed to sum him up perfectly at that moment.

'Don't make me come get you, boy.' Jeff seemed a little angry now, and waved a beckoning hand at him.

Chuck understood perfectly, even though he didn't hear so well. He could feel his heart pumping in his throat. The ARC pad lay on the girl's desk between him and Jeff. That bitch. If she hadn't stolen his job, he wouldn't be standing there now, squeezed so hard between his job and his theft and the Lucky Eight and his disappointment and Jeff – who was now watching him with unseemly hunger – that he could hardly breathe.

Chuck had come top of his class at Texas State. That meant he was at least smart enough to know he had no way out. As Lyle had discovered before him, he couldn't report Jeff. Even if he stopped stealing the certificates for the fidgety guy with the gun, Jeff could get him fired. If he got fired, the Lucky Eight would suck him in like quicksand. He'd never get the smell of fried pork out of his clothes and he'd be married off to the gaunt child he'd been pointed out to in the old village – a child with lice in her hair and shit stains on her thighs.

So, at last, it was Chuck's 3.9 grade point average that made him slowly walk round the desk towards Jeff.

Jeff smiled and hitched open his belt.

Chuck kept his eyes on the desk where the pad and the tampons mocked him.

That whore. Somehow he'd make her pay for this.

20

Kitty looked up and smiled at Tom for about the twentieth time. She was starting to look strained.

Tom didn't smile back this time, just shrugged. He knew Pete was deliberately keeping him waiting. And the longer he waited, the more shit he knew he was in. If he'd needed any further clues, he had only to look past the smile to the pity in Kitty's eyes.

However, if Pete was hoping to put him on the defensive with a game of corporate chicken, it wasn't working. The longer Tom sat in the low vinyl chair, the angrier he got. He could feel it happening to him and could do nothing about it. He was angry at Pete for the forty-minute wait when he'd left Ness at LAX to fly here, straight after arriving from South Africa; he was angry at whoever had run them off the road and murdered Pam Mashamaete and the others; he was angry at every leak in every pipeline and tanker between DC and Anchorage; he was angry at Lenny Munro for being the egotistical tight-ass he was; and he was angry at himself for pretty much everything else that was shitty in his life. For some odd, unbidden reason, this included making Lucia cry. And when *that* thought popped into his head, it made him so angry he wanted to shoot someone. His own conscience was fucking betraying him now! She was history, and not even a big piece of history – a tiny, sharp pebble in the shoe of his memory that made no difference to the whole but pricked at him nonetheless. Why the hell she kept cropping up in his far more urgent mental processes, he was at a loss to explain. He wished fervently he'd never met her so that he wasn't wasting energy on thinking about her.

The phone on Kitty's desk buzzed and she murmured into it, then looked at him.

'They're ready for you.'

As he passed her desk, she said, 'Play it cool, Tom.'

Her voice was serious and Tom knew she was only looking out for him but, right at that moment, it was water off a duck's back to him. He shrugged a noncommittal answer and yanked open the door.

Pete and Lenny Munro were sitting on the same side of Pete's desk, like Munro was some kind of familiar.

'Hi, Tom,' said Pete, and he sounded tired.

Munro said nothing, just fixed Tom with a cold glare.

'Hey, Pete. Lenny.'

Munro flinched at Tom's easy tone and Tom mentally chalked a mark up to himself. Munro wanted Tom grovelling on his knees, begging Pete for forgiveness. Well, fuck him, thought Tom, with another comforting little bolt of anger: he might be brought to his knees in this meeting, but he sure as hell wasn't going to start out that way. He and Munro theoretically were equals. Munro probably thought he was the superior right now because Tom was in job-limbo, but Tom figured he'd always have the edge on Munro on brains alone, so he wasn't about to give him any undue respect just because he was getting twice the money, all the work, and was so far up Pete's ass that only the soles of his shoes were showing.

Tom knew he was meant to take the uncomfortable seat in front of Pete's desk that completed the triangle, so instead he wandered across to the bookcase on the opposite wall and leaned against that.

Pete sighed. 'Tom, you know why you're here.'

'Actually, I don't.'

Munro's face reddened. 'Don't play the innocent, Patrick!'

'Thank you, Lenny. I'll chair this meeting,' said Pete, a little sharply, and Munro pursed his lips tightly.

'The *Pride of Maine*.'

It sounded oddly old-fashioned to hear the plane's whimsical name uttered in the context of an official investigation. '*Pride of Maine*' sounded like something that had gone down with Orville Wright at the helm.

'What about it?' said Tom, flatly.

'You've been conducting a wholly unofficial investigation into probable cause.'

'What about it?' he repeated.

'Probable cause has already been established in that case, as well you know.'

'So the paperwork shows,' he said blandly.

Munro shifted and Tom saw his fingers tighten on the arms of his chair. The chair Tom was supposed to be sitting in did not have arms: that was another clue about the hierarchy in this room, his objective mind thought distantly.

Pete was full of sighs today. 'Tom, whatever your personal feelings about the LAX case, you have overstepped the mark. Simple as that. You have disregarded the wholly legitimate findings of a fellow professional, calling his judgement into question, you must have groundlessly raised the hopes of Mr Stern's friends and family, and you have most certainly pissed off the staff of CalSuperior, who have made an official complaint about trespass, industrial espionage and wanton destruction of property.'

The espresso attack. Tom almost smiled.

'All this,' Pete continued, 'on top of your existing probation for previous infractions.'

NTSB-speak really ratcheted Pete's vocabulary up a notch or two, thought Tom, simultaneously realizing he'd barely been listening to the tongue-lashing. He only knew it was a bad one from Munro's smug look. Bastard. The flames of anger licked higher in his belly.

'You're a fucking maverick, Patrick,' Munro spat, finally unable to hold on to his own anger.

Pete turned to him immediately. 'Lenny, would you wait outside?'

'What? Why?'

'Please?'

Munro got up and stomped round the desk to the door. Tom ignored his going but, once the door had shut behind him, he sat down in the bad chair. 'Maybe now we can talk.'

'Tom. This bullshit's got to stop. Your career's in the crapper and Munro's flush-happy. I'd be justified in kicking you out of this office without a job, and he knows that. It's what he wants.'

'Is it what *you* want?'

'There's a point where what I want becomes pretty much irrelevant. We're *this* close to that point.' Pete held up his thumb and forefinger: from Tom's angle, they looked like they were touching.

'Pete . . .' Tom started, then sat back in the chair and briefly considered how much he should tell his boss. Fuck it, he thought. He really had nothing left to lose. 'Pete, Munro's report is wrong. I'm not saying it's all his fault – even though he is a fucking asshole. I think the *Pride of Maine*'s compressor was ripped apart by a flaw in the fan disc or the flange bolts.' He put the bolt on Pete's desk. 'That's a flange bolt from the engine of a 737 that went down in South Africa. I know I'm not on planes right now, but I need NTSB resources to have it tested to see if it's bad.'

Pete said nothing, just stared at the bolt, so Tom licked his lips and pressed on. 'Something shifted. Something gave way before the engine let go. There was play on the disc, Pete.'

Pete looked surprised, then wary. 'How do you know?'

Tom blinked slowly. This was the hard part. 'The South African 737 had fretting between the disc and shaft flanges. Something sent it off-centre. Whether the bolt failed, or the disc failed, it was enough to throw the whole thing out.'

'You think.'

Tom said nothing. He felt in his guts that he was right. Fuck qualification and caution.

Pete picked up the bolt and turned it over slowly in his fingers, his eyes learning the story that the scoring and the crank-shafting told – as Tom knew they must.

'Have they had the disc tested?'

'It was stolen.'

'Stolen?' Pete's expression was surprise and disbelief rolled neatly into one.

'Yeah, stolen. I was run off the road on my way to look at it, and their investigators were killed in a fire the same night.'

Now Pete sat back in his chair and cocked an eyebrow.

Tom unfolded the paperwork for the *Pride of Maine* disc. 'The fan disc from the two jets came from the same batch at WAE – 501.'

Pete raised his eyes to look at Tom sharply. 'Can you prove it?'

'I saw the South African paperwork.'

'Where is it?'

'It was stolen too. By the same people who stole the fan disc and set the fire.'

'Says?'

'Says me, Pete! Says *me*! Fuck!'

Pete sighed so loudly it was almost comical. 'Jesus, Tom, you *have* no say! You have no paperwork, you have no witnesses, you have no official investigation statements. You have one miserable flange bolt out of a possible twenty. How the hell am I supposed to cover your ass based on that kind of non-evidence? How the *hell*? Lenny Munro's investigation's papered up to the eyeballs.'

'Well, I'm sorry that a fucking mass murderer screwed up my ability to produce paperwork!'

'That's not what I'm saying and you know it! Listen, Tom – this pipeline thing won't last for ever. Just keep a low profile, don't piss people off and I'll recommend your reinstatement. We need you, and the board knows it. But this *Pride of Maine* mess—'

'Pete. I know it's a mess. I know it! But just cos it's a mess doesn't mean there's no truth in it! I mean, maybe it's a mess *because* it's the truth – maybe the mess is just someone trying to cover that up.' He realized he was pleading and didn't give a shit. 'Pete, please. When did I ever let you down?'

'Only all the fucking time!'

'That's personal shit. That's my big mouth. On probable cause, I mean – when did I ever let you down on probable cause?'

Pete didn't answer because Tom was right. He'd never let him down on probable cause.

'I'll do it on my time, Pete. I'll do it between pipeline jobs. All I need is you not to hassle me for it, a few resources, and to know that Munro's off my back.'

Pete LaBello wished for the thousandth time that he'd retired before the Tom Patrick shit had hit the fan – as he'd always known it would some day. He'd as good as promised Lenny Munro that he'd fire Tom today. And when he'd said it to Munro he'd meant it. He couldn't see any way back for Tom. Not then, anyway . . .

'It can't be official. Munro would go over my head.'

'I understand.'

'He might go over my head anyway. He hates you like haemorrhoids.'

'I get it.'

'You have to be discreet. A goddamned sight more discreet than you've been so far.'

'Okay.'

'And you've got to apologize to Munro.'

Tom's face protested. Pete cut him off: 'Right now. In front of witnesses. It's the only way he'll lie down for this – and you know you owe it to him.'

'Shit.' Tom glowered at his sneakers and snaked an angry hand round the back of his neck, scraping at the prickles of hair. 'Okay. Fuck it. Okay.' He stood up. 'As long as you know I don't mean it.'

Pete couldn't help smirking at that.

'What about the CalSuperior complaint?'

Pete thought about it. 'I guess I can make that go away. Their pride's hurt, that's all. The guy who called me up sounded like he was going to cry.'

Tom smiled tightly. 'Lowell Dexter?'

'Yeah.'

'Prick.'

'Yeah.'

Tom nodded, looking around the office, the fingers of his left hand splayed and resting lightly on the desk. His eyes finally travelled back to Pete's. He took a deep breath and went for broke. 'What about this bolt? If I put in an Eddy current test request Munro will be all over me again.'

Pete looked at him in amazement for a moment, then shook his head. 'Unbelievable.' He sighed for the final time that day. 'I'll get it done.' He put the bolt into a Ziploc bag, then saw that Tom had something else to say. Something he was obviously having enormous difficulty with. The man's face was a textbook example of inner turmoil. He was actually sweating, for Chrissake!

Pete hoped desperately that Tom Patrick had the sense to shut the hell up and take what he'd been offered: he had no more to give and he sure as hell wasn't in the mood to dredge up any more favours.

But he felt his heart sink as Tom opened his big fucking mouth to say . . .

'How's Ann?'

Tom came out of Pete's office and Lenny Munro immediately turned to him, his eyes as hostile as a cornered pig's.

Tom grinned at Kitty and was gratified to see her face light up as she realized he was still in a job.

'Shit!' Munro had read the same thing on his face. 'Pete! What the *hell*?'

Pete stood in his office doorway and braced himself. 'Come back in, Lenny.'

'You're kidding me, right? You didn't can his ass?'

Tom cleared his throat politely, fighting every instinct to rub Munro's nose in it. He noticed that heads were turning towards them from every corner of the open-plan office as Munro's voice rose.

'Lenny. Please. We'll discuss this in private.'

'Fuck you, Pete! And fuck you too, Patrick!' Munro was tight with fury. Tom could even see the redness boiling through his pale crew cut.

'Munro!'

Lenny Munro realized he'd gone too far. With an effort that even Tom had to admire, he straightened himself up and walked towards Pete's office, his eyes glinting, his jaw working under his shaking, flushed jowls.

As he passed, Tom put a hand briefly on his arm to hold him in place and spoke before he could change his mind. 'Hey, Lenny, I'm sorry I fucked with your investigation,' he said, loud enough for everyone to hear. He could see Munro was surprised, but also that he was still angry and desperate to have his say and – in an uncharacteristic moment of charity – Tom decided to let him. He raised his eyebrows and stood still in invitation of the man's best shot.

Munro glared at him, his fists clenched tightly at his sides, and gave it to him. 'There's no *i* in "team", asshole!'

That was his best shot? Tom snorted, then told him, 'Yeah, but there's a *u* in "cocksucker".'

Kitty squeaked and Munro swung at him and Tom ducked under it, wondering vaguely where the hell his mouth had found *that* one, and Pete and two other men grappled Lenny Munro into the office before he could murder Tom Patrick in a room full of witnesses.

21

CANDICE HOLMES HADN'T been able to get a seat next to her boyfriend so she twisted in her belt and looked at him. Carlo smiled hazily at her. He'd taken a Valium to help him sleep on the flight from Savannah to LA and it was already kicking in.

'Tired?'

'Hmm. Sleepy.'

She held out her hand to him and he made the effort to take it, holding it under his own on his thigh.

'Did you bring the birthday present?'

He nodded, his eyes starting to close.

'Did you call your dad about the crane thing?'

'Bulldozer.'

'What?'

'Bulldozer,' he said slowly. 'Not crane.'

'Big yellow thing with wheels?'

Carlo grinned and nodded again, almost imperceptibly, with his eyes now shut. Candice thought for the millionth time how handsome he was. They'd been together for three years, so she figured if that feeling hadn't worn off by now, it was never going to. As she often did in a crowded place, she looked around her at the dozens of other men on the flight and decided, as she almost always did, that Carlo was the best-looking guy in the room. *Her* Carlo.

She felt his hand loosen on hers and his breathing deepen as the plane's engines started to whine in rising anticipation.

She slid her hand from under his and sighed. Six hours alone, six hours away from Carlo, stretched before her. She didn't mind him taking the Valium: he was a bad flier and preferred to sit the whole experience out. She appreciated that he was coming with her to LA on a family thing. The least she could do was let him get drugged up to the eyeballs.

As the thrust pushed her back into the seat, Candice smiled. She loved that feeling of power all around her just as much as Carlo hated it. She pulled a book out of the seat pocket in front of her. The book she should have been reading was *Stone Cold: The Geology of the Antarctic and South Georgia*, but she'd snuck *Little Women* on board in a fit of feminine nostalgia, and now she flipped to the bookmark. Candice hated turning down pages: she'd been brought up better than that. If she didn't have a bookmark, she'd use a piece of thread or a scrap of paper. When she'd first met Carlo, she'd thought they couldn't be compatible because she'd found him using a piece of chewed gum as a bookmark. She'd even talked it through with her mother, who had sighed and told her nobody was perfect and 'At least Carlo's reading, Candice. Lots of men don't!' Candice smiled to herself at the memory. Carlo still used gum in his own books but never in hers, and that was good enough for her.

She mentally snuggled down to enjoy four sisters whose lives had precisely nothing in common with her own.

They were over Oklahoma – and Amy was drawing pages

and pages of noses – when Candice's world came apart with shocking speed and utter finality.

There was a sound like a locomotive hitting the inside of a tunnel wall and *Little Women* was ripped from her hands just as the air was ripped from her lungs and for a second she was staring not at the heads of the passengers in front of her but at the whole Earth, lit softly by dawn, spread out below her as if she were an astronaut on re-entry.

She registered wonder at the view, and horror at the view.

Her last conscious thought was that she hoped Carlo was strapped in. Then she and seventy-seven others plummeted the rest of the twenty-seven thousand feet in burning cold oblivion.

22

BECAUSE HE WAS at the airport, Tom called Halo as soon as he disembarked from the DC flight. Halo took a break and came over from Hangar Four.

They met at a coffee shop on the concourse. Tom had an espresso in a private toast to Lowell Dexter. Halo surprised him by ordering something with a lot of whipped cream on it, most of which transferred itself to his top lip at the first sip and stayed there.

Tom brought him up to speed on what had happened in South Africa.

Halo's eyes widened, and Tom realized his reaction was appropriate. Some serious shit had gone down in the Karoo. He'd been a little distracted by his injury and by sheer horniness, and this was the first time he'd recounted the full events in sequence to a third party.

'How can there not be an investigation into the fire?' Halo was as outraged as Tom had been, but now, with time and resignation dulling his anger, Tom rubbed his face tiredly.

'It would be pointless. Their idea of forensics is to sweep all the evidence up with a dustpan and brush. *CSI Timbuk-fucking-tu*.'

Halo looked sombre. 'You should light a candle for them or something.'

Tom's head jerked in surprise. 'What?'

'For Pam and the others. In their memory.'

'Light a candle for six people who died in a fire?' Tom snorted. 'And I thought I was sick!'

Halo hadn't thought of that. He felt stupid. 'You know what I mean.'

'Not really.'

Halo heard dismissal in his tone and shut up about the candle. 'So, what's next?'

'You get cheap flights, right?'

'Cheap enough.'

'Want to get me one to Texas?'

'What's in Texas?' Halo asked suspiciously.

'Oil. Beef. WAE.'

'The engine plant?'

'Thought I'd see them about the batch number. Take a look at their papering systems.'

Halo nodded and sipped and Tom enjoyed the fact that he had a proper whipped-cream Fu Manchu going. How could he not feel that?

'Okay,' said Halo. 'Just let me know when. You may have to be on standby, though.'

Tom shrugged. South Africa had almost wiped him out in more ways than one. Standby was a small price to pay for a small price.

'You going through their paperwork on the fan discs?'

'I'll do what they let me. I can't specify the *Pride of Maine* or it'll get back to Munro and then I'm flipping burgers.'

'So you gotta be discreet?'

Tom inclined his head and Halo grinned.

'I bet you never done discreet before, right?'

'You bet right.' Tom yawned. 'Any news on your friend?'

'Niño?' Halo shook his head. 'Sylvia's going nuts.'

Tom couldn't muster any empathy for Sylvia. His thumbnail was still black.

'Cops don't give a shit. Thought the union here might help but they're assholes too. Shit.'

Silence stretched between them.

'So,' Tom started haltingly, 'you okay?'

Halo was surprised.

'Yeah. Good. I guess. Vee and Katy are great.'

Tom didn't know where to go from this point. He hadn't with Pete and he didn't with Halo. Getting to the question alone had sapped his meagre stock of etiquette.

'How about you?'

Tom shrugged.

'Still getting some?' said Halo, teasingly.

Tom shrugged again, but this time with a small smile on his lips that made Halo laugh as he got up.

'Give me a call when you know you're going to Texas. Or anything I can do in the meantime.'

They stood up to leave.

'Hey, Ole Man River . . .' Tom tapped his own upper lip.

Halo touched his and felt the cream moustache. He wiped it off on the sleeve of his coveralls and grinned his thanks then walked away.

Ness was waiting for Tom when he got home. She was asleep in her little Lotus, despite the cramped cockpit. He'd hoped but hadn't expected that she would be there. There had been no declarations during or after the mind-blowing sex they'd had in Cape Town. No unwise endearments on his part; no wistful longing on hers. They'd parted with a hot kiss at LAX the day before, and he'd stayed to catch the next flight to DC. His track record meant that every time he kissed a woman goodbye, odds were that it was for the last time.

But the fact that she was here now meant she was prepared to ride along with him a little longer, even in the absence of words of love, promises of commitment or even an acknowledgement of continuing interest.

He liked her more and more.

A wrinkle of worry between her eyes made her look very young. He tapped on the window and she opened her eyes, unfocused and wary until she found his face and smiled. She opened the door.

'Bad dream?'

'Huh?'

'You looked a little worried there.'

'Oh. That. Nothing.'

'You coming in?'

'Actually I came to ask you if you could play a game.'

'You could have called me for that.'

She didn't answer.

'You coming in?'

She gazed at him challengingly, her chin lifted defiantly. 'You gonna play?'

'After you come in.'

She struggled. 'I shouldn't.'

'I know.'

They searched each other's face, neither in any doubt of what was being proposed.

'You'll have to be quick,' she said.

'*You*'ll have to be quick. I could come right here on the sidewalk.'

'You kiss your boss's ass with that mouth?'

He smiled ruefully. 'And how.'

She got out and locked the car.

True to his word, Tom didn't waste time leading her through to the bedroom. Besides, he had a sneaking suspicion he hadn't made the bed before leaving for South Africa. Remembering he hadn't cleaned the kitchen for a while either, he turned to Ness the moment they got inside, and pressed her back against the front door with his mouth and hips.

His cell rang. 'Shit.'

He and Ness locked eyes, then she looked away, leaving it up to him. There was an LA number on the display that he didn't recognize. His hips still pressed against Ness, he answered it.

'Tom?'

The voice was a woman's, but very small and frightened – almost like she was about to cry. Tom couldn't identify it but got a sinking feeling. He took a step backwards. 'Yeah?' he said warily.

'It's Lucia.'

Tom felt all the breath stop right where it was in his lungs and windpipe. Nothing moved in his frozen system for a good five seconds while his mind fired with lightning speed. How had she got his number? Then he remembered giving it to that sleazeball club manager, thinking there wasn't a snowball's chance in Hell that he'd pass it on to her. People! Always coming through for you even when you wished they hadn't . . .

'Tom?'

He let his breath out. He didn't look at Ness – aware that she was staring at him. He turned his back to her and could almost feel her gaze harden.

'Yeah, what?' He knew he sounded unnecessarily harsh – but what the fuck was she calling him for?

'I think my sister just got killed in a plane crash.'

'Oh.'

He could hear she was trying not to cry, trying to hold things together, but the cynical part of him – the large cynical part of him – shouted about mindgames and manipulation. He hadn't heard about any plane crash! Did she even *have* a sister? She hadn't mentioned one. Although, of course, family and friends were hardly common conversational currency when you were in the middle of paying for sex in a Motel 6.

A noise from Lucia brought him back. It wasn't manipulative tears – it was the noise of her clearing her throat to try to sound more normal. That didn't exactly match his cynical profile, did it?

'Hold on.'

He crossed the room to the TV and surfed until he found shots of smoking wreckage.

The caption running along the bottom of the screen said the American Airlines 737 had gone down outside Tulsa, and that all seventy-eight passengers and crew were feared dead.

Tom glanced at Ness, who looked away from the TV to him.

'Tom? I'm sorry to call you but . . . can you find out for me? American won't say, and my mother . . .'

She tailed off and Tom listened to the taut silence.

226

'What's her name?'

'Candice Holmes. She was with her boyfriend, Carlo Alienti.'

He glanced at the phone display. 'You'll be at this number?'

'Yes.'

'I'll do what I can.'

'Thanks.'

Tom hung up and looked at the TV while he decided what to tell Ness.

'Another 737?' She gestured at the screen, and he realized she must think that the call had been from work. Relief washed over him.

'Yeah.'

They watched the pictures. The sound was muted, the shots of the wreckage interspersed with eye-witnesses waving their hands at the sky and with what looked like phone-cam footage of two distant blobs falling out of the air to disappear behind a barn and a galvanized-steel windmill. Then back to the smouldering crash site.

'They need me to work,' he lied.

She was silent for a long moment. So long that Tom turned to look at her. She was watching the TV but he saw a struggle on her face. 'What about the game?' she asked.

He turned his palms up in a brief but unmistakable gesture of can't-be-helped. 'I'm sorry.'

Suddenly she was smiling sexily, and slid round behind him, encircling his waist with her slender golden arms. Tom felt her breath at the base of his neck. 'I have to call the air-line,' he said. 'Do a bunch of things.'

It was a kiss-off but Ness was apparently made of sterner

stuff. Her hands brushed gently over his crotch. 'One little game?' She left a hand on his groin and pushed the other under his shirt, running her nails lightly across his ribs to his nipple, making him grunt. Lucia and her dead sister started to seem misty and minor as blood dropped out of his head so fast that all he could hear was a roaring like Niagara as it passed his ears.

He turned to kiss her, to touch her – but she withdrew and picked up her purse where she'd dropped it by the front door.

'Come on, Tom. One game. Then we can come back here and I'll take care of you.' Her eyes dropped to his jeans as she spoke. Then she raised them and he saw the tease lighting them up.

What little sense he had left sparked into anger. Anger at her for leading him by his dick, and anger at himself for being led.

And, for Tom, anger would always beat sex when it came to his own internal version of Rock, Paper, Scissors.

'Sorry,' he said.

As he had in the Karoo, he thought he saw an answering flash of anger in her eyes. Maybe she'd heard Lucia's small voice on the phone; maybe she knew he was lying. Too late to do anything about that now. If she'd heard, she'd heard. If she knew he was lying, she knew. He wasn't about to back-pedal and try to make it right with her.

Suddenly Ness just looked disappointed and he thought maybe he'd been wrong about the anger. He was no judge of emotions, especially in women.

'I'm sorry too,' she said.

'Why?'

'I shouldn't have pushed you. I know your job's important to you.' She opened the door and he joined her, putting a hand on the curve of her hip, holding her there.

'You're important to me, Ness.'

She looked away from him, and then at the floor. 'Am I?'

Tom knew he shouldn't say too much. No promises. No false expectations. He'd learned that anything he said when he had a hard-on was liable to come back to bite him in the ass.

Instead he took the safe option of bending to kiss her neck where it met her shoulder. The skin was flawless and soft and, for a fleeting moment, his blood tried to struggle into a U-turn to head south once more. He broke the contact, and let go of her.

She didn't move away from him immediately, which he figured was a good sign. Then she gave him a small, hurt smile over her shoulder, and hurried to her Lotus. He shut the door before she drove away, not wanting to indulge in the domesticity of waving her off.

*

With his NTSB badge number, Tom was quickly able to establish contact with the American Airlines family liaison team. 'I have two names I want to check off the record,' he told the flustered woman, who identified herself as Sandy Arbright. 'Candice Holmes and Carlo Alienti.'

'Hold, please,' said Sandy, but didn't put him on hold so he could hear her huffing and puffing through paperwork, then checking with colleagues about seat allocations. He got the impression that Sandy was more confused than he was about the crash.

'I don't see . . . umm . . . I don't see those names, sir.'

'Are you sure?'

'Umm . . .' Apparently Sandy was not sure.

'How are you spelling Candy?'

'Not Candy. Candice – C-A-N-D-I-C-E Holmes. That's H-O-L-M-E-S.'

That meant Lucia was Lucia Holmes, he thought idly. Unless she came from one of those fucked-up families where all the kids had different fathers and a dumb mother. But something told him not.

'Oh, Holmes!' said Sandy, pronouncing the *l* as if Tom was an idiot to have missed it. He bit his lip. He knew how these things worked. Sometimes you had to be nice to stupid people, which he found almost impossible. But, for Lucia's sake, he refrained from telling Sandy to fuck off back to blowing her boss between trips to the water-cooler, and agreed: 'Holmes. Yes.'

More rustling. More whispering. If Tom had been a panic-stricken, terrified, potentially bereaved relative he'd have driven to AA corporate HQ and personally shot Sandy's dopey head clean off her shoulders.

'Er, yes, I do have a Candice Holmes listed. Savannah to LA.'

Or not, thought Tom. Savannah to a field in Buttfuck, Oklahoma, at five hundred miles an hour.

He kept that feeling out of his voice when he asked after the boyfriend. Sandy, who had been thrown by Holmes, was beside herself with Alienti, especially as Tom was not a hundred per cent sure how to spell it.

'We have an Allen. A Marjorie Allen from Pittsburgh.'

Tom clenched his jaw as Sandy went through the passenger list as if it was a Sears catalogue.

'Oh, and a Jennifer-Jo Bonetti. That's Italian. Are you sure that's not it?'

'Alienti. Carlo Alienti. A man.'

'A man,' mused Sandy, and Tom almost screamed as he realized he'd just given her *carte blanche* to re-examine every man's name as a possible match for the boyfriend.

'Was he sitting in 22C?'

'How the fuck should I know?'

Sandy turned from dumb to frosty in one swift second. 'There's no need for attitude, sir. I'm just doing my job.'

'Well, do it better.'

There was a gasp of outrage and Sandy apparently turned to a colleague to complain about Tom. There was a muffled response – and then the unmistakable sound of her hanging up on him.

'Fuck!'

Tom hurled his phone against the wall – and wished he hadn't, even as it left his hand. He heard a crack as it hit and bounced across the floor in two pieces.

'*Shit. Fuck. Asshole!*'

His neighbour banged on the wall and he yelled, 'Up yours, Shaeffer!' at the stucco as he examined the phone.

He'd killed it.

*

Tom removed the Sim card and slipped it into his pocket. From his landline, he called the Sawmill in Santa Ana, without any great hope that they'd give him Lucia's number. He told them it was NTSB business but the woman on the phone sounded mightily bored by his so-called business, Lucia's alleged dead sister, and any further attempts he would ever make to wangle one of her dancers' personal numbers out of her. In some underused recess of reason in his mind, Tom couldn't blame her, but that didn't stop him swearing as he slammed the phone down and grabbed his car keys.

He stopped at the door and went back to put on his NTSB jacket, cap and badge. They gave him the right to demand information from multi-national corporations and government agencies. Fucked if he was going to let a sleazy strip joint off the hook.

Tom came off the Garden Grove freeway on Euclid and headed south. He took a left on to the road bordered by strip malls that became progressively more downmarket. Ralph's was a beacon of corporate success surrounded by a hundred Thai cafés, copy shops and pawnbrokers. He passed the Motel 6, which looked even sadder in daylight than it did in the dark, and swung into the parking lot of the Sawmill. It was at the back of the club – a clever ploy so that the men who went there were hidden from the road when they got out of their cars.

Tom noticed a dark blue '67 Thunderbird pull into the lot behind him. He tugged on his cap, checked his ID and got out of the Buick.

Swift, strong hands on his upper arms propelled him forward, making him stumble even while they held him up.

'Hey!' He tried to dig his heels into the pitted surface, but the two men who had him were strong and professional.

Even given the circumstances, Tom couldn't bring himself to yell, 'Help,' but he did yell, 'Fuck!' very loudly as he tried to twist away, and felt the side of his face explode in pain as something hit him. He didn't pass out but it took all the fight out of him in a second, and he could only stagger and drag between the men as they cuffed his hands behind him, then hurled him roughly into the trunk of the Thunderbird and slammed the lid.

23

RIDING IN THE TRUNK of a car was bad in lots of ways that Tom had never imagined it would be. For a start, it stank of gas, a smell that Tom had always quite liked, as he had those of dog food and garlic. But he'd tried dog food and it tasted like boiled garbage, and garlic was only okay in your food, not in anyone else's. In this concentration, when he couldn't just walk away, the smell of gas made him feel sick and dizzy. Although that sock in the jaw hadn't helped, he was pretty sure.

Tom felt around with his hands and feet and touched a plastic gas can behind his back. Great. He managed to manoeuvre it down to his feet, but the smell was barely less pervasive.

Then there was the comfort factor. Until you took the up-holstered seat out of a car and lay down with only a strip of thin felt between you and bare metal, you couldn't really appreciate how rough the ride was. He couldn't get comfort-able. There was a lump right in the middle of the trunk which could have been the bolt holding the spare tyre, and he didn't have enough room to move away from it completely. He could feel it now, digging into his hip.

Without visual warnings of sudden turns and stops so he

could brace himself, he was rolled back and forth like a pebble in a can, now with the top of his head pressed against the side of the car as they swung left, then thrown forward against the seat-backs as the driver braked, and banged against the lumpy metal of the lock and tail-light housings.

To distract himself, Tom tried to concentrate on where they were going – like people did in movies – but soon gave up. Who gave a shit anyway? He'd find out where they were taking him when they got there.

With his hands cuffed behind him, Tom fiddled with the trunk's lock but without a lever it was pointless. He managed to lift the thin felt lining but all he found were a couple of metal cavities that had probably once held the car's jack and toolkit. These guys were thorough. Or had lost their jack and toolkit. Either way it was bad news for Tom.

But the lights . . . In modern cars, the tail-light housings were sealed modular units but in older cars . . . Maybe there was something there.

In complete darkness, rolled and rocked by the vehicle's movement, Tom's fingers found the catch that released the left tail-light access hatch. He prised it off, and was faintly illuminated by the daylight filtering through the coloured plastic of the brake-light and indicator covers. The light was filtered again through the bulb surrounds, but he had enough to work by.

He could see now that the Thunderbird was a pretty rudimentary piece of assembly with gaping holes and flimsy wires. Even his shitty Buick had a more solid-looking back end. Thank God for low-tech cars.

Tom curled himself round so that his feet were against the brake-light assembly and his shoulders braced against the back of the rear seat. For the first time in his life, he wished he wasn't six two.

With a sharp movement, he kicked hard into the brake light, crunching the connectors and bulbs, and buckling the thin metal plate against the coloured plastic. His head was pressed up and against the seat as the car stopped. Tom prayed they weren't at their destination yet – prayed he'd get another chance at kicking out the light. He made a hurried pact with a God he didn't believe in . . . He heard a couple of muffled voices inside the car, but couldn't make out the words.

Lights changed or the road cleared, and the car lurched forward again, making Tom's knees bend as his feet pressed back against the rear of the trunk.

He uncrossed the mental fingers that had kept him vaguely honest in the eyes of non-God, and went back to work.

He shuffled away from the lights to get the maximum leverage and kicked again. This time the plate broke and cracked the glass. It sounded cacophonous to him and he held his breath. But the car didn't slow, and he didn't hear any surprised tones from the men up front.

He kicked again and yelped in pain. His foot had gone right through this time, smashing the brake light out, but the sharp edges of the plate – curved outwards by his assault – tore into his ankle and shin like a bear trap. Trying to pull his leg back only made the metal dig more deeply into his flesh.

A new wave of nausea washed over him and he swallowed. The last thing he needed in this trunk was a puddle of nice hot vomit.

Tom breathed hard. He peered down and saw that his All

Stars sneaker was now protruding from where the brake light used to be. If they were in traffic, surely someone would see it. Surely – having seen it – they'd report it. He hoped and hoped and tried to wiggle his foot around so that it might attract attention, but only his foot was outside the car. If his leg up to the knee was hanging out there, the chances of it being seen increased exponentially . . .

Gritting his teeth against the pain, Tom braced himself and shoved his leg further out of the car. The jagged metal sliced a red-hot groove up his shin almost to the knee, and the shattered plastic of the brake light ripped into his calf. Tom's head and back went cold and prickly with the pain, and he felt a clammy sweat break out on his forehead.

He lay there on his hands in the dark, one leg crooked against the back of the trunk, the other dangling bloodily out of the tail-light, his jaw aching and his ribs heaving. He felt pathetically small and weak, and wished someone would make all this go away. What a fucking baby.

He made a poor – and painful – effort to wave his injured leg around.

Nobody saw.

Nobody reported it.

Nobody came to his rescue.

*

'What the fuck is *this*?' The man's voice was bemused, angry – and unnervingly familiar. Tom blinked back to consciousness in gushing sunlight as the trunk lid rose. At first, he could see the men only as silhouettes, blinded as he was by the brilliance of daylight.

He remembered what he'd done and the nerves kicked in. The taller man leaned down into the trunk to look at how he had kicked through the tail-light. As he did, he shielded the sun so Tom could see him.

Mr Stanley. The Honolulu leg-shaker.

Fear gripped Tom like something physical, holding his throat shut in an iron fist, and clutching his chest.

'Fucking little shit! Look what he did to my car!'

Stanley punched him. Tom saw it coming and turned, but it still connected with his ear, making it ring like a fire bell. Then Stanley started to drag him out of the trunk, careless of the metal and plastic biting into his flesh.

Tom screamed as pain shot through his leg, panicked that Stanley might just keep pulling and twisting until the muscle was stripped clean off the bone and left behind in the trunk of the Thunderbird.

'Hold on.' That was the other man. Thank God for him, whoever he was.

Stanley let him go and stepped back. The other man leaned over him. He was older than Stanley, but wider in the shoulders. He had a shaven head and wore a dark blue suit with a pale blue tie. He peered at Tom's leg, then up at his face. 'What a goddamn mess,' he said, and grinned. Tom saw he had strange, sharp little yellow teeth that made him think of a weasel.

He stepped away again and Tom's fear rolled back that Stanley would be left to his own devices. But Stanley stood and glared at him while Tom felt a door of the car open and then shut. The Weasel came back with a tyre iron. So they were thorough, not careless. Somehow, having the answer to his earlier question failed to delight Tom.

The Weasel inserted the iron into the tear in the metal housing, and levered the edges away from Tom's leg. Tom bit his lip and groaned, but held as still as he could while the sharp metal worked back out of his flesh.

'You pull it out now?'

Tom nodded enthusiastically. He welcomed any non-interventionist policy now that those tin-can edges were out of the way. He pulled his leg slowly and carefully back inside the trunk, trying not to notice the amount of blood that had soaked his jeans from the knee down. He hissed as an errant movement made a fresh gouge in the top of his ankle, but finally he was free and lay panting with relief.

The Weasel reached in and grabbed his arm, and Stanley helped him pull Tom roughly over the tailgate, his ribs, hips and knees banging hard against the metal. He half fell into pale, sandy dust that immediately took him back to the Karoo, and from there it was only a half-synapse-fire from thinking of Pam and the others, screaming in a blaze that had been 'bound to happen one day'.

But it had happened *that* day.

And this was happening now.

And he didn't believe in coincidences.

The men were obviously waiting for him to get up, so he made the effort, holding on to the back of the Thunderbird, then sagging against it, resting his injured leg, his head hanging over his chest.

'What do you want?'

The Weasel smiled sharply. 'You'll find out.'

Tom wished he hadn't bothered asking. Wished he'd saved his energy and dignity, what little of both he had left.

Stanley grabbed a handful of his T-shirt and twisted it up

and under his chin so Tom had to look him in the eyes. He saw Stanley's desire to hurt him writ large there and, with his wrists still cuffed behind him, felt the vulnerability of his exposed abdomen and groin. He turned and brought his injured leg up reflexively in a weak gesture of protection. Stanley laughed and jerked him forward, making him walk.

Tom watched the barn approach with spiralling apprehension. This was the place where whatever was going to happen would happen. And he was limping towards it, complicit in his own fate.

He glanced around. Gum trees pressed over the barn, with scratchy yellow grass between them. Rattlesnake grass and low scrub. He could be anywhere between Santa Ana and Mexico. If he ran now they'd catch him before he got ten feet.

Having only just got used to the light, he was stopped dead by the darkness just inside the barn. Before his eyes could adjust, Stanley shoved him forward and he stumbled to his knees.

'Have a seat, Mr Patrick.' The Weasel was in control now, it seemed.

Tom saw a lightweight wooden chair, and sat in it. The Weasel slid a plastic tie around one of his wrists and fastened it to a strut at the back of the chair.

In the shadows he made out farm equipment. An old tractor and indeterminate bladed implements to hitch to it, their formerly bright-painted surfaces faded to dirty blues and dull reds. He could smell hay somewhere. How he knew it was hay, he had no idea. He couldn't remember ever having seen a bale of hay, but somewhere in his brain the smell of hay was stored and recognized.

The floor under his feet was dirt, just the wilderness cleared and built over with no concession to improvement.

Tom was almost embarrassed by the cliché it presented. He'd been kidnapped and was about to be interrogated or killed in a barn. It was so cheap Hollywood. Okay, a warehouse would have been worse, but once you realized a barn was just a warehouse for hicks, all the shame of predictability returned.

'Mr Patrick,' said the Weasel.

For a crazy second Tom wondered if there was any mileage in denying that he was Mr Patrick, but one brief look at Stanley convinced him otherwise: the man was just itching for an excuse to get physical with him.

'Mr Patrick?' said the Weasel again, with a little note of impatience.

'Yes, what?' said Tom, even more impatiently. He wanted to know what they wanted to know so he could start to make decisions about his own future. Or lack thereof.

The Weasel blinked in surprise and threw a sardonic glance at Stanley. 'Little feisty, ain't he?'

Stanley didn't laugh.

'I don't think he knows what feisty means,' said Tom, and instantly cursed his mouth to Hell and back. This was not the time or the place to make snappy remarks.

Stanley hissed through a tight jaw but the Weasel only shrugged.

'Mr Patrick, we wanted to make something clear to you.'

Tom nodded. He was on board.

'When you're asked to play cards, you play cards.'

Tom looked at him in utter surprise. 'This is about cards?'

'Of course.' The Weasel sounded put out. 'You mean

there's other reasons you would be thrown into the trunk of a car and tied to a chair?'

'No. I mean . . . No.'

'So, you get the picture? When you're told to play, you play.'

Tom's brain wanted very badly to say 'yes'. But something kept his mouth – usually the most reliably eager part of his entire anatomy – stubbornly shut. He'd thought this was about the *Pride of Maine*. If it was just about cards, how bad could it possibly get?

'You understand?' There was an edge to the Weasel's voice now, and Stanley's dark eyes burned into him.

Still his mouth stayed silent and his brain started to catch on. Who the hell were they to tell him what to do? So he'd agreed to play cards. So fucking what? Now he was un-agreeing. Let them find someone else to launder their ill-gotten gains.

Fuck 'em.

'No.'

Stanley gave an unexpected bark of laughter, and shot an amazed glance at the Weasel, who dipped his head towards Tom as if he couldn't have heard him right. 'No? Did you say no?'

'Yes.'

'Yes you mean yes? Or yes you said no?'

'Yes I said no.' He tried to shrug but it was difficult with his hands still tied to the chair. 'I have a lot on right now. I can't just stop my work to play cards whenever the mood takes you. Get someone else.'

The Weasel took a step back with surprise on his face. He and Stanley looked at each other.

'He has a lot on right now!' The Weasel was genuinely astonished.

'Do you know who you're fucking with?' It was the first time Stanley had spoken since the car, and Tom saw the warning look the Weasel shot his way.

'No. And I don't want to.'

Stanley reached for him but the Weasel's hand on his arm was enough to stop his forward motion.

'We know your *work*, Mr Patrick,' said the Weasel, and Tom had the impression he was choosing his words with care. 'We know you have your job to do.'

Tom nodded. Good.

'But we also know you're working on something . . . less official? Something that has nothing to do with your career at all. Some personal crusade, in fact, that would probably only harm your career if you were to continue to pursue it.'

How did they know? Why did they care? He didn't answer the Weasel, but glared at him. The man smiled back serenely.

'Surely it would be in all our best interests if *that* matter were sacrificed. Then you could play cards *and* do your . . . job.'

Anger flared in Tom. The Weasel had said 'job' as if it were in quotation marks, as if it meant nothing, was just a joke they all shared.

'Fuck you.'

It wasn't clever or funny, as Sergeant Konrad would no doubt have confirmed, but it conveyed the venom that Tom felt appropriate.

The Weasel sighed and jerked his head at Stanley, who stepped away into the shadows behind Tom.

Tom started to sweat in earnest. Having Stanley somewhere behind him was disturbing. Hell, it was downright scary. Tom figured he didn't have to admit that to anyone else but he might as well admit it to himself.

There was a brief shuffling sound in the darkness and then Stanley reappeared.

Tom let out his breath with an audible grunt of shock. 'Ness!'

She was cuffed, like he was, but also gagged with duct tape, and her grey eyes were wide with fear.

'Ness?' This time the word was a question and an apology on his lips. But her eyes didn't reassure him and his heart pounded against his ribs. A minute ago this was all about him. He hadn't even considered that Ness might be compromised if he didn't play poker. No wonder she'd tried so hard to convince him. He swallowed at the memory of her hands on him, and felt ashamed at his petulant response when he'd realized it was just a tease. It had been much more than that to her, apparently.

Now Stanley held her in front of him, glaring at Tom over her head.

'Don't hurt her.' He wanted the words to come out as a threat but they sounded like begging. What could he do if they did hurt her? What kind of threat did he represent, cuffed and bleeding in a barn in the middle of somewhere no one could hear them scream? Tom felt a dizzying sense that his life until this moment had been nothing but a sham – a make-believe life of job and sex and food and people – and that reality was finally rearing its ugly head. This was the only part of the whole thing that he really had to concentrate on; the only part that mattered.

'Oh, you like her, do you?' said Stanley, his eyes glittering dangerously.

Tom said nothing. He didn't want to give Stanley more ammunition than he already had.

'You like this?' Stanley gripped Ness's right breast hard, making her wince.

'And this?' He ran the same hand between her legs. She grunted and pulled away. Stanley followed her and back-handed her so hard that she fell heavily on her side. Tom tried to jerk to his feet but the Weasel shoved him down roughly.

Stanley panted over Ness, Tom seemingly forgotten. Ness was looking up at him as if she couldn't quite believe what was happening to her. Tom willed her to look at him but she held Stanley's gaze in what looked like surprise as much as fear. Tom could see the red mark around her right eye, and felt sick.

He didn't love her. He didn't think he loved her. But he couldn't just sit there and watch her suffer if it was in his power to stop it.

'I'll play.'

'What?' said the Weasel.

'I said I'll play. Anytime you want.'

'There, now. See how easy that was? Pity you couldn't have made that choice before . . .' He waved a hand vaguely at Ness.

Stanley hauled her to her feet. He'd knocked the duct tape off her mouth and it hung limply from her cheek. She was biting her lip in an attempt to keep from crying, but it wasn't working and tears were rolling down her face. 'Did I hurt you?' he asked mockingly. Before she could react he slapped her face, drawing blood from her lip and fresh tears from her eyes.

'Hey! You got what you wanted. Let her go!' Tom felt fury burning in his guts and knew that some of it was because he could do nothing. He was all talk in this situation.

Stanley ignored him and gripped Ness's bare upper arms so hard that, even in the half-dark of the barn, Tom could see the tanned skin going white under his fingers. Stanley lifted her nearly completely off the ground, looked intently into her face and hissed, 'Remember this.'

Then he let her go.

Ness staggered but stayed on her feet. Her hair had come loose and hung in wayward strands around her face. Her shoulders heaved with sobs, and blood mingled with tears dripped off her chin.

Stanley turned back to Tom and grinned. 'There's something I want you to remember too,' he said. He glanced at the Weasel. 'Stand him up straight.'

Tom wished he didn't know what was coming.

24

THE BITCH'S NAME WAS Annette Lim. She was twenty-five, pretty, smart, funny, caring and – in another time and place – would have been the perfect girl for Chuck Zhong to take home to meet his parents. Except she'd already gone home to meet Scott Redman's parents, and they'd decreed her to be most satisfactory. In fact, out of his son's earshot, Scott's father had been heard to say that Annette was too good for him.

Scott wasn't Vietnamese, but Annette's parents didn't require that he should be. They had been in America long enough to understand how love blurred national frontiers and stormed racial barriers.

Scott was a good guy. And a big guy. One of the things Annette loved most about him was that he was six foot five, weighed 265 pounds and could – and sometimes did – sling her over his shoulder like a caveman. For a young, liberated woman who'd graduated from MIT and was trying to play men at their own engineering game, cavegirl surrender was a fun and sexy game, so they played it often.

But right now, Annette and Scott were at an early showing of *Pulp Fiction* at the art-house theatre near Lee Park. Scott was a Samuel L. Jackson man and Annette had a weird little thing going for Christopher Walken that only Scott knew and was allowed to tease her about. So, despite the casual violence, it was the perfect date movie. They'd seen it before, of course, so they could neck in the Harvey Keitel scenes and not lose the thread.

After the movie Annette felt like dancing, so they went to Sugar Sugar, a diner with a dance-floor on Kennedy strip. Scott was big but graceful and the two of them twisted and jitterbugged until their entrées arrived. He had steak tartare, she had clam chowder, even though the clams must have been frozen. Unlike her parents and her parents' parents, Annette Lim had never been fishing, so she didn't know what she was missing.

Which is sometimes the perfect state of being.

As they got into his car, Scott asked her to come back to his place.

'I can't. I need to be in early tomorrow to finish up a report.'

'What report?'

'A technical report.' She smiled.

'Ooh, talk tech to me, baby.'

Annette giggled. Scott was a landscape gardener: what he knew about planes she could write on a grain of rice. 'Great steel bird in the sky has pretty shiny beads in its belly that might go on the fritz if me no go in early tomorrow.'

Scott stopped for a red and pulled her into his shoulder so he could nuzzle her hair, which smelt of vanilla. 'Or late tonight?' he suggested.

*

Nicholas Nicholas held up a bread doorstep. 'Peanut butter and jelly?'

They had started swapping food. Nicholas was a sucker for his Chinese dumplings, and the kiddies' comic-book lunch-pail he unashamedly carried always held food designed to make anyone feel patriotic, even a first-generation Chink who was being shafted by America in many and various ways, thought Chuck Zhong. He shook his head and pushed his lotus-seed buns across the desk at Nicholas. 'Have 'em. I'm not hungry.'

It was true. Since Jeff had started . . . sexually assaulting? Abusing? Orally raping? Chuck shifted uncomfortably, squeezing the vile words from his mind, not wanting them to settle, germinate and possibly blossom there so he could no longer ignore them.

Since Jeff had started . . . *messing* with him, he'd lost his appetite and subsequently weight. From being the first person in the Zhong family to appear well nourished, Chuck knew he now looked more like one of his stinking native cousins than a modern Chinese American who'd graduated top of his engineering class.

Chuck had washed his mouth out and done his teeth already tonight. He kept a toothbrush and paste in his uniform pocket for just that purpose. But the taste never completely left him. He knew it was psychosomatic; he knew it was impossible that, after the three long-weekend days when he didn't see Jeff, he should suddenly be aware of the taste of him in his mouth. But that was what happened. Chuck would be eating chilli dogs at the mall or shovelling pork and fried rice at the Lucky Eight Sunday buffet ($8.99 All You Can Eat!) when that salty bitterness would flood his mouth and he'd have to swallow the bile that had risen in his throat and pretend that something had gone down the wrong way.

Now Nicholas Nicholas grinned at him through the sweet white dough. 'You got AIDS or something, man? You skinny as an Af.'

'Fuck you, man.'

Nicholas's grin snapped off and he turned to the CCTV screens, dropping the bun on the desk, like he wouldn't touch it again. Chuck felt bad. He knew Nicholas meant well, but that AIDS crack – that was all he fucking needed planted in his brain. What if Jeff had given him AIDS? What if the weight loss was about that, not about his sudden disinterest in food?

Fuck.

He wanted to punch something or somebody. He wished it could be Jeff but he was afraid that if he stayed here that somebody would be Nicholas H. Nicholas.

He snatched up his flashlight.

'You doin' rounds again?'

'So?'

'I din't mean nothing, man,' Nicholas said defensively.

'I know. I fucking know. It's me, man. I'm fucked up.' It was as close as he could get to an apology when he felt so fiercely that none of this was his fault.

He banged open the security-office door and strode down the corridor, not even turning the flashlight on, daring the dark to mislead him.

He wanted out.

He had tried to get out.

After the second time, Chuck had waited until the man

250

with the gun had given him his cash, then said, 'I can't do it any more.'

'Sure you can.'

'I can't. They've tightened up security.'

'You *are* fucking security!'

The man had laughed meanly, his bad skin dimpling awkwardly. Chuck almost backed down but didn't. The thought of Jeff made him straighten his spine and keep his voice calm.

'I'm not doing it any more. There's a new guy. Nicholas. He drives a '99 Civic. He'll do it.'

The man had gripped his shirt-front so fast and so hard, Chuck never saw it coming. His feet lost proper contact with the ground and he stumbled, held up only by the man's fist and the tips of his own toes.

'You'll do it,' the man had said calmly. 'You'll do it or you'll watch your mother scream and sizzle in the deep-fat fryer of that greasy fucking hole they call a restaurant. I'll put her fucking face in there. By the time I get through with her she'll look like a fucking *won ton*, you slimy little Chink, you hear me?'

Chuck heard him.

Chuck could hear him again now, loud and clear, the words pounding in his skull, like a headache, making him feel queasy and watery-bowelled.

He crossed the production-line gantry without even glancing at the half-formed engines he'd wanted so much to build, to improve, to beautify with his first-generation brilliance.

The canteen was a blur, with thrumming vending machines spotlighting the curled sandwiches and sad fruit that was all that was ever left at night.

Then long dark corridors like tunnels with no light at the end of them. If this had been somebody else's life, Chuck would have laughed at the metaphor. This being his life, he never got close to cracking a smile.

There was a light on in Engineering.

Maybe Nicholas had come up for something. He must've used the front stairs, direct to Engineering. Chuck would have to chew him out for leaving the screens un-monitored. That was why they were called monitors, Lyle had told him redundantly when he'd started the job, what felt like a million years ago.

Chuck sighed. He already felt bad about telling Nicholas 'Fuck you' earlier tonight; he wouldn't say anything about the screens.

But it wasn't Nicholas in Engineering.

It was Annette Lim.

*

Annette had gathered all she needed for the report. Scott was waiting in the parking lot with the engine running and half a hard-on. She smiled to herself at the thought. She'd been a virgin until she was twenty-three. Scott had been her first and, the way they were going, he'd be her only. The thought didn't disappoint Annette: it made her feel lucky that she hadn't given it up for some dolt who wasn't worth it. She and Scott had tiptoed round the subject of marriage by comparing hypotheticals and commenting on the relationships of friends, families and celebrities. They both knew they were on the same page and Annette knew that it was only a matter of time before Scott asked her. Every time he

252

squeezed her hand, every time he went quiet and thoughtful, her heart skipped a beat. And even though it hadn't happened yet, she knew it would, so every time he failed to screw up the courage, it just added to her anticipation and secret store of happiness.

Sure, she earned more than he did but it didn't bother either of them. She'd worked hard to get this job, denied herself plenty to get through school with a 4.0 GPA. Her mother was a fiend for denying herself pleasure, and that had rubbed off on her only child. Annette was a poster girl for delayed gratification, and when she'd got the WAE job and met Scott the same week she'd moved to Texas, it had seemed that all the delaying was suddenly paying off big-time, gratification-wise.

Every time she came into the engineering office, she got a little thrill that sometimes brought a sheen to her eyes and made her nose tingle. She knew she had a long way to go before she was at the top of her profession, the way she'd been top of her MIT class, but she also knew that her characteristic diligence, coupled with real talent for the job, meant she wasn't lying to herself about getting to the top.

Annette occasionally lied to others about her abilities, but she never lied to herself. Her natural modesty dictated that any compliment paid was a compliment skilfully deflected, but it was also a compliment stored up and taken out later to be examined like a rare jewel. She had quite a collection.

But if Annette Lim had had a gun put to her head, she might finally have admitted that everything was not perfect with her life. The imperfection was tiny and probably inconsequential, but it niggled like a hangnail.

Someone messed with her stuff in the office.

Just a few days after she'd arrived someone had taken her tampons.

When Annette had gone into the single-stall ladies' room that she alone used, with the intention of getting a tampon from the machine on the wall, she'd found the floor awash and the toilet bowl bulging with white cotton wadding and blue string. She'd spent twenty minutes digging swollen, mushy tampons and plastic applicators out of the pan in a panic that at any moment one of the cleaning crew might appear and compound her humiliation.

The only other women who worked at WAE were Cindy and Jennifer in Reception, and they used the ladies' room near their desk downstairs.

Since then, she had found a postcard Scott had sent her from Vegas crumpled in the wastebasket, a coffee ring on a report she'd completed and left in her out-box, and she had almost suffered a fertility setback when a nut on her swivel chair had apparently worked loose.

The other engineers seemed to like her. Jennifer and Cindy seemed to like her. The other rookies, Neil Abbotsham and Jerry Gobereski, seemed to like her. But somebody didn't, that much was plain, and it gnawed at Annette's sense of well-being. She hadn't told anyone about it. She hadn't told Human Resources and she hadn't told Scott. Scott was a gentle man in every respect, but Annette knew he'd insist that she made a fuss about it, and she didn't want to do that. She'd never done that. She'd experienced male jealousy before in high-school physics classes and at MIT, and she knew that the best thing to do was to keep her head down and wait for it to pass. Things always did.

Annette looked up as someone opened the door of her office. 'Oh,' she said. 'Hi.'

The guy gave her the creeps but she tried not to show it. After all, there was no reason for the security guard, whose name-tag boasted the very un-Chinese name of Chuck, to wish her ill. She just didn't trust security guards the way some people didn't trust circus clowns. And this particular guard just had something about him. Something that made her wary.

Chuck said nothing, just blinked at her. He opened the door wider and looked around the office as if checking for enemies.

Annette stood up, keen to be out of there and already thinking of Scott waiting for her in the car. She moved towards the door.

Chuck saw the papers in her arms. 'Taking work home?'

Annette was relieved to hear a normal question come from the guard. She smiled ruefully. 'You know how it is.'

'No. I don't.'

She was surprised by his slightly hostile reaction to what was, after all, just by-the-numbers small-talk. Screw him, she thought, with an unaccustomed little wave of anger. He was a security guard: he should be making her feel secure, not uncomfortable.

'Well,' she said, 'good night.'

Chuck stepped smoothly between her and the doorway. Annette felt an electrical flicker of disquiet pass up her spine and burn on her ears. She met his eyes in surprise, then ducked her head submissively low. She had not come this far in a man's world without knowing when to make concessions, and her mind raced as she made this one.

What did he want? Why was he doing this? Was he the one who didn't like her? The answer seemed suddenly clear. But why? The first surge of confused panic gave way to more sensible flashes: Scott was in the car. She was not alone. He wouldn't dare do anything. She would tell. In the morning she would tell. She would get him fired. She would feel bad, but she would get him fired. This was too much.

With her anger came strength.

'Excuse me, please,' she said, surprising herself with the steadiness of her voice.

Chuck said nothing. He could see the report was on rudder-servo assemblies. He'd done his senior-year final paper on rudder servos: 'Rudder Valves – Faults, Failures and Fine Tuning'. Dr D'Agostino had told him he loved the alliteration. He'd got an A–.

'Rudder-valve assemblies,' he said mildly.

Annette felt a rush of relief. He wasn't being threatening: he wanted to talk shop. The guy just had no social skills, was all. She could handle that: she'd been surrounded by science geeks with no social skills since graduating from high school. Relief washed over her, like a cool breeze on a hot day.

'Yes.' She smiled up at him.

And he hit her with Neil Abbotsham's backstroke trophy.

25

SAFETY – WHEN THEY'D both expected to be dead at several points during the day – brought more tears to Ness and cold anger to Tom. Mostly at himself. His inability to protect Ness filled him with frustration and made him long stupidly for a big gun and a second chance.

He had put her in his perennially unmade bed and sat with her as she sobbed. She flinched when he touched her shoulder, and he didn't blame her. He was relieved when she slept so that he didn't have to pretend to be strong for her.

What a fucking joke *that* was.

She had been the strong one. He had leaned on her narrow shoulders as they stumbled away from the ware-house-for-hicks, his balls protesting at every footfall; she had sat him down beside the two-lane blacktop and flagged down a truck; she had concocted the story of carjackers and escape to account for their injuries; she had kept it together for both of them.

His only contribution had been a pained expression of thanks for the ride, and the donation of a quarter so they could call a cab to the gas station off the 710 freeway, where the cheerfully incurious trucker had left them.

At the hospital he'd been steadfastly ignored as his leg bled steadily on to the floor, until someone who looked like an angry janitor fetched a junior doctor to stitch him up.

Dr Joi was young and pretty but her name was deceptive. She had closed his wounds with all the finesse typically shown by a Civil War field surgeon. If Ness hadn't been with him, Tom would've left halfway through the twenty-eight clumsy stitches. Or cried. Possibly both.

Now he lowered himself gingerly to the couch and tried not to think about the shambles his life had become. He felt for the remote under his right buttock and clicked on the TV. The plane in Oklahoma, smoking in the darkness now, reminded him cruelly that Ness wasn't the only woman he'd let down today.

And Chris Stern's widow? a mean little voice in his head taunted. Tom was annoyed at the voice. He hadn't let Vee down today, for Chrissakes! Letting Vee down was just an ongoing situation that would probably never be resolved.

When the mean little voice tried to bring Sylvia Alvarez into it, Tom rebelled and rolled off the couch with a wince.

It was three a.m., six a.m. in DC. He picked up his land-line phone and thumbed through a barely used address book. Sometimes old technology was the best.

He found the number he wanted scrawled in pencil in a margin. He hadn't used it in a long while but he punched it into the handset now before he could think too hard about it.

To his relief, Kitty was awake. She told him that Lenny Munro was lead on Oklahoma.

'Great. Just what I needed.'

'Sorry, Tom.'

'Ah, fuck it.'

'You okay? It's, like, three a.m. there.'

'Yeah, I'm fine. Can't sleep.'

'You should take a pill or something.'

'Has that dick got a prelim cause?'

'Gee, Tom, it's only sixteen hours old!'

Was it really only sixteen hours? Lucia's call seemed like a hundred years ago.

'Off the record.'

'Off the record, it's only sixteen hours old.' Kitty lowered her voice: 'You know I'd tell you.'

'Thanks.' He sighed. 'You got any jobs lined up for me? Pete's car sprung an oil leak? A grease fire at McDonald's?'

'Tom . . .'

'Figures.'

'Are you okay?'

He hated the note of concern in her voice. 'Fucking great. Never better.'

Again the silence.

'Thanks, Kitty.'

''Bye, Tom.'

Tom hung up feeling worse than he'd felt before he called. He would have swallowed what was left of his pride and called Munro anyway, if he'd thought for one second it would do any good. He wondered how long Lucia had waited for him – how long she had trusted he'd come through for her – before she'd given up and started calling the helpline herself, dealing with Sandy.

By now, he thought, Lucia must know one way or another. He hoped for the best for her – and feared the worst.

He flicked through the channels until he found a

documentary on whales and watched humpbacks migrate, hoping it would help his mind stop picking relentlessly over the events of the day.

Ness had seen him weak. He hadn't been able to help her or himself. He'd made empty threats of outlandish vengeance. He went hot as he thought of the desperation and helplessness that had forced them from him.

The whales had swum all the way from the South Pacific to northern California, dodging orcas all the way, before Tom cleared the self-pity and emerged at the brutal remembrance that he wasn't that good at poker.

And if he wasn't that good at poker why did they care so much if he played?

Surely they had a dozen other players of his calibre who would bite their arms off to earn money at their dissolute hobby.

Why him? Why threaten *him*? What was in it for them? What would make it worth their while to kidnap a federal officer and rough him up?

Then there was the Oklahoma crash. Another 737. Another faulty fan disc? Lenny Munro on lead was going to make it almost impossible for him to find out. Would Pete feed him information? Would Kitty? He remembered her tongue in his mouth and wondered how much leverage that still gave him. If any. Sex was a volatile currency.

Sex led him back to Ness. She knew Stanley – she'd told him way back while he watched butter glisten on her chin. She knew him, but he'd still hit her. Why?

Questions spun pointlessly in his tired mind as the humpbacks completed their journey, then turned and headed south again – as if any of them knew what the hell they were doing.

*

The throbbing of Tom's leg roused him twenty minutes after he'd fallen into a fitful sleep on the couch. He woke thinking of Lucia, wondering if she'd gone to Oklahoma, whether her family were with her, whether Candice and Carlo had been found, whole or in the little shreds of road-kill meat he had seen at crash sites, identifiable only by DNA testing. Was Lucia giving blood at this very moment to discover which dribble of ground beef was her sister? Or had Candice worn a watch bought for a birthday? A pendant with an inscription? A bridge from a Savannah dentist who'd be woken to check his records?

Not for the first time, Tom wondered how he'd be identified if he met a sudden, dismembering death. It always depressed him to think that, unless he somehow stayed united with his credit card, there wasn't much to mark him out from the crowd. Cheap watch, no wedding ring, all his own teeth. He had a short white scar beside his left eye – a humiliating reminder of crashing his car while he was in the middle of his driving test – and he'd broken his leg in two places playing basketball in college, so he supposed someone somewhere might still have the X-rays. He hoped so. He doubted his appendectomy scar would make him an instantly recognizable corpse.

Tom wished he could make amends; wished there was something he could do for Lucia and her family. He toyed briefly with the idea of asking Pete to send him to Tulsa to help with the investigation but knew he'd be as welcome there as a red-headed stepchild.

New TV pictures had come in from Oklahoma and Tom rolled himself upright to see them properly aligned.

The plane had gouged a brutal crater in a ripe corn crop. What hadn't been pulverized or driven into the Oklahoma soil hulked and smoked like a truculent teenager.

The high corn masked any view of the ground around the wreckage and he felt a grudging nudge of sympathy for Lenny Munro. The site was a bitch. You wouldn't be able to see ten feet through the corn; agents would have to walk between the tall rows, marking debris, flagging body parts, charting mayhem. Investigators would only ever be able to get a proper look at the pattern of the crash from a helicopter, and from carefully gridded maps that would take days to complete.

Even so, a tingle ran up his neck and the backs of his ears prickled with realization. From this new angle, he didn't need a map or a close-up to see that Flight 823 had suffered at least one major breach where the fuselage joined the leading edge of the starboard wing.

In a sudden motion that made him wince as his feet hit the floor, Tom moved to his desk and impatiently jabbed his computer into life.

He suppressed the guilty image of Ness crying, silver tape hanging from her bruised cheek, as he ran through his favourites – an eclectic mix that included NTSB.gov, PokerStars.com and Slutz.net.

The NTSB site drily informed him that the crash of Flight 823 was already under investigation. Standard stuff.

Slutz.net told him that 36DD Suzy wanted to suck him dry. Standard stuff.

The Boeing website was apparently ignorant of the loss of Flight 823. Standard stuff.

Nothing.

Out of habit, he hit the next site on his bookmarks bar.

The WAE homepage was its standard tedious self – but for one black-outlined box containing a snippet of news.

The WAE family is sad to announce the death of one of its engineers. Recent recruit Annette Lim, 25, was an asset to the company with a promising future and will be sorely missed by friends and colleagues at our Irving, Tx, plant.

Vaguely interested, Tom Googled Annette Lim and sat up straight in his seat, wincing at the jab of pain from his balls, but suddenly very far from self-pity.

From *Irving Online*:

AP – A 25-year-old woman was found dead Friday at the WAE plant in Irving, Texas.

Irving City Police Detective Ronaldo Suarez said engineer Annette Lim had extensive head injuries and was already deceased when paramedics arrived at the plant, which makes airplane parts, most notably the engines for Boeing 737s.

Det. Suarez added: 'We have a weapon and we have a suspect in custody. He is a Chinese-American male who works as a security guard at the WAE plant. He was arrested at the scene and is currently under police guard in hospital.'

Tom's eyes dropped to the photo of Annette Lim. No wonder the site had run it – she was a babe. Had been a babe.

Oh, what the hell – for all the interaction Tom was going to have with her, Annette Lim was still a babe and now would be for ever. He had always been in favour of leaving a good-looking corpse.

He drummed his fingers on the desk, staring at Annette Lim.

WAE. His gut told him there was a connection although he couldn't yet see it.

He got up and stood awkwardly at the doorway to his bedroom, resting his right leg, and listened to Ness breathe gently.

He looked at the luminous dial on his alarm clock: 04:27.

By 04:35 Tom was in a cab on his way to LAX.

*

Unlike Tom Patrick, Halo Jackson had some friends. And when his cell phone rang at five thirty, waking Vee despite the speed of his reaction, Halo seriously thought that, unless one of those friends was in dire need, he would have to kill the caller.

He was somehow unsurprised to hear Tom Patrick's voice.

'Halo?'

'Yes! What?' Halo muttered, as angrily and as quietly as he could.

'Can you get me that cheap ticket to Irving?'

'It's half past five in the morning!'

'Sorry,' said Tom, not sounding it. 'So, can you get me a ticket or not?'

'*Now*?'

'Yes.'

'No!'

Halo wished his cell was an old-fashioned phone so he could slam it down on Tom instead of just digging his thumb unsatisfyingly into the red disconnect key.

'Who was that?' Vee rolled into his side.

'Tom Patrick.'

Vee's silence reminded him of why they knew Tom Patrick – and *that* reminded him that he was in bed with the widow of his best friend.

'About Chris?' Vee had remembered it too.

Halo was about to say, 'No,' when the penny dropped. The sudden jolt out of sleep had left him without awareness of anything but his own name and the warmth of Vee's smooth thigh alongside his. Now he also remembered the 737 crash yesterday: 737 engines were made by WAE. In Irving, Texas.

'Shit,' he said, and groped for his cell phone again in the darkness.

26

CHUCK ZHONG'S PARENTS visited him every day, even though he wished they wouldn't. His tentative grasp on their native language and their confusion and dismay over what he was supposed to have done were added burdens he could really have lived without right now.

At the arraignment they'd sat clutching each other's hands with identical looks of baffled incomprehension on their faces – like someone had ordered a number 562 at the Lucky Eight.

He knew they wanted him to look at them, wanted him to tell them what was happening. But he couldn't do it. Couldn't meet their eyes; couldn't explain. He could barely comprehend that he had killed Annette Lim. It seemed so far-fetched. Not like something he would – could – ever do.

Every time he thought about it, he would get to the point where he had picked up the swimming trophy and swung it at her face, and laugh. Just laugh. It couldn't be real, could it? That he had hit her – 'multiple times', they called it – then looped his belt around his own neck and tried to hang himself from the doorknob.

Laughable.

Someone told him that Nicholas Nicholas had

resuscitated him, which explained the faint taste of lotus-seed buns that Chuck had had on his lips when he had finally come back to full consciousness in the emergency room.

It had added to the surreal feeling of utter disbelief.

But as the days passed, the nightmare remained unbroken by a new morning, and Chuck started to realize that his life was effectively over. Quite possibly literally over, given Texas's jab-happy attitude to lethal injection. It was a terrible dark heaviness that left him cold and sweaty and fluttery with panic at regular intervals. He tried not to think about it but it was everywhere, all the time.

In hospital he'd been questioned by the grossly fat Detective Suarez, who was smart and had a knack of un-settling Chuck, even while Chuck feigned memory-loss, PTSD and – as a last resort – sleep.

'You a virgin?' barked Suarez.

'No!' It was the first question he'd answered truthfully since Suarez had arrived. Damn him!

'Anyone vouch for that?'

Chuck blushed and gave him Verity's name. Suarez looked at him with barely disguised amusement, as if the thought of someone like Chuck screwing someone named Verity only proved his virginity point for him. Chuck felt a flash of anger. He wanted to tell Suarez just exactly how and when he'd had sex with Verity Stringer; that *she*'d made the first move on *him*; that they'd once done it in the baseball dugout after he'd taken a catch in the outfield that had made him wish time could stand still; that *he*'d broken up with *her* – admittedly getting in just under the wire, but still.

Fuck this fat Mex.

'But you were hot for that girl Annette, right?'

'No. I need a doctor. Can you call a doctor? I don't feel so good.'

Suarez ignored that. 'Gimme a break. I've seen pictures. Man, she was even a hot *corpse*. You were hot for her and she brushed you off.'

'No.'

'What's wrong? You queer?' yelled Suarez.

Chuck winced and flushed. 'No!' He shifted uncomfortably and wished Suarez would shut the hell up.

'So why'd you beat her brains out through her nose, then?'

Chuck bit his lip. He knew why he'd beaten Annette Lim's brains out. In his own head he could grasp the logic of it – could sympathize with the way he'd been backed into a corner and then squeezed there, first by the Lucky Eight, then by Human Resources, then by the man with the gun and then, most humiliatingly, by Jeff. He'd been squeezed until he'd just . . . popped.

The thought of how his life had spiralled away from him made Chuck feel dizzy and, with a wave of nausea, he realized he'd lashed out at the one person who least deserved his fury. If he'd killed Jeff or the man with bad skin who'd made him piss his pants in terror, he could have pleaded his own case with a somewhat clear conscience. But killing Annette Lim was an act of pointless knee-jerk petulance that Chuck could not justify, even to himself.

That was when he started to cry.

Detective Ronaldo Suarez smiled. He loved this bit. The bit where they broke down and confessed. It was the only part of his job that was ever remotely like *NYPD Blue*. He was never likely to chase down a suspect, but sitting in a chair watching one cry suited him just fine; he knew his limitations.

But Chuck Zhong knew his limitations too. He knew that Suarez would eventually get what he wanted out of him. But he was also smart, and not so wrapped up in the nightmare that he didn't know that that gave him a certain amount of leverage. Sure, he'd killed Annette Lim – there was no getting away from that now – but the reason he'd finally snapped was a lot more interesting than the age-old one of pretty girl rejecting dumb boy.

Chuck's thoughts were a little formless, but somewhere through the mist in his mind he caught tantalizing glimpses of Jeff being raped in the showers while he awaited trial for sexual assault, and of the man with the gun pissing his *own* pants, as vaguely drawn cops worked him over.

In his current ice-cold position, these images warmed him a little. More than that, with his world, his life and his self-respect stripped from him, his dreams were all he had left to call his own.

So he stopped answering Suarez's increasingly loud questions and rang his bell until a nurse came and hustled the fat detective out, like a bee bothering a bear away from honey.

Then Chuck spoke to his court-appointed public defender – a cherubic-looking man of sixty – and asked about a deal.

27

TEXAS WAS HOT. Tom had thought the Karoo was hot, but he'd been wrong. Texas was like a griddle underfoot, with cartoonish waves of shimmering air rising above the ground. His All Stars actually stuck to the sidewalk, making an embarrassing *schwick-schwick-schwick* as he walked up to the glass doors of the City of Irving Police Department.

Inside, the air-con hit him like a bucket of iced water and within seconds he was shivering.

'Detective Suarez?'

The desk sergeant raised his eyebrows without looking up from his paperwork. 'He's busy.'

'Yeah, I know. I may have some information on his case.'

The desk sergeant peered at him now, blatantly sizing Tom up, from his sweat-dampened hair to his melting sneakers, then finally resting wearily on the NTSB badge in Tom's hand. 'You steal that?'

Tom was too sapped to retaliate. 'No.'

The desk sergeant sighed and jerked his head at a row of plastic chairs. 'Take a seat.'

The desk sergeant did nothing to prepare Tom for Ronaldo

Suarez. And Tom thought he was a man who really needed some kind of advance warning: maybe a lackey running ahead of him with a red flag.

Suarez weighed 317 pounds. He wasn't tall and he wasn't muscled, just obscenely fat. His big round face was topped with a dark crew-cut, and contained black eyes that glittered in slits between his low brows and his high, fat-filled cheeks, making him look as much Chinese as Latino. His nose and mouth were corralled between those cheeks and several chins that bounced on a blue shirt the size of a Texas sky.

Despite his size, Suarez bustled through the double doors at speed, glanced at the desk sergeant for directions and stuck out a giant hand for Tom's to get lost in. 'Detective Suarez,' he said, looking Tom square in the eyes, and every first impression Tom had been gathering was blown away by the sharp intelligence in them. 'How can I help you, Mr Patrick?'

'Maybe I can help you.'

'Well, that would be a nice change.' Suarez grinned at him, showing what looked like milk teeth in his broad head. 'Come with me.'

Tom followed him at speed back through the double doors and past dozens of cramped cubicles separated from each other by the flimsiest of frosted-plastic partitions.

Suarez's cubicle made no concession to his bulk. It was the same size as the others, with the same-sized chair, which he lowered himself into with a sharp hydraulic exhalation. 'Pull up a seat.' He gestured at an empty cubicle across the aisle and Tom grabbed the back of a chair and rolled it opposite the detective. When he sat down, their knees were almost touching.

'So, what do you know, Mr Patrick?'

'This Annette Lim? Who's the guy you've got in custody?'

'Kid named Chuck Zhong. Security guard at WAE.'

'Do you know why he killed her?'

'Not yet.'

'What's he said?'

'Not much. He's only just gone down to Hutchins from the hospital. On suicide watch. Tried to hang himself after he did it. Another guard found him and CPR'd the shit out of the guy. That's why he's not downstairs right now. I've been allowed limited access so far and he's not talking, but I was going over again later to have another crack. So, Mr Patrick, when do we get to the bit where you help me?'

Tom grinned. He liked the direct approach and had a gut feeling that he could trust Suarez. He stood up and rolled his chair back across the aisle. 'You want to grab a bite?'

'You buying?'

'If I must.'

*

For a fat man, Suarez ate very little. Tom wolfed an eighteen-inch pizza while the other man poked at a chicken salad.

'Diet,' he explained needlessly.

'They don't work,' said Tom. 'When you start restricting food intake, the body goes into a protective mode that slows the metabolism to preserve every calorie.'

Suarez looked at him warily. 'Are you shitting me?'

'I saw it on the Learning Channel.'

'Fuck this, then,' said Suarez, and flapped his hand at a

272

waiter. 'Bring me a goddamn bowl of chilli. And fries.'

As they ate, Tom told him about the *Pride of Maine*, about South Africa, about the fan disc and the flange bolts, about the paperwork pointing back to WAE. 'And now this,' he finished, dropping sugar into his black coffee.

'You think it's connected?'

Tom shrugged.

'Seems like a long shot,' said Suarez. 'She was a pretty girl – it may just have been a sex thing.'

'We won't know until your suspect starts talking.'

Suarez sipped his coffee with surprising delicacy. 'And then what?'

'If it's connected, you've got motive and we share information. If it's not, you just had a rare experience.'

'Oh, yeah?' said Suarez. 'What's that?'

'A free lunch.'

*

'My man wants to make a deal.'

They'd hardly got back through the door of the Irving station house.

Suarez looked surprised, then glanced at Tom, who raised his eyebrows hopefully.

The old, baby-faced lawyer Charles (never Charlie) Lumsden had been around too long to play games. If Chuck Zhong wanted to make a deal, Suarez knew that meant there was a deal to be made. He led both men into an interview room cluttered with McDonald's debris, which smelt, appropriately enough, of old fries.

Lumsden put his tatty briefcase on the table but none of

them sat down. 'He'll confess to killing the girl but claims temporary insanity.'

Suarez squeaked out a snort of disdain. 'Yeah, I know temporary insanity. Disappears as soon as you zip up.'

Lumsden came nowhere near the bait. 'He says he was being blackmailed by a colleague.'

'Why?'

'He was stealing from the plant.'

'Stealing what?' Tom asked, ignoring Suarez's slightly territorial glance.

'Nothing much,' said Lumsden. 'Nothing of value.'

'Then what's the big deal? Bit of blackmail can't have been enough to drive him crazy,' said Suarez.

'Seems this colleague was sexually assaulting my client in return for his silence.'

'Sexually assaulting?' Suarez plainly needed more.

'He was being forced to fellate him,' said Lumsden, stiffly.

There was a short, grease-scented silence while they all grappled with the unwanted mental image.

Tom recovered first. 'For stealing nothing of value? Bullshit!'

'My client has an aeronautical-engineering degree. It seems he had expected to get a job with WAE in a more illustrious capacity. Any allegation of theft – however small – would mean an end to his dreams.'

Tom made a face. 'And blowing some guy wouldn't? Sounds like it'd be the end of any dream *I* ever had!'

'Anyway,' said Suarez, 'how come he takes it out on the girl? How does she fit in?'

Lumsden sighed. 'Apparently he feels she filled the job that was meant for him.'

'Now that's what I call motive!' Suarez said, with happy satisfaction. 'Who gives a shit about who blows who, or why? I got him just on that!'

'That's true,' said Lumsden. 'But that's where the deal comes in. In return for consideration . . . Mr Zhong feels that he may be able to help expose a bigger picture.'

'Of?'

'It seems the thefts from the plant were to order, and had been ongoing for quite some time. Years.'

'Theft of what?' Tom butted in again impatiently.

Lumsden looked uncertain, as if he was suddenly worried the cards he held might not take the pot after all.

He cleared his throat tightly. 'Paperwork.'

Suarez threw up his arms and almost laughed. 'You've got to be kidding me! He wants a deal on a cold-blooded murder and all he's got to offer in return is fucking *paperwork*?' He drew breath to pour further scorn on the deal, then stopped abruptly and looked at Tom, whose eyes had suddenly become quite feral, like those of a wildcat that's spotted its prey.

'Paperwork,' said Tom, softly.

*

While Suarez and Tom were following Lumsden's three-year-old Mazda towards Dallas and Chuck Zhong, that same Chuck Zhong was being summoned from his cell.

'Zhong. Visitor.' The guard pronounced it 'Zong'. Chuck was used to it. He got up with a sigh and went to meet his parents.

But it wasn't his parents.

It was the man with the gun and the bad skin. He was sitting on the other side of the polycarbonate barrier on the nasty hard-backed chairs they provided – like visitors deserved punishing, too, by association.

Of course, he didn't have a gun right now, but Chuck still stopped dead and stared when he saw him. The guard gave him a nudge between the shoulder-blades to get him going again.

Chuck felt goose-bumps flare on his chilled skin as he sat down. It took him a half a minute to get up the guts to look the man in the eyes and pick up the phone.

The man slowly picked up his phone but said nothing.

'Hi,' Chuck said stupidly, like they were buds.

The man's eyes were dark and cold.

'I wanted to show you an old friend,' he said.

'Sure,' said Chuck, nervously – as if the guy needed his permission.

Without looking away from Chuck, the man reached into his pocket and brought out a photograph. He pressed it against the barrier with his big hand and Chuck cocked his head to look at it.

For a second he couldn't quite make it out.

When he did, he felt his bladder convulse and struggled against the urge to piss himself again.

The photo was of Lyle – Lyle of the Suzuki 4×4; Lyle who had serviced Jeff Bukelo before him; Lyle who'd almost cried when he'd lost his job.

Not to mention his life.

Lyle was naked in the picture. Naked and bloody from the jagged barbed wire that dug into his flesh as it bound his

276

wrists together, his arms to his torso, his knees and ankles to each other.

There was a bloody pulp where his penis had once been and Chuck felt a sick pull to explore with his eyes where it might be now . . .

'He had a big mouth,' said the man, and Chuck had the answer to any question he might have had.

And that's why, by the time Tom Patrick, Charles Lumsden and Ronaldo Suarez reached the TDJC facility at Hutchins, Dallas, the deal was already dead.

28

JEFF BUKELO LOOKED at Ronaldo Suarez and felt superior. It wasn't a rare feeling for him, but usually he felt superior because of the power he wielded, like a stick, over others: his mousy wife, his two cowed children, his security-booth colleagues. But Suarez made Jeff feel superior because he was much, much fatter than him.

Jeff was a good size himself, with a beer gut that spilled over his work pants, but he always told himself that his weight helped him to dominate others, which it pretty much did. But this cop was a fucking barrel of fat, and that made Jeff feel pretty damned good about his own relatively svelte figure.

Of course, he'd have felt even better about it if the cop hadn't brought along a sidekick, who was as thin as a god-damned whip, but you couldn't have everything in life – nice though that might have been.

Jeff appraised Suarez – and the other one whose name he'd already forgotten. His piggy little eyes shone with low cunning. He figured he was ahead of this particular game. He could smell desperation on the detective.

Suarez hit play on a bulky old police DVD and Jeff watched Lyle's head bobbing in his lap.

'Recognize THIS?'

Jeff saw the slim man blink defensively. Seemed Suarez's interview technique was to batter a suspect into submission with sheer volume.

He shrugged. 'Jealous?'

'Yeah,' the fat man said unexpectedly, 'I wish my wife was that good.'

'So? Divorce her.'

'What say we ignore the sexual-assault charge and you tell us WHAT they were stealing and WHO FOR?'

Jeff jabbed a forefinger at the television. 'I already got my pay docked for that!'

'BIG FUCKING DEAL!' shouted Suarez. 'I'll put you in a cage full of perverts so fast you won't know if you got your pay docked or your GODDAMNED TAIL!'

Jeff glanced at the whip but the man just watched him steadily through lazy green eyes. It gave Jeff a little twinge of irritation that this guy never spoke. What was this? Bad Cop, Possibly-Even-Worse Cop? Fuck 'em both.

'I don't give a shit.' He waved a finger at the screen. 'That there is consenting between two adults. Lyle says anything different and he's a fucking lying little queer.'

'What about Chuck Zhong? Is he a lying little queer too? Huh?'

'I never touched him.'

'That's not what he says.'

'Then, yeah, he's a lying little queer too. You got evidence? You got another *tape*? Then go fuck yourself. Both of you.'

The slim man stood up slowly and Jeff turned his attention to him. 'Okay, here we go,' he drawled. 'Loud cop, dumb cop. I get it.'

The thin man barely looked at him. Instead he took a pad of Post-its from his pocket and peeled one off. Jeff's eyes found the camera in the corner of the room bare seconds before the man reached up and covered the lens.

Jeff swallowed hard, suddenly not so sure he'd played this quite right.

The man wandered over to him, seemingly without focus, then punched him so hard in the nose that he fell backwards off the metal chair with a loud bang.

Jeff Bukelo's size had generally spared him the indignity of being punched in the nose. He couldn't remember the last time it had happened and for that he was suddenly very grateful. It hurt like a motherfucker.

Before he could properly appreciate that, the thin man grabbed him by the sideburns and yanked his head round to watch the TV. Jeff yelped and, in passing, caught a disturbing look from Suarez, which made it plain that he wasn't going to come to his aid. He wasn't going to stop the assault; wasn't going to play Good Cop.

'You think your wife'd like to see that tape, Jeff? You think your kids would? Little Marlee and Jeff Junior? You think "consenting adults" is gonna cut it for them? *Do you*?' The man shook Jeff by the chops, making him howl.

'I'll sue you, you sonofawhore! I'll see you kicked off the fucking force for this!'

The slim man started laughing and Suarez joined in.

'Oh, yeah?' said the man gripping Jeff Bukelo's face. 'You got a *tape*?'

29

NICHOLAS NICHOLAS SHOWED Suarez and Tom to the engineering office where Annette Lim had been killed.

'Shouldn't you be at home?' said Suarez, not shouting.

Nicholas shrugged. 'I had a few days off. Better to work, I think.' He frowned around the office from the doorway.

Tom spoke to Nicholas without looking at him: 'What's your middle name?'

'Hudson.'

Tom ducked low under the police tape stretched across the doorway. 'Ah, well, two out of three ain't bad.'

Nicholas Nicholas smiled a little.

Suarez struggled to bend double under the tape but couldn't make it. 'Fuck.'

'You want I should cut that for you, Detective?'

'Nah. I looked round before they taped it off. Let the fucking limbo kid have his turn.'

As he had in a heat-hazed half-barn half a world away from Irving, Texas, Tom skirted his objective as if a direct approach might scare it off. He'd seen it the moment Nicholas opened the door – the pad of certificates lying on the desk – and his heart had knocked against his ribs like it wanted out.

'Is this how you found it?' he asked Nicholas Nicholas.

'Pretty much. 'Cept for the body, y'know.'

Tom and Suarez nodded almost unconsciously in sympathy.

Finally Tom moved to the pad.

'Those them?' Suarez said and Tom grunted back in the affirmative.

He leaned close to the pad as if clues might be written on the forms. Each one had space for a serial number in the top right-hand corner. Each one would eventually be stamped with the number of an approved WAE part as it rolled out of Quality Control.

Or not.

Not if it was stolen first. Then it could be matched to anything. Any cheap, low-grade Tonka-toy part from anywhere in the world.

And here was the beautiful thing: the paperwork was all that made that piece-of-shit part worth top dollar. Once the parts were papered, airline companies trusted that they had been manufactured to the highest standard. So a fan disc manufactured for a hundred and fifty dollars in a Shanghai sweatshop or a Rio slum would fetch three and a half thousand from Boeing or Airbus, on what was supposed to be one of the most tightly controlled and safest markets on the planet.

The part would look the same. It would feel the same. An experienced engineer would receive it from a reputable source and check the paperwork. Then he would place the fake part into the bowels of a passenger-jet engine and put a flag on the computer that it should be inspected every thousand cycles, replaced after twenty thousand.

And it would fail at twelve.

'You okay?'

Tom looked up to see Suarez eyeing him intently, and realized he was shaking. He sat down in Annette Lim's chair. 'Yeah. Fuck.'

The serial numbers on Annette Lim's pad did not include 501. But those forms would have been taken from another pad two, three, maybe four years earlier. There was no doubt now in his mind that the paperwork on the flawed fan discs had come from WAE; no doubt that it had been stolen.

'That what you were looking for?'

Tom nodded mutely. He didn't trust himself to explain the pictures that now crowded into his head.

Pictures of rudder servos jamming, relays sticking, flaps ripping loose.

Pictures of planes splitting open in the skies and bodies showering to Earth like bloody confetti.

'You okay, man?' Suarez repeated.

'I get you some water or something?' Nicholas Nicholas was staring at him too, plainly concerned.

'Yeah,' said Tom, dully. 'I need a drink.'

*

Tom drank to get drunk. Suarez listened to his fears while he watched over him, like a hen over a day-old chick, then drove him from the bar to a motel near the airport.

The detective insisted on coming to the room with him and was surprisingly tender in making him drink about a gallon of water before helping him into bed.

When Tom woke around four, desperate for a piss, he

found Suarez snoring loudly while wedged bolt upright in the only easy chair in the room.

Even Suarez was a goddamned wife, thought Tom. But sometimes that was nice.

He shook the big man awake. 'Hey, Suarez. I'm okay. I'm not gonna drown in my own sick. Go home, man.'

Suarez got up, half asleep, and stumbled to the door.

'Don't forget to fingerprint the ARC pads,' Tom reminded him.

'I'll give you a call,' mumbled Suarez. 'We'll work it out.'

'Yeah,' said Tom. 'We'll work it out.'

Tom was still a little drunk, but even that wasn't enough to let him imagine in his wildest dreams just how he, the goofy Halo Jackson and the corpulent Ronaldo Suarez were going to work out *this* fucking mess.

*

Tom couldn't get back to sleep. Because it was a Motel 6, he thought of Lucia, which made him feel guilty.

Ah, screw her, he told himself.

Then he remembered her sister was dead and he felt guiltier.

He sighed and checked his watch.

04:22.

He should call Ness, let her know where he was, that he couldn't get a plane out until tomorrow, make sure she was okay.

But he didn't.

He checked his watch again.

04:29. This was pointless.

He got up, walked to the airport, and paid a fine for leaving his rental car outside Irving police headquarters. Because he felt like shit, he bought five Dunkin Donuts in an attempt to soak up the booze, then settled down in an orange plastic chair where the angles were deliberately wrong to deter sleepers.

Even so, he was dozing again when his new phone rang and Pete LaBello told him to go to Oklahoma where a pipeline had ruptured and killed some cows.

Tom could barely focus to scribble down a few details, then got up shakily and traded in what was left of his LA ticket for one to Tulsa.

While he waited for the over-bright girl behind the counter to rearrange his flights, Tom surreptitiously sniffed his armpit and sighed at the thought of getting straight on to a job without even a brief stopover at home. No fresh underwear for him.

What a goddamn life.

30

DEAD COWS DIDN'T sound like much over the phone but the reality took Tom's breath away. Literally. He covered his mouth and nose and glanced at Everard Goby, the farmer and owner of the cows.

Goby nodded sadly. 'I'm used to it now,' he said quietly.

There must have been five hundred.

'Six twenty-five,' said Goby, like a mournful agricultural mind-reader.

The Oklahoma sun had wasted no time in bloating the bodies to almost comical proportions so that each dead cow looked like a helium-filled carnival balloon, stomach monstrous and legs akimbo.

Tom thought of photographs he'd seen of Jonestown, the bodies crammed together in death, carpeting the jungle floor, swollen so far beyond the bounds of human dignity that they were merely cloth-splitting Sumo curiosities. He wondered whether Jonestown had smelt like this, and his still-tender stomach clenched.

To distract himself, he squatted at the head of the nearest cow, a big animal with long red eyelashes and a chestnut-and-white hide that cried out to be pinned to a ranch-house wall. The cow's huge bluish tongue had been pushed from its mouth, making it look faintly ridiculous, like a cartoon character that had been hit with a frying pan.

Tom felt sorry for the cows, and stupid for feeling that way, but there it was.

'Went in the well,' said Goby resignedly. 'Fine one day. Dead the next.'

Tom peered into the well with the farmer, then swung his leg over the buzzy little trail bike Goby had provided and followed in his dust to the point about a mile away where the overground pipeline had split and oil had flowed into a carefully maintained water-course.

Tom shook his head at the vagaries of bad luck. If the pipeline had split ten yards either side of where it had, the oil would have soaked into the dust instead of pouring into Everard Goby's water.

He sighed and Goby nodded, acknowledging the irony, the implied sympathy and the sheer unfairness of the whole situation.

It was sad for Goby, but Tom wished everything he did was this simple. Oil in the water. Oil comes from a pipeline. Pipeline leads right to the culprit. Unless Farmer Goby had taken an axe to the pipeline for the insurance money, there were no grey areas here, no mysteries. And he'd seen the photos at the farmhouse before they'd left for the dusty pasture. Photos of fat bulls wearing blue sashes, like Miss Oklahoma, champion calves and ribboned heifers, all accompanied by an Everard Goby who was cheerful and modestly triumphant, rather than the man beside him now – grey, beaten down and filled with sorrow in a way that only Mid-Western farmers and displaced Native Americans really seemed to have mastered.

If Goby had done it for the insurance money he'd eat his appropriate NTSB cap.

Still, he called his office to get the oil pump stopped and told Goby he'd come back tomorrow in his coveralls and boots to look at the breach properly. Tom often leaped to unusual theories, but he never leaped to conclusions.

Goby's wife insisted on feeding him before he went back to the motel; the steaks were thick, the coleslaw home-made, and the two sons friendly and respectful, but Tom still wasn't concluding a damn thing. Anything was possible. He'd once investigated a light-plane crash where it turned out the pilot had stuck a screwdriver through his own fuel tank before taking off and heading out into the Pacific Ocean with his wife and children on board. Seemed the guy had picked up HIV from his girlfriend, and had decided to spare them all his shame. The egomaniacal asshole.

It was only when Goby's eldest boy – a raw-boned twelve-year-old – mentioned the 737 going down on a schoolfriend's property that Tom realized he was not only twenty-four miles from Tulsa, but almost equidistant from the place he'd mentally labelled Buttfuck, Oklahoma.

*

Buttfuck didn't disappoint. The place closest to the downed jet actually turned out to be named Crossways, but was otherwise just as Tom had imagined it: a collection of about ten run-down farms, each defined by a different hunk of rusting machinery in the yard, along with the regulation cars on bricks, dilapidated henhouses and stringy, angry dogs on lengths of worryingly frayed rope.

A few hundred yards west of 'town' he came to the first blue-and-white tape swinging in the slow breeze.

He saw the downed plane before he saw the circus surrounding it. The wreckage sat in the ripe yellow cornfield, surrounded by what looked like old ashes someone had tossed from a fire grate. A few lumps here and there, but mostly just scorching and black and dust scarring the crop.

Cars were parked along the dirt shoulder for what seemed like miles. Cop cars – state, local and Highway Patrol – TV trucks, shiny rentals, dirty rust-buckets, Cherokees, Chevy trucks, compacts.

The human content of the cars was dotted about the landscape. Tom knew there were only three kinds of people around a crash site: the workers, the bereaved and the ghouls. They were easy to distinguish from each other. The professionals moved purposefully, towards the crash, away from the crash, instruments in hands, heads together in businesslike discussion. The bereaved stood in quiet, loose affiliations, barely moving, sometimes embracing each other, but always looking at whatever they could see of the wreckage with dull eyes, as if staring long enough could change reality – like it would all be okay on the action replay. The ghouls craned, shifted position and talked too loudly of what they'd seen on TV and how they knew it was a bad one. They picnicked and put toddlers on shoulders so they could see better; they wanted blood. People were never happy till they'd seen blood, and once they had, they still weren't happy. They withdrew then, pale and miserable and chastened by their own ghoulish need, or self-righteous and angry that they hadn't been protected from the sight they'd driven miles to see. There were kids here, after all!

Tom drove past slowly and spotted Lenny Munro in a knot of serious-looking men. Munro was sunburned and appeared tired already.

Tom kept driving until he reached the last of the cars parked on the shoulder, then pulled in and watched the operation with trance-like fascination before he slid his phone from his pocket and called Pete.

'Pete?'

'Tom.'

'You got the results on that bolt?'

'You finished that job?'

'I'm there now.'

'Then how come I just got a call from Munro to say you're at his crash site?'

Fuck.

'Way to be discreet, Tom.'

'Screw that – if you hadn't expected me to take a look, you wouldn't have sent me out here in the first place. A fucking five-year-old could have pinned down the dead cows!'

He waited for Pete to deny it, but it didn't happen. He took a breath and said, more placatingly, 'Look, I just drove past. There was no more I could do at the farm today. I've already told Sunoco to turn the pumps off and I have to go back tomorrow to take a closer look at the breach.'

He heard Pete make an all-purpose sound of disgruntled acceptance so pressed home his advantage: 'The bolt?'

Pete sounded tense. 'The lab found evidence of crank-shafting—'

'I knew it!' Crank-shafting meant the bolt had been bent by the force of the flanges moving across each other. If that movement had happened suddenly, the bolt would have

290

been sheared in two; crank-shafting meant there'd been repeated or continuous pressure against it for a period before the let-go.

'Looks like the disc strained against it,' said Pete.

'Enough to allow play?' Tom's chest was tight with tension.

Pete hesitated only briefly. 'Yeah. Enough. Maybe a little more than enough.'

Tom stared through the dusty windshield of the rental Toyota and felt himself fill not with satisfaction but with anger.

The fan disc was flawed. Now he could couple that with the theft of the ARC forms, he felt justified in putting two and two together to make four – where 'four' was equal to 'fake part'.

He didn't have kids but if he ever did have kids and one of them was found curled round a shit-stained toilet, dead of a heroin overdose, he imagined this was how he'd feel about the dealer who'd sold the kid the fatal hit. A low, thrumming anger that chilled the Oklahoma heat and sucked a little light out of the world.

He squinted in his mirror at Lenny Munro, who stood, hands on hips, surrounded by people who wanted answers from him. Too distracted, busy and pressured even to put sunblock on his already-peeling nose.

The site was tough. Clues would be hard to come by. Solutions even harder . . . 'Give it to Munro,' he said quietly.

There was a short, disbelieving silence. 'You sure?'

Tom knew what Pete was asking. The bolt was his – only his. His lucky break, his hunch . . . his ticket back, maybe. They both knew it.

'Yeah, I'm sure,' he said, and hung up before he could think about what he'd be losing.

He hated Lenny Munro. But right now Munro – and Lucia – needed that bolt even more than he did.

*

Ness called him the next morning while he was straddling the Sunoco pipeline like a long, shiny mustang as it jumped Everard Goby's water-course and galloped off across the plains. 'Hi,' she said. 'Where are you?'

'Hi, Ness. You okay?' he sidestepped. Neatly, he thought.

'I'm fine. Where are you?'

Or not so neatly.

'Working.'

'Where?'

Shit. She was like a dog with a bone.

'Does it matter?'

There was a long silence during which – despite his general lack of insight into the female psyche – Tom could tell she was deciding whether or not to hang up on him.

She didn't. He was almost disappointed.

'They want you to play,' she said tightly. 'Can you get back by tonight?'

Tom stared about him at the bloated cows. Two hundred yards away, Goby was scooping up a former ribbon-winner in the bucket of his tractor, like so much garbage.

He did a quick calculation and found he could get back by tonight, but still felt aggrieved enough about it to demand, 'Do I have to?'

Her silence told him he did.

*

Tom was in Departures when he saw Lucia. She walked past with an older woman and a young man and their eyes met. Then she looked quickly away, clearly hoping his gaze had been casual, unfocused and unrecognizing.

If he hadn't screwed up helping her, he would have felt fine about pretending he hadn't seen her. As it was, he felt he owed her an explanation. He was on his feet and going after her before he had any idea what he was going to say.

He saw the trio take seats at the gate for a flight to Savannah. He stopped twenty yards away and reconsidered. Telling Lucia what had really happened to prevent him calling her back suddenly sounded like 'the dog ate my homework' on steroids. Like he was not only unreliable, but a hopeless fantasist to boot.

But while he was hesitating, Lucia saw him again and this time she didn't look away. This time her expression was hostile. It told him quite clearly to fuck off.

Walking away now would be a capitulation. So he went over to her and said, 'Hi.'

The older woman, whom Tom presumed was her mother, looked up at him with bloodshot eyes, her blank expression speaking of sedation. Tom noticed she wore white summer gloves, like someone in an old movie. The young man between her and Lucia looked tired but suspicious.

'Hello.' Lucia's tone was neutral but he could see the barely suppressed panic in her eyes.

Tom nodded politely at her mother and ... What? Her brother? Boyfriend? He knew the next thing he should be saying was 'I'm sorry for your loss' but those words had never sounded right in his mouth and he felt victims' relatives could tell that, so he'd long since given up on them.

'Did they find the bodies?'

The expressions on three faces informed him that his preferred choice of words was hardly a humanitarian alternative.

'They didn't find anything. Not yet. They told us to go home and wait. So . . .' Lucia glared at him like it was his fault. Everything in her voice and body told Tom to go but, for some reason, he stayed.

'I'm sorry,' he said instead. He hoped she knew he meant about the phone call as well as about her dead sister.

'I don't think we've been introduced.' The young man had read Lucia's tone too, and his own was abrasive as he got to his feet.

'It's okay, Louis,' said Lucia, but Louis continued to bristle quietly, so Tom stuck out his hand.

'Tom Patrick. I'm a friend of Lucia's from LA.'

'College friend?'

'Yeah,' he lied. Keep it simple. 'I'm sorry for your loss.' The words fell unexpectedly from his lips, and sounded as insincere as they always did to his ears but for some reason they seemed to mollify Louis, who dropped his hard-eyed stare.

'Yeah. Thanks, man.' He sat down again. Tom waited in the ensuing silence.

'This is my mother and my brother,' Lucia said grudgingly. Tom had seen this before: the truly well-brought-up could no more dispense with the social graces than fly to the moon. Tom had once been punched in the eye by a bereaved husband who'd prefaced the blow with 'Mr Patrick? I'm sorry to trouble you . . .'

Lucia's mother nodded at him minutely and said, 'Pleased to meet you,' but obviously didn't give a shit about meeting him or anyone else any more. Louis had slumped again and was staring at his own hands.

Tom looked at Lucia. 'Can I buy you a drink?'

Her eyes widened and he realized his words echoed those he'd used in the club that first time. Before the Motel 6. Before he'd held her smooth-skinned body against his. Before she'd . . .

His face must have betrayed some kind of acknowledgement of his own stupidity because she said, 'Sure.'

They went to the coffee bar closest to the gate. Now that she was no longer hostile, Lucia just looked dog-tired and very young.

'I couldn't call you back.'

She shrugged, like she hadn't really expected him to anyway, and that bugged him enough that he told her the truth. Or the truth without touching on his relationship with Ness. Why he left that out, he wasn't sure – as if a whore gave a shit who her clients went home to.

She stopped meeting his eyes around the point where he told her he'd been bundled into the trunk of a Thunderbird in the Sawmill parking lot, and he knew he'd lost her. From that point on, the story seemed unreal, even to him.

At the end, he said, 'You think I'm lying.'

She was drawing idly in the foam on her cappuccino with a wooden stirrer.

'Look,' he said, and pulled up the leg of his jeans to show her the freshly stitched lacerations. 'And my car's still in the lot behind the Sawmill. At least, it should be. The black Buick, remember?'

She half smiled: 'That beat-up old car.'

'Believe me now?'

'Look, I don't even care.'

Of course she didn't. Her sister was dead. Why should she give half a good goddamn whether he called her or not; whether he told the truth or not; whether he was alive or dead.

'Can I get your number again?' He pulled a pen and a five-dollar bill from his pocket.

She looked wary.

'In case I can help.'

He knew that was a lie and hated himself for how easily it came to him. He wrote the number on the bill when Lucia gave it to him in a tired voice.

As she spoke, he let his eyes drop to her V-neck T-shirt and saw the start of her firm little breasts there, then forced his gaze elsewhere. Ogling the bereaved would be a new low for him, and he'd only just caught himself.

'Listen,' he started. 'About your sister—'

'Let's not talk about it, okay?' she said quickly.

'Sure.' He wondered what the hell they were supposed to talk about instead. Her schoolwork? Her pool-hustling career? Read any good books lately? Fucked any nice johns?

'I need to go,' she said. 'My mother's flight is boarding.'

'You're not going with her?'

'Louis is. I'm going back to LA. I got to work tonight.'

He jerked his chin at her mother and brother. 'Do they know where?'

'What do you think?' There was no anger in her voice, only contempt.

He shrugged apologetically.

296

'Yeah,' she said wearily, and stood up.

'I'm going home too. You want to try and sit together?'

'I want to be alone. Thanks for the coffee,' she said, and walked away. Well brought up, even in the face of his crassness.

He saw her briefly later as they boarded but her eyes were fixed on the back of the woman in front of her, and she worked hard at not looking around.

*

He met Ness in the parking lot of the Bicycle Club. Her cheek was swollen and her eye half closed. 'Don't stare,' she said.

'Okay,' he said, but couldn't stop.

'I'm not coming in with you.'

'Okay.'

She held out three rolls of cash to him. He knew now it was thirty thousand dollars. 'Change up one at a time. If you go through the twenty, change up five, then only change the last five if the tide's turning your way.'

'Okay.'

He felt awkward. He wanted to touch her face and tell her soothing things but neither would help. Just looking at her made him feel weak and useless, and the fact that she barely made eye contact with him didn't bolster his self-esteem.

'Don't be fooled by pocket pairs.'

She was trying to lighten the mood, he knew, but he just opened the door and unfolded himself from the Lotus.

'And keep your mouth shut.'

He ignored that. There were no guarantees. 'Where shall I meet you?'

'Right here,' she said.

Tom almost hoped he'd lose so badly that they wouldn't want him to play any more.

He played recklessly for the first hour but luck smiled on him anyway and bumped the first ten grand up to sixteen. Halfway through the second hour he remembered his rent was due, his pay cheque wasn't, and he'd put a flight to Oklahoma on his credit card that wouldn't be redeemed as expenses for at least two months.

His attitude changed but his luck didn't. Five hours after he'd left her, Tom woke Ness with a tap on the passenger-side window, slid into the car, and handed her eighty-nine thousand dollars. He'd never even broken the second bankroll.

She smiled lopsidedly and he felt some of the weight of the past few days lift from him. 'Fifty-nine thousand dollars' profit, Tom.' She gave him a mock-grumpy look. 'You couldn't make it an even sixty?'

He gestured resignation with his hands: 'The tide turned. I got out of the water.'

She handed him his ten per cent.

'Buy you a doughnut?'

To his surprise, she accepted.

*

She ate two glazed doughnuts, then followed him back to his place where he put clean sheets on the bed, then made slow, careful love to her, mindful of the bruises on her face and arms.

It was a long time since Tom had felt so tender in bed. Long before Ella had left, their lovemaking had become perfunctory and hollow. But Ness's new vulnerability made him take care – and he'd forgotten how good it could be when care was taken. She cried when she came, which confused him, but then she immediately pulled him up and into her body, so he figured it couldn't be anything too bad, and his own release was intense.

He still knew he'd messed up. But he hoped this made up for some of it.

It would have to.

Fucked if he was saying sorry to two people in one day.

31

Ness left while he was still asleep, which made him feel part whore, part relieved. Breakfast small-talk was not his thing.

He lay for a while thinking of the feeling of being inside her, and of the $5,900 he'd earned the night before, and couldn't remember when last he'd woken to such a sense of well-being.

After a shower, he called Halo and asked for a ride to Santa Ana to pick up his car.

'It's my day off,' complained Halo.

'That's lucky,' said Tom, cheerfully.

Halo whined for a bit while Tom ignored him, but finally agreed to come over. It was only after he'd secured his agreement that Tom told him he had made progress on the investigation.

'What?' said Halo, suddenly interested.

'See you in a half-hour,' said Tom, and hung up.

Halo took forty minutes, just to show Tom he wasn't some goddamn kiss-ass Thai bride. He'd had to park up the street for those extra ten minutes, which was boring, but what the hell.

'Fixed your mirror,' was all Tom said by way of greeting.

'Well, hello to you too,' countered Halo, and pulled into traffic.

'Stop for breakfast if you want. I'll buy.'

Halo passed three diners before pulling into Rosie's on Bellflower.

'What was wrong with the other places?' Tom asked.

'They're kinda cheap,' said Halo.

'You're so fucking petty,' Tom said mildly, as he got out of the car.

'Why are you limping?'

Tom waited until they were served before telling him about the Thunderbird, the barn and his trips to Texas and Oklahoma.

When he'd finished, Halo leaned back in his chair and gave him a suspicious look through slitted eyes. 'Man, I don't know. Either you just had, like, Three Days of the fucking Condor, or you been out of your head in Tijuana.'

Tom picked up the cheque. 'Talking of which, your buddy show up?'

'Niño? No. Sylvia's going nuts.' Halo toyed with his coffee spoon. 'She blames you, you know.'

'Whatever,' said Tom. Sylvia Alvarez could blame him for global warming; he didn't give a shit. He frowned at the cheque. 'Did you have a fruit salad?'

'To go.'

'Jeez! You want me to get your groceries while I've got my wallet out? How about dinner and a fucking movie?'

Halo doggedly ignored his sarcasm. 'I mean, she's in the middle of decorating and all, and Niño just ups and runs off. Cos of us going round there. I mean . . .'

Tom stopped in the middle of counting out a tip, and grinned suddenly at Halo.

'How much wallpapering d'ya do?'

'Nothing!' Halo protested. When Tom wouldn't stop grinning, he gave up and admitted, 'Jus' the living room.'

Tom waited.

'And the kitchen.'

*

The Sawmill wasn't open and the Buick was the only car in the lot. He hoped Lucia had seen it there last night and known he wasn't lying. About that part, at least.

'So what do we do now?' Halo said, as he pulled up alongside it.

'You mean what do *I* do now, right? Cos as far as I can tell, you just sit around and fuck your dead friend's wife while I get my ass kicked.'

Halo shook his head and murmured, 'Dick,' under his breath as Tom got out of the car. 'I'll wait until it starts,' Halo said.

'Smartass.'

'You should take better care of that car.'

'It gets me from A to B.'

'When it's not stuck at C,' said Halo, but the Buick gave a polite cough, then turned over wheezily, and Tom gave him the finger by way of thank you and goodbye.

He half thought of hanging around Santa Ana until the Sawmill opened at seven but he couldn't think of anything to fill the time until then so drove slowly back to Long Beach, his leg complaining every time he put his foot on the gas past fifty.

Driving so slowly was mind-numbingly boring so to spice up the journey he called Ronaldo Suarez.

'Hey, Tom, I was just gonna call you,' said Suarez.

'Oh, yeah? I was thinking about Nicholas Nicholas.'

'Same here,' said Suarez.

'With Chuck gone—'

'They might approach him to steal the ARC forms.'

'Exactly.'

'Great minds!' said Suarez.

'And fools,' Tom reminded him. 'You get any prints off the pads?'

'Chuck Zhong's prints were on all three pads in that office but not on any of the pads in the senior engineers' rooms.'

'Maybe he figured the new kids would take the fall if missing paperwork was discovered.'

'Probably true.'

'Anyone else?' asked Tom.

'Yeah, got Lyle Parker on two of the pads, and a previous guard, Steven Jones, on one.'

'So the dockets are what they were all targeting.'

'As far as we can tell.'

'What does WAE say?'

'I got them going through their records looking for missing batch numbers. They're pissed. Not sure they'll tell me, even if they find them.'

'Why don't you subpoena them?'

'Can't. Not from my end anyway. I've got one body, one confession. That's a good trade-off to my boss. I can make the other stuff look like loose ends for a while, but really it's just for you.'

'Don't. I'm filling up,' said Tom. 'Talking of which, how's the diet?'

'Much better now I'm eating again.'

They both laughed. Then Tom got back to business. 'Any leads on who they were selling them to?'

'Nope.'

'Zhong still not talking?'

'Wouldn't even come out of his cell for me.'

Tom thought for a moment. 'You tried leaning on the consenting adult?'

'Yep. Says he doesn't know and doesn't want to know.'

'I don't blame him. Those guys must've been scary to keep Zhong stealing even after that redneck started . . . y'know?' He chewed his lip. 'Hey, have they filled his job?'

'I don't know. Why?'

'Should stake out the new guy too, just in case.'

'The NTSB going halves on manpower?'

Tom knew Suarez was only half joking. Surveillance cost bucks. But Tom also knew this was the best chance he'd have of picking up what had become a cold paper trail after the collapse of the deal with Chuck Zhong. The thought of getting on a plane back to Texas filled him with a premonition of homesickness, but he told Suarez he'd be back soon to help out in person.

'Just you?' said Suarez.

'Don't push your luck.' Tom hung up and called Pete LaBello.

'What now?' said Pete, warily.

'I've got a serious chance of tracing those fake parts.'

'Tom, every six months we get a container of fake parts stopped at some port somewhere.'

'Yeah, but these aren't being stopped. They're getting through. Anyway, the parts aren't important. It's the paperwork that opens the doors – that's what gets the parts into planes – and it's the paperwork I'm on to now, but I can't do it on my dollar any more. I've been putting my hand in my own pocket on this for months and I'm cleaned out.'

He was hardly lying. He had rent and credit-card bills to pay, and what was left wouldn't last through the next month.

There was a heavy silence in DC. The longer it went on, the more hopeful Tom got.

'I'm sorry, Tom. I just can't do it. Not when Munro's report on the *Pride of Maine* is already a matter of record. How can I okay expenses on a closed case?

He sounded genuinely sorry but Tom felt prickles of anger run up the back of his neck. 'Fuck sorry, Pete! And fuck you!'

'Tom—'

'Pete, I got thrown out of CalSuperior on my ass like a goddamned *drunk*. I went ten thousand miles to South Africa and almost got killed finding evidence that I then *giftwrapped* and gave to Lenny fucking *Munro* of all people! I went to Texas on a hunch and my dollar, and now it looks like that hunch might be about to pay off and maybe – just maybe – we can stop thousands of people risking their lives every time a 737 takes off. And you won't pay my way because of office fucking *politics*?' Tom actually laughed – it sounded so stupid to him. 'I like you, Pete. But you're being a gigantic asshole!'

Pete LaBello was a patient man. He was a kind man. And he was a decent man. But he was a man – not a saint.

305

'You're this close to being fired, Patrick!' he shouted across the continent. 'This fucking close!'

'Fuck that!' yelled Tom. 'I quit!'

'Good!' Pete yelled back – a little less certainly.

Three thousand miles away, Pete LaBello frowned at the sudden sounds of the wind, the clatter, the angry horns and the terminal crunch – all of which he correctly interpreted to mean that Tom Patrick had thrown his phone out of a car window on a Californian freeway.

*

By the time he swung the Buick into his street, Tom had gone from buzzing with adrenalin, through slight discomfort and on to regret. But he'd lingered there only momentarily before rebuilding to self-righteousness, and from that there was a well-worn path to angry bitterness.

He couldn't believe he'd been forced to quit. Quit the only thing he loved; the only thing he was really good at. Not to mention the only legit thing he got paid for – albeit badly right now.

He'd thrown away his phone partly in frustration but also because he knew that he might otherwise have called Pete right back and withdrawn his reckless words. Tom's pride had taken a battering over the past eighteen months and he knew that what little he had left had spurred him into quitting, but the only apparent alternative was continuing to be sidelined while waiting to be fired.

Jumping before he was pushed was a sour little victory; a sharp diamond in his shoe.

Tom lifted his hip so he could search his jeans pocket. He pulled out a handful of crumpled bills, change and fluff, and saw that the bill he'd written Lucia's number on was still there. Now all he needed was yet another phone, he thought, and the anger swelled in him again.

He squealed to a halt outside his condo, jerked the parking brake furiously and registered the black Lotus parked across the street. He got out and slammed his door, ignoring the other car, but Ness caught up with him as he reached his front door. 'Hi,' she said, searching his face. 'What's up?'

'I quit my job.' He yanked open the door and stormed in, leaving it up to her as to whether or not she followed.

She did, her brow creased. 'Why?'

He hesitated. Suddenly the only reasons he could give for surrendering his career sounded weak.

Politics.

Pride.

Petulance.

The anger left him instantly, and left him empty. He crumpled on to the couch. 'Because I'm an asshole.'

She raised her eyebrows and half smiled, and he remembered just how spectacularly beautiful she was.

'Thanks for not arguing,' he said drily.

She smiled properly then and sat beside him, close, facing him, one hand snaking gently round the back of his neck, the other smoothing circles on his chest. Tom felt himself calming, perspective returning.

'Is it about the *Pride of Maine*?'

'Among other things.'

She nodded carefully. 'What happened with Lemon's bolt?'

307

They'd called it that between themselves. A small private joke that now just bit into him, like salt in a paper cut.

'I had my boss check it out. It was damaged before the engine let go. Looks like there was play in the fan disc. Maybe a fault in the actual alloy made it loosen round the bolts and start to move. I don't know.'

'Is that why, the night of the fire, they took the paperwork on it from Pam's car?'

'No doubt.'

'Where's the bolt now?'

Tom hesitated again. Now, the gift of his only bargaining chip to his arch rival seemed the height of stupidity. 'I gave it to Lenny Munro.'

'The other investigator?' Ness couldn't hide her surprise. 'The one who wanted you fired?'

'Yeah,' he mumbled. He gave her a hang-dog look. 'Please tell me you weren't sleeping with me for my brains.'

She laughed then and kissed the side of his mouth. 'No,' she said huskily, 'not for your brains.'

Her hand slid down his stomach and into his jeans. He turned and kissed her, his own hands finding their way under her T-shirt and across her hot nipples, feeling her breath thickening in his mouth, as his was in hers. He nearly passed a smart comment about her devotion to Richard, then surprised himself by thinking better of it. He pushed her down on the leather and forced his knee between her legs, pushing himself into her hip as he slid her skirt up her smooth thighs.

'Why?'

'Uh?'

She turned her head away from his lips. 'Why did you give it to him?'

Tom took a moment to refocus. 'What?'

'Why did you give Munro the bolt?'

'Cos I'm stupid.' He ducked his head to suck the nipple he'd just exposed – but she held his head off her.

'I'm serious.'

He saw that she wasn't going to shut up about it. 'Because he's investigating the Oklahoma crash. The site's a nightmare and I thought he could use the help. I wasn't doing anything with the bolt except trying to buy my way back in. He needed it to maybe find probable cause.'

She stared at him, assimilating the information.

'If you're quite finished, can I suck your nipples now?'

She smiled but he could see she was still distracted. What the hell. He decided to just get on with it and let her catch up, so he dipped his head to her breasts once more, feeling the dizzying air of unreality that this woman – this beautiful, perfect woman – was letting him do this to her. The thought made him groan and press himself against her more firmly, feeling the heat build in him. He needed her naked – and fast. He started to drag her panties down her hips.

'Tom,' she said.

Jesus! Did she never shut up?

'What?' he muttered breathlessly.

'Ask him to speak to your boss.'

'What?' He didn't understand what she was saying. Ask who? What boss?

'Lenny Munro. You gave him the bolt. You helped him. Now maybe he'll help you get your job back.'

Tom actually laughed in her face.

Then he got off the couch with a sigh, went into the bathroom and slammed the door.

*

The flight back to Irving was a bumpy one. Tom tried not to grip the armrests but by the time they landed, on what felt like wagon wheels, he was queasy and already drained by his second trip to Texas in a week.

32

NICHOLAS NICHOLAS WAS a hero, but he didn't feel like one. The memory of finding that girl – that poor girl – had leached every ounce of pleasure out of the high regard in which he was suddenly held at home and at work.

He'd been offered a month off with counselling – more for insurance purposes than sympathy, he was sure – but he'd turned both down because if his mother ever found out he was seeing a shrink she'd consider that bringing up six children alone, steering them around crime and into worthwhile employment, plus helping to raise eleven grandkids so far would all have been a terrible waste: one of them had turned out crazy anyway.

Nicholas grinned at the thought, then sighed. People at work knew him now. He was no longer just a uniform in a booth as they passed. People said hello. Smiled. Gave him cheerful waves. That was good in one way, of course, but in another every hello, every smile, every wave was a reminder of why he was suddenly somebody. And he didn't want reminders: all he wanted was to do his job and forget Annette Lim's face, caved in like an empty rubber mask; Chuck Zhong's vomit-flecked lips under his; the boyfriend howling like a giant toddler in the parking lot . . .

Nicholas shook himself out of that night and back into this one.

The new guy seemed okay: Raoul Estanza, 'but you can call me Rollo'. Nicholas didn't know whether this was because Estanza liked the name Rollo or because he'd had 'Raoul' mispronounced so often that he'd given up on his own identity.

Nicholas liked his own name. It had something about it. A bald man in a bow tie had once told him it was a 'slave name' but Nicholas had no truck with that, and he'd like to see the emphatic little man try that line on his mother and see how far he got.

Jeff came back from the can, wiping his hands on his pants.

Nicholas didn't like Jeff. He didn't know why, but he suspected something was going on. He'd occasionally watched Chuck make the rounds on the monitors – only because it was mildly more interesting than watching dark, empty rooms – and there had never been anything too weird about them. Once he'd seen Chuck take something off a desk in the engineering office and throw it in the trash.

Then, a week after Nicholas had started, Jeff had started making the rounds too. Nicholas hadn't been at WAE long enough to know whether that was usual. But what he did know was that one night, when Chuck and Jeff were both making the rounds (although they'd left at different times), he'd idly hit the button for the engineering-office camera and found it blocked. Not dead, but blocked by something not 100 per cent opaque; light filtered through, but nothing as defined as even blurred shapes was visible. Nicholas had slapped the monitor and run through other cameras on it.

Everything else seemed to be working fine: it wasn't the monitor. And when he rolled back round to the engineering-office camera again, there it was, gloomy and dark without light enough now to filter through a fishing net, let alone anything else.

So someone had been in there, and someone had covered the camera.

Why, Nicholas Nicholas could not even hazard a guess. But he did notice that while Jeff carried on being his usual domineering dickwad self, Chuck Zhong – who made *dim sum* to die for – started to look wary, fretful and thin.

He didn't know either of them that well, and did make one clumsy move with a poorly judged crack about AIDS that almost had Chuck snapping his head off. It was only then that Nicholas really considered whether Chuck and Jeff were . . . What would you call it? Lovers? That sounded far too normal and okay-by-God to be right, but that was the word he settled on.

And immediately shied away from and tried never to think of again.

After that, whenever he was alone in the booth, he switched off the camera in Engineering. If that kind of thing was going on in there, he didn't want to know about it.

Which was why there was no recording of Chuck Zhong killing Annette Lim, for which Nicholas was grateful, even though the cops had been incandescent with frustrated rage.

Nicholas mused for the millionth time since that night about the fleeting nature of existence, then discovered he hadn't eaten a doughnut he'd bought as a special pick-me-up. As he crammed it into his breakfast-hungry mouth he mused instead on how something so simple could give so much pleasure.

*

Texas enjoyed the perfect climate for about forty-five minutes after sun-up and it was in this warm, fresh brilliance that Nicholas Nicholas said goodbye to Rollo and to the day guys, Vern and David, and walked across the parking lot.

Two men watched him from a nondescript rental parked in the long shadows of a line of conifers that WAE had established to shield the plant from aesthetically offended commuters.

Nicholas unlocked the rusty door to his Civic.

In the moment between the lock clicking open and him withdrawing the key, he heard a tiny scuff on the asphalt behind him and felt his neck prickle in ancient warning.

He swung round, heart racing.

But the low sun in his eyes meant he never saw their faces.

*

Ronaldo Suarez was watching Tom Patrick throw up barely digested airline food in the airport parking lot when he got a call from Toby Uncle, the youngest, cheapest and – it was turning out – dumbest cop he'd been able to find for the surveillance detail.

'Uh-huh,' he said.

Tom straightened and leaned against Suarez's police-issue

Chevrolet. He felt something press against his arm and took the towel Suarez was offering; it was thin and old and smelt of dogs. He spat on the ground a few times then wiped his mouth, only vaguely aware of Suarez's half of the conversation.

'How long ago? . . . Okay . . . Where are you now? . . . How could you fucking lose them? . . . Okay. Okay . . . Go back there. I'll be fifteen minutes.'

'We gotta go,' he told Tom, pressing his own gut down so he could squeeze behind the wheel.

'You want this?' Tom said, holding up the towel as he slumped into the passenger seat.

'You keep it.'

Tom dropped it out of the window as they pulled away. 'Goddamn planes.'

*

The men who took Nicholas Nicholas from the lot only made him suffer ten minutes of abject terror before dumping him back at his car and driving away, but as he sat beside his little beige compact he thought he'd never feel safe again. Even the death of Annette Lim had not shaken him like this. Annette Lim was not supposed to be able to protect herself. She was not a man. She was not *him*. But, in less than a quarter of an hour, Nicholas had had his idea of personal security turned upside down.

He tried to stand and found his legs were jellied with fear, so instead he leaned against the door of the Civic, feeling the warming metal comfort his back and one cheek.

He heard a car and half opened his eyes. In this new world

315

of his, where nothing would ever seem unexpected again, he was not in the least bit surprised to see Detective Suarez and the skinny guy who'd been with him before striding purposefully across the blacktop towards him.

*

'So,' said Suarez, with the air of Detective Columbo summing things up, 'they took you, they put a gun in your mouth, they told you they could shoot you, or you could steal the paperwork for them and make plenty of money – your choice.'

'Yes,' said Nicholas Nicholas, shakily.

'What did you choose?'

Suarez, Tom and Nicholas all turned slowly to look at Toby Uncle, who blushed to the very roots of his wispy blond hair and mumbled, 'Sorry.'

'And then they dumped you back here.'

'Yes. Just before you showed up.'

'Goddamn *planes*!' Tom muttered furiously. If he hadn't thrown up in the airport lot, they'd have reached WAE in time to see Nicholas dumped – in time to catch the men who'd dumped him. He knew it and he knew Suarez knew it, although he'd been good enough not to say it.

Nicholas dabbed at the lump on his forehead. It wasn't bleeding but he kept touching it, then looking at his fingers.

'Do you know where they took you?'

'I was face-down on the back seat the whole time. With a guy on my legs.'

'The guy who put the gun in your mouth?'

'Yes.'

'Did they have local accents?' said Suarez.

'No. Just American.'

'Can you describe them?'

'I didn't see the driver hardly at all. So I don't know.' Nicholas frowned in concentration. 'The other guy. He was white. Umm. Black hair, I think. Taller than me. Strong build. I didn't see much of him either, didn't get a good look at his face.'

'Even when he put the gun in your mouth?'

'I had my eyes shut.' Nicholas said it like they should have guessed that – like, if they'd been in his place, they *would've* guessed that.

Tom had never had a gun put in his mouth but he figured Nicholas was probably right.

Suarez sighed, and Nicholas seemed to feel bad that he hadn't been more helpful.

'He was kinda fidgety,' he offered.

'Fidgety?'

'Yeah.'

'Great,' snorted Suarez. 'Uncle, get an APB out on a fidgety white guy.'

'Yes, sir,' said Uncle, keen to make up for his earlier stupidity. He actually turned back towards his car to put out the call, before he apparently realized he'd just compounded his sin. 'Fuck,' he berated himself quietly.

Nicholas remembered. 'He wore stupid red boots.'

Tom felt like he'd been knocked off a pier with a plank. He had a sense of free-falling through a vacuum and his breath left him with an audible rush that made the others turn towards him. When he finally found his voice, it was strangled. 'Stupid red *cowboy* boots?'

317

'Yeah,' said Nicholas Nicholas, in surprise. 'Stupid red cowboy boots.'

*

When Worlds Collide.

Tom had seen that movie on TV once after a long session at the Normandie. Now he couldn't get the title out of his head as he tried to get a grip on the two worlds – cards and work – that he'd thought were entirely separate, but which he now discovered were somehow swirling tightly around each other, like twin stars connected by a pivotal point: the leg-shaking, red-boot-wearing Mr Stanley.

Mr Stanley, who'd beaten him up after folding three of a kind.

Mr Stanley, who'd thrown him into the trunk of his Thunderbird.

Mr Stanley, who'd slapped Ness so hard that he'd knocked the duct tape clear off her mouth.

All those things were about the world of cards.

So what the hell was Mr Stanley doing here in his world of work? Somehow involved with a paper trail that led all the way back to the *Pride of Maine*? And all the way forward to . . . what? To whom?

And if he was involved in the *Pride of Maine*, where did his involvement stop? Halo Jackson? Pam Mashamaete? Buttfuck, Oklahoma? Tom's head spun.

And what about Ness?

I know that guy. He's an asshole . . .

Ness knew Stanley; they worked for the same people. If Stanley was involved in more than the cards, did that mean Ness was too? He felt sick and dizzy at the thought and tried to take a mental step back so he could see the bigger picture instead of these fuzzy, half-formed bits that teased as much as they told, but it was impossible.

Ness under him on the hood of the Honda, bathed in headlights, then suddenly walking away.

Ness holding her phone, as though she'd just made a call from the room they'd shared in De Rust.

Waking in Cape Town to find her holding the bolt.

But there was also Ness bravely grabbing at Lemon's tether as the big bird thundered past her.

Ness's warm mouth sliding down him as his hands burned.

Ness, tear-streaked and bruised, with duct tape hanging off her cheek.

It was too much. Every time he thought he was making sense of it, it got away from him again.

He stood in a daze and watched Toby Uncle take Nicholas Nicholas away in his unmarked car to look at computerized mug shots. Tom had told them Stanley's name and described the Weasel, just in case they were still paired up. But he'd said no more.

Now, with the sun starting to hurt their eyes, Suarez turned to him. 'So, you gonna tell me what you know about this guy?'

The same question had been buzzing through Tom's head, along with all the other craziness. There was no way he could tell Suarez everything: what he'd been doing in the card clubs was illegal.

'I played cards against him once. In LA. He's a real sore loser.'

Suarez waited for more – obviously aware that there was more to be said – but Tom just shrugged.

'That's a coincidence,' said the detective.

'Yes,' agreed Tom, flatly. 'But a lucky one.'

'For me, maybe. For you? I'm not so sure.'

Suarez squeezed himself back into the driver's seat and waited for Tom to get in beside him.

*

Tom called Ness from the airport. 'Hi.'

'Hi, Tom. Where are you? Your phone's not working.'

'Yeah, it got broken.'

'Again.'

'Yes.'

'So where are you?'

'Texas.'

There was a nervous silence.

'When are you coming back?'

'Now.'

'Can you play tonight?'

'Sure.'

'Good,' she said, relieved. 'I'll meet you at the Honolulu at nine.'

'Okay. Hey, Ness?'

'What?'

Tom wanted to ask if she was betraying him, if she and Stanley were in this together. And if they were, just what the hell 'this' was. But he suddenly knew that he needed to see her face when he asked her.

'Looking forward to it,' he said instead.

'Me too,' she said, and Tom could almost hear the sexy little smile that went with the words.

She might have been lying.

But while there was half a chance she'd still fuck him, Tom sure as hell wasn't leaping to any conclusions.

33

Tom's head hurt from thinking so he took two Valium and slept until a perky attendant woke him on an almost-empty plane in Los Angeles. He stumbled through Arrivals and caught a fifty-five-dollar cab ride home, where he dived on to his bed and slept again.

He didn't hear the phone, but when he finally woke, the machine blinked two new messages at him. The first was a halting silence and then a gruff, faintly familiar voice, saying, 'You there, Patrick?' before hanging up.

The other message was from Kitty, who told him she was sending him the forms he needed to finalize the termination of his employment with the NTSB. Then she paused and said, 'I'm so sorry, Tom,' in a rush.

The phone rang and Tom picked up.

'Patrick?' The same voice as on the first message.

'Yes?'

'It's Lenny Munro.'

Tom said nothing. He had nothing to say to Munro until he knew what Munro had to say to him. Maybe not even then.

The silence thrummed between them.

'That bolt,' said Munro. 'It's a big help.'

Tom was stunned that Munro had apparently called to thank him. He wasn't sure he could have done as much. 'Good,' he said, sincerely. 'Is that what your incident's looking like?'

Munro gave a humourless snort. 'This incident's looking like a nightmare.'

'I noticed.'

'Yeah, well. Can't say for sure yet but it looks like the number-two engine disintegrated without warning and before impact. We haven't found the fan disc yet but when we do we'll take a real close look.'

'I hope that's it.'

'Yeah. Me too. Shit.'

There was a weary silence and Tom felt hollow. This was what he'd given up: a job he loved so much that, even when he was talking about a shitty detail with a man he thought was an asshole, he was still captured by the quest, heart and soul.

Eventually Munro spoke awkwardly: 'You busy?'

'I quit,' he said flatly. It covered everything.

'Yeah,' said Munro, but didn't do the little dance on his grave that Tom had expected. Then he sighed. 'Still. I could use your help on this one. Even unofficially.'

Tom didn't even repack his bags. He stuffed $2,300 in hundreds into his jeans – all that was left of his winnings, all that was left of his savings – and got back to LAX less than twelve hours after he'd left it.

He bought a ticket to Tulsa and a pre-pay phone. He called his service and arranged to have his calls forwarded to the new number. Then he entered Ness's number on the contacts list.

He should call her to let her know he couldn't play tonight.

But he didn't.

34

IT HAD RAINED IN Oklahoma, and what brought relief and free irrigation to most brought mud and misery to the site where Flight 823 had come down. The ashes had turned to black soup, and slick-shiny pools hid inch-deep shallows, or trenches: the unwary could only tell one from the other when they fell in them up to their hips.

Tom parked much closer to the action this time because the rubberneckers had packed up their picnics and gone home, although there were still plenty of bereaved family members left to keep vigil over the cornfield. They mostly stayed in their cars, though, leaving only the investigators to brave the weather in slick raingear, dripping ball-caps and shiny rubber boots.

Tom hadn't brought his raingear so he just zipped his jacket up to his chin and hunched his shoulders as he splashed through the blackened muck, past whippy red and green marker flags, to Munro.

The man looked up from under the peak of his cap, his face lined with tiredness. A long way from the last time they'd seen each other in Pete LaBello's office. There was a moment's hesitation and Tom could see Munro was thinking the same uncomfortable thing. Then the man stuck out his hand. 'Tom,' he said, 'thanks for coming.'

And that was all it took.

Munro led him to the bogged-down trailer he was using as an on-site command centre. 'Fucking place,' he said. 'Ninety-five degrees in the fucking shade for a week and now this.'

It could have rained for forty days and forty nights and Tom would still have been happier than he had been since the Learjet.

Munro caught him up as they walked. 'Command centre's at the Holiday Inn in Glenpool. There's a room reserved for you, if Kitty's done her job. Debrief every night at six, then show and tell at seven. You might want to give that a miss.'

He didn't look at Tom and his voice held no judgement but Tom understood. He was welcome to get together with the team to discuss the day's progress; less welcome to have any contact whatsoever with the public and press at the subsequent meeting. Couldn't blame Munro for that. 'Sure,' he agreed easily.

It hadn't escaped him that Munro had said Kitty had made a reservation for him: that meant he was on expenses that must have been okayed by Pete when requested by Munro. He wondered if he should acknowledge that in some way, but Munro had moved on.

'Boeing's playing it close to their chest but I don't think they're hiding anything. Alpa's being a pain in the ass as usual. So I didn't tell them about the bolt.'

At that, Tom grinned: the manufacturers and airline companies always hoped it was pilot error, while the pilots' union was rabid in defence of its members, alive or dead. The Airline Pilots' Association sent representatives to every crash investigation, just as determined to establish mechanical or systems failure. The NTSB investigators were often more like referees at a boxing match, caught in the middle, trying to hold the two adversaries at arm's length. Except this referee also had to keep the press and bereaved families in the picture, deal with any local issues the crash may have thrown up, and all while conducting an investigation into why the hell the plane had fallen out of the sky in the first place.

Not telling the Alpa representatives about the bolt was technically justified until it had been thoroughly investigated. But it was also a mean little bit of payback that Tom heartily endorsed.

They climbed the two muddy metal steps into the draughty trailer and stood for a moment, dripping on to the filthy linoleum.

'This is Mike Carling and Bryce Potts from Arlington, and you know Jan. Tom Patrick.'

From their surprised, stilted greetings, Tom was left in no doubt that they all knew he was already halfway out of the door. But even that realization wasn't enough to burst his happy bubble. Wherever he might be in a week's time, he was *here* now.

He trailed into the office after Munro and took the seat he waved at, then pulled it up to the Formica desk where Munro clicked a laptop into life.

There was a grid map on the screen: the crash site showing clusters of numbered green blocks, wreckage spread in a rough fan-shape covering about four square miles. A simple depiction of what must already have amounted to thousands of man-hours picking through dirt and corn, bush and trees.

Munro leaned across Tom to fire up the laptop in front of

him too. Another grid map, this one with red triangles spread over a similarly wide area.

Bodies. And parts of bodies.

'How many'd you find?' Tom nodded at the triangles.

'There were seventy-eight souls on board. We got about two hundred and twenty bits so far. Thirty-four whole, or nearly whole, bodies, and the rest everything from heads and legs right down to dog food.'

Tom thought of Lucia and Louis and their mother in her little white gloves, waiting for news of Candice and Carlo.

Dog food.

'There's a bunch of trees here maybe a mile long, a quarter wide.' Munro tapped the screen. 'Chopper's no good for that. Sure to be more in there but we haven't had the manpower yet. I've asked the state police to lend a hand but they're taking their time putting it together.'

Tom nodded his understanding of the daunting logistics of the operation. 'You got the CVR?'

'It gives us nothing. The pilots never knew what hit them.' He touched a key and Tom heard the voice of a dead man passing the time of day.

'. . . Jean. So I'm thinking, what's the point of even going then?'

'Too right,' said the co-pilot.

'You want to trim that a little?'

Tom listened to the tiny sounds that meant the co-pilot was adjusting the trim. The black box – the one that held the computerized records of every technical change in the plane – would tell them exactly what he'd done at that point. Whether it had made any difference.

'So we didn't go.'

'You didn't miss any—'

The voices were steamrollered by a huge, indeterminate noise. A mechanical roar – a cacophony too loud and confused to be interpreted by mere ears. Then, frantic but faint, as if they were already far from life, the pilots' last words . . .

'Oh fuck—'

'Jesus. I—'

And then nothing.

However many times he listened to those recordings, they would never fail to affect Tom. What was most shocking about them was their very mundanity, the complete lack of foreknowledge in the pilots' conversations, in their voices. Until the bad thing happened, there was just . . . ordinary life. He'd listened to hundreds of hours of cockpit voice-recorder sound and had never heard a flight-crew member say, 'I have a bad feeling about this,' or 'We're all dead.' Even when they knew it was past sensible, the pilots always kept trying, fighting, hoping. He'd never heard one take his mind off trying to pull out of a terminal dive to shout, 'Tell Ruby I love her!' Or 'The safe deposit key's in my sock drawer!'

Tom understood it. If the billion-to-one recovery manoeuvre paid off, then Ruby would only want to get married, and a new hiding place would have to be found for the key. It was human nature: men liked to keep their options open even as they plummeted towards oblivion at 500 m.p.h.

But, just once, he wished he could hear something astonishing on one of those goddamned tapes. Something that gave a clue to an awareness of the fact that a portal was opening up between life and death – between one reality and another.

'My God – it's full of stars!' The line from *2001: A Space Odyssey* was his fantasy CVR benchmark, but all he ever got was 'Shit', 'Fuck' and the ubiquitous 'Pull up! *Pull up!*'

It was an undignified way to die. Confused, terrified – and with your always-useless last words recorded for the posterity of the inquiry room and transcribed in brutal black-and-white for *The Orange County Shopper* or Channel 2 Tampa's *Top-of-the-Hour News*.

He realized Munro was staring at him and wondered what he'd missed. Munro repeated his question: 'So what do you want to do, Tom?'

The guy was giving him a choice?

Tom felt the eyes of the other three investigators boring into him, no doubt just as amazed. He felt gratitude swelling inside him, like a brittle old seed dropped into water. 'Anything you want. Just tell me what you need.' He was astonished to find that he meant it. He owed Munro for this. Big-time. Sure, Munro thought he was the one repaying a debt, but Tom knew that, although he'd passed on the bolt via Pete, he could never have done what Munro was doing for him right now: treating him with respect, instead of like a rookie.

Munro nodded thoughtfully, swivelling slightly in his chair. Then he yanked open a drawer and took out a scuffed wallet. He peeled off two hundred dollars and handed it to Tom. 'For starters, you can go back into Glenpool and get yourself some raingear. Come in and start fresh tomorrow.'

Tom took the money silently. He sincerely hoped Lenny Munro was going to punch him in the face next, or he was in serious danger of getting all misty.

'When we find the fan disc, that'll be the time you'll really

330

come into your own. But until then, just do what you think would be most useful. Let me know what it is so I know where you are if I need you.'

Tom nodded again, not trusting his voice, unable to look Munro in the eyes. Instead he fixed his gaze on the little red triangles. Some poor bastard would be out there now, trying to add to that map. Finding the bodies was the shit detail in air-crash investigation. Picking up arms, peeling scalps off asphalt, checking random shoes to see if they still contained feet.

Once, near Milwaukee, he'd stepped on an eyeball.

Tagging-bagging-and-flagging was an exhausting, soul-destroying attempt to identify flesh that used to be people. All enhanced by the constant reminder that some day, somewhere, someone was going to be picking your teeth off the freeway, pulling your flaking body from under the pier, covering their nose over your fetid, piss-soaked, bed-ridden corpse.

Tom looked Lenny Munro square in the face. He wanted to apologize for calling him a cocksucker. But what he said was: 'I'll look for bodies.'

*

The Holiday Inn had a laundry service. Tom stripped off everything he was wearing, bundled it up with every other item of clothing in his bag, and called for it to be taken away. When the maid came to his door, he paid for the full express service, including pressing, even though it was only for jeans and T-shirts. He asked what she could do with his All Stars, which were covered with mud, and she seemed quite confident about them, so he let her have those too. If there was a fire now, he thought, he'd have to escape in his new galoshes.

He showered, then threw himself on to the bed and slept almost instantly.

He woke from a nightmare on a sweat-soaked sheet, still naked, and was so disoriented that he looked around for Ronaldo Suarez, before remembering that a lot of muddied water had passed under the bridge since the giant detective had watched him sleep in another motel room a thousand miles away.

Tom lay on his back and blinked at the illuminated face of his watch. It was nine p.m. in LA. His nakedness reminded him of how vulnerable he'd felt in the barn.

A soft knock on the door made him flinch and rise quickly from the bed. He peered warily through the spyhole and saw the maid with his clothes. As he opened the door, he remembered he was naked and grabbed one of his galoshes to cover himself. The girl blushed and Tom patted his ass before he remembered he didn't have his jeans on; he had to back away from the door to get a tip off the dressing-table, despite her stammered protest that it really didn't matter, that it was her fault for coming back so late but she knew 'you din't have no other clothes to put on, sir'.

Tom finally managed to tip her without committing an arrestable offence but it was a close thing.

When she'd hurried away, he buried his face in his clean clothes, wondering when last he'd felt and smelt so clean. It made him think of a fresh start, and all the pleasure leaked from the feeling.

He didn't want a fresh start: he just wished he'd done better with the start he'd already made.

*

The rain had only got worse and Tom was glad he hadn't skimped on the raingear. What had seemed needlessly bulky when he'd pulled it on four hours ago now seemed like the most sensible purchase he'd ever made.

Even though the trees gave him some cover, rain plopped loudly on to his breathable Gore-Tex hood and the peak of the cap he wore under it. The strip of woodland was untended and overgrown, and Tom wondered what the hell it was doing between the acres of corn all around. He used a light metal pole to prod about in the stands of whippy new hazel and tired old thorns between the patchy yellow grass that was slowly sinking into the fresh, unaccustomed mud.

He had bags, tags and flags in the pack slung over his shoulders, but all he'd found so far was a paperback of *The Da Vinci Code*, open and face-down in the mud. He'd flagged it anyway, in case prints matched a passenger, and moved on, treading carefully, his eyes sweeping slowly around, up and down, adjusting to the dull light seeping through the canopy, and readjusting to the darkness of the undergrowth, as he criss-crossed the strip with a grinding patience that made him want to throw down the pole and run around shouting.

In the next hour, he found two seat cushions, a twist of metal and rubber he recognized as cabin window framing and, sitting atop an old stump, like a mythical woodland offering, a single-serving utensil bag containing plastic knife, spork, salt, pepper, sugar, paper napkin and toothpick. Tom didn't know what time it was – peeling back the layers of waterproofing was too much hassle just to look at his watch – but he figured it was a sign to have lunch. He squatted on the trunk of a downed tree and did just that, opening the utensil bag with his teeth so he could use the salt on the tasteless gas-station sandwich he'd bought, which turned to mush in the rain faster than he could eat it.

The afternoon passed in the same excruciatingly slow way. He added a suitcase to his list of booty, tan leather, with a businessman's array of shaving kit and carefully filed paper-work inside. He found a child's T-shirt with 'Princess' on it in glitter; he found seven mini-cans of Coke and one of 7-Up; he found a hand and part of a forearm. The forearm had freckles and pale, curly hair on it, and a twenty-four-hour Swatch was still strapped to the wrist. Tom noticed that it was almost five p.m. The light would be going soon; he'd come back tomorrow. He photographed the arm, making sure that the watch could be easily identified, then sealed it carefully inside a bag to prevent predation, flagged it and entered its location on the GPS.

As he stood up, he caught a flash of red between the trees.

With anticipation rising in him as the red thing grew in his obstructed vision, Tom dropped into a gully, jumped what had become a little stream, and slipped and slithered up the other muddy side. He skidded near the top of the bank and scraped his injured leg against a root. 'Fuck!' The pain flared. He gripped a branch and stood on one leg for a long second, doubled over, panting at the dirt.

He straightened up slowly and stopped dead, his harsh breaths frozen in his chest.

In a small clearing, four people were sitting in a block of airline seats.

As if in a dream, Tom moved towards them – no longer aware of the rain or the mud – hearing only the ticking of his pulse in his ears.

They looked so alive.

That was impossible. Wasn't it? They had to be dead. And yet there they were, each sitting upright, the one closest to him in a red sweatshirt. From that angle – behind them – they looked as if they were waiting for the in-flight movie to start.

Tom reached the seats, his heart bumping so wildly in his chest that it made the strip of Oklahoma trees into a jungle filled with warring natives.

He took a breath, as if he was about to dive into a deep pool, and looked down.

They were all dead, of course.

The young, dark-haired man closest to him – the one in the red sweatshirt – had his head twisted to one side and his mouth open, as if he was asleep and snoring. There was blood around his mouth and nose where his lungs had imploded upon the sudden loss of pressure.

The older man beside him had lost an arm below the shoulder but his face was unperturbed.

Tom took a pace forward and looked across at a chubby man, whose head had dropped so far forward that he appeared to be closely examining the twin stumps his legs had become just above the knees. Two bits of shiny blue-white bone protruded rudely from the meat and the tattered remains of his beige old-man slacks.

The girl who sat beside him was Lucia's sister.

Tom grunted as that certainty hit him like something physical.

Candice Holmes had been pretty in the same soft, unassuming way her sister still was. Her hair was pulled back in two neat clips and the leaves and pieces of twig that decorated it looked deliberate, rather than the result of her 120 m.p.h. fall through the forest at the end of a 27,000-foot drop. Her head was thrown back against the rest, and her golden-brown eyes were open and filled with rain that spilled over and ran, like little rivers of tears, across her cheeks. A smear of blood at one corner of her mouth had been almost washed away by the rain.

Tom sat down heavily beside Candice, feeling the cold wet earth tug at him, suddenly aware once more of the sound of the rain dropping through the trees around him. The girl's slim brown arm hung gently beside her seat, a silver bracelet with a single charm on it falling over the back of her delicate hand. The charm was of a penguin. He reached out and touched it, the backs of his fingers sliding against her hand. Her skin was cold, but so was his in the unseasonable rain.

Tom let go of the penguin, then sat for a while and held the dead girl's hand while the rain dripped from the peak of his cap, and cried from her eyes.

*

As soon as the progress meeting was over, and Munro and Ryland had gone to speak to the press and families, Tom went back to his room and called Lucia on the phone he'd picked up at the airport. He'd also taken out insurance, feeling smug that he would almost certainly be claiming at some point. He called three times, twice hanging up before the phone could start ringing in LA. Finally he found his balls.

'Lucia?'

'Yes?'

'It's Tom Patrick.'

Silence. Then, 'Oh. Hello.' Cold but polite.

'I'm in Oklahoma.'

Instantly, the coldness left her, along with the strength, and when she spoke again it was with the voice of a frightened child already on the edge of tears. 'Yes?'

Tom felt like a shit: Lucia had obviously thought he might be calling for more selfish reasons, even at a time like this. Apparently she thought he was that big an asshole.

'Did Candice wear a silver bracelet, Lucia?'

'She had a bracelet . . . with a penguin on it.'

He knew there was no easy way to do this, so went straight for the quickest. 'Then we found her body. I'm sorry.'

Lucia started to cry and he waited in silence, hating this. He could tell she was trying to control it, and wanted to tell her not to bother, but she clearly wanted to talk through it, and made a reasonable job of it.

'Was she. . . did she . . .'

'There wasn't a mark on her.'

'Don't lie to me!' Her anger surprised him.

'Lucia, I swear. She was still strapped in her seat. She looked like she was sleeping – I couldn't believe it. She looked so alive, I sat and held her hand. That was when I noticed the penguin.'

Lucia sobbed, and suddenly Tom wished he'd flown back to LA to tell her.

'Are you alone?'

'. . . the Sawmill,' he managed to decipher.

'Is there someone at home you can be with?'

'I have to tell my mom.' She hitched painfully, 'How can I tell my mom?'

'You want me to call her?'

'No. I need to do it. I need to tell her.' She was crying loudly now, and Tom felt his own throat tighten at the sound of her raw grief.

'Why don't you speak to Louis first? Ask him to tell her. He's right there with her, isn't he?'

She made a little sound that he interpreted as agreement.

'Go home, Lucia. Call Louis, then go to bed, okay?'

'Okay,' she gasped, between sobs.

'Get drunk. Something. I'll call you later.'

'Okay.' The word tailed off and she hung up in a burst of fresh weeping.

Tom stared at the phone in his hand, wondering why the hell he'd said he'd call her later. Wondering why the hell he didn't regret saying it.

*

He went out to get food and ran into Munro, Carling, Potts and Jan Ryland in the lobby. The rain had stopped so they walked to a local steak bar where Tom ordered catfish – the only thing on the menu that wasn't red meat.

Munro ordered beers and nobody questioned it when Tom ordered another just minutes later.

They'd all found bodies; they all understood.

Carling, Potts and Ryland continued a tease that had obviously been going on all day about another case in another town. Munro barely joined in, but smiled and nodded as he ate, and made sure they all had what they wanted.

Tom ate slowly and quietly, but was glad to be in the company of the others, who were keen to regain normality, if only for a couple of hours before bed. It rubbed off on him: he was soothed by the noises of the bar, the clinking of glasses, laughter from another table, the pan-piped Simon and Garfunkel, which, on any other night of his life, might have led to a scene with a waiter but tonight allowed him to feel like he was drowning gently in middle-American nothingness. It was the land that taste forgot, but it was a warm and cosy land, distant from vomity card-room carpets and guns in mouths and young girls who should have been in LA with their sisters but who were instead being zipped up in black rubber and trucked slowly to the makeshift morgue on the local high-school basketball court.

He even felt a wishy-washy sense of burgeoning goodwill towards Lenny Munro. The guy wasn't all uptight asshole, after all.

He started to tell him about the Avia Freight connection, to check the batch number on the fan disc when he found it, but Munro waved it away. 'Tomorrow, Tom. We'll talk about it then. Have a drink.'

Tom ate half his fish, but drank all his beers, and laid his arm across Jan Ryland's shoulders to steady himself as they strolled back to the Holiday Inn. Now that the rain had stopped, the returning heat was sucking it off the blacktop in wisps of steam; the humidity and the drink made him feel warm and flushed.

They stopped in the light spilling out of the lobby so Mike Carling could finish his cigar.

'Hope that's the end of the rain,' said Munro.

'Don't let these farmers hear you say that,' said Potts. 'Round here that's blasphemy.'

Carling drew on his cigar and Tom watched it glow orange and black like a microcosmic planet, new and molten in the dark. He felt calm and content and knew he'd sleep well in his good-smelling shorts and clean hotel sheets. He'd call Lucia first. He'd done what he promised her he would – he'd found her sister – even if it was a week late. That had to count for something, didn't it? He thought it did, and that made him feel good.

'I'm turning in,' said Jan.

Munro grunted as if in agreement, and stumbled sideways. Tom put out an arm automatically to steady him but Munro's knees gave way and Tom found himself stumbling too, dropping to the ground with the man in his arms, trying to break his fall.

'Hey, Lenny, you lightweight!' said Potts.

Carling laughed and bent to help them both up.

Tom looked down, fuzzily confused by the blood on Munro's neat blue shirt, suddenly unnerved by the way the man's head lolled on his thigh.

It was only when he heard the squeal of tyres as a car peeled out of the hotel lot that he realized Lenny Munro had been shot.

Tom was running before he even knew he'd stood up.

In the dark and sodium-light the Jeep was big and black and reflective, glimmering in the night. He sprinted at an angle across the lot to intercept it at the stop light and, for a few heady seconds, he closed on it. Then it got away from him again.

He vaulted a low wall and cut another corner; horns blared as he raced down the white centre line, fifty yards behind the car in traffic. Forty yards.

Thirty.

His feet pounded, his breath tore painfully through his lungs and he thought dimly of joining a gym. The Jeep slowed. For a crazy moment he thought it was going to stop for the red light, and the problem of what he would do with it when he caught it loomed large.

And then, when he could almost reach out and touch the back of the vehicle, he saw the passenger window slide down, a narrow bar of dead black opening in the liquid mirror of glass, and the muzzle of a gun point straight at him.

Tom dived to the side and felt something spit into his face as he hit the ground. He rolled behind the Jeep, out of the firing line, and lay panting, his nose pressed against the asphalt. Then his world turned from black-and-red to brilliant colour as the reversing lights blazed on.

If the driver hadn't hit the gas so hard, he'd have run Tom Patrick over, like a Virginia squirrel. As it was, the wheels spun and shrieked and smoked for the split second it took Tom to register what was happening and throw himself out of the way, rolling against the kerb. Then he was up and running again, but away from the Jeep this time, across a grassy bank, through a McDonald's drive-thru, over a chain-link fence, wrenching his shoulder, scattering trash. He heard no sounds of pursuit but wasn't taking any chances. He hurtled down an alleyway and skidded on to a well-lit street filled with restaurants, including the steak bar they'd left a lifetime ago. Immediately he forced himself to walk. Dozens of people were spilling out of bars and eateries, and cars drifted softly by.

He was wearing a black hooded top; he ripped it off so he was in just a white T-shirt. Cars passed him and he dared not look round. At any second he expected to feel white-hot bullets. His leg screamed furiously at him, but he tried to minimize any limp. He straightened and walked back to the main drag.

He emerged half a block up from the Holiday Inn, where blue and red lights now flickered lazily over the body of Lenny Munro.

35

A NURSE PICKED CHIPS of asphalt out of Tom's cheek and forehead. He winced and the doctor smiled cheerfully. 'You're lucky she's not picking a bullet out of your eye socket.'

Tom stayed quiet. There were few things he hated more than happy doctors; he wasn't encouraging this one.

'As for your leg . . .'

The stitches in his calf had been torn free. His freshly laundered jeans, socks and sneakers lay in a bloody pile near the door.

The doctor irrigated the jagged tear, humming a tune, then pushed his glasses down his nose so he could look over them to thread a needle.

'I need to make a phone call.'

'When I'm through here.'

'How long will that be?'

'Not long.'

'How long is not long?'

'Soon,' he said, and dug the needle into Tom's leg.

'Shit!'

'I know.' The doctor grinned. 'It really hurts, doesn't it?'

* * *

Tom left the hospital in somebody else's pants. Somebody who was shorter and a lot fatter than him and who, Tom imagined, was also probably dead.

Jan Ryland had been waiting for him, so he hadn't been able to call Lucia, and they drove back to the hotel in virtual silence. They said good night at her door and she hugged him. 'I don't understand it,' she said flatly. 'Why Lenny?'

'Yeah,' he said noncommittally, although disturbing answers had already taken root in his mind.

Lenny Munro might have been a random victim. Or he might have been a target before Pete had given him the bolt. Might have been either. But Tom doubted both. And if Munro had become a target because of the bolt, then Tom had to look at the people who had known he had it.

Pete LaBello. Ryland. Carling. Potts.

And Ness Franklin.

He let go of Ryland and stepped back. 'Where's the bolt, Jan? From the South African jet?'

She looked confused. 'I don't know.'

'Where did Lenny keep it?'

Her brow furrowed. 'In the trailer, I guess. Or in his room. He wouldn't have wanted it getting mixed up with 823 wreckage.'

'Which is his room?'

'Two nineteen.'

*

Upstairs, there were still a few cops outside Munro's room. Tom showed his ID and told them what he was looking for and why. He didn't have time to mess around.

Sniffing a motive, a young detective in a suit and tie introduced himself as Sean Hapgood. 'Someone was sure looking for something,' he said, and opened the door to 219.

The place had been turned over. No drawer was unemptied, no closet unraided. Lenny Munro's few clothes and many files were hurled about as if a twister had passed through.

'Shit,' said Tom. If the bolt had been here, they'd have found it. 'We have to check the trailer at the site.'

Hapgood agreed readily, much to his relief – he was so drugged up he didn't think he could drive. Tom picked up the trailer key from Jan Ryland, and Hapgood drove him to Crossways.

They both splashed through the mud to the trailer, Tom clutching his big pants in front of him to avoid losing them. He needn't have bothered with the key. They could see the door was ajar from twenty paces.

'Shit,' said Tom again.

Inside everything had been scattered, broken or stolen. Paperwork had been thrown about and trodden into the muddy floor. Disconnected laptop cables told their own story.

Hapgood held one up. 'Computers?'

Tom thought of the work that would have to be painstakingly repeated and could only nod mutely.

He kicked a few drawers aside but knew there was no point in looking for the bolt. If it had been here, they would have found it.

But that didn't mean they *had* found it. The wan hope flickered in him, even though he couldn't think where else it might be.

The painkillers the jolly doctor had given him were wearing off: his leg ached and his face burned.

He dragged himself through the mud back to Hapgood's car and was embarrassed when the cop shook him awake at the Holiday Inn.

By the time Tom finally slid between the fresh hotel sheets in his good-smelling shorts, the experience had lost a lot of the comfort he'd expected from it a bare six hours before.

*

A knock at his door woke him at eight a.m. and he felt a hundred years old as he stumbled out of bed on his stiff leg, with a head like a hot, ringing bell.

Pete LaBello stood in the hallway. 'You look like shit.'

Tom saw the truth of that in the genuine shock on his boss's face. He stepped back from the door to let him in, and sat down on the edge of the bed.

Pete took the armchair. 'Jan called me.'

'Yeah.'

'I can't believe it. Lenny Munro.'

'Yeah.'

'It's fucked up.'

It certainly was. 'You want a coffee or something?' Tom offered vaguely.

'No, thanks.'

There was gaping silence as Pete picked at the stitching on the armrest, avoiding Tom's eyes until he could no longer hold it in. 'You think it's about the bolt?' he asked quietly.

Tom started to nod – and before he knew it he was crying like a kid lost in a supermarket, tears running down his nose and dripping from his chin, his chest heaving with sobs born of tension, frustration and guilt that had been going on for months before he'd marked Lenny Munro for death by the one altruistic gesture he could ever remember making.

He pressed a hand to his stomach, as if he could somehow force it all back inside, but it made no difference. Even the embarrassment of crying in front of Pete LaBello couldn't make it stop. All he could do was sit there and wait for it to end.

When it finally did, he blew his nose into yesterday's T-shirt and murmured, 'Fuck.'

Pete got up, sniffed and cleared his throat. He still sounded a little hoarse when he said, 'I'm taking Lenny's wife to the morgue to ID the body. I'll see you later.' He briefly laid a hand on Tom's bare shoulder, then left.

It was only after he'd gone that Tom finally got round to wondering whether the bullet had been meant for him.

After all, he was the one who wouldn't let the *Pride of Maine* go. Even when Stanley and the Weasel had as good as told him to drop it, something inside him had dug in its heels and refused. Maybe the only reason he wasn't lying dead on a slab right now was because they hadn't known he was going to be here. Lenny had called and he'd left. Hadn't told anyone. Not even Ness.

Tom frowned with the effort of making sense of it all and slowly came back to Stanley and the Weasel.

He pulled on his only other pair of jeans and called Halo, who answered sounding like a confused drunk. 'Yeah. What?'

'Halo, it's Tom.'

In an LA where the dawn was only just breaking, Halo

Jackson leaned over to check his alarm clock. Tom beat him to the verdict.

'It's six a.m. I'm sorry.'

Something in Tom Patrick's voice made Halo more concerned than angry. ''S okay. What's up?'

'The guy who grabbed you outside Vee's house that night.'

Halo frowned, readjusting. 'Yeah?'

'What did he look like?'

'He was white. Strong. Big.'

'Don't bullshit me, Halo. I don't care if you got beat up by a fucking Girl Scout. What did he look like?'

Halo reconsidered. 'He was strong,' he insisted. 'But he wasn't that big. Maybe my height.'

'Or a bit less?'

'Maybe.'

'Maybe older than you?'

'Maybe,' Halo said grudgingly. 'A bit.'

'Was he wearing a suit?'

'Yes!' said Halo, surprised by his sudden recollection. 'Yeah, he was! And a tie. Why?'

There was a brief silence.

'Tom?' said Halo, louder. This time he heard an answering grunt. 'Tom? You think it was about the *Pride of Maine*?' He held his breath, aware that Vee was awake and watching him.

'Isn't everything?' said Tom.

*

Tom's stomach churned, part shock at the previous night's events, part excitement. Bits of the jigsaw were slowly emerging from the darkness and starting to drop into place. Finally he had enough to start putting the puzzle together, even though he couldn't yet see the picture he was trying to build. At least he was convinced now that pretty much all the pieces were from the same puzzle.

He knocked on Jan Ryland's door and she opened it in pink pyjamas, still with bed hair.

'We working today?' he asked, without preamble.

She shook her head. 'Why? You got somewhere to be?'

'LA. Not for long, though.'

'It's okay.'

'Did the cops tell you about the trailer?'

She sighed. 'Yes. We'll have to start again.'

He handed her the key and turned away.

'Tom?'

He looked back at her.

'Last night. Thanks for going after them.'

He shrugged and walked away. He wasn't about to take credit for trying to catch Munro's killers when he might as well have painted a bull's-eye on the man's chest.

He went back to his room and packed.

As Tom was throwing his gear into the trunk of his rental in the hotel lot, Pete pulled up and helped a woman he knew must be Lenny Munro's widow out of his car. He glanced around for someplace he could duck out of sight but his heart sank as Pete saw him and raised a 'hold-on' hand.

He clicked the trunk closed and slowly walked across the lot, noticing that police tape now cordoned off the corner where the Jeep had been parked last night. Next to the space was a police cruiser, a bored-looking cop securing the scene.

'Tom Patrick, this is Gloria Munro.'

Lenny Munro's wife was a small, homely woman with laugh lines round every one of her features. Even now, she smiled at him with real warmth and held out her hand for shaking. The words 'sorry for your loss' stuck in his throat and he could barely look at her as he mumbled, 'Hello.' He wondered how often Lenny Munro had told his wife what a prick he was.

'Mr Patrick, Pete tells me you went after them. Thank you so much.'

He nodded dumbly and she squeezed his hand, as if he was the one who'd just lost his life partner.

Tom noticed that she held a clear plastic Ziploc bag in her other hand. Lenny Munro's personal effects, as collated by the Tulsa Police Department morgue, stuff he must have had in his pockets. He could see Munro's cheap leather wallet, a watch, a couple of slips of paper.

And Lemon's bolt.

Right there. In the bag.

Munro must have kept it on him. Stuffed it casually into a pocket, little knowing that *this* was what they wanted; *this* was what he was going to die for.

Tom almost whooped in relief and had to resist the urge to yank the Ziploc out of the grieving widow's grasp and tear it open right there in the parking lot. It took all his restraint.

'Will you join us for a drink, Tom?' Her eyes shone with gratitude through the pain, and he thought that if he'd known Gloria Munro before all this, maybe he'd have liked Lenny more.

'I have to go,' he said.

'It was so nice to meet you.'

'Sorry for your loss,' he finally managed to croak out,

feeling the empty formality of those by-rote words more fiercely than he ever had.

He walked back to his car, got in and quickly drove away before they reached the front porch where Lenny Munro had died.

He wanted them to see him go.

*

Pete LaBello's retirement date seemed to be receding, rather than getting closer. Like some Hitchcockian vortex, he could see it spinning away from him, just out of reach of his grasping fingers. On days like today he thought he'd never get there, that his personal Hell was to remain on the brink of retirement while all the time his job became more and more complex; more and more surreal.

The thing with Tom Patrick had been bad enough; now here he was sipping red wine over dinner with what remained of the Go Team and Lenny Munro's widow. To add to the weirdness, it was Gloria Munro who was holding them all together. No doubt it would hit her later: a week from now, a month from now, a year from now, she'd be pressing a cantaloupe at the grocery store and realize her husband Lenny – boring old Lenny who wore button-down shirts and kept pens in his top pocket – had been gunned down by men in a big black Jeep, like some rap star. But for now Gloria Munro was being mother to the stricken Jan Ryland, the silent, tight-jawed Mike Carling and Bryce Potts, as they took for ever over their salads so they wouldn't have to speak to one another.

Pete sighed and took another sip of red wine. He didn't

even like red wine – it gave him a headache – but he needed something to stop him staring endlessly at the tablecloth as Gloria tried to draw them out of themselves, leading by example with a tender little story of how Lenny had screwed up on an early case and immediately mailed a letter of resignation. Gloria had chased after the mailman on her six-year-old daughter's Barbie bicycle to beg for the letter back.

They all smiled, although Jan's chin wobbled.

Pete knew *he* should be doing this. It was his job to keep them on track, to steer them carefully back to normality, to remind them there was work to be done. But it was hard. Gloria had lost Lenny Munro, sure, but in an abstract way from a thousand miles off; Jan and Mike and Bryce had watched him die at their feet. Mike and Bryce didn't even have the macho comfort of having followed Tom Patrick's brave – stupid – gesture in running after the killers and getting a face full of ricochet for his pains.

Pete's heart seemed to have done nothing but sink steadily over the past year; it was nothing new to feel it drop again now as he realized his team was good for nothing on this investigation. He'd have to bring Jan back to DC and send Mike and Bryce home to Texas. Have them brief new agents. Start again. He would begin working on it in the morning. The press and the families would understand a short delay, but no more than that. He wished he could hand it to Tom Patrick but that brilliant sonofabitch had backed them both into the same corner and then jumped before Pete had been forced to push him.

Pete wanted nothing more than to throw down his napkin, push back his chair and get the hell out of there. But Gloria was still doing her best to help them all through the meal, and if she could stay through her grief, he could find no excuse to go.

Finally it was over. They all feigned fullness so they could skip dessert, and Gloria hugged each of them as if absolving them from the sin of still being alive.

Pete walked her to the first-floor room he'd had Kitty reserve. 'Will you be all right?' he asked, at the door.

'I'm sure I will be. You've been so kind.'

'We all liked and respected Lenny very much.' It wasn't strictly true, but at a time like this, Pete almost felt it might have been. He pecked her on the cheek and she opened the door.

And screamed.

In the darkness a shadow skittered across the room.

Pete pushed past Gloria, yelling, 'Go get help!' and went after the man. He cracked his knee on the bed as he rounded it, swore, and stopped briefly at the sharp pain.

The man was behind the drapes now, half out of the window. Pete made a grab for him, missed, and the shadow dropped out of sight.

If it had been anyone's room but Gloria Munro's, Pete would have let him go and been relieved that he'd done his bit without having to confront anyone. But he owed Lenny Munro's widow more than that. He clambered out of the window, snagging the leg of his pants on the catch, and fell heavily – on to something that grunted as he knocked the air out of its lungs.

'Shit.'

The man shoved Pete off him, groaned and rolled unsteadily to his knees. 'You nearly killed me!'

Pete lay on his back, winded, staring up at Tom Patrick.

Tom grimaced and held his ribs where Pete's elbow had dug in. He got slowly to his feet. 'Jesus! Aren't you supposed to be retiring?' He sucked in his breath and doubled over with his hands on his knees.

'What the hell are you doing?' Pete squeezed out.

Still breathless, Tom slowly held up the bolt. 'I don't know,' he said frankly, then jerked a thumb over his shoulder at the window they'd just come through. 'I think I'm saving her life.'

The two men stared at each other in the darkness. Then the light went on in Gloria Munro's room.

Tom turned and ran.

36

ONLY PETE LABELLO knew he had Lemon's bolt. That was good: the fewer people who knew about it, the fewer people were in danger. So Tom felt a little guilty when he called Halo as soon as he landed at LAX, met him at the same coffee shop as before, and told him someone had tried to steal it.

Halo listened, then reduced it to its constituent parts like the organizer he was.

'The *Pride of Maine* disc is gone. The South African disc is gone and the Oklahoma crash . . . ?'

'Too early to tell. But if they'd got the bolt we couldn't have linked Oklahoma to either of the other two incidents. No pattern without the paperwork or the physical evidence.'

'Could it be the bolt that's fake?'

'It's not logical,' said Tom. 'Why take the same risks to fake a six-dollar bolt when you can fake a three-grand disc? And stealing the South African jet's paperwork clinches it for me.'

Halo nodded slowly.

'Don't tell anyone else about the bolt,' Tom warned.

'Why not?' said Halo. 'It's evidence. That's a good thing, isn't it?'

Tom had to tell him about Lenny Munro, which made

Halo go all quiet and stare into the ridiculously frothy coffee Tom had bought for him while he'd waited for him to make his way up from his evening shift in Hangar Thirteen.

'I won't tell anyone,' agreed Halo.

'Not even Vee.'

'Are you shitting me? Specially not Vee.'

'From now on, we shouldn't have contact unless it's an emergency,' said Tom, almost cringing at the melodrama.

But Halo didn't laugh at him, just nodded silently.

They sat and sipped their coffee. Halo got a little moustache but this time Tom didn't find it even vaguely amusing. Instead he just tapped his own lip and Halo wiped his mouth on his sleeve.

'So,' Halo said eventually, 'I guess it was *Three Days of the Condor* after all.'

'I guess so.'

'Makes me wonder what happened to Niño.'

'Yeah,' said Tom. It made him wonder what had happened to a lot of people.

*

'Where have you *been*?' Ness's voice was half angry, half relieved.

Tom remembered a time when he'd been eight and had missed the school bus and, for some now-forgotten reason, decided to walk the five miles home just for the hell of it. When he'd got there, after dark, his mother had said the same words in the same way, then slapped him hard in the face, before holding him so tightly he'd thought he'd never breathe again. He didn't know which was more scary: her anger or her love.

'Away,' he said.

She hesitated, then apparently let it go. 'Can you play?'

'I just walked in.'

It was true. He'd picked up the ringing phone before he'd even put his bag down. But she didn't offer an alternative.

'When?'

'Three hours. At the Honolulu.'

He sighed. Paying rent on this place was a joke – he might as well take a lease on a black vinyl chair at LAX with a weekend place up at Mount Poker Table. 'I'll see you in the lot.'

'Okay,' she said, and hung up.

Tom let out a long breath. Ness had turned to quicksand under him. He didn't know how deep it was – he didn't know if there was anything to grab on to to keep from being sucked down. He didn't even know if sinking into her would be good or bad. He thought of the last time they'd been together, when they'd made love and she'd cried, and tried to recapture the tenderness he'd felt for her then, but it eluded him. All he could feel now was an uneasy wariness, which reflected back at him from her.

He hadn't asked what had happened when he'd been unable to play the last time – hadn't even called her to tell her – but she was still alive and talking and apparently in the same line of work, so he assumed it was nothing too bad.

He wanted to see her, though.

He wanted to see her face when he told her about Lenny Munro.

*

He'd forgotten to call Lucia back before leaving Oklahoma. It wasn't his fault: so much had happened.

He called her now.

'Lucia? It's Tom.' He could hear her breathing.

Then she quietly hung up.

37

HE PULLED THE Buick into the spot beside Ness's Lotus in a far corner of the Honolulu parking lot, and got out. She met his eyes and gave a neutral smile that made his stomach tighten. He folded himself into the little car. 'Hi. How are you?'

She nodded and handed him two rolls of hundreds.

'Are you coming in?' He looked at her face and saw that there was no sign of the old bruising or any new marks.

'Yes.'

'Good.'

'Why didn't you come last time, when you said you would?'

'I had to work. You were okay?'

She ignored his question. 'But you quit,' she said.

'Lenny Munro called me. He needed help.'

She frowned slightly. 'The man you gave Lemon's bolt to?'

'Yes.'

She nodded, remembering, her face giving nothing away: 'Did you ask him about your job?'

'I didn't get a chance,' he said. 'Someone killed him.'

She stared at him, searching his eyes for a lie – as he was doing with hers. 'Why would someone kill him?'

She didn't look like a liar: she looked genuinely puzzled.

He never took his eyes off hers. Just shrugged.

She bit her lip and frowned some more, her eyes focusing on something he couldn't see, off in the distance. She was still beautiful, he thought. It was hard to believe anyone so beautiful could do ugly things. He didn't want to believe it.

'Where's the bolt now?'

Her words stabbed him, like a knife in the heart. The hope he realized he'd been clinging to was ripped from him and he was set adrift on a sea of angry sadness. He'd been going to work up to asking her about Stanley. Stanley and the Weasel. How much she knew about them, their connection with the *Pride of Maine*, *her* connection . . .

He didn't need to.

He'd just told her Lenny Munro had been killed.

And all she wanted to know was where the bolt was.

'I don't know,' he lied softly.

*

Tom was still in a kind of hurt shock when he sat down at the No Limit table with Ness's twenty thousand dollars. He barely registered the other players, although Ness had run an eye over them before approving the table, and told him to watch out for a skinny Japanese girl with a Minnie Mouse tattoo on the back of her wrist. She was new on the scene.

His mind churned through options and possibilities, all of which twisted back on themselves to become traps and pitfalls in his thumping, free-floating thoughts.

Ness had betrayed him. He'd trusted her, and she'd betrayed him. They'd made love until she'd cried and she'd still betrayed him. He didn't know how far back that betrayal went, but a bullet in Lenny Munro's chest was far enough.

He thought again of South Africa. Of the way she'd tried to distract him – hell, the way she *had* distracted him – with sex. Her hand on him in Lettie Marais's big, lumpy bed; her thighs pressing him close to her heat as he yanked desperately at that stupid button-fly in the middle of a hot Karoo night; him waking to find her holding the bolt after they'd fucked for the first time in the Table Bay Hotel.

Finally he could see the angles.

The phone in her hand in De Rust. Not for a call to *Richard*, but to somebody *else* – to let them know about the fan disc. Its importance and its vulnerability.

The car that had knocked them into the Karoo and hadn't stopped. If he'd gone after it, instead of fumbling to get inside Ness, maybe he'd have been able to stop them taking the fan disc. Ness had delayed him long enough with the promise of sex, then taken the opportunity of the sudden headlights supposedly to come to her senses, and get back in the car.

If he hadn't woken when he had in Cape Town, would she have walked out with the bolt and left him asleep in a post-coital haze? Flown home alone? Or just thrown the bolt in the harbour and returned to their warm bed to give him one for the road?

He could see it all now.

Tom was dealt in but barely registered his cards.

The only angle he couldn't see was the hospital. He couldn't see how events at the hospital had helped her cause. The fan disc was gone; the bolt not yet discovered; the paperwork stolen; the investigators dead. He was no longer a threat. As far as Ness was concerned, it was mission accomplished.

Then why sit and read to him? Why smooth things over with the doctors and nurses he'd rubbed up the wrong way? Why take him in her mouth? The selflessness jarred. He couldn't reconcile it with his new image of her: of a chrysalis splitting open to reveal not a butterfly but a smooth, dead-eyed deceiver.

In less than an hour, the first ten thousand was gone. Most of Tom's chips now sat in front of the Minnie Mouse girl, the huge piles making her look even smaller. With grim satisfaction, he changed up the second roll and Ness leaned down to put her lips against his ear. 'Get your mind on the job.' She sounded tense.

Fuck you, he thought, and bet recklessly on pocket fours in the face of a possible straight flush that kept three other players in to swell the pot.

A four came up on the river and Tom scooped three and a half thousand dollars.

It turned the tide. Playing stupidly, he started to win steadily. He played every hand, whether it was any good or not. Two hours later he had thirty-three thousand more than he'd started with. He picked up his cards – a two and a seven off-suit – and bluffed with gusto. Ness first put her hand on his neck, then dug in her nails to stop him. He winced, but didn't throw in the hand. Hating her, he raised and re-raised until even Minnie Mouse caved in under pressure and he stole more than fifteen thousand dollars from the table.

Ness gripped his neck and hissed angrily in his ear, 'I'll see you in the car.'

He didn't watch her go, just grinned, picked up six-jack off-suit and took another flyer.

Players started to leave the table as they watched Tom's luck spiral outrageously. Minnie Mouse and a quiet young man wearing a Raiders cap stuck in there. Both were good players. Both made the percentage calls – calls that would have won them pots if they'd been playing someone wholly rational.

Right now, that wasn't Tom.

He took the table for another big pot, bluffing crazily on the promise of a flush, which never came through. The Raiders fan was wiped out and Tom won six and a half grand.

Tom was not himself. Otherwise he would never have flipped over his cards to show that he'd beaten them all with what had finally amounted to a pair of threes on the turn.

'You cheat!' Minnie Mouse said vehemently. A ripple of unease went through the players: there was no question of Tom having cheated, but it was not an accusation that was ever made or taken lightly at a poker table.

Everyone looked nervously at Tom, who snapped, 'You loser.'

'Fuck you. You cheater!'

The dealer, a pretty, round-faced Vietnamese girl, signalled to a floor man and two security staff hovered closer than before.

The dealer shoved the cards into the shoe, drew out the freshly shuffled pack and dealt quickly, but Minnie Mouse spat at Tom in Japanese. She snatched up her cards, muttering furiously. Steaming, she made a stand.

Tom stoked the pot to four thousand dollars; the other

players dropped out one by one again but the girl kept pace, throwing her chips down with clattering anger each time, muttering under her breath and finally going all in, turning over pocket jacks with jack high on the table.

Tom showed her his pocket queens, and when another came up on the river, he stood up and grinned meanly at her shocked, pale face, then went to the pay window as if in a harsh, noisy dream.

Behind him the security men threw the now-hysterical Japanese girl out. He didn't look round, but he heard her shouting receding as the cashier counted out almost $112,000.

He declined the offer of a cheque.

He declined the offer of an escort to his car.

He stepped out from between the plastic palm trees into the sultry California night and looked to the left-hand corner of the lot, where he could just see the low roof of the Lotus and the higher one of his Buick beside it. Then he turned right on to the strip and caught a cab.

'Where to?' the driver said.

'Santa Ana,' he replied.

38

THE SAWMILL WAS FULL. Tom couldn't get a seat anywhere near the stage so he stood at the bar and watched the dancers over the other patrons' heads while he knocked back two Jack Daniel's in quick succession, then made the third last.

Despite the whiskey burning slowly through his veins, he felt shaky now the win-high was gone. In the cab he'd reorganized the money so it wasn't in cumbersome rolls, and divided it into equal flat slabs, but $112,000 was still a lot of money to stuff into one pair of jeans and a leather jacket, and now he was aware of it padding him, bulking him up, chafing his thighs and tickling his ribs when he moved.

As the high left him, only the bitter anger remained – joined by fear. He hadn't known what he was going to do when he left the Honolulu until the very moment he walked away from Ness instead of towards her. Everything he'd been through in the previous eighteen months had built up to that point, his future chosen on a patch of red carpet laid on asphalt between two plastic palm trees. He'd made a spur-of-the-moment decision that he was going to have to live by for ever.

There was no going back.

They might already be at his condo, turning it over, looking for the bolt, looking for the money, looking for him. He didn't care. There was nothing there he loved, and the place usually looked like it had just been tossed by the cops anyway.

Going to Halo was not an option. Tom needed to keep as far away from Halo as he possibly could right now. He couldn't go to the police. The money straining his pockets condemned him like a confession. A dozen people at the Honolulu could testify he'd sat down with twenty thousand dollars he hadn't earned, and the hand of a known criminal associate on his shoulder. The money gave him options but it also made him a target.

A *bigger* target.

Every road seemed closed to him but this one. Tom's mind tried to skitter away from just why he'd made his great escape to a strip club in Santa Ana instead of flying to Omaha or Oregon, building a shack and raising pigs or hunting Bigfoot for the rest of his anonymous life.

Lucia.

He told himself he wanted to see how she was holding up after the death of her sister, but the truth was that he just wanted to see her. Any place. Any time. Any reason.

Or no reason at all.

As if she'd heard his thoughts, Lucia came onstage with another black girl, and his heart lurched as it never had when he was bluffing his way to a stolen pot. Never had with Ness.

She looked slimmer. Too much slimmer. That's how she's holding up, Tom thought sadly. It was only a week and already she'd lost weight.

She started to dance, her eyes closed to preserve her privacy as her body became public property.

The other girl was more obvious, with a high, tight ass and hard silicone breasts, but for once the customers seemed more drawn to Lucia as she made her body a sinuous, sensuous wave of soft beauty.

When the music ended, dozens of hands reached up to touch her and to stuff bills into her G-string. Tom saw a middle-aged man grip her thigh hard as she knelt in front of him, and saw her wince, before smiling emptily over his head and taking his money.

Tom found himself at the stage. He pulled the man back by the shoulder, breaking his contact with Lucia.

'What the fuck?' the man said, then backed off when he saw the look in Tom's eyes.

'Lucia.'

She looked surprised, then angry. Then blank. She rose carefully and turned her back on him, taking bills from men on the other side of the walkway.

'I need to talk to you.'

The music started again and two new girls walked out, hips thrust forward, shoulders back, lips parted. Lucia ignored him and headed backstage.

Tom jumped on to the stage and went after her, followed by the angry shouts of the other customers.

He grabbed her arm. 'Lucia—'

Strong arms choked off his next words and he was yanked clear off his feet. Lucia's face registered uncertainty before disappearing from his view and he found himself looking up into the lighting rig as the man who'd grabbed him round the neck, and somebody else, lifted him like a log and carried him roughly through a series of dark, sharp-edged corridors until he felt the night air on his face – and then the hard reality of the parking lot as they dropped him without bothering first to set him vertical.

Big hands grabbed the lapels of his jacket and the man, who reminded him very much of post-diet Ronaldo Suarez, dragged Tom's wincing face to within an inch of his own. 'Don't. Touch. The fucking. Girls.' He dropped Tom hard, so that his head bounced on the broken asphalt, and walked away. Dimly, Tom heard the back door of the Sawmill bang shut.

He lay there, getting his breath back.

As kick-outs went, that wasn't such a bad one. And the money had broken his fall.

He started to laugh. It was true – his head hurt but nothing else did; the bolt in his jeans pocket had dug into his hip a little but otherwise he was too well padded to have suffered any injury. The thought made the laughter bubble up even more strongly and he lay there and laughed at the moon until, again, he could barely breathe, then slowly got to his feet and put his fingers to the back of his head. There was blood, but not much.

He didn't know what to do now. Where to go. His car was back at the Honolulu; his condo was a no-go zone.

He wandered down the strip and broke into his $112,000 to buy a bucket of Kentucky Fried Chicken and a Coke, a transaction so meagre that it set him laughing once more, so that the staff and few other customers watched him carefully while he ate.

Then he went back to the Sawmill, upended a trash can and sat on it for two hours until Lucia came out of the back door.

'Lucia. I need to talk to you.'

'I'm busy.'

She walked past him towards a beat-up Mitsubishi Colt.

'Are you okay?'

She ignored him and went to unlock the car, fiddling to get the key to engage.

'I know I said I'd call you.'

'It doesn't matter.'

'Yeah, it does. And I was going to. But someone got killed. Shot.'

She looked at him with borderline contempt.

'I swear,' he added, like a fifth-grader.

Why did this always happen to him around her, this feeling that he was unworthy? She was a pole-dancing whore, for Chrissakes, not Mother Teresa.

The answers came back at him with slick ease: because she'd left a refund on a Motel 6 pillow; because she'd whipped him at pool and still made him laugh; because nobody really watched her dance but him; because her mother wore white gloves; and because he'd held her dead sister's hand in the rain. All those reasons and more jumbled through his head while she managed to seat the key correctly and open the car door.

'Lucia,' he started, ready to convince her with the un-believable truth. She stopped half in and half out of the car and looked at him, impatient, angry, hurt. He changed his mind.

'I need your help,' he said.

It was the truth too, but it was also the one thing he knew she wouldn't refuse him, and he burned with the shame of sinking low enough to take advantage of someone's impeccably good manners.

*

She drove past the Motel 6 without a glance. Tom knew because he watched her.

She wasn't going to cut him any slack.

'Everything I'm going to tell you is true,' he said, and she slid an appraising look his way, then concentrated on the road again.

'Okay,' she said, 'then I'll believe it all.'

This time he left nothing out. Almost nothing.

She took Harbor Boulevard to Warner, then swung a left and a quick right, and pulled up outside a low stucco apartment block. They sat there until he finished up with stealing evidence from a grieving widow and $112,000 from what he had to assume was the Mafia, or the Russian Mafia, or the Irish Mafia. Some ethnic, scary mob, in any case.

'I've only left one thing out,' he told her finally, 'and that's to protect somebody else.'

She nodded slowly. 'Why are you telling me this?'

'I told you. I need your help.'

'But why me?'

'I—' He stopped. 'I just . . .' He didn't know what to tell her. Didn't know what to tell himself.

She nodded again. 'Let's go inside.'

Her apartment was tiny but neat and tastefully furnished. She dropped her purse on the couch and disappeared into the kitchen. 'You want coffee?'

'Please.' He stood in the doorway between the two rooms and watched her. 'How's your mother?'

Lucia used a carved wooden scoop to measure the coffee grounds into a black-and-chrome espresso machine. 'If you don't mind,' she said quietly, 'I'd rather not talk about my family with you.'

He felt slapped. Hard. It was a new twist in his humility training.

'What happened to your face?' she said, turning her back to him.

'When I went after the men who shot Munro . . .' it seemed so foolish and unimportant now '. . . I fell.'

'Do you want cream and sugar?'

'Sugar. Thanks.'

They sat down, she on the couch, he in a small leather armchair.

'I don't know what I can do for you, Tom.'

'I don't know either.'

'You must have had some idea when you came to the Sawmill.'

He glanced around the apartment. It was barely big enough for one.

'Do you need a place to stay?'

He wanted to say, 'No,' but he had to say, 'Yes.'

'Okay,' she said. 'For now.'

'I can pay.'

'I don't want that money.'

He felt embarrassed. 'It's all I have.'

She was staring at the wall. 'Then stay for free.' She drained her cup and got up.

'You got some blankets or something? For the couch?'

'You can sleep with me. *Sleep.*'

'Sure,' he said. 'Sleep.'

Man, that humility thing was really getting a workout tonight.

*

By four in the morning, he was all ready to check into a motel. Sleeping with Lucia was impossible. He'd never known that if you did nothing with it a hard-on could last all night. It was a case of ignorance having once been bliss.

Bliss newly defined was Lucia in the little white panties and crop-top she called pyjamas. She was apparently so moved by his sexy presence that she fell asleep before he'd even got out of the bathroom. He slid under the covers beside her, lay on his back, and watched the ceiling fan revolve for the next two hours while his groin ached. Im-fucking-possible.

Only the fact that her sister had just died stopped Tom from putting a careful hand on her breast and seeing how things went from there. At four thirty he conceded defeat and shut himself in the cramped bathroom. He came as quietly as a prisoner, then crept back to bed.

''Kay?' she mumbled, making him jump.

'Yeah,' he said.

Still half asleep she turned over to face him and murmured, 'You're an asshole, you know that?'

'Yeah,' he said again. He didn't know whether she meant for lying beside her all night with a hard-on, for jerking off in the bathroom, or just in general, but right now he thought she was probably right on all counts.

Even so, Lucia fell asleep again with her head on his chest and her right hand curled loosely on his hip.

Tom sighed and decided to write off the night's sleep.

If he hadn't, he wouldn't have heard the front door open.

Just as the sky started to turn cobalt from navy, the soft metallic click made him hold his breath, his ears straining. The smallest squeak of hinges would have gone unnoticed, except that he was already quivering like a pointer, all senses alert.

He rolled over and put his hand on Lucia's mouth and his lips next to her ear, barely whispering, 'Lucia. Wake up.'

She tensed against him.

'Somebody's here. Is there another way out?'

She shook her head.

'Stay here. Don't move.'

She nodded. He let go of her mouth, slid silently out of bed and behind the bedroom door. He felt naked and vulnerable in just his shorts. His eyes darted around, in search of a weapon, but there was nothing. He winced as the tender back of his head nudged a picture frame.

Now he could hear the tiny creaks that told him someone was moving across the living room. He put his eye to a crack in the door and saw the shadowy figure of a man rounding the couch. Just one man.

He glanced at Lucia. She was still in the position he'd left her in, but he could see the dawn light reflected in her open eyes as she watched him, watched the door.

Carefully, Tom turned to the wall and lifted the large picture off its hook. Close up, he could see it was a psychedelic print of John Lennon wearing little round glasses and a T-shirt reading 'Give Peace A Chance'.

As the intruder entered the bedroom, Tom shifted his feet so he was firmly braced. Then, as the man cleared the edge of the door, he swung the glass-fronted print into his face.

The glass shattered loudly and the man dropped with a cry of pain and surprise, but only to one knee. Tom tried to raise the print and hit him again, but the man grabbed one edge of the frame and held it down, over his own head, so Tom couldn't even punch him satisfactorily. Even as his right fist tried to circumvent John Lennon, the man grabbed him round the knee and toppled him backwards on to the wooden floor, the air jerking out of his lungs in a painful jolt.

This is going badly wrong, thought Tom.

Then Lucia stepped on his arm as she jumped off the bed and tried to grab the man round the neck. 'Get out of my house!'

The intruder lashed out at her and she crashed against something with a squeal of pain. The man had his knee in Tom's stomach, a surprisingly effective anchor. It left his hands free to shove Lucia away again as she came back for more. This time he twisted her arm first and she screamed, which gave Tom the impetus to buck the man off him.

They wrestled messily on the floor, each trying to get on top of the other, snatching hair, wrists, ears. Tom grabbed at the man's clothing; the man grabbed at his skin, which was infinitely more painful. The man got on top of him; Tom found a stubbled cheek against his clenched teeth and bit hard, tasting blood, feeling sick that he'd done it, less than human. The yowl that came from his opponent was just as animal.

And suddenly a gun was pressed against his face – cold and hard and frightening. Tom stopped fighting and let go of the man, who turned out to be Mr Stanley.

Of course it did. Who else would it be?

The man with the gun was the Weasel. He smiled down at Tom. 'Mr Patrick. How are you?'

Tom spat Stanley's blood out of his mouth. 'Not great,' he panted.

The Weasel's smile widened.

'Bastard bit me!' said Stanley, clutching his cheek. He drew his arm back but the Weasel put up a hand.

'Not yet,' he said.

Tom twisted his head to look around the room. 'Where's Lucia?'

Stanley sat back on his haunches so Tom could see her lying on the floor beside her dressing-table, apparently out cold.

'Is she okay?'

'Why don't you worry about how *you* are? And how you're gonna be?' said Stanley, as he stood up.

'How did you find me?'

Stanley grinned. 'It's always easy to follow a man who's following his dick.'

Tom said nothing.

'Where's the money?' asked the Weasel.

Still Tom said nothing.

This time the Weasel stepped on Tom's face and pressed it sideways against the wooden floor so he was staring at Lucia's bare, still foot. He dug the barrel of his pistol into Tom's ear. He flinched more in anticipation than in pain.

'Where's the money?' the Weasel said again, calmly.

'And the bolt,' Stanley reminded him.

'Yeah. The money and the bolt.'

Tom felt helpless. Helpless and stupid. He couldn't lie, much though he wanted to. He knew that anyone else he accused of having the bolt would be in mortal danger.

'I've got the money. I don't have the bolt.'

'Bullshit,' said the Weasel, sounding amused. 'We were watching the hotel. We saw you fall out of Mrs Munro's window. Smooth technique, by the way.'

These were the men who'd shot Lenny Munro.

Stanley kicked him in the ribs to speed things along, and when Tom got his breath back, he said, 'In my jeans.'

Stanley snorted in derision and picked them up. The Weasel took the gun out of his ear but kept up the pressure on the side of his face. Tom watched Stanley pat down the pockets and pull out slabs of cash. Then he did the same with his leather jacket. 'Is it all here?'

Tom decided they wouldn't miss the cost of a KFC bargain bucket, so he nodded with difficulty under the Weasel's shoe.

Stanley dipped his hand into the jeans pocket again and drew out the bolt. He squatted down and waggled it in front of Tom's squashed face. 'You don't even have the sense to hide it.' He shook his head in wonder. 'You're such an asshole.'

'So I've been told.'

Stanley stuffed the bolt into his own pocket.

The Weasel pushed Tom on to his side, wound a plastic zip tie around his wrists and pulled it tight. 'Okay, then,' he said. 'On your feet.'

Tom rose, achingly. It seemed to be all he'd done lately. He longed for a time when he was just suspended from work, on a losing streak at cards, and his girlfriend had dumped him. They seemed like halcyon days.

The Weasel gripped his biceps. 'Come on.'

'Can I get dressed?'

'No.'

Stanley bundled the jeans and jacket – still full of money – under his arm. 'Where you're going you won't need any clothes.'

'Swimming?' Tom asked, but without any edge.

He glanced back at Lucia, but was dragged roughly out of the apartment and into the cold of the deep blue dawn.

Stanley's Thunderbird was parked near by and he jingled his keys in his hand as they approached it.

The Weasel pushed Tom's chest against the passenger side and he winced at the cold metal against his skin and the hard ring of the gun barrel against his neck, holding him in place.

Stanley opened the back door. 'Get him in.'

'Put him in the trunk,' said the Weasel.

'Not after what he did last time. Six hundred bucks that cost and there's still blood on the lining.'

'For fuck's sake, just put him in the trunk!' hissed the Weasel, glancing at the sleeping houses around them.

'Fuck that. He can go in here. He's cuffed.'

The Weasel sighed. 'And if some cop looks in at a stoplight and pulls us over for having a half-naked guy tied up in the car? Put him in the fucking trunk, Stanley, and let's get the hell out of here!'

'It's not your car.'

'Jesus *Christ*!'

'Let me get dressed. Then I won't be half naked,' suggested Tom, helpfully.

'Shut up.' The Weasel fisted the gun into the back of his head so hard that his nose banged painfully on the Thunderbird's vinyl roof.

Two sets of headlights came slowly towards them from the direction of the sunrise.

'Get him in the fucking car before someone sees us!' said Stanley, forgetting to keep his voice down.

The Weasel looked at the approaching lights.

'Shit!' he said irritably. He dragged Tom off the car and threw him face-down on the back seat. 'Happy now?'

Stanley said nothing, just got into the car. The Weasel joined him.

The seats were soft, aromatic black leather and Tom determined there and then to piss on them at the very least before this journey was over.

He hoped Lucia wasn't dying because of him. The thought brought a wave of self-loathing and fury that he'd put her in danger. He should have been smarter than that. So what if he'd needed a place to stay? He'd had one hundred and twelve thousand stolen dollars in his pocket: he could've sprung for a bed for the night somewhere that hadn't involved dragging her into all this.

But he'd wanted to see her. Needed to.

Selfishly.

'What the hell are these dicks doing?'

Tom dimly registered the Weasel's words, right before all hell broke loose.

The Thunderbird rocked as the doors were yanked open. Someone gripped him by the hair and dragged him, yelping, onto the asphalt. He caught a glimpse of Stanley on the ground beside him, a gun just inches from his nose, and thought, Thank God, the cops, before he was toed on to his back, and he realized that the new assailants were Japanese.

A young man, in dark glasses despite the sunless sky, pointed a gun at him and said, 'This him?'

'Yes!'

It was Minnie Mouse.

'Tha's him. Tha's the cheater!'

'I'm not—' He stopped fast when Dark Glasses cocked the gun.

'Where's our money?'

'It's not your money. I won it.'

'He cheats!' cried the girl.

'Fuck you,' he said angrily. 'You lost. You played like a drunken teenager!'

The girl stamped a sharp heel into his shoulder. 'You steal my money!'

'Where's our money?' added Dark Glasses.

'That's not his money!' He heard the Weasel say. 'He stole it from us! If you take it, you're fucking with the wrong people, my friend!'

Someone round that side of the car said, 'We're not your friends and we don't care who we fuck with, so shut your big mouth.'

Tom sighed inwardly. These people – probably Yakuza – just wanted the money. If he gave it to them, there was a good chance they'd all go away. Unlike Stanley and the Weasel, who wanted far more from him than mere recompense.

'Let me go, and I'll tell you.'

Dark Glasses glared at him – presumably – from behind his ridiculous shades. How the guy saw anything was a mystery. Then he raised his gun against his cheek like some cheap-movie hood, and stepped away from Tom.

Someone rolled Tom on to his stomach and cut the tie on his wrists. His arms had gone a little dead, and he could barely push himself off the asphalt. Someone else put a strong hand around his elbow and helped to tug him upright.

Tom stepped over Stanley, who looked up at him with furious eyes, and retrieved his clothes from the front footwell.

One by one, he drew the slabs of tightly bound money from his various pockets, and set them on the roof of the Thunderbird. 'That's it,' he said.

Dark Glasses jerked his head at one of the others, who re-checked the jeans and jacket to make sure that Tom hadn't held anything back.

'This is it all?' The young man seemed unwilling to be handed the money so simply after they'd come prepared for trouble.

'I spent a little,' Tom admitted.

'Oh, yeah? On what?'

'This car.'

'*Sonofabitch!*' Stanley lashed out at Tom with his feet, and received a swift blow to the face from his personal captor. It didn't knock him out, but it temporarily shut him up.

The young leader nodded slowly. 'Okay,' he said. 'Take the guns and the car too.'

Now they had their orders, the crew moved efficiently, frisking the Weasel and Stanley, removing two hand-guns from each and a hunting knife from Stanley, binding their wrists in the same way Tom's had recently been bound, transferring the money to their own cars. Minnie Mouse watched the proceedings sulkily, her arms folded across her non-existent chest, until the leader got into the Thunderbird and whistled for her to come, like a dog.

First she stepped over to Tom and glared up into his face. 'You cheater!' she spat at him. Tom could see the truth in her eyes, and the bravado she needed to keep that truth hidden. But he was more grateful for the Yakuzas' interruption than angered at the girl's lies, so he just told her quietly, 'Get a new job.'

'Fuck you,' she said, but she didn't look at him when she said it, just tossed it over her shoulder as she got into the Thunderbird.

They drove away and Tom shivered, gooseflesh raised over his naked torso as the invisible sun coloured the smog a dirty orange.

He started for the apartment, then glanced at Stanley and the Weasel, both helpless, in the middle of the road, with their wrists and ankles bound. He quickly dragged the silent Weasel to the sidewalk then went back for Stanley, who was apoplectic with rage, grinding his teeth and jerking against his bonds. Tom was a little afraid to approach him, even tied up. The guy was a psycho.

'I'm gonna kill you, Patrick. I'm gonna fucking *kill* you!'

'Okay,' said Tom, reasonably. 'Then I'm gonna leave you in the road.'

He turned away, grabbed his clothes from the gutter, and ran back to Lucia's apartment block, ignoring the torrent of abuse Stanley hurled at his back, but confident that it would wake many a local resident, one of whom was sure to find it in his heart to pull Stanley out of the road so he wasn't squashed by a truck.

Or not. Tom really didn't care.

He burst through the front door of Lucia's apartment and narrowly missed having his head knocked clean off his shoulders by a pool cue. He dropped under the strike and fell on his ass, his arms covering his head – better late than never.

'Lucia! It's me!'

She stepped from behind the front door, still in her so-called pyjamas, her face streaked with tears. She was shivering with fear.

Tom scrambled to his feet. 'Are you okay?'

She nodded slowly, letting the cue hang loosely beside her thigh. Tom took it from her gently and put his arms around her trembling shoulders. 'You have your own pool cue? I *knew* you were a hustler.'

She half laughed but it turned into a sob, which became a flood of choking tears against his bare chest. 'I thought they were going to kill you.'

'Me too,' he said, and shuddered, because he knew they would have. He held her until the sobbing subsided.

Then, as the sound of police sirens broke with the dawn, he said, 'We've got to get out of here.'

39

SUDDENLY $112,000 POORER, Tom considered his escape options while they sat in a diner a few hundred yards from Lucia's place. They obviously knew and loved Lucia in here: the tubby owner smiling and bringing her little extras 'to build you up'. Lucia ducked her head shyly, warmth flaring briefly in her troubled eyes, and Tom wondered how he could ever have thought her anything but beautiful.

*

His landlady, Mrs Roseman, cackled in genuine enjoyment when he asked for his thousand-dollar security deposit back. 'Have you seen your apartment?' She chortled. 'It's going to cost at least that just to replace the broken furniture.'

'But I didn't do that!'

'Well, *I* didn't!' she said, and hung up on him.

*

Halo had no spare cash. He and Vee were redecorating and had paid the guy up front.

'Up front?' Tom exclaimed. 'You know he's gonna rip you off, right?'

'He seems like a nice guy.'

'That's *how* he rips people off.'

Halo sounded hurt. 'At least he's painting the house for the money, not asking for a free handout!'

'Yeah, well . . .' Tom was too tired to fight.

'You okay?' Halo's voice lost its bite and became concerned.

'I'm so far from okay that I'm calling you.'

There was an awkward silence.

'Anything else I can do?' Halo asked apologetically.

'Nah. You've done more than enough. I'm sorry I even got you in this deep.'

'I got myself in.'

'Yeah, that's true,' said Tom. 'In fact, you got me in too, you sonofabitch.' There was no anger in his words, only weariness. 'You're in far enough, so stay right there.'

'Where are you?'

'Here and there. It's best you don't know.'

'Okay, then,' said Halo. 'Take care.'

'I will.'

'Hey, Tom, what happened with that girl in South Africa? Things work out there?'

Tom laughed hollowly. 'Not exactly the way I'd hoped.'

'I'm sorry.'

'Yeah.' Tom sighed. 'Listen, Halo, be careful, okay?'

'What do you mean?'

'They don't think they have any reason to come after you, but that could change. And these guys aren't fucking around.'

A long, worried pause from Halo before he said, 'You think they'd hurt Vee, Tom? You think they'd hurt Katy?' The edge of concern in his voice sharpened noticeably.

'I think they'd hurt just about anyone.'

*

Kitty made excuses until he challenged her on her lies, then confessed that Pete LaBello had ordered her not to put Tom's calls through to him.

'Kitty, it's an emergency. A matter of life and death.'

She paused. Then she said, 'Tom, he's so mad he told me not to put you through even if you said it was a matter of life and death.'

'But I'm not joking! It really is! *My* life and death!'

'I'm . . . sorry, Tom.'

'Fuck!' Tom thought about it for less than ten seconds. 'Can you lend me a thousand dollars?'

There was a horrible, embarrassing silence. Or, at least, it would have been embarrassing if Tom hadn't been past embarrassment now – so far past that he'd have tap-danced naked down the 405 freeway if someone had offered him a hundred bucks.

'Tom, I really can't. My sister—'

'It's okay. Forget it. Sorry I asked.' And he truly was.

'Okay, Tom. Take care.'

'I will.'

He hung up and sipped his coffee. Lucia touched his wrist lightly. 'I have seven thousand dollars,' she said quietly.

He was stunned. He couldn't take her money but, *hell*, it was good to hear she was prepared to do that for him – that

385

anyone still trusted him that much. His throat was suddenly too tight to speak so he just squeezed her hand and shook his head.

*

As, deep down, he'd always known he'd have to, Tom went back to the tables. Except now it scared him even to walk into the clubs. He knew the events at Lucia's apartment wouldn't deter Stanley's people from coming at him again. Whoever he worked for wouldn't just write off the theft of $112,000, even if the Yakuza intervention made his own felony almost academic. He was still on the hook for stealing money he didn't have any more.

The Rubstick was too close to Lucia's place – they'd be sure to look for him there. His only hope was to dodge them around the several clubs in LA. Lucia had gone back to her apartment for some essentials. She'd understood the necessity to get out, but he'd found it harder to understand why she hadn't just taken her seven thousand dollars and flown to Savannah. They had schools there; they had strip clubs there; she'd have been safe there.

Instead, apparently based solely on his selfish decision to ask her for help, she was behaving as if they were in this together. It was beyond reason, and it was humbling.

They'd cruised past her apartment building several times, looking for anyone who might have been waiting for them. Then he went in ahead of her, wishing again for a gun. A gun and a gym membership – the past several months would have been immeasurably eased by either or both.

The door to her apartment had been easily opened,

splinters of wood showing it had been entered since that night by less careful means.

When Tom had gone in and seen the devastation he'd felt a sharp jab of anger. They hadn't even been looking for anything. They had the bolt – they had what they wanted. Or they thought they did . . .

Lucia had passed him with dull eyes and tight lips as she surveyed the ruin of the little home she'd made for herself. Tom wanted to be man enough to tell her to get away from him while she still could, but he was too much of a man to let go of something he wanted so much. She'd packed what she needed – and could still find – into a duffel bag, and hadn't let him carry it to the car for her.

*

Feeling like a bad actor, Tom wore a fake moustache and dark glasses into the Normandie. He spent twenty minutes just wandering about, looking for familiar faces, before changing up a hundred dollars and sitting down. It represented one tenth of all the cash he had left in the world, and he wished he hadn't paid his rent when he'd last won big for Ness.

He wouldn't have had this much if Lucia hadn't paid for the hotel room. She'd done it with a credit card and a fierce glance that had kept his mouth shut. Used to playing with more money – and recently money that didn't belong to him – Tom raised too fast and too high and the hundred dollars lasted all of thirty minutes, despite a couple of small wins.

He changed another hundred and played more conservatively. Three hours later he came away six hundred and fifty in profit.

His phone rang in the parking lot and Ness's name was on the display. He stared at it until she rang off, then flinched when the tone told him he had a new message.

'Tom? It's Ness. Please call me. We need to talk.' She sounded tentative – a little fearful. He almost bought it. Almost felt concerned. But he didn't call her.

He walked to the Best Western where Lucia had been looking forward to seeing him. He knew that because when he knocked she opened the door and kissed him, then ripped off his moustache and kissed him again.

'Ow,' he said, grinning and closing the door behind him.

'You won.'

'I won.'

'How much?'

'Six fifty.'

'Woohoo! I earned too!' She walked over to the nightstand and picked up a fan of tens, smiling and waving it at him. 'Eighty bucks!'

He tried to smile but felt his face stiffen with hurt. 'Good,' was all he could manage.

Realization dawned in her eyes and she lashed out, slapping him hard in the face.

'Fuck you!' she said, and followed up with a flurry of blows and ten-dollar bills. He grabbed her flailing wrists and held her against the bathroom door. She writhed in fury, trying to knee him in the balls. He was too tall for her to connect there, and he twisted his hips protectively, but he winced as she gave him a dead leg, and angrily pushed his full body length against hers to keep her from getting any leverage.

This close, he could feel her breasts against his ribs, her

388

angry breath on his throat as she hissed, 'I won it playing pool!'

Tom didn't care. He was suddenly so hard he could barely breathe, and the feeling of her struggling against him made him groan and press himself into her belly. He dipped his head to kiss her; she dodged his mouth.

'Please don't,' she whispered, and he drew back to see tears in her eyes.

He released her immediately. She turned and slid into the bathroom.

'Lucia?' He heard the door lock.

She didn't come out, even when he said he was sorry. Even when he said he needed to use the toilet.

He ended up pissing out of the window and crawling into bed alone.

He woke around five a.m. to find the bathroom door unlocked and Lucia asleep in the tub. At some time during the night she'd tugged the top cover off him and taken a pillow. He knelt beside her and stroked her hair until her eyes opened warily.

'You'll get cold in there,' he said.

She didn't answer, but let him help her out of the bath and put her into the bed where she fell asleep again almost instantly. He wanted to hold her – if only to let her know he could be trusted just to do that – but felt awkward about getting in beside her, and didn't quite trust himself.

Instead he showered, dressed, put his moustache back on, and drove her little car back to the Normandie, where he put down a hundred bucks and won four hundred and seventy-five before breakfast.

He took bagels and coffee back to the room. Lucia was

awake and worried by his absence. They ate in virtual silence.

Afterwards he sat beside her on the bed, not knowing where to start, or even what he wanted to say to her. Just staring at the wall and then at his feet, and then at the wall again.

'I want you to know something,' she said quietly.

He looked at her, waiting for her to go on. She bit her lip, working up to it.

'What I did with you. That first time? It's the only time I've ever done that.'

'Then why did you do it with me?'

'I don't know.'

'Lucia . . . Last night when I . . . y'know . . . I wasn't assuming anything like that.'

She seemed unsure of his meaning.

'I just wanted . . . I didn't mean to treat you like a whore. I'm sorry if I made you feel like one.'

The two of them sat and looked at the wall for a while. Then he took her hand and was grateful when she didn't pull away.

*

At the Bicycle Club, it was only by lucky chance that he saw the Weasel before the Weasel saw him. The man was coming out of the john, straightening his tie. He had to stop and look down to step around a little cordon marking the place where a waitress had dropped a tray of Chinese food.

In another instant, his eyes once more raked the room, but by then Tom had ducked behind a pillar, grateful that this was the brick-and-mortar Bicycle, not the pillar-less big-top of the Honolulu.

His mind raced. One of Lucia's neighbours had apparently cut off the Weasel's cuffs before wondering why they might be there. Probably Stanley's too. Shit.

He circled behind the Weasel and hurried to the car. Suddenly LA clubs seemed like Fox searchlights criss-crossing the sky – he was sure to be caught in one of them soon.

He was already back in the hotel parking lot when he decided to swing round and make for the 888. The Weasel was definitely at the Bicycle. That took him out of the equation. Maybe they couldn't cover every club every night. The 888 was north of the city. He'd never been there with Ness and had only been there alone once about five years earlier when he'd been in Santa Anita on a Piper crash. Maybe the 888 was safe.

Tom knew the logic was shaky, but he also knew that he couldn't go on picking up a few hundred dollars here and there indefinitely. He was having a reasonable run, but he was staking too low to win a sum of money that would give him options. He needed to take a risk.

And tonight he was in a risk-taking mood.

*

The 888 was smaller than he'd remembered, a low, ugly, industrial-looking building creaking under the dis-proportionate weight of the biggest neon sign Tom had ever seen flashing 888 and two tired, half-burned-out aces. Eights and aces: the dead man's hand.

He felt nervous at first, the unfamiliarity of the place making him jumpy, but he figured it was better to be safe than sorry and took his time at the bar, scanning the room from behind his shades.

After twenty minutes he started to breathe normally, and took his place at a two-four table, figuring it was a good median point for someone who wanted to stake low but win big.

The crowd at the 888 could have come direct from the Normandie or the Honolulu. Tom glanced around his table and saw the usual mix of fat men, college boys, Chinese businessmen and token female – this one a meek-looking grey-haired woman, who might have wandered in from a church social.

Tom didn't care if she'd wandered in from Paradise. He eyed her with the same cold thought as he had the others: I'm going to fucking cripple you.

And that was how he played, with iced anger in his veins that this was all he had left. What he hadn't lost by himself had been taken from him. Everything but a few hundred bucks, his resilience, and a strip of dirty green baize to try to rebuild a life on.

He lost steadily but didn't hesitate to keep changing up more money. It was as if he were going all in with his very life, shoving his heart and soul into the middle of the table and baring himself to Fate.

With only a hundred and seventy-five left between him and a cardboard box in downtown, Tom started to win.

And win big.

He won with the same dogged blankness with which he'd previously lost, pushing, forcing, bluffing, intimidating. Never speaking, even when Church Lady said, 'Well done,' as he scooped a four-hundred-and-eighty-dollar pot towards him.

When he hit two thousand he got up and moved to a six-twelve table and continued to win as if he'd never been interrupted.

At around three a.m. he lost three hands in a row on okay cards, and decided his luck was spent.

He cashed up more than eleven thousand dollars. It wasn't great, but it was enough. Enough to get out of LA. Enough for some breathing space.

It took him almost two hours to drive back to the Best Western and the sky was lightening by the time he got there.

Even so, Lucia must have been awake because, before he could knock twice, the door was opened.

By Ness – with a gun trained on his face.

40

TOM'S GUTS SPASMED. They regarded each other for a long moment. Tom could feel his heart beating in his throat. The muzzle of the gun looked as big and black as a well. Big enough to fall into and disappear for ever. He wondered what it would be like to be shot in the face, whether he'd be dead before he found out, or whether he'd feel the copper jacket burst in his eye and drive a molten wedge through his brain.

He took a breath and raised his eyes to Ness's. 'Where's Lucia?'

A look flashed across Ness's face that might have been hurt, although he was no judge. 'She's here,' she said flatly. 'She's fine.' Then she stepped backwards, lowering the gun.

Tom pushed past her into the room to find Lucia propped up on the bed in her pyjamas, with her wrists and ankles bound. 'Are you okay?' he asked.

'Who's she?' demanded Lucia. Just like a woman.

'She's Ness,' he said curtly. This was no time for hurt feelings. 'Can I untie her?'

'No,' said Ness. 'Not yet.'

'What's with the gun?'

'It's for my own protection.' He said nothing and she

shook her head angrily. 'They're after me now, too, thanks to you.'

'Why?'

She gave a sarcastic laugh. 'I don't know. You think it could've been something to do with the hundred and twenty thousand you stole from them?'

'It was a hundred and twelve. And they stole it back. It's not my fault someone else came along and stole it from them.'

'Strangely, that's not how they see it,' she snapped, and then the sharpness fell away from her: her shoulders dropped and she looked down at the bed, and Tom saw the woman he'd desired re-emerge. 'It doesn't matter now anyway.'

Tom felt his anger waning, and reached to keep it close. 'It doesn't matter? *It doesn't matter?* You betrayed me.'

She shook her head sadly. 'My job was just about the cards, Tom. I swear, when I met you, that was all I thought it was going to be.'

'Is that why you came to South Africa with me? To watch me play cards?'

'They knew you were on the right trail. They wanted me to keep you away from the truth and stay close to you. I was a convenient spy.'

'You knew they were going to steal the fan disc?'

Her silence confirmed it.

'So that little charade out in the desert . . .'

Her eyes slid away from his and colour rose up her throat.

He felt like the biggest kind of fool. 'Yeah, I thought so . . .'

The memories of that night flashed in his head for the millionth time – his desperate schoolboy heat, her sudden cool retreat. The wound to his ego was crippling. He tried to shake it off, feeling all his emotions closing down, apart from bitterness, anger and desperation.

'And the fire?'

'I didn't know, Tom. I swear! I swear to you I didn't know!' Her lip trembled. 'I don't know if you were meant to die there, or even if I was! I was so out of my depth. I had no idea what to do. I was just reacting to whatever happened.'

'And feeding information back to them.'

'I had to! I was already in deep with the cards – I couldn't just go to the cops! You don't understand, Tom. They aren't small-time crooks, they're killers!'

'They sure are,' he shot back. 'You told them Lenny Munro had the bolt and they killed him for it.'

'I didn't know they were going to kill him. I *didn't*! They wanted it back.'

'Well, they've got it now,' he spat. 'Trashed my place and hers and would have killed me too!'

'I know,' she near-whispered. 'I hoped they'd find it in Oklahoma. Then you would've been safe. But they knew you'd taken it.'

'How?'

'I don't know. I didn't tell them. I didn't even know that!' Her eyes glistened with tears. 'I only wanted to protect you, Tom. I told them Munro had the bolt so they'd go after him, not you.'

'Why? Why protect me? What's so fucking special about me, Ness?'

Ness's voice was low, husky, as she said, 'Because when you still had your job, you were useful.'

Tom felt sick. The job he'd fucked up. The job he'd wasted.

The job he'd finally thrown in Pete LaBello's face. It had been all that had kept him alive. Without knowing it, he'd quit a lot more than a job the day he'd tossed his phone on to the Santa Ana freeway. He felt gouged out, only vaguely aware of her still talking.

'It was useful to them to know what was happening inside the NTSB, how close you were getting, whether anyone else took you seriously. What you were doing to track down the parts and the paperwork. When they knew what you were doing, they knew how to avoid you. But then you got too close, I guess . . .'

'Am I still useful, Ness?' he asked, without a shred of emotion.

She sighed as if with exhaustion.

He nodded, understanding.

She turned to open her shoulder bag and held out an airline ticket. 'To DC. Tomorrow. Under your seat you'll find a file with all the evidence you need.'

He glanced round at Lucia. 'Just the one ticket?' He'd said it to hurt Ness, and was pleased when he saw in her eyes that it had. 'Why should I believe you?'

She shrugged. 'It's the truth.'

He put the ticket into his jeans pocket.

'I have to go.' She picked up the gun and put it into her bag. He followed her to the door. When they were hidden from Lucia's view by the bathroom wall, Ness turned to him and spoke so low he almost didn't hear her. 'Be careful, Tom.'

'What do you care?'

She caught her lower lip between her teeth and turned to go. Tom grabbed her arm and spun her back to face him, seeing he was hurting her and glad of it.

'Ness.' He lowered his voice too. 'I get it. I get it all. Except the hospital. The disc was gone. We hadn't found the bolt. So what the fuck was the hospital all about?'

She put a hand on his chest, the warmth of her slender fingers like electricity on him, then tugged her arm out of his grasp, slipped out of the door and closed it quietly behind her.

Tom stared at the fake wood-grain for a long time, then went back to the bed and untied Lucia. He stripped off in silence, then got into bed beside her.

They should get out of there. If Ness had found him, others could too. Tom knew that but he was physically exhausted, and Ness's revelations had corralled his brain into a corner where it ran in small circles and got nowhere fast. He didn't know who to trust, where to go or how all this was going to end, and that sense of fragmentation left him by turn terrified, enraged and – finally – numb.

'Are you angry with me?' Lucia said softly.

'What about?'

'Anything.'

'No,' he said. 'Nothing is your fault. *Nothing.*'

In the morning they dressed in silence. Then he asked if she wanted to go to DC with him.

'Yes,' she said, and looked at him levelly, as if she expected a fight.

'Why?'

She looked away, thinking, and finally shrugged: 'I'm not sure.'

*

They went past the Honolulu and Tom retrieved his Buick, which was sitting on soft tyres and took an age to start. Then he followed Lucia back to her place, where they left her Colt.

At LAX, he bought Lucia a ticket for the seat across the aisle from his own. They were three hours early but had nothing else to do, so sat side by side in complete silence as the airport ebbed and flowed around them.

His phone rang.

'Tom?' It was Halo.

He was immediately wary. 'Hey. Where are you?'

'Hangar Three.'

'What's up?'

There was a pause and Tom heard a muffled voice. When Halo spoke again, his voice was tight with tension. 'Some guy just walked in and asked me to call you. Says he's a friend of yours.'

'I don't have any friends.'

'That's what I thought.'

'What does he look like?'

Halo lowered his voice. 'Dark hair. Bad skin. Cowboy boots.'

Tom ran.

*

The decorator was ripping him off. Halo knew it. Vee knew it. Halo had a sneaking suspicion that even Katy had an inkling. Fuck, even Tom Patrick – Mr Perceptive, Not – had told him what would happen.

Now Halo sighed and felt dumb, which was unusual for him. He usually felt pretty smart. He knew he was smart. Had known it since he was in junior school. But he'd been brought up in Redondo Beach, instead of Watts or South Central, which meant that he'd missed out on acquiring the street smarts most people thought any black resident of LA or New York acquired as a birthright.

Halo's parents hadn't split up. He and his brothers, Chas and Victor, hadn't joined gangs and died in blazes of drive-by glory; his sister, Maddie, hadn't turned ho' and got herself knocked up or drugged up or hooked up with a pimp. They'd all graduated from high school and college. Chas was a realtor in Torrance, Victor designed websites, Maddie arranged weddings at English stately homes. She even spoke with an English accent now, to enhance the experience for her clients. And while Halo was eternally grateful for all that, he knew it left him vulnerable to being shat on by people with more low cunning and fewer scruples than himself.

That was why – despite his 125 IQ – he was being ripped off by a man with a tattoo that read: '*Whose the Daddy?*'

Halo sighed and gripped the handle of his toolbox. Tool closet, would be closer to the truth: it was five feet tall, wheeled, made of galvanized red steel and had his name stencilled on the side: Halo Jackson. Chris had done that for him, he never failed to remember with a pang.

The crew had already started on the 747 next door in Hangar Two, but Halo had been delayed by what he'd tried to keep to a civilized discussion with the decorator, which was why he was only now fetching his tools.

He'd just got the toolbox rattling across the cement floor when he noticed the man walking towards him. The guy didn't have any ID tags and wasn't wearing Day-Glo, a uniform, or coveralls, so he shouldn't have been there. But

Halo wasn't the kind of man to chew the guy out: he was probably just lost.

'Hi,' said the man. 'You Halo Jackson?'

'Yes. Hi.'

The man stuck out his hand and Halo let go of the tool-box to shake it out of politeness. He noticed the man had a half-healed ring of bloody bruising on one cheek that looked suspiciously like a bite.

'I'm a friend of Tom Patrick's.'

'Oh, yeah.' The skin on Halo's forearms prickled. He was almost sure that no one in the world would introduce themselves that way and really mean it.

*

Tom ran. Adrenalin burned through him. He never heard Lucia shout his name; never noticed the blurred faces turn to watch him as he flashed past them, never felt the pain in his tender leg.

The escalator was full of people and luggage. He shouldered past the people; trampled over the luggage, skidded off the end, stumbled, regained his footing. Security guards came at him but he didn't wait to show them his ID, just ran on. He didn't have time to stop, explain, convince. Instead he headed for the nearest check-in desks. American Airlines. First Class. No lines.

He slid under the guide tapes, like Willie Mays, then bounded to his feet and jumped on to the conveyor-belt scales beside an immaculate check-in girl. She grabbed his sleeve with surprising strength for one so manicured, but he wrenched free, making her yelp and shout, 'Motherfucker!'

He dove through the hatch where luggage disappeared, behind a pile of Louis Vuitton that made him think fleetingly of Ness.

The alarms rang. Shouts behind him. He tumbled off the belt in the baggage-handling hall, took his bearings – saw the jagged square of daylight that meant a door, and headed for it under the towering roller-coasters, their little carts filled with bags starting their journeys to all over the world.

Off to his right he saw three security men coming at him, angling to stop him reaching the door. Like a running back trying for the end zone, Tom computed the angles, the relative speeds, the numbers, the gaps.

Fuck. He'd never make it.

They were only fifteen feet behind him when he hurled himself up on to one of the conveyor-belts. His fingers were briefly caught in the chain and he tugged them free, grabbing the edge of the rubber belt as his legs flailed for purchase beneath him and he rose from the floor. A hand snatched at his ankle and he kicked it away. Then he was too high to be caught, although he was still dangling and his fingers were wet with blood, his grip slipping.

He looked under his arm at the men staring up from below, keeping pace with him on the floor as he pulled himself up and on to the belt and leaped from cart to cart, some empty, some containing bags that slowed him a little. But not much. He sprang off trolley bags as though they were little trampolines, heard things breaking in duffel bags and kicked smaller items clear of the conveyor-belt, scattering the men below as they burst open on the cement, like cluster-bombs.

Forty feet in the air, his belt crossed another, and Tom

dropped on to it, almost bouncing off and crashing to the floor thirty feet below. This belt was heading off at right angles to the first, straight towards the door, and had very few carts on it. Tom ran along it recklessly, the extra speed of the belt allowing him to outdistance his pursuers. He hurdled two carts, teetering as he landed each time on moving rubber, rather than solid ground, but kept going.

Thirty yards from the doorway, he approached a long line of luggage and knew his free ride was over. He swung down on to a lower belt running almost parallel, and almost immediately another, tumbling awkwardly off on to the floor.

The security guards were seven in number now, and the nearest was fifty yards away and coming at him fast. Tom was up and running again.

In the doorway, two men in Day-Glo coveralls tossed bags on to caged low-loader trailers. One saw Tom and stepped into the doorway. Tom fumbled for his ID and yelled, 'NTSB,' but was not surprised when the man showed no sign of bowing to officialdom. He blocked Tom, who lashed out – his badge still in his fist – and opened the man's cheek.

'Shit!' The guy clapped one hand to his face, but held on to him with the other, and Tom ripped out of his leather jacket, shook it loose from his arms, and kept going.

Hangar One, Hangar Two . . . He could hear the wail of Airport Police sirens. He ran into Hangar Two, under the wings of a 747, past surprised engineers, ignoring angry shouts, dodged left and crashed through a side door, across the strip of asphalt, and through the matching door into Hangar Three.

Hangar Three was darker than Hangar Two, or the LA

sunshine. Tom willed his eyes to adjust. He couldn't hear for the blood in his ears, the sirens, the pounding of his own heart.

No work was going on in here, no plane, no maintenance crew, the only light the little fluorescent strip over the side door he'd just come through.

'Tom!'

The word was choked off. He turned and saw Halo, Stanley's arm round his throat, a gun to his head, the smaller man arched against his captor, stumbling, trying to stay upright, blood staining his teeth as he grimaced in pain.

Stanley's teeth were all white when he smiled. 'Hello, asshole.'

'Hi,' said Tom. He didn't want to waste any breath. He knew he had a limited supply. He put his hands on his knees, sucking at the air, but keeping his eyes on Halo and half a brain on the clock. He needed to get that flight to DC. Having come this far, he could only trust that Ness wasn't lying to him, that he would indeed find an incriminating file under seat 15C. All he needed was to miss the flight and have some over-enthusiastic National Airport cleaner find it and put it in a dumpster.

He had no time for this shit. 'What do you want?' he said impatiently.

Stanley grinned again. He yanked Halo sideways to remind him of who was in charge and his gun hand disappeared, reappearing seconds later with the bolt. 'What the fuck is this?'

'Um, is it . . . a bolt?'

'The wrong fucking bolt.'

'A bolt is a bolt is a bolt. Surely.'

Stanley slammed the butt of his pistol into the side of Halo's head. Tom flinched.

'You think this is funny?'

'No.'

'You switch the bolt and you think we wouldn't know? We wouldn't come back and *fuck you up*?'

Tom didn't answer. He'd kinda hoped none of those three things would happen.

But now they had, of course.

He'd thought he was being so clever, giving Halo Lemon's bolt, letting Stanley and the Weasel think the slightly battered replacement was the real thing when they took it from him. Now it turned out he hadn't been clever at all, that all he'd done was put Halo in more danger than anyone deserved to be in. He had to put an end to this, fast, before Stanley got any angrier.

'Where is it, Halo?'

Halo coughed as Stanley choked him again. Then Stanley laughed. 'You mean this little shit *has* it? Man! I didn't even need to use him to get you down here!'

Tom ignored him, looking Halo straight in the eyes. 'Come on, Halo,' he said softly. 'You've done your bit.'

'Yeah, Halo.' Stanley grinned. 'Don't make me shoot you in the head. This is a new shirt.'

Halo struggled to speak. 'Fuck you and your new shirt. You're not getting it.'

Tom's world was whirling. He was desperate to tell Halo that maybe – if Ness had been telling the truth – they didn't need the bolt now. That they had other evidence, other options; that they no longer had to cling to one solitary lump of metal. Tom was ready to take that chance if it would save Halo. Lenny

Munro getting shot was bad enough. But he had to admit that he liked Halo Jackson. The thought of watching as Stanley shot him in the head made the *Pride of Maine* seem insignificant. But the thought that Ness had put herself in serious danger to get the file to him made him keep it to himself.

'Chris wouldn't want you to die for it, Halo. Neither would Vee. Or Katy.'

Tears started to run from Halo's eyes.

'Are you fucking *crying*?' Stanley laughed again, and Tom wanted to smash his face in.

The anger he felt at Stanley manifested itself in his words to Halo. 'Fuck the bolt, Halo! Give it up!'

Halo shook his head stubbornly and Stanley jabbed the barrel of the pistol into his kidneys, making him yelp, then shoved him to his knees, holding him up by the scruff of his coveralls, and pressing the gun against his head again.

'If you shoot him you'll never find it!' yelled Tom.

'But if I shoot you both, who cares?' smiled Stanley, and – with complete clarity and calm – Tom knew then that they were both dead, whether Stanley got the bolt from them or not.

But he also knew that going along with the quest for the bolt would buy them more time. More life.

And more life seemed a good goal to aim for.

'Halo, please,' he said. 'Just tell him where the bolt is.'

There was a long moment when all Tom could hear was the sound of the police-car sirens winding down somewhere close by. They wouldn't get here in time: he'd gone through Hangars One and Two first – that was where they'd start.

Halo held up one hand weakly.

Stanley shook him. 'What does that mean?'

'In my toolbox.'

Stanley jerked his head at it, looking at Tom, his meaning clear. He pointed the gun as Tom moved to the toolbox.

'Where?'

Halo's head hung in shame. His voice was muffled. 'Bottom drawer. Under the foam.'

Tom slid it open. Each of Halo's Snap-on wrenches was neatly bedded in its designated foam template. He slid his hand into the narrow drawer, right to the back. The back corner of the foam bedding was slightly raised. Tom peeled it back and felt the lump of metal he'd once cut out of the flank of an ostrich.

Slowly he picked it up.

'Bring it here.'

His mind racing for an escape route, Tom did. Stanley dropped Halo and took the bolt from him, keeping the gun trained on Tom's chest. Halo fell to his hands and knees.

Tom swallowed a lump in his throat. Now was the moment. They'd given up the bolt; they'd run out of leverage. And – unlike Bruce Willis or Brad Pitt or some other better-scripted sonofabitch – he was fresh out of clever ideas.

He looked Stanley straight in the eyes. 'Stanley, I don't know how many other fan discs were in batch 501, but you'd better find them.'

'I don't think you're in any position to give orders right now, do you?'

Tom strove for sincerity, for humbleness, to keep the hatred out of his voice. 'I'm not. I'm just telling you. Even by your shitty fake standards, those fan discs are made in Hong Kong. Whoever you work for needs to know that something's gone badly wrong. People have died. A lot more people will die if you don't get those parts out of the planes they're in.'

Stanley sneered, and levelled the gun at his face. 'I'll be sure to tell my priest.'

Tom sighed. 'You prick.' Dully, he wished he had the energy to think of better last words.

'Freeze!'

Stanley swung round, dropped his stance and fired all in the same movement, the bullet singing off the corrugated-metal wall beside the surprised face of the airport cop, who – with admirable devotion to duty, Tom thought, as he hurled himself to one side – squeezed off two rounds before ducking out of the doorway.

Stanley never hesitated. He charged straight at the door, his gun held out in front of him, like a sabre, and when the cop chanced another look inside, Stanley was just four feet away and shot him right in the face without ever breaking stride.

There was a short silence, then the sound of an engine, a squeal of tyres and a flash of black-and-white as the cop car sped past the open door.

Tom found his motor skills and ran to the side door. Behind him another voice yelled, 'Freeze!'

He threw up his splayed hands and yelled, 'NTSB!' but didn't slow down until he dropped to his knees beside the still-twitching body of the airport cop, who'd done every-thing right except imagine for even one second that any man would be crazy enough to run straight down the muzzle of his service revolver.

Tom heard running footsteps coming at him from all

sides, and turned to hold up his ID, but before he could get there, the first cop to reach him swung his gun into his face, and then what felt like the defensive line of the Green Bay Packers jumped on top of him, all eager to get a little piece before they could remember they were supposed to be the good guys.

At the bottom of the pile – squashed and pummelled – Tom was very faintly aware that he still felt rescued.

*

They didn't want to let him go, of course. A cop was dead, a car stolen, an engineer beaten up, and a foul-mouthed check-in girl's nail broken.

Tom called down his federal credentials, his ongoing investigation, his LA driver's licence and, finally, swore on the life of his mother that he would return to answer questions within twenty-four hours. How were *they* to know she was already dead?

Once Halo, Lucia and a telephonically confused Pete LaBello managed to convince them of various aspects of the truth, the airport cops took a brief preliminary statement, withheld his driver's licence, and reluctantly released him just as the DC flight finished boarding.

They didn't go so far as to apologize, but one of them gave him the number of his dentist, who'd apparently done a great job when his own tooth got broken 'in the line of duty', as he put it. In the line of a fucking rent-a-cop steel toe-cap, Tom thought, but, for once, managed not to say.

Then the American Airlines flight attendants were wary of letting him board because of the blood that kept dripping from his mouth on to his shirt, forcing Tom to swallow it in a pretence that it had stopped, then buy a fresh T-shirt from the gift shop with 'Only in LA' across the front, before they warily stood aside and let him follow Lucia on to what he was unsurprised to see was a 737.

Seat 15C was on the aisle. Lucia was in 15D. Tom noted automatically that they were five rows back from the exit door over the wing. He sat down bare inches above what he could now only hope was the answer to every question he'd ever asked about fake fan discs, and fastened his seatbelt.

41

Tom READ THE SAFETY card assiduously as they taxied. He glanced at Lucia and saw the tension in her. He could have given her chapter and verse on the odds of survival that the seating plan, aircraft type and destination gave them in the event of a crash on take-off or landing, but instead he double-checked his seatbelt, then simply reached his hand across the aisle to hold hers as the thrust pressed them back in their seats and they left LA behind.

For a moment he thought about holding her sister's hand, but Lucia's was warm and gripped his firmly in return.

As soon as the seatbelt sign went off, Tom got on his knees and yanked his life preserver from under his seat. A passing flight attendant stopped and asked if she could help him, but Tom held up his ID and told her he was doing random safety checks. Then he asked for a Jack Daniel's for him and a Coke for Lucia. 'With rum in it,' she said, and gave him a small smile.

'While you're on duty?' the attendant said pointedly.

'Make it a double,' Tom shot back, and she withdrew.

'Why do you have to piss everybody off?' Lucia wondered.

'I don't. *They* piss *me* off.'

The elderly woman in 15B tutted but Tom ignored her.

The file was there. Tom pulled it out with hands that shook. He glanced up and Lucia was gazing at him with bright, questioning eyes. He nodded, hoping his excitement wasn't misplaced.

He sat down and stared at the file. Dull brown manila with old-fashioned pink string fastenings, not as thick as he'd hoped, but still.

He opened it and rifled through the contents. As he did so, the low-grade pessimism that had dogged him for months lifted and he felt his heart bump with excitement.

It didn't take a code-breaker to know what he was looking at.

The first document was an import manifest detailing the importation of twenty CFM56 fan discs, which had landed at San Pedro four years earlier, from an engineering firm in São Paolo, Brazil. The batch number was 501 and Tom grinned.

The next was a bill of lading releasing possession of said fan discs; this was a carbon copy. The company taking possession of the shipment was printed neatly, Avia Freight, and the receiving signature read 'B. Allway'.

Jesus. Bruce Allway: he of the new-smelling carpet and the actress-slash-clerk who got her kicks by baiting the waiting room with porn. Tom could hardly believe the arrogance of the man in signing for the parts himself, not even trying to disguise his involvement behind a front-man. Whether Avia were aware of it or not, Allway's position with the company gave him the perfect cover to match stolen paperwork to fake parts and sell them on as genuine to a range of carriers across the USA.

A dart of self-anger jabbed him, but he discarded it fast.

His mind rapidly replaying their encounter, he couldn't think of anything he might have missed, anything he should have seen to let him know that Allway was involved. The man had been open with him, had handed him the documentation he'd requested with a smile and a handshake.

Tom shook his head at the sheer bravado and flipped to the next document.

It was the purchase record of a single fan disc to American Airlines within months of its importation. Attached to that was the familiar 8130-3 'birth certificate', and also the 'Serviceable' tag showing the date the 501 fan disc had been installed.

Tom was slightly disappointed that there was a paper trail for only a single part in a single plane; he'd hoped for hundreds of documents – enough to ground dozens of specific aircraft. But technically he knew that what he held in his hands was all they needed to convict Allway, at the very least. So what if the work hadn't been done for them? They could subpoena Allway's records, follow the paper trail themselves. And with a charge of mass murder hanging over him, Tom was sure Allway could be made to sing like Doris Day. The arrests wouldn't stop with him: they'd be sure to catch other fish in their net. Bigger fish.

They would. The NTSB. Not *him* any more. But, still . . .

Tom felt lighter. The weight of not knowing lifted from him and a buzz of excitement filled him instead. The thought of laying this file on Pete LaBello's desk, of watching his eyes as he absorbed and understood the import of the information, the knowledge that he'd succeeded instead of failed, the bittersweet pang that Lenny Munro, Pam and her team had died trying to prove something that had indeed been provable all along: they'd all been vindicated now he'd finally got that proof.

He looked round and found Lucia watching him.

'It's all here,' he said, in a rush of dizzy relief.

She smiled at him and reached for his hand. He took it. Finally he had someone to celebrate with. The fact that it was Lucia, and that she was so pleased for him even after all the shit he'd put her through, made him feel drunk with happiness. He got up and knelt in the aisle beside her seat like a man begging forgiveness, which he absolutely was.

'I'm sorry,' he said, shocked at the ease with which it emerged from his mouth.

She half smiled, half frowned in confusion. 'What for?'

'Being a jerk.'

The frown disappeared and the smile widened. He raised his brows in mock-surprise. 'No argument?'

'No,' she said. 'For once we're in complete agreement.'

They laughed and he winced at the pain in his mouth. The frown returned and she touched his lip with the tip of one finger. 'Kiss it better,' she said.

It was not a question so he let her kiss it better until the attendant, who already didn't like him, banged his feet with the drinks cart.

Back in his seat, Tom knocked back his whiskey and felt his body relaxing in a way it hadn't for months. He felt like a leaf that had been clinging to a branch in a storm, finally letting go and enjoying being carried by the wind instead of fighting it. He wondered how the hell he'd hung on for so long against such ridiculous odds. If he had to do it all again, he thought, he couldn't. He'd given it everything he had to give. Now he was empty, but in a good way.

He glanced at his watch. Two hours to DC. Even now he allowed himself to daydream about getting his job back. He didn't want to have to ask for it; in his head he heard Pete – no, not Pete: Pete was okay – he heard the whole fucking board begging him to withdraw his resignation, reinstating him to air crashes. Promoting him? Nah, that was unlikely, even in Fantasyland. He'd be happy to be back where he'd been a year ago, but had been too dumb to appreciate.

He thought about ringing for another drink, but was too tired. He glanced across at Lucia: she was already asleep. A slow, sensuous wave of exhaustion engulfed him and dragged him willingly into its depths.

*

The woman in 15B woke him twenty-five minutes later because she needed the toilet but even that couldn't defuse Tom's sense of well-being. He let the woman out, then sat down, confident that he'd sleep again when she returned. In the meantime, he reopened the file, thrilling to its very existence.

He studied every document anew, then flicked over the last page and frowned.

He'd missed something. An envelope was tucked into a pocket inside the back cover. It was the same manila colour as the file, which was no doubt why he'd missed it previously. Now he slid it free and opened it.

Inside were three Polaroid photographs. Tom squinted, getting his bearings on the first, then stopped breathing. The

415

photo was of Niño Alvarez. Niño Alvarez who had installed what Tom now knew for sure was a fake fan disc in the *Pride of Maine*. He recognized the man's new Timberland boots, but Niño's mother wouldn't have been able to identify him in any other way. He might have been shot in the head, but it was hard to tell; what wasn't hard to tell was that he was dead, and lying on what looked like pine needles.

The second photo was of Garvey, the Pinball Kid. He was on his stomach, face twisted sideways, arms bound behind him with barbed wire. Several strands of the wire had also been tightened around his throat. Blood had squeezed out through Garvey's eyes, and the tip of his tongue poked between his teeth to touch the grey dirt floor of what looked like a barn.

Garvey? Yes. He told.

Tom's stomach flipped at the memory of Ness's words.

The final Polaroid was of Bruce Allway. The middle man. The linchpin. The sudden suspect that Tom had been convinced would sing like Doris Day.

Someone else had apparently had exactly the same thought.

Allway had been hanged by the neck from a beam. His face was blue-black and swollen; his neat tan chinos were dark with piss. Close to his swinging feet was the chair to which Tom had once been cuffed.

'Oh, my God!'

Tom flipped the file shut and looked up at his returning neighbour, who had gone pale.

'What was that?' she cried, making other passengers look round, and waking Lucia.

Tom stood up. 'Ma'am, I apologize for that. I'm a federal

416

officer investigating a case.' He pulled out his tired ID and she looked at it distractedly as if she could still see the other images. 'Are you okay? Can I get you some water?'

She nodded, and Tom saw that the threat of full-blown hysterics had been averted. The woman slipped back into her seat and Tom rang for an attendant. When she came, the woman asked tearfully for a double whiskey and the attendant gave Tom a hard stare, as if she knew this must have something to do with him. 'Would you like to move to another seat, ma'am?' she asked, but 15B shook her head stoically and said she'd be fine.

Tom paid for her drink, a double for himself and another rum and Coke for Lucia.

'Okay?' Lucia was clearly concerned.

He nodded tightly, then stared at the file he'd stuffed into the seat pocket in front of him. His half-hour of pleasure had been sucked up and blown away as if by a twister.

Everything in the documents pointed to Bruce Allway. If the people Ness worked for were setting someone up, they'd done a good job of incriminating Allway with the paperwork. And then they'd killed their fall-guy.

It made no sense. Like the Karoo hospital blow-job, Tom couldn't see the angle. It was as if Ness had dangled a solution in front of him, then snatched it away, like a schoolyard joke. And if that was the case, then the joke must be on him.

But he still had the paperwork. He still had the Polaroids. He probably still had enough to convince Pete LaBello and the FBI to open a full investigation into the fake parts and at least three obvious murders, let alone the links to organized crime.

Why would Ness give him all that when she knew – when *they* knew – that the moment he got to DC, their highly profitable business could come under threat?

The answer came so hard and fast it made his breath whine noisily in his throat.

He was never going to make it to NTSB headquarters. Someone would be waiting for him – maybe at the airport, maybe at the taxi stand.

Maybe he wouldn't even make it to DC.

Tom reached for the file again. From the corner of his eye he saw his neighbour glare, but he couldn't help it: he had to check.

The bill of lading. The transfer of possession. The bill of sale. The 8130-3 . . . His hands shook as he ran a finger down the documents, seeking something he was terrified to find.

This was paperwork for a fake fan disc that had been bought by American Airlines and installed three years ago in a 737-400.

Just like the one he was sitting in right now.

The 'Serviceable' tag listed the ID of the aircraft in which the disc had been installed.

Tom got up so fast he banged his head on the overhead lockers.

'You okay?' said Lucia, suddenly wary.

He put all his reserves of deception into making a smile for her. 'Fine,' he said. 'I'll be right back.'

He strode up the aisle towards the cockpit, suppressing the almost overpowering urge to run. The attendant who didn't like him came out of the galley and bumped into him. Tom glanced at her tag, which read 'Shirley Vickery'.

'I need to speak to the captain,' he said.

Immediately her eyes became suspicious. 'What seems to be the problem?'

Tom lowered his voice. 'There may be a safety issue with this plane.'

'A life-preserver safety issue?' she asked, a little sarcastically.

'No. A we-all-die-screaming safety issue,' he shot back.

'That's not funny, Mr . . .'

He dragged out his ID for what felt like the millionth time. 'Patrick. NTSB.'

She took it and peered closely at it, her pretty lips pursed in suspicion that was far from allayed by the fact that there was a streak of blood on the ID. The baggage handler. Tom cursed himself for not wiping it off.

'Listen, Miss Vickery,' he said, 'I haven't got time to waste here. I need to ask the pilot about this plane's ID. It may be nothing. But if it's something, he'll want to know about it.'

He saw her look past his arm and raise her eyebrows at someone behind him. He glanced over his shoulder to see the chief steward heading down the aisle towards them.

In the good old days Tom could have shoved her aside and forced his way into the cockpit. Post 9/11, that wasn't an option. If he tried it, they'd probably Taser him.

He had to stand and wait, swallowing his anger and his fear.

The chief steward arrived and Shirley handed him Tom's ID. 'Mr Patrick has been behaving . . . erratically, Jim. Now he says he needs to speak to the pilot.'

'Why?' said Jim, and Tom almost screamed with frustration.

He kept his voice low with difficulty: 'There may be a problem with the plane.'

Jim glanced around, just as nervous of alarming other passengers. He ushered them into the galley and gave a concerned frown. At least he's taking me seriously, Tom thought.

'Is that a threat, Mr Patrick?'

Tom closed his eyes and swayed. He clenched his fists so hard it hurt, and felt control slipping away from him.

'It's not a threat,' said Lucia, calmly.

Tom opened his eyes. She was standing at the steward's shoulder, then stepped in beside him. He felt her hand unfurl his own and hold it.

'He's telling you the truth. He's been investigating this for a long time and if he says the plane may be in danger, then I'm sure we're all agreed that the sooner we know whether the threat is real or not the better.'

The animosity left the cramped galley in a heartbeat. Suddenly they were all on the same side.

Jim took control. 'I'm going to search you, okay?'

'Okay.' Tom said.

The man made a good job of patting him down. He took Tom's phone and keys from his jeans and handed them to Lucia, then did the same with his credit cards. Tom felt a stupid urge to protest, just in case the plane went down while he and his cards were disunited, but suppressed it.

'Come with me.'

Tom squeezed Lucia's hand and walked down the aisle after the man.

The steward picked up the phone on the wall beside the cockpit door, shielded his mouth from Tom, and said a few words to the flight crew. Seconds later, the catch on the door was released.

It took the longest five minutes of Tom's entire life to convince the pilot to check the plane's ID on the control and display unit. It matched. Tom's knees turned to water and he sank quietly to the floor of the cockpit, his back against the door. The other four men – who had until now been suspicious and disbelieving – suddenly looked uneasy at what looked like unrehearsed terror.

'We have to land,' was all Tom could say weakly.

The pilot looked at his watch. 'We're only an hour and forty-five from DC.'

Tom shook his spinning head, feeling the hot-cold clamminess on the skin of his neck and back that usually preceded vomiting, but he knew he wasn't going to be sick.

He wanted to shout at them to put the fucking plane down, but remembered Lucia's fast results back in the galley, so tried hard to make his mouth say what his head meant, without histrionics and without obscenities.

'The first fake fan disc blew after four thousand eight hundred cycles. Three men were killed. The second went after only two thousand six hundred. A hundred and thirty-eight people died. The 737 that went down in Oklahoma? We're pretty sure it's the same problem. Seventy-eight people died. The fake in this plane has been installed longer than any of those. It's gone through more cycles. It could let go at any second. It's a miracle it hasn't already.' Tom breathed out at the end of his little speech. The strain of keeping it short and calm made him shudder.

Suddenly everyone's eyes were on the pilot, who chewed his lip.

Tom looked up at him, sweat running into his eyes. 'How many souls on board?' he asked.

'One twenty-seven.'

'Sir . . .' said Tom, when he badly wanted to say 'asshole'. 'If we land now, worst-case scenario is some pissed-off passengers. If we don't and it lets go . . .' He gave a short, mirthless laugh. Then, in the face of the pilot's continuing doubt, he found a cruel little winner on the river.

'I mean, if I'm wrong you can blame me, y'know? It's all on the CVR, right?'

Right. Everything Tom had told them, everything the pilot said or did in response – *or didn't do* – was a matter of record now, whether they lived or died.

'Where are we?' said the pilot, not taking his eyes off Tom.

'Closest is Blue Grass,' said the co-pilot, in a tone that suggested he was suddenly in favour of an immediate controlled descent, as opposed to one where they all fell out of the sky like a plague of frogs.

Fate, thought Tom. He'd get to see those Kentucky high-stakes gamblers and their horseflesh chips up close, after all.

If they made it down.

Jim was holding out a hand and Tom allowed himself to be helped up.

The crew didn't thank him as he left, and he didn't blame them. He was just grateful they were bowing to what they must still consider to be a million-to-one shot just for the sake of covering their asses.

The chief steward escorted him all the way back to his seat, as if he wanted to make sure Tom sat down. But when Tom did, he asked if he could get him a drink. Tom really wanted a drink very badly but decided he'd

422

look like a drunk if he accepted one, so asked for water.

'And I'll have a Bloody Mary,' said the woman in 15B. 'On him.'

The man left and Tom looked at Lucia. She was hiding her fear well, but Tom could still see it on her face. She gave him back his cards, phone and keys silently.

The captain introduced himself cheerily over the PA system and said that, due to unforeseen circumstances, they'd be diverting to Blue Grass Airport, Lexington. A groan and then a babble of angry voices drowned his by-rote apology for inconvenience caused, as the passengers voiced their impotent displeasure.

Tom looked reassuringly at Lucia, and knew they were doing the right thing.

*

It took them just fifteen minutes to get down, with an ear-poppingly steep series of descents. The pilot didn't even take the time to burn off what excess fuel he could, so Tom figured he must have been more convinced now than he'd looked at the end of their conversation.

Lucia was tense again and he hated to feed her fear, but finally he leaned across the aisle, pulling her close so they wouldn't be overheard. 'We're five rows back from that exit door.'

She nodded, waiting for the relevance.

He tried to lighten his tone. 'The pilot is going to ask us to take up brace positions, as if we were going to crash, but that's highly unlikely, okay?'

Her amber eyes flickered.

'If all the lights go out, stay calm. Remember, your seatbelt catch is right here in the middle, okay? Not at the side like a car.'

Her face was set and serious.

'If we have to get out, just remember we're five rows back. That's four seat-backs you have to count in front of you, then turn right to the door.'

'What about you?' she said shakily.

'I'll be doing the same. Just get out and get away from the plane as fast as you can. Promise me, Lucia.'

'I promise.' He saw she was holding back tears and he squeezed her hand.

The pilot told them to take up brace positions, quickly adding that this was just a standard precaution, and Tom let go of Lucia's hand, his heart in his mouth.

He stuffed the manila file down the back of his jeans and covered it with his T-shirt. He'd never had to brace for real in a plane before, and now that the moment had arrived, it felt like a woefully inadequate thing to do, but he did it anyway. He could feel the woman in 15B shaking in fear.

'Crash landings are survivable,' he muttered to her. 'Remember we're five rows back from the door on the right. Brace properly. Visualize yourself getting out. You'll be fine.'

She nodded furiously between her arms, and Tom could hear her teeth chattering.

They hit the ground hard and bounced. People shouted in fear. They hit again with a loud squeal. The lights went out and the braking slammed Tom's head into the seat in front, despite his protective arms.

It didn't matter. They were down. He felt slightly stupid but that didn't matter either. They were alive, and that was all that mattered. He'd rent a car and drive to DC – drive all night if he had to. He wouldn't even wait for his bag. He had the file, and that was all he needed. The file and Lucia.

The pilot had complete control now, Tom could tell. All the sounds were right, all the feelings . . .

With a noise like heavy mortar fire, the 737 tore apart in front of the wings and suddenly they were ploughing into, up and over the forward part of the cabin and cockpit, wrenching it aside and tilting crazily as the rest of the plane thundered over it, then sliding into a manic spin, the Kentucky wind blasting through the cabin with shocking suddenness.

Some people screamed; most just hung on grimly, like he did. He was pressed hard into the woman beside him. She was screaming so high and fluttery he could barely make out the words – pleasejesuspleasejesuspleasejesusopleasejesus . . .'

In his head, Tom replied, ''Sokay'sokay'sokay . . .'

The spin would slow the plane. Slow was good. Maybe they'd make it . . .

Then there was a grinding, squealing lurch and the whole world turned upside down.

42

I~N THE~ L~EXINGTON~ control tower, Dylan Tether watched the
737 lumber in steep and bounce hard.

It hit again – fierce but even – and the pilot braked
immediately. Dylan let out a long, hissing breath. The 737
wasn't going to crash. Not on his watch.

The breath he blew out was 99 per cent relief.

And one per cent disappointment.

Secret disappointment, of course. He was an air traffic
controller and it would never do to let anyone know – *ever* –
that, just once, he'd like to see one of these babies hit the
ground and burst into flames. It might dent folks' confidence
in him, but, boy, that would be something, wouldn't it? Not
that he wanted people to die. Far from it. In Dylan Tether's
well-hidden fantasy, he always allowed for the fact that he'd
undertake some act of such bravery and derring-do that,
'against insurmountable odds' (he could hear the news
reporter shouting in amazement), he would somehow
rescue all passengers and crew by a method that was always
hazy in his mind, but which left him with minor burns and
an heroic (not disfiguring) scar on his face. Across his cheek,
most likely. Probably earned as he dragged the unconscious
flight crew out through the shattered windshield bare

seconds before the cockpit was engulfed in flames.

He was brought back from his crowded split-second reverie by Jackie McKenzie muttering, 'That's the way. That's the way,' as the jet screamed down from flying to rolling.

Four fire trucks and three ambulances raced down the asphalt after the plane, like hungry puppies after a bitch, their sirens yapping and howling at being outpaced. The—

'FUCK!'

Dylan's heart almost stopped as the 737's starboard engine disintegrated in an impossible instant, tore the front of the cabin half off, then the back of the plane ran over it before slewing sideways and starting to spin.

Jesus Christ!

At least the spin would slow—

But before Dylan could complete even his thought, the plane, still travelling forward too fast to bear the force of the sudden spin, flipped on to its side and cartwheeled down the Blue Grass runway.

And Dylan Tether realized, with a sick, sucker-punched feeling, that he was all about the 99 per cent, and wished he'd never imagined for one second that watching a plane hit the ground and burst into flames for real could ever be anything but fucking, fucking terrible.

*

Primed by years of mental rehearsal, Tom opened his eyes and his seatbelt clip at the same time. He fell upwards and landed hard. He grunted in pain and surprise, coughed, sucked in thick air and coughed again. Then all escape bets were off because nothing was where it should have been and the cabin was full of smoke.

He felt smooth plastic under his fingers and slowly realized he was on the cabin ceiling. Which meant the plane was upside down. He rose to his knees and reached around frantically – finally touching a headrest.

His eyes ran and burned and were pointless to open, but he kept trying, kept hoping to see something in the murk. Everything was quiet, as if he was the only person in this nightmare. He tamped down the rising panic, put up his hands and gripped the headrest – his only reference point – as he tried to align his mind's eye with this new, unexpected world. Why had he never worked this one through in his head? He hated himself for not thinking of it.

He was five rows back.

But which way was he facing? He ran his hand over the headrest and got his bearings. That was forward. That was safety. He chanced letting go of the seat to bend and press his nose to what had been the ceiling and was now the floor. He sucked in air that made him cough, then rose to his knees again and groped in the grey tearfulness that had become his vision.

His headrest.

Remember: the way to safety was straight ahead.

He flapped his hand out to one side. Felt a cloth-covered arm hanging down towards him. Wrong side. Lucia had had short sleeves on, a blue T-shirt. This was the old woman in 15B. Tweedy jacket. He reached up and dug about in her lap until he felt the belt buckle, then yanked it open. The woman moved in his arms as he lowered her roughly to what was now the floor. He shoved her towards what he hoped was the front of the plane and left her.

He flailed with his left hand. Nothing. Again. Nothing.

He knelt again and breathed more smoky air. This time it hit him like a first cigarette. He choked and retched and panted and choked some more, gasping and wheezing.

He was running out of time. Lucia might not even be there. She might have got out – he'd told her to, hadn't he? Made her promise.

He should get the hell out too.

He had to check.

This time he chanced half rising so he could feel further. He banged his head on another hard head hanging down. Found two more arms – one wearing a man's watch – the other in wool.

A hand grabbed at his hair and he put up his own to feel it. A man's hand. He grimaced as he tore his own hair out to get away, and groped blindly, his chest burning.

Then a naked arm, a woman's small hand.

Tom guided himself up the arm until he touched the face. He went further up to the cotton-covered breast that fitted neatly in the palm of his hand.

'Lucia!'

He shouldn't have spoken. It took the last of his air. His head started to hurt.

He grappled with her belt. Ripped the buckle open, and she fell on to him. As he went down under her, Tom desperately tried to keep his sense of direction. He thought he had it.

Somewhere he could hear vague sirens but inside it was still so quiet. Eerily so.

On his knees, he gripped Lucia's arm and started to drag her.

A choking, whining sound approached fast, like a ghoul in the mist, and a dark shape trampled over Lucia and fell on to Tom, flattening him with one leg twisted awkwardly.

'Shit!'

The man lay on him, struggling, crying, his feet kicking at Tom's hips for purchase as he tried to get up again. Tom shoved him up and forward.

'Keep going!' he croaked, and the man was gone.

Tom turned his face to breathe close to the new floor but this time there was little more than thick smoke, and his lungs started to burn. He put his hands round his mouth and gulped again, but it didn't work. The air he'd breathed what seemed like hours ago was all he was going to get.

And Lucia hadn't even had that.

His chest screaming from lack of oxygen, his eyes and nose streaming, Tom got to his feet, grabbed Lucia's wrists again, and ran backwards with her, not caring about turning right for the door, or left, or wherever the fuck it was, just running and dragging her through the blazing horror of his juddering lungs until there was no floor, no ceiling, just a swift, airy nothingness, during which he dug his nails into Lucia's wrists to keep her with him, then an odd squishy thump that made him think of throwing himself on to his couch at home. After that, blackness.

*

Major incident teams who'd rushed to the University of Kentucky Medical Center were sadly under-utilized. Hoping with stupid optimism for 127 casualties, they finally saw only fifty-two, ranging from the walking wounded to DOAs.

But it was fifty-two more than they would ever have seen if the starboard engine had disintegrated at 30,000 feet.

Lucia was one of thirteen passengers who arrived not breathing, paramedics keeping them alive in nearly pointless hope.

The paramedics who hitched Tom Patrick on to the ER gurney were confident he'd be okay, though. Despite smoke inhalation and concussion, they'd got him breathing fine in the rig on the way from Blue Grass. Other than that, he didn't even have a break that they could find. He'd dropped out of the ruptured plane straight on top of some guy who'd obviously jumped out right before him. That guy – whose driver's licence ID'd him as Lamarr Sweeter of Falls Church, Virginia – might have been killed by his own fall, or by Tom Patrick's. They figured a coroner would eventually be able to tell but until then they went with the second option, as it was a far better bar-room anecdote.

43

TOM WOKE TO WHAT he assumed must be a hallucination of Lucia's mother sitting beside his bed in her white gloves, her head bent over a big old hardback copy of *Little Women*. He closed his eyes again, then forced them open more fully, and she was still there. He meant to say 'hello' but his throat wouldn't co-operate, so he just grunted. She looked up from the book on her lap, stood up and came over to him.

He tried to say, 'Where's Lucia?' but it didn't sound right even in his own head. Still, it seemed Lucia's mother understood him just fine, because she slapped him so hard in the face that Tom thought she'd broken his jaw. 'Mr Patrick,' she said politely, 'if you ever come near my daughter again, I'll kill you.'

Then she picked up her book and walked out.

Tom blinked at the fire-retardant ceiling tiles and felt a burning in his eyes that heralded tears of relief.

If Mrs Holmes never wanted him near her daughter again, that meant Lucia was alive. Her mother had answered his question with a killer right, but he'd take that news any way he could get it.

*

He woke again hours later to the much more welcome, though just as surprising, sight of Halo Jackson and Pete LaBello playing Rock, Paper, Scissors.

'Hi,' he managed, with far more clarity this time.

Pete raised a peace sign, which Tom surmised was Scissors, and came over.

'How're you doing?'

'Okay.'

'You want some water?'

Tom nodded, then dribbled most of it round the back of his neck. He looked at Halo. 'Why are you here?'

'Nice to see you too,' said Halo.

'How long have I been out?'

'Near enough twenty-four hours,' said Pete, looking at his watch.

Tom jerked upright and started coughing.

'Take it easy,' said Halo.

But Tom wouldn't. He looked around wildly.

'The file,' he choked out.

'I got it,' said Pete, picking it up. 'Relax.'

Tom couldn't. He felt like he was going to cough up a lung. Halo came round and hit him harder between the shoulders than Tom thought was strictly necessary, but it worked, and he spat what looked like slimy black metal-flake paint into his hand. 'Shit,' he panted in disgust.

'Charming,' said Halo.

Tom lay down again, snatching at the air, feeling the panic subside. Pete took the file out of a briefcase he'd laid at the foot of the bed. It was in shreds.

'What happened to it?' Tom managed to gasp.

Pete quirked a little smile. 'Stuffing the evidence down the back of your pants works fine – until some ER nurse has to cut them off you.'

Tom gestured at the file. 'Is it enough?'

'Hell, yes. But it can go higher.' He put the file on Tom's legs and jabbed at Allway's signature. 'This Bruce Allway's the key.'

'This is Bruce Allway,' said Tom, emptying the Polaroids on to the bed.

'Shit,' said Pete. 'Then we're going to have to work harder.'

Tom thought about Ness, but said nothing. If there was any way of getting out of this without revealing his poker-playing activities, he would take it.

'Still . . . it's a start. It's hard evidence.'

'*I'm* hard evidence! Those sick bastards showed me what I've been searching for, then tried to kill me!' He paused then added quietly: '*Did* kill some people?'

'About seventy so far,' said Pete, grimly.

'And that's just in the jet,' said Halo. Tom glanced at him but he was looking at the pictures.

'I'm sorry about Niño, man,' said Tom.

Halo nodded and made a 'what-ya-gonna-do?' face. 'Yeah,' he said, 'well . . .'

Carefully he picked up the pictures and put them back into the manila envelope, then replaced it in the back pocket of the cut-up file. He handed it to Pete.

'Okay,' said Pete. 'Jan Ryland is already on her way to Avia Freight with a subpoena. As soon as we get the list of batch 501 purchasers, we can start grounding planes.'

'Why not right now?' said Tom. 'There are potentially

sixteen more planes out there waiting to fail – seventeen, if Oklahoma was something different.'

'We'd have to ground every 737 in US airspace, Tom. That'd take an act of Congress.'

'Yeah, God forbid lives should be saved just because we can. Christ, Pete!'

'Where's the bolt?' said Pete.

Tom sighed. 'They took it.'

'Again?'

'We can make a case without it, right? I mean, *you* can, right?'

Pete thought it through. 'Maybe. Channings over at the FBI seems to think so. But we're light on physical evidence.'

Halo stood up and, like a conjuror, laid Lemon's bolt on the bed. They all stared at it, as if it might turn into a bouquet of flowers at any second.

'Where the fuck did you get that?' said Tom.

Halo grinned. 'Under the front seat of my car.'

'Then what the hell did you give to that sonofabitch in the hangar?'

'My decoy bolt. Figured if you could have one, so could I. 'Cept I mangled mine better than you did. Better job all round.'

Tom was furious. 'You crazy sonofabitch! You let that bastard come this close to shooting both of us for a useless piece of scrap metal?'

'That bolt's the evidence that can clear Chris. Give Vee and Katy what's theirs. Just in case, I left a note, telling Vee where it was and who to give it to.'

'To me?'

'Hell, no! I assumed you'd be dead long before me. I just put NTSB in DC.'

Tom caught Pete LaBello's amazed look and shook his head. 'Shit, Halo,' he said, struggling to keep his voice even. 'Loyalty beyond the grave. That's above and beyond the call of friendship.'

'Yeah,' said Halo.

Pete picked up the bolt with a questioning look at Halo, who nodded his permission.

'Be careful, Pete,' said Tom.

'I will.' Pete tapped the file on his thigh and headed for the door. 'I have a flight to catch. I'll call you from LA, Tom, and you can fill me in on any other details you think I should know about.' He stared at Tom meaningfully, then shook Halo's hand. 'Good to meet you, Mr Jackson.'

'Same here,' said Halo. 'I hope you and Ann have a happy retirement. Sounds like you deserve it.'

'Jesus!' Tom said irritably. 'How long have you guys known each other?'

'It's called conversation,' said Pete. 'Regular people do it.'

Tom was momentarily silenced, then waved a dismissive hand. 'Ah, fuck regular people.'

Pete flapped his arms in an all-purpose gesture of hopelessness.

At the door he stopped. 'By the way, Kitty said your termination paperwork got lost in the mail, and it would be a whole lot easier for her if you just withdrew your resignation.'

Tom's overstretched heart thudded so loudly, he thought Pete must be able to hear it clear across the room. 'Seriously?'

'Yeah.'

436

Tom's throat was tight and aching. 'Thanks, Pete.'

*

When a nurse came back to check his blood pressure and lung function, Tom bullied Halo into going to find out how and where Lucia was. He came back with the sobering news that she was in a hyperbaric chamber on the first floor.

Tom waited until the nurse had finished and left the room. 'Is she okay?'

'I don't know. I didn't ask anyone.'

'Is her mother with her?'

'I just looked through the glass in the door. There's a nurse and a woman in white gloves.'

'That's her. She was in here when I woke up this morning. Hit me in the mouth.'

'Good for her.' Then Halo looked at Tom properly. 'You're kidding?'

'Nope. Said if I ever went near her daughter again she'd kill me.'

Tom's tone was obviously seeking support and Halo knew he should be condemning an assault on a defenceless man in his sickbed but, really, he couldn't blame the woman. If he'd had a daughter, and she'd shown any interest in Tom Patrick, he'd probably have done the same thing. He skirted that truth and headed for safer waters. 'Did you meet Lucia in South Africa?'

'Not the same girl.'

'You got two women to sleep with you?'

'Fuck off.'

Halo grinned. 'What happened to the other one?'

'She gave me the file. And the plane ticket.'

'Man, you must be *really* bad in bed.'

Tom shrugged. 'Maybe she didn't realize that was the plane.'

'Maybe,' said Halo, kindly, although he looked doubtful.

Tom swung his legs off the bed and tugged the open-assed hospital gown over his head.

'Where are you going?' said Halo.

'To see Lucia.'

'What about Mrs Muhammad Ali?'

'You're coming with me. If she sees I have a black friend maybe she'll like me better.'

'I'm not your friend. I'm just some guy who calls you up and hassles you to work for free, remember?'

'Well, she doesn't need to know that, does she?' Tom picked up his ID, then swayed and had to put a hand on the bed to stop himself falling, his legs weak and rubbery.

'Shit, man, you need to be in bed. Get back in bed.'

'Who made you my mom? Pass me my fucking pants.'

*

The glass in the door that Halo had peered through before was now blocked by what looked like a coat. Great place to put a peg, he thought irritably. He glanced down the corridor at Tom, who was in the nearest waiting area, hiding behind *Quilting Quarterly*. He shrugged helplessly and Tom limped over to him, wearing his smoke-blackened 'Only in LA' T-shirt and a pair of green surgical scrub pants which he'd forced Halo to steal from a closet down the hallway to replace his aerated jeans.

438

'What's up?'

'Something over the window,' said Halo. He was waiting – just waiting – for Tom to ask him to go in and draw Lucia's fierce mother out of the room with some bullshit story she'd believe just because he was black, of course. Well, Halo wasn't doing it. He had his 'No' all ready to go in his mouth, and his 'Fuck you' waiting behind that if Tom pushed him.

To pre-empt the confrontation, he said, 'I'm not coming in with you. You're on your own.'

Surprisingly, Tom didn't argue. Instead he stood and stared off down the corridor for a bit, weighing his options.

Then he sighed and pushed open the door.

Halo's imminent animosity switched instantly to manly support, and he gave Tom two thumbs-ups and mouthed, 'Good luck!'

Halo sat down on a chair conveniently placed outside the door. He really hoped he wouldn't have to go in after Tom and break up a fight between a foul-mouthed aggressive white guy and a little old black lady, cos if that happened, he just knew that somehow he and Lucia's mother would end up in the Lexington drunk tank together.

And she sounded scary.

*

Tom slid quietly into the room, braced for the worst. And found something so far beyond it that he froze in horror.

Stanley stood behind the long white hyperbaric chamber, one hand directing a gun at a cowering nurse and Lucia's mother on the other side of the room, the other lighting the cigarette clamped between his lips.

439

The door clicked shut behind Tom and the sound made them all look at him – even the gun turned to capture him in its sights.

Tom couldn't help noticing that Lucia's mother looked even more annoyed to see him than she had at being held at gunpoint by a stranger. 'I guess this is all your fault!' she snapped.

Stanley laughed and blew smoke in little puffs. 'You bet it is,' he told her, then shook his head at Tom. 'You never did know when to get off a fucking hand, Patrick.'

'Sir,' said the nurse, tightly. 'You need to put the cigarette out *right now*! That chamber is filled with oxygen.'

'Yeah, I know,' said Stanley, without taking his eyes off Tom. 'You could've saved yourself the walk – I was coming up to see you after I got through here.'

Tom was scared to ask but had to: 'Got through doing what?'

'This,' said Stanley, nodding down at the chamber, and – while his right hand kept the gun loosely pointed at Tom – his left started to unscrew the wide cap covering the hatch, which allowed medication or water to be passed to the patient.

'Sir!' said the nurse, with rising panic. 'Sir! You can't do that!'

'Watch me,' said Stanley, and glanced at Lucia's mother. 'Is she a smoker?'

'None of my children smoke,' said Mrs Holmes, curtly.

Stanley laughed again. 'Well, this one's about to start.'

Tom moved slightly.

'Stay where you are, asshole.'

He stopped, but now he could see Lucia's face through the

440

little porthole in the side. She was lying on her back, watching Stanley through the top porthole, her eyes wide with fear. Beside her head he could see a pad of Post-its, which must have been provided so she could communicate with the nurses. The top one had a single word on it.

HELP.

'Listen, Mister!' the nurse said furiously. 'If you open that hatch and the cigarette gets anywhere near it, that whole chamber will go up like a bomb.'

Stanley didn't look at the nurse, but he raised his eyebrows at Tom. '*Feisty*, ain't she?'

Tom ignored the words. Instead he sought the bluff in Stanley's eyes. With a sickening sinking feeling, he could see it wasn't there. He was going to do it. Stanley was going to open the hatch and drop the cigarette into the oxygen-filled chamber, and they would have to watch Lucia burn – if the whole fucking room didn't go up as well. But the chamber was solid steel, and Tom thought Stanley must be pretty sure it would contain the fire at least long enough for him to escape, or he wouldn't be doing this at close quarters.

Tom watched his left hand slowly turning the metal cap. It was almost off. When it was, Stanley would have to put the cap down in order to take the cigarette from his mouth. That was his chance – his only chance.

In an instant, Tom visualized how it would happen. He would feint left, go right, running low so Stanley would have to lean over the top of the chamber to shoot him, grab the metal visitors' chair that was beside the porthole, shield his head with it, throw it at Stanley.

Take it from there.

The cap was almost off. Tom tensed.

Lucia's mother gave a loud cry and hurled *Little Women* at Stanley's head.

It took them all by surprise. Stanley had been expecting a move from Tom, not from a sixty-year-old woman in white gloves, armed with a chick-lit classic. He ducked down behind the chamber, then immediately bounced back up to point his gun at the real danger – Tom.

But before his head even cleared the top of the chamber or his finger found the trigger, Tom Patrick fell on top of him.

The second he'd seen Mrs Holmes make her move, Tom had made his. All thoughts of ducking low, grabbing chairs and throwing missiles fled from his head and he went for the shortest possible route between the two points that were himself and Stanley. He threw himself straight over the hyperbaric chamber.

It was chest-high and he had almost no run-up, plus he was weak from the smoke and his bad leg ached, but he still seemed to take off like Superman, and felt metal bolts and ridges bruise and scrape his belly and hips as he slithered over the rounded shell, his hands locking around Stanley's throat.

They crashed to the floor together, Tom on top, Stanley's head making a sickening crack against the shiny lino. Tom saw his eyes roll back and his grip on the butt of the black gun loosen. He snatched the weapon from Stanley's hand and spun it away across the floor.

When he saw Stanley coming back to him, he picked up *Little Women*. It was like a brick in his hand, and it felt embarrassingly good to smash it into Stanley's face and to watch blood squirt from a freshly opened cut on the bridge of his nose. Felt so good, in fact, that he did it again. He was

442

sure he could knock some teeth out too, so took aim . . .

His hand was halfway to Stanley's grimacing mouth before he realized he was no longer holding the book. He curled his fist and punched the man instead, which was less satisfying, and made him wince as the man's teeth dug into his knuckles.

When he looked up, Mrs Holmes was holding *Little Women*, with an expression of disgust.

Directed at him!

The nurse stood beside her, holding the gun on both of them like someone who knew what the hell she was doing. Even as he watched, Tom saw her flick the safety off with a practised thumb.

This was Kentucky, after all.

Looking over his shoulder as Stanley coughed and moaned, semi-conscious beneath him, Tom saw Lucia's sobbing, gasping face staring out of the side porthole at him, like some shocked alien in a passing spaceship.

'I *thought* I heard something!'

They all turned to Halo.

'Gimme a hand here,' said Tom, and Halo edged between Mrs Holmes and the end of the chamber, keeping a wary eye on the nurse with the gun. 'Step on that cigarette, will you?'

Halo obliged.

'Get me something to tie this bastard with.'

Halo pulled open a couple of drawers and found an Ace bandage. Together he and Tom got the still-groggy Stanley's wrists bound tightly together, then fastened to a metal strut under the chamber.

Tom sat heavily on Stanley's belly, ignoring the grunt it

forced out of his captive. He turned to the nurse. 'Can you call security?'

The woman's eyes narrowed and Tom sighed. He tugged his ID from the scrubs.

'NT—' he started, and then got all choked up and couldn't say the rest because he was so happy and relieved to be able to say those dumb initials and for it still to be true.

'SB,' Halo finished for him. 'He's a federal investigator. You need to call security.'

The nurse, who should really have been recruited by the marines, Tom reckoned, jerked the gun. 'I'm keeping this,' she said. 'So no funny business.' She backed away and picked up a phone on the wall.

Tom turned to Mrs Holmes. 'Lucia needs a doctor.'

As if coming back from a trance, the woman snapped into action-mode and hurried from the room.

Tom knelt forward, still straddling Stanley, and ran his hands through the man's pockets until he found a wallet, then he dropped heavily on Stanley's guts to check through it, making him groan.

'I'm gonna kill you, asshole,' Stanley choked out.

'Again?' said Tom, mildly. 'You're shit at it.' He pulled out a California driver's licence. 'Rickard Westacott Stanley. The Third.' He looked up at Halo and they both spurted laughter.

Tom grinned at the glowering killer. 'Where'd you learn to shoot cops in the face, *Rickard*? Princeton?'

'Fuck you.'

'Whatever.'

He flicked through the rest of the wallet. Cash; credit card in the name of John Ronson; receipts . . . 'These for the expenses you claim on fucking *murder*?' Tom tossed them aside, not waiting for an answer.

Stanley was quiet, watching him. Despite his victory, it made Tom uncomfortable. The look said Stanley knew something he didn't; there was even a little curl to his lip that said something amused him.

Tom finally found it.

A photo of Stanley and Ness.

Arms around each other. Happy together.

Stanley saw the precise moment Tom found the photo written on his face, and laughed. Despite the blood on his nose and in his mouth, he laughed and laughed and laughed, while Tom stared at the photo, his mind spinning back through time, snatching at clues, gutted by realization.

I know that guy. He's an asshole . . .

What's your boyfriend's name?

Richard . . .

The shock and surprise in her eyes when Stanley had hit her in the barn; Stanley's fury as he ran his hands over her breast, between her legs, suspecting that Tom had fucked her, jealous because of it, letting her know she was still his, whatever orders they were under.

'You were just a job to her, Patrick.' He raised his eyebrows towards Lucia. 'Like *this* whore.'

Things went kind of dark and speedy then, and the next thing Tom knew, Halo and two security guards were dragging him off Stanley, while Lucia's mother hit him repeatedly in the back with what was left of her copy of *Little Women*.

44

THE TWO ARRESTING cops grinned happily and gave the thumbs-up to Tom's phone-cam as they held the bandaged Rickard Stanley between them. Then Tom sat on a low wall to watch them push the man's head roughly down into the back of a Lexington Police Department cruiser.

A doctor had checked Stanley out in a manner so cursory and rough that Tom figured he must've been told about the incident with the hyperbaric chamber and the cigarette. He'd declared that Stanley's nose was broken but that his other cuts and bruises were not serious and that he could be released into police custody. He remembered his Hippocratic Oath in time to hand Officer Ridge a bottle of codeine, with offhand instructions about when Stanley should take the tablets.

As the cruiser pulled away, carrying with it a message to contact Assistant Director Luke Channings at the FBI office in DC, Tom flipped open his phone and called Ronaldo Suarez.

'Hey, it's Tom Patrick.'

'Hey. What's up?'

'I'm sending you a photo. Show it to Chuck Zhong. I'm

betting he'll feel safer about talking once he sees this guy is behind bars.'

Suarez gave a low whistle. 'Nice work.'

'Tell him we got the man in the suit too.'

'Nice one.'

'Yeah, well, it's a lie but it'll help. And offer him protection in the joint.'

'You think he needs it?'

Tom sighed. 'I'm amazed he's still alive. These guys go all the way.'

'You sound like you know what you're talking about, Tom.'

He could hear the question in Suarez's voice but was too tired to explain.

'I wish I didn't.'

'Thanks, man. Anytime you're in Irving, lunch is on me.'

'Not at that crappy place I took you to, you cheap bastard.'

Suarez laughed and hung up.

Tom stretched his face up to the sunshine, like a bear emerging from a long winter.

He felt a brush on his shoulder and opened his eyes to see Halo sit down beside him. 'What did she say?' asked Tom.

'You come near Lucia, she'll kill you.'

'Shit! Did you tell her I pulled her daughter out of the goddamn plane?'

'Yup. She didn't believe me. Then said she didn't care anyway, said Lucia wouldn't have been *on* the plane if it wasn't for you.'

'Did you tell her— Oh, fuck it.' Tom waved away his own argument as he realized Mrs Holmes held the over-card every time: Lucia would be fine and dandy if she'd never met him. It was the royal flush of protective motherhood.

'Did you do the whole black thing?'

'No, I didn't do the whole *black* thing.'

'Call yourself a fucking friend?'

'Yeah.' Halo shrugged defensively. 'I do.'

45

IT TOOK TOM three days to clean Lucia's place up properly and to replace what was broken. Now and then he'd start to choke and have to cough muck into his hand until he could breathe again. It was gross, and he was glad Lucia wasn't there to see it.

He'd left her in the hospital. He'd stuck around Lexington for a few days, hung around the hallway where her room was, watched from behind *Quilting Quarterly* and the *Weekly World News* as they transferred her from the chamber to a recovery ward. The whole time, her mother never left her side.

Finally frustrated, Tom had caught a cab to the airport, where one runway was still cordoned off. He'd run into Mike Carling, who was there investigating the crash and seemed genuinely pleased to see him. They shook hands, then Carling hugged him briefly and Tom wasn't even embarrassed. The last time they'd seen each other, it had been over the body of Lenny Munro; both of them apparently felt good that Tom, at least, was still alive.

Carling had been told all Pete LaBello knew, but still pumped Tom for more information as he waited for his flight, jotting down notes in a little black book that made

Tom think wistfully of Sergeant Konrad, Lemon and Harold Robbins.

He'd been allocated a seat ten rows from the exit over the wings. For the first time ever, he didn't care. If the plane crashed now, he'd know that God not only existed, but also wanted him dead real bad.

He left Kentucky without ever laying eyes on a horse.

At LAX he'd paid a hundred and seventy-five dollars in parking fines and then found the Buick wouldn't start so he'd called Halo for a jump. Halo had come over from Hangar Five and they'd had a cup of coffee before going out to start the car.

When Halo admitted he'd been ripped off by his decorator and was having to do everything himself, Tom had managed not to say, 'I told you so.'

Finally, Tom had driven straight to Santa Ana and thrown himself on the mercy of Lucia's landlady, who was suspicious and hostile until he peeled next month's rent in cash from the fast-diminishing wad of his eleven-thousand-dollar winnings. It didn't matter. From next month he'd be back at work on full pay.

*

Every day he worked to put the apartment right. And at night he curled up in Lucia's bed and thought about her.

Twice he called the hospital and managed to get a condition report. She was improving. That was all they would tell him. The third time he called, an officious woman said condition reports on that patient were no longer being released, at the family's request. Tom was torn between petulant anger and grudging admiration for Mrs Holmes, who was apparently covering all her bases when it came to keeping him from scoring.

He had no doubt that she would take Lucia back to Savannah with her when she was finally discharged and would try to keep her there permanently.

But he also had no doubt that Lucia would come here eventually, even if it was just to pick up her stuff. She had photos here, clothes, keepsakes. A yearbook that showed she'd been voted Most Likely to Succeed in her graduating class. Most Likely to Get Screwed Around by Some Selfish Jerk and Almost Die in a Plane Crash apparently wasn't a category.

Pete had told him to take a month off before reporting back to planes. Only his need to put things right with Lucia kept Tom from defying his boss by reporting for duty the day after he left UKMed.

He didn't miss much. Avia Freight had already tagged six fan discs they had in stock from batch 501. They then moved heaven and earth to accelerate Jan Ryland's records search, which led quickly to the grounding of ten more 737s – thankfully before any of them suffered a failure. The records showed that Flight 823 out of Savannah had had a 501 disc installed, and Lenny Munro's final case was closed.

The NTSB jurisdiction ended there.

Now the Feds were all over the case like a rash.

Ten days after Tom had left Kentucky, two agents knocked on Lucia's door, their badges at the ready, and grilled him about how he fitted into the case.

He told them everything he could about fake parts, Rickard Stanley, the Weasel, and the *Pride of Maine*, and precisely nothing about his alternative career at the tables. *They* didn't mention Ness's name, so he figured not mentioning it to them was hardly withholding evidence in a federal case. Although it was, of course, which he tried hard not to think about.

He wondered what they were getting from Stanley, but they wouldn't say, which Tom thought was unduly proprietorial, considering they wouldn't even have *had* a case without him, and that he'd been the arresting agent.

They finally told him the Weasel had been arrested, although they called him Robert Best, and he read between their lines that Stanley was talking and that, somewhere, players much higher up the food chain were being lined up like ducks in a shooting gallery. He could guess at the turmoil as they started to suspect they were in the firing line, that he was still alive; that Stanley might turn traitor.

Tom suppressed the bristling anger at the thought that he was being brushed off. And as the two Feds talked about confidentiality and ongoing investigations, he focused past them and on Lucia's apartment. Each item was something she'd chosen; she was in every part of the modest space, from the renewed John Lennon print to the childlike collection of glass horses on the art-deco bureau. Several had been smashed by whoever had turned her place over, but Tom had found some unbroken, and fixed others with clear glue, and the collection was almost complete again. While he'd bent over the delicate little ornaments, Tom had grinned to find himself caring so much for something so stupid, just because someone he cared for cared for them.

Now, he realized the Feds had stopped and were waiting for his response to being cut out of the loop. With surprise, he found he didn't much care to be in this particular loop any more. They would arrest some people and pat each other on the back.

And a year from now, *another* batch in *another* factory run by *another* gang would roll off an illicit production line with another fatal flaw . . .

So, by way of an answer, Tom just shrugged at them.

Finally he'd found something worth zipping his lip for.

*

Apart from shopping and repairing stuff, Tom just hung around the apartment.

But Lucia didn't come.

Finally restless after three weeks, Tom started going to the Rubstick most days. He lost some but won more, and knew he was a better player now than he'd ever been.

One night he saw Corey Clump. They bought each other a beer and Corey told him the kid with the shades and the iPod had turned up murdered. Said talk around the clubs was that it was over a girl. Tom nodded in tacit agreement, and got a little jag of nostalgia for a time when cards were just fun for him and held no overtones of life and death.

'Yeah, women!' Corey pronounced, in a long-suffering tone, although Tom had never seen him with one. 'Can't live with 'em, can't shoot 'em.'

Tom forced a smile and clinked glasses with him, and wondered whether Ness Franklin was dead.

*

Three nights later he got his answer. He'd just thrown down pocket sixes in the face of a flush when a soft hand touched the back of his neck.

His heart almost stopped and he spun to face her, half expecting to be met with the barrel of a gun.

Even now, she looked good to him.

She smiled at him a little sadly. 'Tom.'

He couldn't speak.

'Winning or losing?' She waved at his chips.

'Cashing out,' he managed, and got up with his racks.

He felt her follow him as he strode to the pay window – would they jump him in the parking lot or follow him home? He hadn't won enough to be offered an escort; maybe he'd ask for one anyway.

She watched him stuff the roll of money into his jeans and smiled. 'Just like old times.'

'What do you want, Ness?'

She hesitated, and Tom saw doubt in her eyes.

'Buy me a drink?'

He almost didn't; he almost walked away. He'd think later that he should have.

But he didn't.

He bought her a whiskey straight and got a Coke for himself. If he was going to get into it tonight, he'd need every one of his reflexes at his immediate disposal.

They were halfway through their drinks before she spoke. 'How are you?'

He laughed with real amusement – had a hard time stopping – and finally answered, 'Fine, thanks – ever since you tried to kill me.'

'I didn't—'

'Know,' he finished for her sarcastically. 'For a smart woman, Ness, you're just a ball of ignorance.'

She looked down the bar, away from him, and Tom thought that if she was pretending to cry, he'd slap her hard and enjoy doing it.

She wasn't pretending to cry: when she looked back at him, she was cool and calm. 'Everybody's running for cover. Stanley's talking. Your security guard in Texas is talking. The operation's falling apart.'

'Good. Where does that leave you?'

'Nowhere.' She sipped her drink. 'That's the thing about being a small fish in a big pool. It's easy to disappear.' Then she lifted her chin at him defiantly. 'Unless you tell the Feds about me.' Her words were a statement but her eyes were a question mark.

'Not yet.'

'You won't.' She smiled. 'If you want to stay out of jail.'

He hated her smug look. He wanted to watch it change as he told her he knew about her and Stanley, but he stopped himself. Never show your hand. Even after winning.

She put a hand on his forearm, running her thumb sensuously across the dark hairs. Despite it all – despite the betrayals and the sex games and the cursed ticket to DC – Tom felt the pull of her.

She smiled sexily up at him. 'You want to take me home, Tom?'

'No, thanks.'

He winced as she dragged her nails lightly across his groin. 'Yeah, you do.'

He caught her hand in his and moved it away from him.

'How's Richard?'

She faltered. Frowned. Hurt creased her brow, and then anger.

He turned and walked away from her.

Her voice rose behind him: 'I faked all my orgasms! Every last one of them!'

Men at the bar stared at them in surprise and amusement but Tom didn't turn round.

'Me too,' he threw over his shoulder, and left.

He stopped on the way home and bought a bunch of flowers and a bottle of Jack Daniel's. One in case Lucia came back, the other in case she didn't.

46

HE LET HIMSELF into the apartment and found Lucia on the couch. He pressed the door closed with his back and leaned against it. 'Hi,' he said.

'Hi.'

She'd lost weight again, and her eyes were huge in her face now. Huge and somehow sad.

Tom was tongue-tied and stupid in the face of her sudden presence.

She nodded at the flowers. 'Are those for me?'

'Yes.' But he didn't move.

'How did you know I was coming?'

'I didn't. I just kept buying them. And hoping.' It was true, even if it did make him sound like some jerk in a romantic movie. Last week's flowers were still in the vase in the window, drooping in green water.

He registered that she still hadn't smiled at him. Surely she should have smiled at him by now. Tom put the Jack Daniel's down on the bureau next to the horses and stepped forward with the flowers. 'How are you?'

'Okay.'

She didn't reach for the flowers, so he laid them on the table beside her. He felt a seed of unease deep in his belly,

457

and ran his hand up the back of his neck before he could stop himself.

'I got my job back,' he said, feeling like a kid presenting his mother with a lumpy piece of C-grade woodwork.

She nodded, then said, 'I'm not staying.'

'What?'

'I'm not staying in LA. I'm going back to Savannah.'

Tom felt like someone was banging a kettle drum in his guts. 'Why?' was all he could manage.

'My mother wants me there.'

'I want you *here*!'

She shrugged as if his desires were inconsequential and, with another pounding drum-roll of nausea, Tom realized there was no reason why she should think anything else. He'd fucked her, he'd failed her, he'd begged favours from her and he'd almost got her killed. Twice.

No, three times.

Jesus, no wonder she wanted to put the width of the continent between them. He had no right to ask her to stay, no right to burden her with his feelings.

'I love you,' he said anyway, hating his own selfishness even as he said it.

She looked away from him then, and Tom thought the absence of an 'I love you' back was the most painful sound he'd ever not heard.

'My mother hates you, Tom.'

'That's what mothers are for. It doesn't mean anything.'

'And I hardly know you.'

'Bullshit! You know me!'

She sighed and tears welled in her eyes. 'Only enough to know that you'd always find a way to fuck up, Tom. Always find a way to let me down. Always find a way to hurt me, even if you didn't mean to.'

He wanted to yell that it wasn't true, that she was wrong, that it wouldn't be like that. But he'd just admitted to himself that she had no evidence to the contrary. And in matters of love, he was learning that actions spoke louder than words.

He wished he hadn't wasted the words now. Without the actions to back them up, 'I love you' was just a cheap shot. A twenty-dollar bunch of dahlias wasn't going to change that. He knew she was wrong, but he also knew she'd made the right decision based on what she'd seen of him. Frankly, he'd applaud her choice – if it had meant anything but him losing her.

His cracked whisper told her the best truth he could muster: 'Then you should get to know me better.'

She nodded slowly.

He knew she understood.

But he also knew that it wasn't enough.

*

He helped her pack. She took the things he'd thought she would – the photos, the clothes, the yearbook, the glass horses. She'd come out on Amtrak; they rented a U-Haul for her to drive home in. She didn't care how long it took: she wasn't flying.

It crossed Tom's mind to offer to drive her back to Georgia. Days and nights on the road, he was sure he could change her mind.

But he wanted her to change her mind by herself.

He hoped it would happen while they were packing.

Then he hoped it would happen when he made love to her the night before she left. She sobbed in his arms for an hour afterwards and he hoped and hoped that she would turn to him and take his face in her hands and tell him she would stay with him.

She finally fell asleep without saying it.

He kept hoping, even as the U-Haul turned the corner and disappeared from his sight. He waited fifteen minutes for it to reappear.

It didn't.

*

Tom sat and stared at Lucia's dormant TV for about a day. Then he drove to Bellflower, turning off the boulevard to where the yards had low chain-link fences. The lawn had been cut since he was last there.

Halo's Mustang dripped on to the asphalt, newly washed.

Tom took fifteen minutes to get out of the Buick, and another five standing on the porch, getting up the nerve to knock, before Vee came round the corner of the house, making him jump.

'Tom!' She threw her arms around him and kissed his cheek so hard he had to take a step backwards.

'Hi,' he mumbled.

'Halo!' she yelled at the house, as she pulled a piece of paper from her jeans and unfolded it. 'This came this morning.'

It was from Air Maintenance Inc. Chris Stern had been exonerated in the loss of the *Pride of Maine*; his pension and death benefits were being reinstated and backdated.

Despite his low mood, Tom smiled.

'Thanks, Tom.'

He'd never heard so much feeling in just two words. He shrugged. 'Thank Halo. He bullied the shit out of me.'

Halo peered through the fly screen with yellow paint on his face. 'Hey,' he said, a little warily. 'What's up?'

Tom took a breath. 'You want a hand with the painting?'

If the offer surprised Halo, he had the good grace to hide it.

'You bet,' he said, and opened the door.

Acknowledgements

Many thanks to Licensed Aircraft Engineer Ross Fraser for his expertise and enthusiasm. Any errors or omissions are mine, not his.

Also to Bill Scott-Kerr and the rest of the editorial and creative team at Transworld, who have been such a pleasure to work with.

I'll always be grateful to James Renn, my partner in crime at the card clubs of LA, and to my mother, who nagged the hell out of me.